Careful of the
Company You Keep

Also by Angie Daniels

IN THE COMPANY OF MY SISTAHS

LOVE UNCOVERED

TROUBLE LOVES COMPANY

WHEN I FIRST SAW YOU

WHEN IT RAINS . . .

Anthologies containing novellas by Angie Daniels

BIG SPANKABLE ASSES

Published by Kensington Publishing Corporation

Careful of the Company You Keep

Angie Daniels

KENSINGTON PUBLISHING CORP.

www.kensingtonbooks.com

DAFINA BOOKS are published by

Kensington Publishing Corp.
119 West 40th Street
New York, NY 10018

ISBN-13: 978-0-7582-1748-6
ISBN-10: 0-7582-1748-X

First trade paperback printing: September 2008
First mass market printing: April 2011

10 9 8 7 6 5 4 3

Printed in the United States of America

I wanted to thank everyone that read
In the Company of My Sistahs
and
Trouble Loves Company
and begged for more

This one's for you.

Acknowledgments

To my new friends and coworkers Tracina Butler and Abigail Buhr, for reading the first two chapters and motivating my ass to write even when I wasn't feeling it.

Shouts out to my writing circle, who always have my back and helped make this ride fun! Dashaun "Jiwe" Morris, whose book is about to blow up. Yo, welcome to the family and much success. Kimberly Kaye Terry's crazy erotic ass. Maureen Smith, my partner-in-crime. The shit's gonna pay off in the end. Trust and believe.

To Tonya Hill and Novia Mearidy, just because y'all my girls and for putting up with me all these years. I love y'all!

To Maureen Hunter, my Jamaican friend, who I forgot to mention for all her help with *In the Company of My Sistahs*. Luv you, too, gurl!

I love hearing from all my readers. When you get a chance please visit me at www.angiedaniels.com or drop me a line at angie@angiedaniels.com.

1

Renee

There are a lot of things I expected to face in my life. Walking in on my husband with his dick stuck in another man's ass was not one of them.

Shock was an understatement. I couldn't think. I couldn't breathe and damn near choked. All I could do was stand there and watch John and another man racing to the finish line in *my* bed. They were so busy fucking neither of them heard the bedroom door open or noticed me standing there.

Think, bitch, think!

Inhale. Exhale. I knew I had to do something quick, fast, and in a hurry because any second now and the moment would be lost. I reached down to my waist, removed the cell phone from my hip, and aimed it in their direction.

"Cheese, mothafuckas!"

As soon as both of them fags looked my way, I pressed the camera button on my phone.

Priceless.

John jumped back so fast, he tripped over a shoe and fell flat on his ass. "Renee! What the hell?"

"My words exactly. You should have taken that booty bandit shit to a hotel." I moved in for a close-up and pressed the button again.

John held up his hands in a panic. "Hold up, baby! I can explain."

I glared at his fat ass. "Save it for someone who cares, because I don't give a fuck."

At a loss for words, John just sat there breathing heavily while Shemar scrambled for his pants. I looked at him and rolled my eyes in disgust. To think, I've been fucking his faggot ass for the last couple of weeks. Angrily, I snatched the first thing I could get my hands on—a bottle of scented lotion—and tossed it across the room and got pretty boy on the side of his head.

"What's wrong with you?" Shemar shouted, then ducked out of the way before my hairbrush got him in the forearm.

"What's wrong with me?" *Oh no, he didn't just ask me that.* "What's wrong is finding you . . . bent over . . . like some bitch . . . with my husband fucking you!" I tossed John's aftershave, and it hit the wall and shattered. "What's wrong is knowing my husband . . . *my husband* . . . fucked you in the bed that *I* bought!" I kept on screaming and throwing shit at the two of them.

John's eyes grew wide with guilt. "Renee, please, let's talk about this," he pleaded.

"We ain't got shit to talk about!" I screamed. Was he smoking crack? What could he possibly have to explain? I moved over to my dresser and started throwing everything in reach. I snatched up a bottle of Diamonds perfume and was about to toss it when I remembered how much I paid for it. I put it down and grabbed the cheap shit instead. By now I was throwing anything I could get my hands on in their direction, including a pair of three-pound dumbbells I kept on the floor in the corner. Both of those bitches were bobbing and weaving and trying to cover their heads. "As soon as you get dressed, get the fuck outta here!"

"We ain't going nowhere!" Shemar screamed like a little bitch. "Tell her, John. Tell her you're my man now and this is . . . this is *your* house!"

John looked over at Shemar and cut his eyes. "Shemar, this is not the time."

Shemar propped a hand at his waist. "The hell it ain't. What have we been talking about for the last several months? You promised we'd be together, and I'm tired of waiting. Dammit, John, you belong to me!"

What the fuck? I couldn't believe this gay shit. The longer I looked and listened, the angrier I got. I reached for a pair of scissors and lunged at Shemar, who saw me coming and hurried into the adjoining bathroom and slammed the door. I was moving so fast the blades stabbed the wood. I yanked the scissors free and headed toward John, who ducked, then grabbed my wrist and wrestled the scissors out of my hand.

"Let me go!" I screamed. I balled up my fist and started beating him across his face and chest. And just like a bitch, he let me tear his ass up.

"Go ahead, Renee. Do what you have to do, but it's not going to change anything."

"Fuck you!" I shouted, then swung hard and got him in the nose. Finally he grabbed my hands and I jerked away from him. I was breathing so hard I was hyperventilating. Leaning over, I placed my hands on my knees and tried counting to ten to catch my breath. "How . . . could . . . you . . . do this to me?"

John moved and took a seat on the end of the bed, holding a T-shirt up to his nose. It was bleeding. *Good*.

"As soon as you calm down, we can sit down like two adults and talk." I could tell by the tone of his voice that he never expected me to find out this way.

"I said we ain't got shit to talk about! I've been tolerating your itty-bitty limp-dick ass for the last five years, and this is how you treat me?" No wonder his dick half worked when we made love. Part of me felt like laughing—and probably would later, because this was the excuse I'd been waiting for to finally get out of my marriage—but right now, it was too humiliating for words.

"I can no longer hide how I feel."

"You sick bastard." I was so mad I didn't realize until I saw John holding the side of his head that I had hurled my wooden jewelry box at him.

"Quit it, Renee!" he ordered and tried to reach for me, but I jumped out of the way.

"Fuck you, John!"

I was too through. I had to bite my tongue to stop from telling him how I really felt about the last five years of our marriage. Big Mama taught me a long time ago not to bite the hand that feeds you, and I needed John to keep supporting me until I could figure out a plan. The best way was to play on his sympathy by making him think I was hurt to discover our marriage was over. No, I wasn't hurt. I was pissed the fuck off. "How could you do this to me?" I forced myself not to blink so my eyes would become misty, and tears eventually appeared.

"I . . . I never expected you to find out this way. I'm really sorry. How—"

I cut him off before he could finish.

"Sorry, my ass!" I screeched. "Both of y'all get out of my house!"

"Bitch, this is my man's house!" Shemar screamed from the other side of the bathroom door.

"Faggot, shut the hell up!" I ran over and kicked the door and hurt my damn toe. I screamed at the top of my lungs, then started pacing the length of the room.

John just continued to sit there holding his head with one hand and applying pressure to his nose with the other. I removed my cell phone from my hip and went ahead and sent those pictures to my e-mail address just in case one of those gay mothafuckas decided to get bold and try to snatch the phone. My hands were trembling with anger.

"What're you planning to do with those pictures?"

I rolled my eyes in John's direction. "Nothing just yet, but if you *fuck* with me, I'm going to send them to everybody, including your uppity-ass mama."

I expected him to lunge from the bed and snatch the phone from my hands, because the last thing John wanted was to tarnish his image. Lenore never did think I was good enough for her son. Shit, if she only knew.

However, instead of wrestling me to the floor, John just sat there like a bitch with his hands on his lap, looking at me like what I saw happening never really happened. As if it had been my imagination. "Quit trippin'," he finally said.

"Trippin'? Trippin'!"

He gave me a dismissive laugh. "Yes, Renee, trippin'. It's not that big a deal."

"Oh, it's not? Okay, then let me show you how big a deal it is!" I ran across the room to the large walk-in closet we shared and started fumbling on the top shelf. John must have heard me loading his gun because he hurried into the bathroom with Shemar and shut and locked the door just in time. I aimed, and a bullet pierced the wall only inches from the door.

"Renee, what the hell are you doing?" John screamed. "Put that gun down!"

"Shut the hell up!" I yelled and shot at the door again. Shemar was screaming at John to "control that crazy bitch." I pulled the trigger again and screamed, "Shut up, punk, before I give you something to cry about." He must have realized I was serious because everything got quiet. "That's more like it. Now listen and listen good. I want both of you gay mothafuckas out of *my* house by the time I get back. Otherwise, I'm shooting y'all fags for real!" I decided it was time for me to bounce before one of the neighbors called the police.

I couldn't get out of that house fast enough. I took the stairs two at a time and grabbed my purse from the table. A retired couple who lived across the street was standing on the porch. As soon as they saw me coming out the door with a gun in my hand, they raced back in the house.

I climbed into my Lexus and peeled down the driveway and onto the street. A mile up the road, the tears began to fall and I angrily wiped them away. "Don't you dare cry over that gay bastard."

I was driving, thinking over everything that had happened, and trying to figure out how in the hell I missed the warning signs. I hear women all the time talking about how they had no idea their man was on the DL, and I always say to myself, "what the fuck ever." The signs were there. Hell, most of the time I could spend five minutes with a man and could tell he was gay. Yet I had no idea about my own husband. But then ours was a weird relationship from the start.

Our marriage was a one-night stand that turned into a five-year commitment. We'd barely dated a month before he proposed. My ass was unemployed and about to be homeless. With two little kids, that was not an option. So when John proposed, "marry me now and love me later," I jumped at the opportunity.

And that's what your stupid ass gets.

Yep, I should have left him years ago. Quit talking about it and be about it, that's the shit I say to my friends all the time, yet I didn't follow my own advice.

I was ten miles from home, speeding down the highway, when my cell phone rang. I looked down and saw I had a private call. *I bet you five dollars and a Long Island iced tea it's John's gay ass.*

"What?"

"I'd appreciate it if you'd not share those pictures." He said the words so slowly that it gave me an eerie feeling.

"That depends," I stated calmly.

"Depends on what?"

"On how much you plan to pay, mothafucka!" Even with the windows down and the wind whipping across my face, I could hear Shemar yelling something in the background. "Tell that fag to shut the hell up!"

John covered the mouthpiece and mumbled something, then came back. "Sorry, he's upset, too."

"Who give a fuck how that fag feels?" I screamed. This was some straight-up soap opera shit.

"Don't be like that," he scolded.

"Don't tell me what the fuck to do before I come back over, shoot both y'all gay asses, and then plead temporary insanity."

"Listen, Renee, we can work this out if you'd give us a chance. I love you, Renee, but I'm not going to lie to you, I love Shemar as well. You didn't mind sharing me before, so what's different about now?"

"It was *your* idea to start swinging with other couples, and it was *you* who thought you weren't satisfying me sexually, so you invited Shemar to fuck me while you were in the room watching. Nowhere in that conversation did you say you would be fucking him as well. Huh? Tell me, John, because not once in the five years that we've been married did you mention anything about being gay."

"I'm not gay," he barked defensively.

"Then what the fuck would you call it?"

There was a brief pause before he answered, "I would call it . . . liking variety."

"And I call it liking dick!" I was screaming so hard the lady in the next car was staring nervously at me. I flipped her off for not minding her own business. "I'm divorcing yo gay ass. And according to our prenuptial agreement, if either of us catches the other in a compromising position, the other gets paid. And I'm getting ready to milk yo ass!"

"And what about the men you've been with? Remember, I have home videos," he reminded me.

"Yeah, and your bitch ass is in every one!" I was no fool. From the first day we started trying to add a little flavor to our marriage, I made sure every time John pulled out the camcorder, he was in that home movie as well. All the things that we had done with Shemar and the others started racing through my head. Hell, I even sucked Shemar's dick. *Oh my goodness! I'm going to be sick.* I was so nauseous my dinner tried to come up. I choked, then pushed that shit back down.

"Are you okay?"

"Hell nah! What the fuck? I just walked in on you fucking another mothafucka in his ass and *you have the nerve to ask me if I'm okay*?"

My response was met by a wave of silence.

"Renee, I don't know what else to say other than I'm sorry and hope we can work this out."

"What the hell is there left to work out?" This shit was so unbelievable I didn't know what to think or how to react, and that's rare for me. Never in a million years would I have expected to walk in on my husband, or any man for that matter, banging another one in his ass. I don't even watch boy/boy adult videos. I got sick watching *Brokeback Mountain*. "I want my monthly allotment doubled and don't even think about canceling my insurance benefits. You got one hour to pack yo shit and get the fuck out of my house. Oh yeah . . . and take them sheets with you!" I screamed, then ended the call.

Tears were running down my face. I don't know why I was crying over that fool.

John had never been good in bed. His thing is too little and he spends more time tweaking my damn nipples like they were knobs to a transistor radio than anything else. Nevertheless, he was rich and I told myself it was a small consequence for everything he had given me. Big-ass house. New ride. Private schools for the kids, and money in my own personal bank account. In exchange, all I had to do was give him some pussy three times a week. It was easier in the beginning, but the last three years, I started feeling like it was too much damn work. Hell, if I wanted a job, I would have gone out and applied for one. So to escape, I started writing and was now a published best-selling author of erotic romance. What I wasn't getting in my bed, I was getting in my books, and plenty of it. And when that was no longer enough, I started fucking around with every Tom, Dick, and Jerry I came in contact with. But after a while, I still wasn't happy.

Somehow, John sensed my misery, and two months ago, he invited Shemar to our bed for a ménage à trois. I thought *cha-ching*, I had hit the jackpot. Shemar and I would fuck while John sat back, beating his meat and watching. Then John and I started swinging with other couples. The husband was banging me while John was poking the man's wife. I thought I was getting the best of both worlds. Only the joke was on my black ass.

I guess I can't blame anyone but myself. I should have known that it was too good to be true. That's what I get for thinking I was getting something for nothing. I'd been talking about leaving John for years, and now that the time had come I had to quit talking about it and be about it. Starting right now, my life was beginning anew. A tear streamed down my cheek because I wasn't sure if I even knew where to begin.

2

Danielle

I turned the burner down low on the stove, then moved up to my daughter's room to tell her it was time for dinner. After knocking on her door and not getting an answer, I stepped in and found the room empty. Hearing water running in the bathroom at the end of the hall, I realized Portia was taking a shower.

Seeing dirty towels on the floor, I reached over and grabbed them. No wonder I can't find half my damn towels. They are here, buried in Portia's room.

I reached for a large gold bath towel and something dropped. Looking down, I spotted a small leather-bound book. I reached for it, flipped it over, and realized it was Portia's journal. Staring at it, I was tempted to open it, but I try to respect my daughter's privacy . . . most of the time. But curiosity got the better of me and after several seconds I had convinced myself that I'm the mother and had a right to know what my teenage daughter was up to, because the majority of the time she was up to no good.

"I'll look at just one entry, then I'll put it down," I murmured to myself and flipped to the center of the book.

I saw Ron's dick today. He wasn't too happy that I walked in on him, so I played it off and stepped out of the bathroom. I've never seen a thing with the skin still on it. But dang, it was big! I promise you I'm going to get some of that before the school year's over.

Hell to the no.

Stunned, I flipped forward several more pages.

Tomorrow my mother is working evenings and I plan to finally make my move on her boyfriend. The plan is to come running out of my room butt naked, pretending I saw a spider.

Fingers shaking, I turned the page.

I can't believe Ron rejected me. Even after I told him I loved him he tossed it back in my face and said he loved my mom, not me, and that I needed to find a boy my own age. I hate him! I hate him! Just wait, I'm going to get him back.

My hands were shaking as I flipped to an entry dated the day after I broke up with Ron.

Well, my plan worked. Mama believed me over Ron and put his butt out. Hee-hee! You should have seen his face. That's what he gets for treating me that way. Now Mama thinks I'm pregnant by Ron when I'm really carrying Demetrius's baby. Yuck! That was the worst sex I've ever had. I sure hope my baby comes out looking like me.

I didn't even know the journal had slipped from between my fingers until I heard it hit the floor. For the longest time I just stood there, stunned, knowing good and well what I was reading better not be true. But it was.

My daughter had lied.

Everything went still as my world started spinning.

Slowly I lowered onto the bed and took several deep breaths to calm my nerves because what I wanted to do was to run down the hall to the bathroom and snatch Portia's wide ass out of that shower. The only thing stopping me was the fact that she was pregnant and I didn't want to be responsible for two dead bodies.

Ain't this a bitch? I believed her. Even when something in the back of my mind kept telling me something wasn't right about my daughter's story, I believed her anyway because she's my daughter and that's what mothers are supposed to do, stick by their children.

How was I to know that when she described my man's uncircumcised dick, the reason she knew what it looked like was that her hot ass had barged into the bathroom and seen it? Not because Ron had been sleeping with her.

It was like a sick joke.

For the first time in my life I could understand how a woman could murder her own child, because that's exactly what I wanted to do. The only thing stopping me was that I didn't own a gun and that Portia was pregnant. *Dear God, Ron isn't even the father of her child. She lied to me! Ron never touched her.* He tried to tell me she was lying, yet I refused to listen.

The pipes grew quiet, which meant Portia had turned the water off. I returned the journal to where I had found it underneath a towel and quickly exited her room before I did something crazy. I then moved down the hall to my bedroom and made two calls and simply said, "Get over here or I'm killing her ass," then went downstairs to wait.

Fifteen minutes later, I was down in the kitchen walking laps around the table with a butcher knife in my hand, still contemplating murder. Portia came bouncing down the stairs in shorts and a T-shirt, looking like any typical sixteen-year-old. "Mmmm, Mama, that smells good! Is it time to eat yet?"

I glanced over at her lying ass, wanting so badly to take that pot of hot spaghetti sauce and fling it at her head and burn the shit out of her. *Hummph!* And then we would be even, because Portia had burned me good with all her lies.

"Why don't you set the table?" I suggested between gritted teeth.

She nodded obediently, then moved over to the counter and reached inside the cabinets. I watched her work, wondering how someone who looked so innocent could be so slick. A beautiful full-figured girl built like a woman since fifth grade. I had no idea until recently she knew how to use every last curve to get what she wanted.

"Set an extra plate. Your grandmother is coming over." *And she better hurry, because I don't know how much longer before I snap.*

"Mama, I'm so glad Ron doesn't live here anymore. I really enjoy having you all to myself again."

That's because I kicked his ass out. *Breathe, girl, breathe! She ain't worth it.* Ten, nine, eight, seven . . . I was seconds away from flinging that knife across the room when thank goodness the doorbell rang.

Portia dashed off to answer it. I took another deep breath, then pulled the garlic bread out of the oven. My mama entered wearing a worried look on her face. I placed a finger to my lips, halting any questions. "Let's eat."

We all took a seat, Mama to my right, Portia directly across from me. I waited until we were all eating before I broke the silence. "I decided to call the police."

Portia's eyes grew wide.

"For what?" Mama asked with concern.

I continued eating and didn't even bother looking her way. My eyes were glued to my daughter's face. "I'm filing charges against Ron for rape."

Mama nodded in agreement. "About time! I told you you should have done that the second you found out. Hopefully it's not too late."

Portia reached for her Kool-Aid and took a sip.

Uh-uh, she wasn't getting off that easy. "We probably won't be able to go to court until the baby is born because they're going to need DNA evidence. Once they have that and are able to prove the baby is Ron's, it's off to prison for the next twenty years." My eyes got small and never left hers.

Portia squirmed uncomfortably on the seat. "Can't we just leave it alone?"

"Why? I should have pressed charges against him the minute I found out, but instead I wanted to protect you."

She lowered her head, trying to avoid eye contact.

Mama pointed her fork at her granddaughter. "Listen to your mama. What that man did was against the law." She started shaking her head. "Lord knows I had a bad feeling about that thug living in this house. I just knew something bad would come out of this."

"B-But I . . . I don't want to have to face him in court," Portia stuttered nervously.

I just bet you don't. "You don't have to. The lawyers can put a case together without you if they need to. As soon as we get done eating, we're going down and file charges."

Portia dropped her fork and started frantically shaking her head. "Mama, they won't believe me . . . I know they won't," she insisted.

"Why is that?" I asked quickly.

"Because . . . Ron isn't the only one I've slept with. There's a chance this might be someone else's baby."

I couldn't believe she was admitting what I had said all along—she was a slut. I wanted so badly to scratch her eyes out for lying. "Well, I guess that's a chance we'll have to take."

"I don't want to." Portia sat back in her chair, arms crossed and lips poked out.

I raised my voice to ensure she knew who's boss. "Since when do you have a choice? This is my house, and that was a grown man . . . *my man* you were sleeping with. I'm going to make him pay!" *Damn, I should earn an Oscar for my performance.*

"Why does it always have to be about you? What about me?"

I wanted so badly to knock her upside her head. "I'm not even about to get into it with you. We're pressing charges as soon as your daddy gets here."

Her face dropped. "My daddy? I'm not doing it!"

"Why is that?" Mama asked, clearly confused by what was going on. "Don't you want to get the man who did this to you?"

A single tear ran down Portia's face as she tried to appear innocent. "I'm scared of what he might do to me."

"Since when? You weren't scared before," I replied with a rude snort. I was already sick of playing this charade.

Portia just pursed her lips together and looked away.

"Be nice, Danny," Mama warned under her breath.

I don't know what I was thinking when I asked her to come over, because no matter what I said, Mama was going to side with Portia. "I think the reason she doesn't want to press charges is she's lying and she knows that once we start the proceedings, the court is going to find out."

"I'm not lying!" Portia insisted but didn't bother to look up from the table.

"Oh really?" I said. "Hold that thought." I quickly moved up the stairs and came back a few moments later with the journal in my hand. As soon as I stepped inside the kitchen, I tossed the book onto the table. "Now try again. Tell your grandmother why you don't want to press charges."

Mama looked from Portia to me and back to Portia. "Baby, what's she talking about?"

Portia looked increasingly nervous. "I-I don't know."

"She's lying, Mama! Ron didn't rape her. It's right there in that book. She had a crush on a twenty-two-year-old man and he wasn't thinking about her hot ass so she lied to break us up."

Mama couldn't hide her disappointment. "Is that true?"

"No." She finally looked up at me.

I could no longer hold back. I sprang from the chair, jumped across the table, and tried to grab my daughter by her neck, but Mama rose out of her seat in time to keep me back. "You better be glad you're pregnant, because otherwise I would beat your mothafuckin' ass!" I screamed.

Portia jumped from her chair and was in the corner, shaking and crying like someone had died. Tears weren't going to save her this time.

"You need to pack yo shit and go home with your grandmother. You're not welcome back in this house. As far as I'm concerned, you're no longer my daughter."

Mama gave me a light shove, then shook her head at

my rude behavior. "Sweetheart. That is not the way to react to a situation like this. We can work this out, I know we can."

"Mama, there is nothing to work out!"

"Young lady, don't you take that tone with me." Mama gave me that look that told me I wasn't too big for her to still whup my ass. I pursed my lips and moved over near the sink.

She then started jumping in my shit about how I shouldn't have been messing with a man twelve years younger than me in the first place and that I needed to try and be a better mother. God, I could feel a migraine coming on with a vengeance. All I wanted Mama to do was take Portia home with her so I could go and find Ron and make everything right in my life again.

I heard a knock at the door. Before either of them could move, I raced out and flung the door open to find my ex-husband, Alvin Patterson, standing there. He immediately moved into the house.

"What's going on?" he asked, looking around frantically. "You called screaming and I couldn't understand a word you were saying."

"I'm putting your lying ass daughter out of my house." I folded my arms across my chest and glared at Alvin waiting to see what he had to say.

"For what?"

My mother moved into the living room. "Hello, Alvin."

His face brightened at the sight of her. He and Mama have always been close, even when I wished they weren't.

"Why don't we all have a seat and talk about this like adults?" Mama suggested.

"There is nothing else to talk about," I replied with a defiant tilt of my chin.

Mama nudged me in the hip. "Yes, there is, now *sit*!"

I growled in protest but took a seat when it was the last thing in the world I wanted to do. Time was ticking. The only thing on my mind was going to find Ron and trying to work things out between us.

Alvin took a seat on my couch and rested his elbows on his knees. "Okay, I want to know what's going on. Where's Portia?"

"Probably still in the kitchen crying," I replied with a snort.

Puzzled, he looked from Mama back to me. "Why? What's going on?"

Mama intervened. "I sent her up to her room."

"Can someone please tell me what's going on?" Alvin repeated.

"She lied. All this time she'd been lying, claiming that she was pregnant by my man."

"What! Pregnant by *your* man?" He shot out the chair. "I thought she was pregnant by some little boy at school."

"She is, but she lied and said it was Ron!"

Alvin shook his head with disbelief, then looked over at me like it was all my fault. *I can't help it if he's having a hard time accepting that Portia is no longer his little girl. Maybe this will help bring him out of la-la land.* "How do you know she's lying?"

I wanted so badly to hit him. What in the world did I ever see in him? "Because I read her journal."

"Read her journal?" He took a step toward me and gave a strangled laugh. "You're putting her out because of something she wrote in a journal." Alvin shook his head and looked as if he wanted to say something else and would have if my mother hadn't been sitting there. "I'm going to go and talk to my daughter." He took the stairs two at a time and I heard him knock on her door.

"This has gotten out of hand," Mama said, trying to sound calm, but I could tell she was not happy. Well, too damn bad.

"No, the only thing out of hand is my daughter, and I don't want to deal with it anymore."

"Danielle, you can't keep turning your back on your daughter."

"Mama, I love Ron more than I've ever loved a man."

"And you'll probably love a handful more. What's wrong with Calvin? He seems like a wonderful man."

Just the mention of Calvin Cambridge caused me to sigh with despair. "He is a nice guy, but he's just not Ron." I hated that I was going to have to break Calvin's heart. We'd only been dating a few weeks, but I was going to get Ron back. I felt a flutter at the pit of my stomach. I couldn't wait to see him.

Mama snorted rudely, then rolled her eyes. "Ron is history. And it's probably for the best."

"The best for who? Definitely not me." I rose and moved into the kitchen to start cleaning up. As soon as Alvin finished talking to his daughter, I was putting everybody out of my house and going to find Ron and make everything right.

"Danielle, you need to go upstairs with Alvin and talk to your daughter."

I pursed my lips and tried my best to keep my temper. Mama hadn't even been here an hour and already gotten on my last nerve. "Mama, I really would appreciate it if you would stay out of this. This is between me and Portia."

"Then why did you call me over here? Huh? That's

what I want to know." She planted her hands at her hips and started tapping her foot.

I groaned inwardly. "Because I know I would have killed her if you weren't here."

She kept trying to reason with me, but I wasn't having it. I wanted them all out of my house so I could leave.

Mama shook her head. I know she didn't agree with the way I raised my child. Too bad. I never wanted my daughter to turn out like me and my siblings. A bunch of spoiled brats. We grew up in a middle-class family, and Kendall, Constance, and I got everything we wanted with a pout and a few tears. Portia acted the exact same way, which was why she had my parents wrapped around her little finger. As a little girl, I had thought the behavior cute, but over the years I learned that my child was a manipulator, and I've done everything in my power to nip that shit in the bud.

"Since you're not listening, I guess I'll go upstairs with Alvin."

"Mama!" I cried, halting her from moving upstairs and making the whole matter even worse than it already was. As soon as she saw those tears, she'd start taking up for Portia's lying ass, and I wasn't having it. "Go home."

"What?" she cried, shocked.

"I said, go home. Let me and Alvin handle this."

She released a heavy sigh. "Fine. I got sense enough to know when I'm not wanted."

I watched her leave, then took a seat and waited for Alvin to come down the stairs. It was another thirty minutes before he came with his hands tucked in his dark dress slacks. Part of his uppity attire. He was too good to simply wear jeans. When we were together that's all he owned. Portia followed, came halfway down the stairs, and took a seat.

"Well?" I asked impatiently. "So how are we going to handle this situation?"

Alvin started popping his knuckles. He knows I hate when he does that. "I need a moment to get my temper in control, because after what my daughter just told me, I'm ready to go to jail."

"Jail?" I barked as I glanced over at the smirk that she quickly shut down. "I told you before you went up the stairs that girl is lying."

"And you heard what she said. She isn't lying."

Portia dropped her head.

"She's lying. That's all your daughter knows how to do is lie."

Alvin was so angry, he was shooting venom. "Face it. Your man messed with my daughter and I'm going to have his thug ass arrested." He glanced over his shoulder. "Portia, honey, go get your things. You're going home with me."

Obediently, she moved up the stairs.

Uh-uh, no, he didn't just come in and make my ass look like I'm the one to blame. I sprang from the chair. "Make sure you take all your shit, because you ain't coming back here!"

Alvin stood there and rocked on the back of his heels. "You sound like a fool."

"No, you're the fool believing your daughter, but then she gets it honest so that explains it all."

"That's the reason why we're not still together."

"We're not together because I left your sorry ass." I put my fingers in his face and he had the nerve to laugh at me.

"I blame you for our daughter being pregnant."

"What! How is her spreading her legs with some nappy-headed boy my fault?"

"If you were giving her the guidance she needed instead of chasing after all those young thugs, none of this would have ever happened."

I started laughing because I was so angry and because he sounded crazy as hell. "Go right ahead and press charges against Ron, and I'm going to let the entire world know what kind of tramp your daughter is."

"Yes, well . . . and I'll let the world know that if you weren't so busy dating men half your age, this would never have happened in the first place."

"No, if she'd kept her legs closed then none of this would have happened." I was too through with him. "Listen, I don't have time to be arguing with you. I've got something to do." I turned on my heels, grabbed my keys and my purse from the living room.

"Where you going, to find that nigga?"

I pierced him with an icy look. "Don't worry about me. Just take your daughter and be out of my house by the time I get back."

I hurried to my Durango, then peeled out of the parking lot and immediately put the car in drive. My cell phone rang and I looked down to see it was Mama. I didn't feel like hearing her mouth because for once in my life, I knew what I was doing. I loved Ron and he was my man and from now on, he had to come first.

I just don't know how I could have been so stupid. Something in my gut had told me my daughter, who had a habit of crying wolf, wasn't telling the truth, but no, I listened to my friends and did the motherly thing and believed my daughter's word, even though deep down I knew something wasn't right. Even after Ron pleaded his innocence.

See, my daughter had been a problem since she started high school. Meeting men over the Internet. Running away, accusing a college student of raping her. Portia had been out of control. And when she accused Ron of seducing her, I believed he fathered her child no matter how much it hurt me, because it was the right thing to do. *What a fool I was.*

As I drove, I thought about the last several weeks and had to blame my boo as well. *Damn you, Ron!* If he had told me months ago that Portia had walked in on him coming out of the shower, then I would have known how Portia knew he was uncircumcised. Instead, everything had spiraled out of my control and left me with no choice but to believe my daughter. What mother wouldn't? I know several hos that put their men before their kids. I know of a girl in Portia's class who had tried to tell her mother her stepfather had been sexually abusing her, but her mother refused to believe her and kicked her out onto the streets. Two days later, the girl hanged herself. It had been all over the news. And that was why I had chosen to believe Portia.

Angry tears streamed down my face as I made a right at the corner and then a left.

I met Ron about two and a half years ago. Shop & Save was running a sale on ground chuck and there wasn't any left in the bin. I rang the bell for the meat department and Ron came out. My tongue was hanging out of my mouth. He was fine as all get-out. Tall, dark, sexy, and a white-toothed smile dripping with charisma. After he brought out a family pack of meat, he asked for my number. That night he called, and by Friday, we'd gone out on our first date. It never bothered me that I was twelve years his senior. Hell, I'd dated men younger than that before. Cornrows braided straight back, jeans hanging off their butts, long white T-shirts and Timberland boots—there wasn't anything sexier. I didn't know why I was attracted to those types of men. It wasn't that I liked young dudes. I just had a thing for thugs, preferably one with a job. As an LPN, I could have dated and probably married a doctor by now. Instead I wanted a man like Ron in my life and I was going to do whatever it took to get him back.

"He's gonna forgive me. He's gonna forgive me." I chanted that over and over as I drove, and by the time I made it into town, I was sure that he would listen to what I said. After all, Ron loved me as much as I loved him. We've split up before but always managed to work it out. A smile curled my lips. Yes, everything was going to be okay, I was certain of it. We had been together two years strong before Portia fucked everything up.

It didn't matter what anyone said. Ron was one helluva man. My man. Maybe he didn't have a legit job and was forever in court for one thing after another. None of that mattered. I loved him and if, correction, *when* I got him back I'd stand by my man and tell all them haters to kiss my ass. I'm serious, there was just too much time invested in our relationship to just walk away. And that wasn't happening.

As I headed east on Providence Road, I started planning the rest of the evening. We definitely needed an entire night of make-up sex. Hopefully, he would just pack his bag and come back home. *Hmmm.* I would have to remember to drop by the store on my way home. Ron loves getting up in the middle of the night looking for Twinkies. What my man wanted, my man would get. I even planned to take off tomorrow so we could sleep late and then spend the entire day and night together.

I started smiling and was shaking with excitement as I neared my destination. I was finally going to get Ron back, and this time I wasn't going to let him go.

I pulled up in front of his mother's place in the hood

and cursed under my breath when I saw his sister Ursula's raggedy Honda in front of the house. Damn, that skank always did something to piss me off. I felt like pulling off and coming back another time. The only thing stopping me was that I needed to say what I needed to say to Ron as soon as possible so he could start packing his shit and head on home with me. Yep. It was going to take a lot more than Ursula's big mouth to stand in my way.

I climbed out of my SUV, moved past the unkempt yard littered with beer cans, and knocked on a screen door that was hanging off the hinges. As soon as Ursula swung open the door and saw me, she turned up her nose.

"Uh-uh. No, yo skinny ass didn't just knock on my mama's door!" she snarled.

I rolled my eyes at her. She got a lot of nerve talking about someone with her big forehead. "Where's Ron?"

Ursula posted her wide ass in the door. She wore a size twenty and was at least four inches shorter than me. "What the hell you need Ron for?"

" 'Cause I need to talk to him, that's why."

She rolled her neck as she spoke. "My brother ain't got shit to say to you."

"Ursula, this doesn't have anything to do wit you. This is between me and yo brother."

"Guess what? I'm making it my business." She propped her hand on her waist. "Mama!"

A few seconds later I heard someone dragging their feet across the floor.

"What's all that noise on my goddamn porch?" Nita said as she moved to the door. Sponge rollers in her hair. Dingy-looking housecoat and raggedy house shoes she wore every day, even to the grocery store. As soon as Nita spotted me standing on her porch, she bunched up her squinty eyes. "What yo boney ass want?"

"Nita, I came to talk to Ron."

"You got a lot of nerve showing up here. He don't wanna talk to you."

I glared at one and then the other. "I don't have time to be fooling with either of yo ghetto asses. I came to speak to Ron!"

"Bitch, don't be on my porch yelling!" his sister screamed.

I noticed the neighbors next door had come out of their house and were standing on the porch listening to the exchange. At least there would be witnesses if anything was about to go down. "Go get yo brother and I won't have to scream."

Ursula made a show of pulling off her jewelry. "Mama. You would want and go get the Vaseline."

I took a step closer and she took a step back. I laughed. Ursula couldn't fight and knew it. Hell, everyone knew it after she got her ass beat down by the woman her baby's daddy was now living with.

Ursula and I started shouting in each other's face. Nita got a big kick out of the whole thing and moved out onto the porch, took a seat, and lit up a joint. By the time I had my fist balled up and was ready to take a swing, Ron came to see what all the commotion was about. His right arm was in a sling and his face looked like meatloaf.

"Can we talk?" I said between breaths.

He didn't answer, just opened the screen door and stepped out on the porch. Tears burned at the backs of my eyes. Damn! My brother Kee had done a number on him.

Only seconds after Portia told him Ron had raped her, Kee tracked Ron down in Church's Chicken parking lot, yanked him out of his car, then beat him down with a crowbar. Rumor had it that Ron had been in a coma for three days.

"Can I please talk to you in private?" I asked. I was trying not to smile but was so glad to see him. I wished what happened to him never happened, but I had every intention of making it up to him as soon as we got home. *Hmmm, maybe I'll grill us some steaks.*

Ron moved out toward the curb, then turned and lit a cigarette. "All right, talk."

I glanced over at the porch where his mother and sister were both watching. I glared at them, then turned back toward him. "Can we go somewhere more private?"

"Nope," he answered as he took a puff. "You either tell me whassup or I'm out."

Damn, he wasn't making this easy for me, was he? I turned so my back was facing them. "I know you're not the father of Portia's baby."

Ron tossed a fist in the air so fast, I jumped back, afraid he was trying to swing at me. "I told you from the get-go *I ain't touched that girl*!"

"I know, I know, and I'm *soooo* sorry I didn't believe you."

"Are you sorry for yo brother and his boys jumping my ass? That's what I want to know." He glared at me.

"Yes, I didn't mean for any of that to happen."

He took another puff. "So . . . if I held you down while my cousin Twin came over and whupped yo ass, we'd be even, right?"

Hell nah! His cousin just got out of jail for attempted murder and was crazy as hell. I glanced over my shoulder at his people and rolled my eyes. "Listen, I'm trying to apologize."

Ron leaned forward and the muscle at his jaw twitched the way it did anytime he was pissed off. "And what's that supposed to solve? You and I were trying to do the damn thang, but you wanted to believe that trick over me even when I swore to you on my daddy's grave I ain't touched her mothafuckin' ass." It was quite evident in his face that he couldn't stand Portia.

"She *is* my daughter."

"And I *was* your man."

I smiled, then put on my seductive voice. "And as far as I'm concerned you're *still* my man. What can I do to make it up to you, boo?" Even beat up he was fine as hell. I was ready to beg if I had to.

"You betta not forgive her!" Ursula yelled from the porch as she passed the joint back to her mama. I glared at her and wanted so badly to pick up a brick and toss it at her wide forehead. "What you looking at?" she asked.

"You, bitch! Now what?" While I waited for her to respond, I watched a yellow Mustang pull up in front of Nita's place.

Ron leaned over and gave me the look that I loved so much. "I need to know how sorry you really is."

I returned my attention to him and took a step forward so our thighs brushed. Damn, he smelled good. "Boo-boo, I'm very, very sorry."

"You are? Well, check this out. You know what I want you to do?" He leaned in closer. If I didn't know better, I would have sworn he was going to kiss me.

"What, boo?" I asked while licking my lips.

Before I saw it coming, Ron cleared his throat and sent a big wad of spit that landed on my cheek. "You can get the fuck out of my face! That's what you can do. You lucky I don't hit women, 'cause I feel like stompin' yo ass."

"Hell naw!" Ursula shrieked.

It was then that a woman with long blond locks climbed out of the Mustang, chuckling like a hyena. "Baby, you ready?"

"Yeah, I'm ready." Ron tossed out his cigarette butt, then turned on the heels of his white sneakers and hopped into the car.

Spit slid down my cheek onto the concrete. Ursula and Nita screamed with hysterical laughter. The neighbors joined in. I was so embarrassed I climbed into my Durango without saying a word and headed home to find it empty.

3

Renee

Five months later

We were already pigging out on homemade chips and salsa when my girl Kayla Sparks finally arrived at El Maguey. She headed in our direction and I have to say, she looked fabulous in a wool pantsuit she bought last weekend at Lane Bryant. Her face was glowing with excitement. Shit, I ain't mad. With a man who was not only wonderful, but *fine* as hell, life for her was definitely sweet.

"Hey, sorry I'm late, but my boss waited until four-thirty to tell me he wanted me to get a letter out tonight." Kayla slid on the bench next to my partner-in-crime Danielle Brooks, then reached for a handful of chips. "What I miss? I know y'all were gossiping about somebody."

I met her gray eyes from across the table. "Yeah, John's faggot ass. He's been blowing up my phone all day."

Kayla gave me a weak smile. "Maybe it's important."

Danielle laughed. "Yeah, and maybe he's no longer screwing that fag and wants to get back together."

"Won't know unless you talk to him," Nadine Baker singsonged.

I glanced at all three of them, then stuck up my middle finger. "Fuck y'all. We don't have anything to talk about. Unless of course he's ready to give me a divorce so he and *Shemar* can get married."

Nadine gave a cross between a laugh and a snort. "You're sick."

"No, John's the one who's sick. Booty bandit."

Danielle started laughing and we all joined in. It felt good being able to finally laugh about this shit, because five months ago it wasn't that funny.

I sipped my drink and glanced at my girl Nadine, who was sitting to my right. Sick? How the hell could she talk about anybody? Her big-titty ass just came out of the closet less than three years ago and was now trying to have a baby with her woman. "Nadine. What happened at the clinic last week?" Her face dropped and I almost felt sorry for bringing it up. Remember I said almost.

"Jordan lost the baby."

Okay, now I really did feel sorry for her. The couple had spent thousands of dollars trying artificial means of inseminating Jordan, who was in her early thirties and wanted desperately to have a baby. Nadine already had a grown son and was knocking on forty. I knew they could afford it, but damn, enough was enough. I already told Nadine what to do. She just doesn't want to listen.

Kayla gave her a sympathetic look. "I'm so sorry. What are you and Jordan going to do now?"

Nadine shrugged. "We're looking at some other options."

Danielle looked over at me with a raised brow. I

reached for another chip, then repeated what I've suggested so many times I was starting to think that maybe Nadine was hard of hearing. "I already told you what to do. Find a sperm donor who's willing to do it the way it's meant to be done. Some plain old-fashioned fucking."

"Renee!" Kayla's high yellow ass turned three different shades of red.

I gave them all an innocent look. "What's the big deal? It's not like Jordan hasn't ever had dick before. Why keep wasting all that money? Shit, give that money to me and *I'll* find you the perfect man. Then all Jordan has to do is let that mothafucka fuck her long enough to bust a nut, then send his ass on home."

Kayla shook her head like I was one of her kids. "Girl, do you know how many diseases are out there?"

I gave her a dismissive wave. "So have him go get tested first. It's a helluva lot cheaper. Buy that negro a six-pack and a box of chicken and he'll be happy as hell."

Danielle choked on her drink and laughed along with me. Unfortunately, we were the only two who thought the shit was funny.

I could see the shock on Kayla's face. "You're stupid." Leave it to Kayla's holy ass to find something wrong with what I said.

"I think it's a wonderful suggestion." I turned to Nadine. "You and Jordan really need to give it some thought, seriously. Go rent that Spike Lee joint *She Hate Me* and you'll see what I'm talking about."

Nadine stared down into her drink as if she was embarrassed to reply. "To be honest, Jordan is so desperate, she's actually thinking about doing what you suggested."

See, I'm really not crazy. "Good."

The waiter arrived and Kayla ordered a virgin drink. As soon as he left, she clapped her hands merrily together. "Well, I've got something for all of you to gossip about."

Leave it to her to try to change the subject. "What?" I asked.

"Jermaine proposed."

"What?" We all squealed like teenagers.

Nadine's smile returned. "Oh my goodness! When did this happen?"

"Last night. I've been dying to tell someone but I wanted to tell all three of you at the same time." Kayla reached inside her purse and removed a platinum three carat diamond ring and slipped it onto her finger. She must have taken it off before walking into the restaurant. That's definitely what I called bling-bling.

I was impressed. "Hell nah! That shit is blinding!"

Kayla was beaming with pride. "This ring is so heavy I'm afraid my finger is going to fall off." She giggled.

Nadine gave her a scolding look. "Shame on you. I am so happy."

"So am I. I never thought this day would come."

"Let me see." Danielle reached for her hand and took a closer look. "It's beautiful! I knew there was a man out there for you. You just needed to find him."

Tears started running down Kayla's cheeks. "I know. Jermaine is the best thing to ever happen to me."

My eyes started to burn and I frowned. "Quit before you make me cry."

"Shit, she's going to make us all cry," Danielle replied as she dabbed at her eyes.

Kayla was one of my closest friends. She had come from a dysfunctional household with a mother with low self-esteem and a habit of letting men use her. Kayla and her sisters inherited her traits. Kayla went through life letting men take advantage of her and ended up with two lowlife baby daddies. After a dead-end relationship with a shady Baptist minister who ended up murdered, Kayla finally came to her senses and realized love had been standing right in front of her. She was just too stuck on stupid to notice until five months ago.

The waiter returned and took our orders. We'd been coming to this authentic Mexican restaurant for so long I knew the menu by heart. By far, El Maguey has the best margaritas and tamales in town.

"So when is the big day?" Danielle asked after our waiter moved to put our order in.

Kayla rested her elbow on the table, wearing a dreamy smile. "I don't know. We talked about getting married in September, but I really don't know if I can wait that long." She paused and dropped her eyes to the table. "I'm afraid if I don't marry him tomorrow something is going to happen and I'm going to lose him."

I pursed my lips and rolled my eyes. "Kayla, that man loves you. Shit, the size of your ring proves that. Quit thinking so negative."

"I know. I know. I just can't believe that something this good is happening to me."

"Well, believe it, girl," Danielle said with encouragement.

Kayla gave us an uncomfortable look, then reached for another chip.

That's Kayla for you. Always thinking that she doesn't deserve any goodness in her life. That's from years of fucking around with a no-good penis-dick minister who told her that her fat ass wasn't worth a damn.

Kayla is a *big* girl. Always has been. But she is a beautiful woman, especially on the inside, even though she doesn't think so. Hell, look at Mo'Nique—that sistah is fat, but so beautiful and confident and can dress her ass off that you forget about her size and all you notice is what's on the inside. Kayla has so much going for her. She's got a vanilla complexion, gray eyes to die for, and long cinnamon hair. She's just a healthy girl, but like I tell her all the time, men like a woman with a little meat on their bones. Hell, look at me, I'm thick—ass, legs, and no breasts.

Nadine touched Kayla on the arm. "It's your big day. When would *you* like to get married?"

Kayla shrugged.

"How about a June wedding?" Danielle asked as she tapped an acrylic nail on the table.

She frowned. "No, my cousin's getting married then."

"Okay, how about July?" Nadine suggested.

I nodded. "July is nice. It's also one of the busiest times of the year. If you're going to do a July wedding, then we're going to have to start planning right away because March is right around the corner."

Danielle agreed. "Yep, that's five months away."

"I'll help." Nadine was so excited you would have thought it was her gay ass getting married.

"Hopefully all of you will help me," Kayla replied, then glanced around the table. "I can't do this without my three best friends."

We all nodded in agreement.

Here it was, one of my best friends was getting married while my ass was one step away from divorce. I guess I could be a party pooper and say marriage is for the birds, but I know that isn't true. I just haven't found the right man yet. But damn, how long is it going to take? My ass has already been married three times.

4
Renee

We ate, drank, then made plans to meet over the weekend to start planning the wedding. I headed home and glanced down at my phone, and John's number flashed on the screen. "Die, bitch!" I screamed. What the hell did he want? As usual, I let it go to voice mail.

I'd be lying if I didn't admit to being scared. Hell, after years of fucking around on my husband, then wondering what the hell I was thinking when I agreed to marry him in the first place, here I was finally free and I was scared shitless. Now don't get me wrong. The last thing I needed was to be married to a booty bandit. Nevertheless, here I was at thirty-eight, starting over and nervous about failing my children. I'm a failure at love. After three husbands, I just wasn't in a rush to go down that road again. Mario was my high school sweetheart; we lasted long enough to conceive two kids. The second one was military. I was married to Troy six months before I discovered his stupid ass was also married to someone else. And then there's John. Other than the legal formalities, as far as I was concerned, he and I were through. But his calling me was just making matters worse. I wanted to move on and start a new life, but his punk ass just wasn't willing to let me do that.

After I caught John and Shemar together, he moved into an apartment while I stayed in the house long enough to sell it. John tried to reconcile, but my attitude was we didn't have shit to talk about except how to split the money.

When I moved back to Missouri, I purchased a three-bedroom house on the north side of town. Smaller than I was used to, but it was all mine and I didn't have to share it with some booty-bandit mothafucka. Hell, my ass is even working a part-time administrative job on campus. Having a job took some getting used to, but at least I have the flexibility to work on my erotic novels when there isn't shit else to do in the office, and I like that. Which reminds me, I have a book due in three months and need to put some fire under my butt if I'm going to meet my deadline.

I turned onto my street and noticed a black woman was standing off to the side waving her hands frantically in the air. I pulled up beside her and rolled down my window.

"Sistah, can you help me?"

I took in her Goodwill wardrobe and the slobber running down the side of her mouth. Her eyes were as yellow as her teeth. Ugh! I leaned back in the seat. That bitch better not slobber on my Lexus. "Help you with what?" I tried to focus on her eyes and not her mouth, but that wasn't easy to do.

"I don't get my food stamps until Friday and need some money to get some vegetables."

She looked like she was ready for her next crack fix.

"Sorry, I don't have any money. I'm trying to hang on until payday."

"Okay."

I was amazed at how easily she gave up. Anyone on drugs would have kept begging and pleading until I either cussed their ass out or gave in. Instead, she turned and walked up the gravel driveway to a raggedy duplex that looked like it had seen better days. I drove off feeling guilty because I had almost fifty dollars in my purse and enough in my checking account that I could have spared five dollars. But I knew that she would be like a stray dog. Once you gave her something, her ass would keep coming back.

Even though I drove off, she was heavy on my mind. I don't know, but something in her eyes reminded me of my mother. Bernice Brown was bipolar with a crack habit. I haven't seen her since Tamara was five. We were all at Big Mama's house having Christmas dinner when my mother came waltzing in drunk and smelling like a skunk. Mom had been MIA for the last six months. My aunts and uncles all acted like it was every day she came in carrying a half-eaten sweet potato pie. My older sister Lisa and I stopped eating and glanced at one another. Mama was in rare form that day. Singing, laughing, talking loud, obviously she had stopped taking her meds. Big Mama refused to believe anything was wrong with her daughter and moved to the kitchen to fix her a plate. After dinner, Mama disappeared again.

It had been a pattern since we were teenagers. One day we came home from school and found a note on the door that said she went to Washington, DC, to find work. It was two months before she returned, and by then my stepfather had come down to take Lisa and my younger brother Andre back to Chicago to live with him. Paul never liked me, so I wasn't invited to go. I stayed in the house until all the utilities were turned off, then moved in with my kids' daddy, who was jealous and possessive. I put up with him for four years. Then when he started trying to beat me upside my head, I decided it was time to go before I spent the next twenty years behind bars for murdering his ass. That was a lonely time in my life. My mama gone, Lisa and Andre far away. My stepfather never cared for me and rarely let me see my brother and sister and screened my calls. I heard him once say he didn't like me because "she acts like her damn daddy." I found that ironic since I didn't even know my real daddy. He had been murdered when I was too young to remember.

Our relationship has been strained ever since, and while Lisa was alive she did everything she could to try to bring me and my stepfather together. Even when she was struggling with ovarian cancer, she made me promise to reach out to Paul and I tried, for Lisa, but now that she's gone, I wrote him off like a bad debt. As far as I was concerned, I couldn't care less if I ever saw either of my parents again. Although it would be nice to at least know that my mother was okay.

I pulled into the garage then stepped into the house where my kids were sitting at the dining room table playing a game of Monopoly.

My sixteen-year-old daughter, Tamara, sprung from the chair. "Mama, you ready to go driving?"

I rolled my eyes. I've been slowly teaching Tamara how to drive, but after she ran my car through the garage door two weeks ago, I don't think my nerves could take it. "Tomorrow. I've been out drinking."

She turned her nose up at me. "You're always getting drunk."

"Girl, be quiet. I ain't had a drink all week." I'll admit I've been drinking a lot more lately. Shit, I'm stressed. But what the fuck? I'm married to a fag.

I looked over at my tall eighteen-year-old son, who was probably stealing money from the bank while Tamara's back was turned. "Quinton, I thought you were working tonight."

"I was, but it was slow so they sent some of us home." He worked at Popeyes Chicken.

I shrugged, grabbed my mail from the table, and let them get back to their game.

"Mama, John called my cell phone looking for you!" Tamara called after me.

Ugh! I wish that booty bandit would leave me alone. I fell back on my bed with a scowl and stared up at the ceiling fan above me. What I needed was some dick. It was time for a girls' night out.

5
Danielle

I spent Friday evening arguing on the phone with Mama. It's been five months and nothing has changed. I still can't understand how she could take sides with Portia when it was clear who was in the wrong. Is Mama not understanding what she did? My daughter had lied about sleeping with my boyfriend and had pretty much ruined my life. No, she can't come back and live with me. Is she crazy? That would be like Portia getting her way. As far as I'm concerned, she can just keep on staying with her daddy.

As promised, Alvin filed rape charges, and just as I had been trying to tell his dumb ass all along, Portia waited until the day before the case was to go to trial to admit she had been lying. *Told you so!*

Ron was released, which was a good thing. I was all prepared to testify on his behalf even though he doesn't want to have anything to do with me.

My friends think I'm stupid for turning my back on my daughter, but I don't agree. Portia's lies caused me to lose my soul mate. I would do anything to have him back. Really. If Ron called and told me he'd take me back, I would have him. I know he isn't perfect, but Ron is everything I love in a man. A thug to his heart. He knows the streets, and let's not forget the brotha is no joke in bed. Sure, he had a bunch of kids, and bitches be calling me at all hours of the night. I dealt with the BS because I believed my man was worth it. The only reason we weren't still together was because my daughter had described my man's dick. Not too many brothas running around uncircumcised, but Ron was one of the few. Not that it affected his performance in any way.

The last five months have been miserable. I feel lost without him. Even though I have a new man in my life, all I think about is getting back with him. I've left him messages. Dropped by his mother's house, but he never responds to any of my advances. I know after five months it's time for me to try and move on, but it's hard.

I reached in the back of my closet looking for something to wear. I hadn't been out in months and it was definitely time for me to get out of the house. With Ron and Portia both gone, unless I was spending time with Calvin, I was usually bored and lonely. Yep, I was definitely ready to get a drink. Who knows, maybe I'll meet someone new tonight to take Ron off my mind.

Yeah, right.

In a small town like Columbia, Missouri, there wasn't anyone worth meeting because chances were they had already gone through half the skanks in town. And after my breakup with Ron, I wasn't sure if I was ready to handle another thug just yet. Right now I needed a dependable, no-stress relationship, and that was Calvin.

Speaking of Calvin . . . I glanced over at the clock. He

was prompt and should be calling just about . . . now. I reached over and grabbed the phone before the second ring.

"Hello, may I please speak to Danielle?"

I rolled my eyes. He knew good and damn well I was the only one living in the house. I didn't know why he always tried to act all professional and shit. Sometimes it pissed me off so much.

"Hey, Calvin. How's the conference?"

"Long and boring." He's a university police officer and was in California attending a CSI training seminar. "I can't wait to get back and hold you."

I smiled. "Me either."

"What do you have planned this weekend?"

"Me and the girls are going out tonight."

"Don't have too much fun," he warned with laughter in his voice.

"I won't. Are you doing anything fun tonight?"

"Me and a couple of the boys are going out and Regina's tagging along."

I chuckled. Regina was the new administrative assistant in the department and had a mad crush on Calvin. "Maybe I need to be worried about you being in Cali with another woman," I teased.

"Sweetheart, you don't have to worry. There's only one woman for me." His voice sounded sexy as hell. "I can't wait to get back on Sunday. I hope you're ready."

"Ready for what?" I asked as if I didn't already know.

"You know what."

I chuckled. "I'll be ready."

"Good. I'll call you tomorrow, love."

"Okay."

Calvin was such a nice guy. And so faithful that I never had to worry about him messing around. Regina didn't have a chance in hell of taking my man from me. Damn, if only I could love him the way he deserved. We've been together over six months and I'm crazy about him and the sex is good, but my feelings for him are nothing like what I felt for Ron. If I could feel like that with Calvin, I would have the perfect man. I wanted that heart-stopping, can't-be-without-my-man feeling that I used to have. I like a man who knows the streets and doesn't have a problem telling me what he wants in and out of bed. I'm not sure if anything other than a thug would ever do. Some people saw it as a problem. I saw it as simply having a preference.

6

Renee

Tonight was not at all like I had planned. Kayla didn't want to go out because she was going to spend the evening with her fiancé, and Nadine and Jordan were too busy making baby plans. What the fuck! Couldn't either of them put their lovers aside for just one night so that the four of us could hang out for old times' sake, but *noooo,* and I had to go out with Danielle by my damn self. I knew the minute I told her the other two weren't going what club she was going to pick.

Athena's.

I can't stand that place, but without my cheering team to back me up, it was either go with her or go out by myself.

It was after eleven when I stepped through the doors, and immediately I felt like I had just stepped inside Chuck E. Cheese's. Nothing but a bunch of goddamn kids. What the fuck? That's what happens when you live in a college town. Students were back after a three-day weekend, and everyone was out trying to get their drink on. I walked in, late of course. Danielle had paged me an hour ago to tell me she was heading over early so she could get a table. So she was in here somewhere.

I strolled in wearing a long-sleeved blue-jean jump-suit and four-inch gold platform shoes. I'll admit the music was jumping and people were everywhere. I could barely get through the door. As I moved around the room looking for Danny, I saw a few cuties looking my way and even smiled at one until I noticed the sweatshirt he was wearing said *RBHS Class of 2005.* Rockbridge High School. What the hell? He was nothing but jail bait.

I pushed my way through the crowd looking for Danielle. I don't know why her ass couldn't have just waited until I had got ready so we could have came to-gether. It's bad enough I even have to be in this motha-fucka.

Moving through the crowd, I passed a group of girls who barely looked sixteen. The shit they were wearing was downright nasty—skirts that if they bent over showed all their *assets* and bras they were trying to pass off as shirts. One girl had rolls around her stomach and was running around with a bra that was at least two sizes too small. If that had been Tamara, I would have snatched her ass off that dance floor and taken her home.

I slowly made it around the building. All anyone did in this place was walk around in a fucking circle and try to be seen. I just wasn't in the mood.

I managed to get around a fat chick and made my way over to the bar. I slid onto a bar stool and while I waited for the bartender, I rocked my hips to the beat of the music. 50 Cent was putting it down with his new sin-gle. I loved that song, and from the looks of it so did several others. A tall, skinny bartender came and took my order, then came back with my apple martini. I took a sip. Delicious. I tossed another dollar on the counter.

Glancing across the bar, I caught a dark-skinned brotha trying to get my attention. *What the fuck ever*. His ass was busted and definitely too damn old to be in a place like this. He was definitely somebody's grandpa. I rolled my eyes, to make sure he got it loud and clear that I wasn't the least bit interested in his tired-looking ass.

I was taking a sip when I felt a tap on the shoulder. I glanced over and my mouth dropped.

"Oh my God, Landon!" I swung around and gave him a hug. "When you move back?"

He smiled and appeared pleased that I noticed he'd been gone. In a town this small, who the hell wouldn't.

"I've been back from Germany almost five months."

"You still in the military?"

He shook his head and said with pride, "Retired army."

I nodded and took in everything he had to offer, and that was a whole helluva lot. Landon had been one of those misfit kids in school who always seemed to hang with the girls. He didn't act gay and shit, just one of the girls. Senior year, he started dating Tonja's ass and she had his nose so wide open, he followed her around like a lost puppy. A week before graduation, she dumped him and next thing I heard, right after graduation, he had joined the military. Over the years I had seen him from time to time, but this was the first in two decades we had a chance to strike up a conversation. I'm glad I came out. 'Cause Landon was finer than a mothafucka!

He was wearing a typical military cut. Hair was higher on the top than the side but low just the same. A navy blue turtleneck emphasized every muscle in his chest and his arms. His jeans were loose but not enough to hide his massive thighs. White sneakers set off the look.

"What are you doing here?" I asked. "Trying to catch a case with the jail bait in here?"

He frowned. "Nah, Hodges dragged me in here with him."

I nodded knowingly and followed the direction of his eyes to his boy standing at the other end of the bar trying to spit at one of those young-looking girls. Hodges was one of those who refused to admit his ass was hitting fifty.

Landon grinned. "I should be asking what you're doing in here."

"I'm meeting Danny."

He chuckled and I joined in. He knew my girl's taste for young thugs as well as I did.

"Have you seen her?"

He pointed to the back of the room. "She's sitting over there."

We stood there staring at each other like two damn fools. I could have continued, but the last thing I wanted was for him to know just how attracted I was to him. I don't run after men. I like to be chased. "Thanks. I'll holla at you later."

"You do that. Save me a dance."

I reached for my drink, then turned and walked away. At least something good was coming out of this night. I moved to where Danielle was sitting. She was wearing this cute Rocawear jean outfit she bought while we were in St. Louis shopping last week.

There were only two chairs at her table, and neither was empty.

"Hey, whassup?" I asked with my eyebrow raised as I

looked down at Mavis's crackheaded ass sitting across from her.

"Whassup, Renee?" she asked as she rose out of my seat. "You got five dollars?"

I backed up and raised a finger to my nose because I could smell her breath from where I was standing. "Yeah, here." I reached inside my pocket and slipped off a five. Anything to get her ass away from me. She didn't even bother to say bye as she dashed off into the crowd. "Ugh! What you doing talking to her?"

"Girl, you know her ass is a booster. She's going to come by my house tomorrow with some new DVDs that just came out."

"Oh, well, if she's got anything good, hook me up."

Danielle nodded, reached for her drink, and took a sip.

"Guess who I saw coming in?"

"Who?" she asked.

"Landon."

Danielle's eyes widened. "Landon Lawson? Hell nah! I heard he was back."

"Yep, and he looked good as hell."

She gave me that look that said *I know something you don't.* "Girl, you know he's been messing with Leslie's wide ass since he's got back."

She had my attention. "Leslie who?"

She smirked and reached for her drink. "Leslie Harris."

My eyes grew large. "Hell nah."

She sucked her teeth. "Yep, but I heard she started stalking his ass, so he quit fooling wit her."

Leslie came out of high school a year ahead of us and was one of those that I never cared much for. She spent too much time in the club getting drunk instead of home taking care of her three kids. I heard she didn't like me. Why, I don't know, and really couldn't care less.

"I saw her in here earlier, so don't let her see you talking to her man."

"Fuck Leslie's ass."

"All right, don't say I didn't warn you," she teased.

I pursed my lips and swung around in my chair. Danielle knew I wasn't scared of that ho. One thing I don't do is back down.

While sipping my drink, I waved at people I knew as they moved around the building. Like I said, the place is one big circle, so at some point everyone came around at least once. Sure enough I saw Landon, and shortly after Leslie was coming up behind him. I shook my head. One thing Renee doesn't do is sniff after a brotha. When it's over, it's over. If we decide we want to fuck after that then it's a mutual decision. But I'll be damned if I ever stalk a mothafucka that doesn't want me.

"Danielle, look."

I pointed to the bottom of Leslie's boot. She was dragging a long piece of toilet paper. We both fell out laughing.

I sat there for the longest time watching Leslie watch Landon. What Leslie needed to do was go home and change her damn clothes. I don't know why fat people always feel they have to throw on a miniskirt, especially when their thigh is wider than their waist.

Danielle lightly kicked my leg underneath the table. "Nae-Nae, here comes David."

David Lavell. Short, chocolate mothafucka and one of Columbia Police Department's finest. He looked fabulous in dark slacks and a white polo shirt and white sneakers. But then he looked good in anything he wore. He had a body made for clothes. I tried to give him some last year, but his crazy-ass wife came banging on the door of our hotel room. If I had gotten some before she had interrupted maybe I wouldn't still be angry.

"Whassup, Renee?" He gave me his devilish smile and held out a hand. "Come dance with me."

I shook my head. "Hell nah! So your wife can come over and start trippin'? I don't think so."

"She's not here and if she was, she wouldn't trip about me dancing with a friend."

Before I could object further, he took my drink out of my hand, placed it on the table, and led me out onto the dance floor. The music had slowed down to Fantasia's new cut. I allowed David to pull me in his arms. I ain't gonna lie, the married mothafucka smelled good as hell.

He brushed his lips against my ear. "You know I regret what went down with us."

"No, you don't, 'cause if you did, you wouldn't have gotten me in that mess in the first place." I leaned back so he could see my eyes as I spoke. "How could you set my ass up like that?"

"I didn't mean to. Really," he pleaded.

"Yeah, you just forgot you and her were together," I replied sarcastically.

"Nah, I just was pissed at her."

"And you tried to use me to get back at her?"

He offered me an apologetic smile. "Something like that."

Laughing, I shook my head, then rested it on his shoulder again. That was something I would have done, so I guess I couldn't be too mad as long as that shit never happened again.

"So you want to go to the hotel after we leave here so I can tap that ass for real this time?"

"David, shut the hell up!"

He tossed his head back with laughter. "You know I can't help myself when it comes to you. Renee, you fine as hell."

True that, but I wasn't even going to go there with his married ass. One thing Renee Moore doesn't do is intentionally mess with someone else's husband. Your man, yes. Your husband, no. Even though I don't attend church on a regular basis, I know that there is a God up there in heaven and if He says do not to be drooling over someone else's husband, then I know better than to disobey Him. Adultery is a sin, which I have been committing for years on my husband, but that situation was different and as far as I was concerned didn't count. But I never ever mess with someone else's husband. I didn't like that shit when I caught my husband in bed with another man, so I wouldn't want to see anyone else have to go through that kind of shock, ever.

We danced two songs before I looked over to see Landon. He was leaned up against the bar flirting with some female. As soon as he spotted me, he whispered something in her ear, then headed my way. With his eyes, he asked me to dance. I thanked David, who didn't look too happy, and moved toward Landon, who wrapped his arms around my middle. Together, we moved to the beat of the music, neither of us saying anything. I closed my eyes and got caught up in the moment.

"Your body feels so good next to mine."

That shit was corny, but for his fine ass I'm going to let that pass. "You feel good, too."

"Here we are twenty years later. Who would have ever guessed we'd be attracted to each other?"

I chuckled at his confidence. It was something the old Landon never had. "Who would have ever guessed?"

"Ima keep it real, I have always been attracted to you, even back then."

"Really?" I said like I didn't already know.

"Yep. I was such a cornball back then. Highwater pants, thick glasses."

"Yep." I laughed.

"I knew back then there was no way I could step to you without having you laughing in my face."

I shrugged. "You were like a brother to me."

"And now?" he asked, studying my face. He licked his lips and I felt my body quiver.

"Now . . . when I look at you I don't think about my brother."

"That's what I wanted to hear."

We chuckled and then I rested my head on his chest and closed my eyes. For the first time since I left John's tired ass, I felt that maybe there was a chance for me to finally get it right.

It was during the next song that I got this feeling someone was watching me. Sure enough, I opened my eyes and spotted Leslie from across the room staring at my ass. I locked eyes with her, then ran my hand up and down Landon's back. Oh, the look on her face was priceless. It took everything I had not to start laughing while I rained light kisses along Landon's neck.

"Mmmm, that feels good," he murmured.

I continued to smile over at Leslie, daring her to bring her big booty onto the dance floor.

"You better quit before you start something," Landon whispered against my ear.

I pulled back and stared up at him, then draped my arms around his neck. "Oh, I'm definitely trying to start something," I purred and looked over my shoulder to make sure Leslie was still watching. She was.

"What do you have in mind?"

I smiled up at him. "After the club. My place. I think we have a little catching up to do."

He looked surprised by my response. "Sounds like a plan."

The song ended and I released him and headed back over to where Danielle was sitting and talking to some short, bald dude. When I got up closer, I recognized him. Christopher Thomas. He and Danielle had dated while in high school.

"Whassup, Nae-Nae?"

I jumped back when I noticed his top teeth had packed up and moved the fuck on. "Hey, Chris, what's been up wit you?"

"Just trying to hold it together."

If his teeth were any indication, he was doing a poor job at it.

He looked from me to Danielle. "I was just trying to get your girl here to go out with me."

I smirked, reached for a chair at the next table, and pulled up a seat. "That sounds like a good idea. Danny, why don't you go out with him?" She gave me a look that said *help me out* but I pretended not to notice. "Chris, Danielle loves Red Lobster."

"Bet! I can take you there tomorrow night. I think they are having all-you-can-eat shrimp." He wagged his thick bushy eyebrows, then slid an arm around her shoulders. "How 'bout it, Danielle? You want me to pick you up?"

She removed his hairy arm. "I don't think so."

I intervened. "What you riding these days?"

He stuck out his chest with pride. "A Geo Metro."

"Geo Metro?" Danielle and I said at the same time.

"Yep." You would have thought he said he owned a BMW.

I shook my head with pity. "I thought they stopped making them in the nineties."

"They did. I have one of the last ones that ever came off the assembly line. I don't know why they stopped. They are economical. Even with gas prices, I can ride all day for little or nothing."

"That's wonderful." I turned my head to hide my laughter. Chris was definitely a winner.

"Come on, Danny, let's dance," he suggested.

Danielle choked on her drink. "Uh, I'm not feeling up to it."

"Okay, I'll leave you alone as long as you save me a dance and promise to think about dinner."

Danny nodded. "I'll think about it."

Chris said good-bye, then moved into the crowd with his pimp-daddy stroll and I howled with laughter.

"You need to quit playing so damn much. Ain't no way in hell I'm going out with him."

I was cracking up. "He used to be the love of your life."

"That was a long damn time ago. Now his ass looks tired as hell."

We laughed, then leaned back in our seats and enjoyed the music. We were on our third round of drinks when Landon pushed through the crowd and joined our table.

"What's going on, Danny?" They hugged and he took the chair beside me.

"Damn, boy! The Army definitely does a body good." She looked him up and down. "I should have snatched you up when you asked me to the spring dance our sophomore year."

He gave a nervous laugh that used to sound so goofy but now was quite sexy.

For the next couple of songs, we sat there talking about the old days, laughing and shooting the shit. Danielle kicked my leg under the table. Damn, that was a bad habit of hers.

"Uh-oh, here comes trouble," she said.

I followed the direction of her eyes in time to see Leslie heading our way. I struggled to keep a straight face. She huffed over to us and slammed the palms of her hands onto the table in front of Landon.

"Landon! We need to talk," she demanded.

Danielle mumbled under her breath. "Uh-uh, no, she didn't."

"Oh, but yes, I did," she replied, spacing each word evenly, then bored her eyes at Danielle to show her she wasn't scared.

Danielle gave her a dismissive wave and pointed to the other side of the club. "Y'all need to take that shit over there."

I started laughing 'cause I ain't think Leslie had it in her. But here her big ass was, leaning over the table all in his face waiting for Landon to acknowledge her.

He finally shook his head and got up. "Excuse me a minute."

"Yeah, *excuse* him," she replied sarcastically. Leslie stormed off and Landon followed.

I called after him. "Go handle yo business, boo! I'll be right here when you get back." Danny and I exploded with laughter. "She would want to do something about her breath."

"That wasn't her breath. That's her armpits."

I started waving my hand in the air. "Hell nah! She smells sour as hell."

"I can't believe Landon was screwing her."

I sucked my teeth. "At the looks of things, he probably still is."

I watched the two of them in the corner going at it. Leslie was definitely feeling some type of way seeing him with me, but then most women do. *Whatever!*

My eyes traveled around the room and I spotted several people I knew who were too damn old to be in this place, but then who was I to talk. I had no business being in here my damn self. This was definitely a college hangout spot.

I looked over at the door and my mouth dropped. "Danny, ain't that Ron?"

"Where?"

I pointed and she practically broke her neck trying to see who was walking through the door. The expression on her face confirmed my suspicions.

I ain't gonna lie, Ron is delicious in a thuggish kinda way. Tootsie Roll dark chocolate. Tall with a muscular build. Straight-back cornrows. He had on low-rider jeans and a white T-shirt.

"Who's that girl he's with?" From across the room she looked vaguely familiar.

"I don't know and don't care," Danielle answered with straight attitude. She tried to act like she didn't care, but her eyes reflected her anger and I could tell she was still hurting over him. I tried to cheer her up. "Girl, that bitch's weave is whacked."

Danielle laughed. "Right."

I rose. "I'm going to go and get another drink. You want one?"

She nodded, yet her mind was more on Ron and his date with the bad hairdo than on me. "Yeah. A drink would be great."

"Coming right up."

I shook my head. I don't know why Danielle can't just move on. Men like Ron ain't the kind you marry. They're the kind you simply fuck. Even if her daughter hadn't lied, Ron was a piece of shit. He ain't never been able to hold on to a job for long and spends too much time in the street. I wouldn't touch his dick with my worst enemy's pussy.

1

Danielle

I watched Ron with that bitch on his arm. I didn't want to stare, but his walk demanded my attention. I hadn't seen him in five months and just the sight of him caused old feelings to resurface. There was something about him that did things to me. He had obviously moved on, yet I couldn't help feeling jealous the way the two of them were hugged up. I felt hate. I felt love. I felt like going over and demanding that bitch leave my man alone. Luckily, I remembered he no longer belonged to me. *Damn! Am I ever going to get over him? It's been months, yet he's all I can think about. I am so pathetic.* I don't know if I'll ever love anyone like him. I wasn't sure if I even wanted to.

"I know who that is," I heard Renee say when she returned to the table with our drinks.

I should have known Renee was going to bring Ron back up when she returned. Knowing her, she went over to the bar just so she could get a closer look. "Who?" I asked, trying hard to sound like it didn't matter one way or the other.

"He's with that bitch Rosalyn."

The name didn't ring a bell. "You know her?"

Renee nodded and took a sip. "Yep. She used to mess with my cousin Dirt. Straight ho. I heard she's got the package."

"Which package?"

She pursed her lips. "Herpes."

"Hell nah!" I couldn't help but feel relieved by what she said even though it was probably just one of the hundreds of rumors floating around this little-ass town.

"Danny, if that's what Ron wants, then so be it."

That was easy for her to say. She left her husband because she caught him fucking another man in the ass. The only reason Ron and I weren't still together was because of my daughter's lie. I wanted so badly to get out of my seat and over there and talk to him. *Don't you dare do it!* Fine. Besides, I'm sure Renee would kick my ass if I even tried.

I sipped my drink and watched the two of them walking around the building, he in front and she right behind on his heels. As much as I hated it, they looked good together. She had more curves than a cul-de-sac. Full breasts. A wide ass and a narrow waistline. She was wearing low-rider jeans and a midriff sweater that showed off her belly ring. Ron was wearing loose-fitting jeans and a T-shirt that couldn't hide the massive muscles in his arms and chest. I wanted to reach out and take a bite. He had bowed legs. Dammit! Just knowing someone else was now riding *my* dick was hard for me to accept. Instead, I was left feigning for him and thinking if he would just give me one more chance things would be so much different.

My nostrils flared. It wasn't fair! I had waited almost two years for him to grow up and get a job. And as soon as he had gotten himself together and things in our relationship had just started to get better, my daughter stepped in and fucked everything up.

"You need to quit staring before he notices."

I blushed. I should have known Renee was watching me. "Damn, am I that pathetic?"

"Danny, I know you ain't still trippin' off of Ron. After he spat in your face, he would be the last man I'd want to be with."

I took a sip from my glass, ignoring her comment, and was glad when David came over and led her back out onto the dance floor. Sometimes my best friend gets on my last nerve. What she'll never understand is that it doesn't matter how long I date Calvin, I will never get over my one true love. No one can make me feel like Ron does. The brother was slinging dick for days, and nothing beats being in bed with a thug.

I forced myself to look around the room but my eyes kept landing on Ron and that ho he had on his arm.

If Portia hadn't lied, we'd still be together.

Or maybe not.

I released a heavy sigh. Maybe it was time for me to let go and move on. After all, it was Ron's loss. I had been a hell of a good woman to him for over two years, and up until the last couple of months all he had done was use me. My utilities had gotten turned off so many times even though Ron claimed he had paid the bill. Then there were the calls from his baby's mama in the middle of the night. For real, he wasn't even worth my time and I wasn't sure why I still wanted him, but I did.

Just get over him.

I looked over in time to catch Ron looking in my direction and quickly turned my head. The last thing I wanted him to know was that I still loved him.

Renee returned, reached for her drink, and brought it to her lips, then started bobbing her head. Everything was going to be all right. I could feel it. *As long as you stop staring at Ron.*

Focusing on the opposite side of the room, I spotted a tall, thuggish-looking brotha with Hershey's chocolate skin. Good God Almighty! I had never seen him before in my life, and I thought I knew everybody. My heart started pounding. And when he glanced over in my direction and the two of us made eye contact, I wiped my mouth to make sure I wasn't drooling all over myself.

Renee noticed, too. "Goddamn, the cutie is sweating your ass."

"And I'm checking his ass out, too."

It wasn't long after, he walked across the room and stopped right in front of our table, and I thought I was going to fall out of my chair.

"Hey, sexy, you want to dance?"

I was tongue-tied. All I could do was sit there and stare at his sexy gold-tooth smile.

Renee intervened. "Hell yeah, she wants to dance."

Nodding, I rose from my seat and followed him out onto the dance floor. The last time I was caught slow dancing in the club with another man, Ron had come over and started a fight. I glanced over to the right to make sure Ron wasn't paying attention. He wasn't.

"What's your name?"

I smiled up at my partner and wrapped my arms loosely around his waist. "Danielle. Yours?"

"Chance."

Ooh, his name was just as sexy as he was.

I leaned against him, and together we swayed side to side to the beat of the music. I gazed up into a pair of mesmerizing hazel eyes. Damn, could the brotha possibly be any finer? "You new in town?"

"Yes and no," he began with a pearly white grin. "I went to school at Lincoln University and used to kick it up here all the time."

"Where'd you grow up?"

"St. Louis. But I've been back a month. If I can find myself a good woman I'd have a reason to stay." The music slowed down and Chance pulled me snugly into his arms and I closed my eyes and smiled. Damn, it felt good being held by him. Why couldn't it be this way with Calvin?

When the song ended he pulled back slightly and stared down at me again. "I'll let you get back to yo girl. But first put your number in my phone just in case you try to sneak out before I get those digits."

I smiled and tried to hide my excitement. The last thing I wanted him to know was how much I was feeling him.

"Holla at me before you leave."

I nodded, then sashayed back to the table and caught Ron staring. I tossed my head back and laughed all the way back to our table. Good for his ass.

8
Renee

I went and got another round of drinks even though I knew good and well neither one of us needed another. But what the hell? You only live once, and I knew I wouldn't be back in this place again anytime soon. Although I have to admit I was having a hell of a time with the few folks in this place that were my age. I returned to the table just as Danielle came back and lowered onto the seat.

"Who the hell was that fine mothajumper?"

"His name is Chance."

"Chance?" I frowned as I watched him move around the bar. "Where's he from?"

"St. Louis, can you believe it?"

"St. Louis?" Something about him suddenly seemed familiar, but I couldn't put my finger on it.

"What?"

"I don't know. I was wondering if I knew him." There was something about him, but there was no telling. I knew a lot of people. "So whassup with him?"

"Nothing really. I gave him my number so I'll see if he calls me."

At least she gave him her number. I thought with Ron being in the room she'd be scared to even try to step to another. The last time she did, Ron's ass clowned Calvin. He stole on that negro before he saw it coming. Hee-hee! That was some funny shit. That's a good sign. Maybe she was ready to move on. And it's about damn time. Ron just ain't worth losing sleep over.

I looked over and saw Landon heading our way. Leslie was nowhere in sight. "Whassup?" I asked as if I hadn't been watching him since he left our table.

"I'm so sorry about all that." His apology seemed sincere.

"Whassup with you and Leslie? 'Cause inquiring minds want to know."

He shrugged like it was no big deal. "That's the past."

I rolled my eyes. "Must not be, the way she was sweating yo ass."

Danielle gave him a hard look. "I think you need to go on back over there with her, 'cause Ima have to whup her ass if she come over here trippin' again."

"She left."

I smiled. "Good, then have a seat."

9

Danielle

I waved Renee good-bye. I should have known she was going to take Landon home. Hell, I wasn't no hater. If I had my way I would have been inviting Chance home with me. But as I followed the crowd out of the club, hoping to run into him again, I couldn't find him. Hopefully he'll call me— soon. In the meantime, I would have to go without getting any dick tonight.

You can always pull out your vibrator.

Hell no. I needed something tonight that a piece of plastic could not give me. Something rough and dirty that only a thug could offer.

I reached inside my purse for my keys and crossed the street. Everybody was coming out of the club, and both the street and sidewalk were crowded. Nobody appeared to be in a rush to go home. Neither was I, but where else did I have to go?

When I got close to my vehicle, I almost tripped on the heel of my boot when I spotted Ron leaning against the hood of my Durango smoking a blunt. Cops were circling the area, but leave it to him not to give a fuck.

My heart soared when I realized he hadn't gone home with that slut. *Bitch, you gotta play it cool.* I couldn't let him know how happy I was to see him waiting for me. Instead of running into his arms like I was dying to do, I ignored him and walked around and unlocked my door.

"Yo, whassup?"

I simply shrugged. "What's up wit you?"

"Nothing," he said and took another hit. "Where yo nigga at?"

Oh, he had noticed. By the frown on his face, I knew it pissed him off. *Good.*

"I don't have a nigga."

Ron dropped the blunt to the ground and put it out with his foot. The whole time I stood there with the door open, waiting. I knew I should get in and just pull off but I couldn't, because this was the moment I've been waiting for.

"Want some company?" he finally asked.

"I guess," I said. It took everything not to smile.

"Yo, it's either yes or no."

I rolled my eyes and climbed in. Ron was always trying to run things. "You can either come or you don't."
Please come. I was already staring down at his crotch.

"Yeah, aw'ight. I'll be there in a few."

Nodding, I pulled away, and as soon as I reached the corner, I stopped my SUV long enough to scream "Hell yeah!" at the top of my lungs, then tried not to get a ticket as I sped home to change my sheets.

10

Renee

I pulled into the driveway, raised the door to the two-car garage, and signaled for Landon to pull into the spot beside me. The last thing I needed was for the neighbors to be knowing what's going on at my house.

I'm an undercover freak. Tamara was staying the night with a friend and Quinton was spending the weekend at his father's. I was free to get buck wild without an audience. Otherwise, I would have had Landon pay for a hotel. And not a cheap one, either.

The door lowered, I climbed out. Landon came around beside me.

"You live in a nice neighborhood."

What did he think I lived in? The hood like that rat, Leslie?

I just smiled, moved toward the door, and opened it. He followed me inside and gave a wolf whistle as he looked around. "Damn, Renee! You living large."

I love when people compliment my house.

"Shit, maybe I need to write a book."

I get a kick out of how people think just because you write books you've got to be rich. And I'd be damned if I corrected him. With the money from my separation agreement, I was able to afford a house I was proud to call my home. But I didn't invite him over for a tour. I wanted to get to know him better, if you get my drift.

I reached inside the refrigerator, removed two Coronas, and signaled for him to follow me into the family room. While he got comfortable on my leather couch, I went over to the stereo and turned on the "Quiet Storm." I moved over to that couch and took a seat, putting just enough distance between us but close enough that I could reach over and caress his thigh. For a long time, neither of us said anything and just enjoyed the music. Atlantic Starr was singing "Secret Lovers." I hadn't heard that cut in years.

"I can't believe I'm here with you," Landon said with a sheepish grin.

"Neither can I." I can bet Leslie is madder than a mothafucka. Hee-hee!

"What are you smiling about?"

"Nothing."

"Oh, so you're not going to tell me what's on your mind." He tried to tickle me and I jumped back out of his reach.

"Hey!" I laughed. "I didn't say that."

"Then tell me. What're you thinking about?"

"I'm wondering when you're going to shut the hell up and kiss me."

"You said nothing but the word."

He took both our drinks and set them on the floor, then leaned forward and pressed his lips to mine. Mmmm. Yummy! They were soft and he knew how to give just enough tongue without getting all sopping wet. I moaned when he snaked an arm around my waist and pulled me against him. I locked my hands around his neck and leaned in closer. I could feel my body responding to him. *Now that's what I'm talking about!* A brotha with looks and skills. Landon was a passionate kisser who cared about making sure I was enjoying it as much as he was.

I closed my eyes while he nibbled and licked at my neck, each touch sending chills down my spine. I could tell he liked to take his time, while I was ready to get busy. I slipped my hands beneath his shirt and caressed his pecs. Oh, but they felt good. His hand slipped under mine and he unclasped my bra and reached inside to caress my itty-bitty titties. *Oooh, yesss!*

Eager to get this show started, I broke the kiss and pulled his shirt over his head, then removed my own.

"Do you want to go up to your room?" he suggested.

"Not just yet," I whispered. Rising, I stood before him, reached for my zipper, and removed my jumpsuit and stood before him in a pair of lace panties.

"You're beautiful."

"So I've been told."

He pulled me back down on the couch. The whole time he was kissing me, my mind was racing with possibilities. Little Landon Lawson had grown up to be a man.

Never one to let a brotha think he has the upper hand, I flipped him onto his back and allowed my tongue to travel from his neck across his pecs while he palmed the cheeks of my ass.

"Damn, you're sensual," he moaned.

Okayyy, that shit sounded gay as hell, but 'cause he's sexy, I'd let that comment pass as well. But one more of those and I was going to slip him John's address, then show him the door.

I slid my tongue down his fabulous abs and followed

the trail of hair to the band of his boxer briefs. I love the way they look on a man, especially if he has large legs. And Landon's thighs are massive. And that's not the only thing. That bulge in his briefs was enough to make me salivate. Anxious to see what was inside, I instructed him to raise his hips. I lowered his underwear and wanted to shout. *Oh, hubba bubba, Landon, go grab that rubba!*

"Mmmm, Daddy, you're full of surprises."

He beamed, and he had every reason to be proud.

I got down on my knees on the floor and instructed him to hang off the edge of the couch. With his legs spread, I moved between them. As soon as he was comfortable, I licked a path up one inner thigh and then the other, teasing and drawing closer to the tip each time but never quite reaching him. Landon lifted his hips, trying to get me to lick the head of his big black snake, but I refused. Don't he know by now I do things at my own pace, and damned if I'm going to rush. Besides, I like to make a brotha beg.

"Please, Renee. Suck it."

See what I'm talking about? "Not yet," I said and blew on the tip. He squirmed. I chuckled. I teased him a little longer, then captured the head between my lips and lightly sucked. Oh, he was moaning like a baby now.

I lowered and swallowed him whole, released him, then took it slowly in and out of my mouth, sucking and releasing, taking him deeper and deeper and releasing again.

"Oh, hell yeah!" he said.

"You like that?" I asked between slurps.

"Hell yeah. Take all that dick."

But can you handle it, I thought as I released him and slid my tongue around to his balls and nibbled at one and then the other. He arched off the couch. I wrapped my fist around the base and my hand traveled up and down his length while I kept my lips at the head sucking. He rocked and tried to take my head deeper but I wasn't having it. As soon as I thought he was on the verge of coming, I released him and rose.

"Where you going?" Landon asked, looking desperate as hell.

"To my room."

I didn't even have to look over my shoulder to know he was right behind me.

11

Danielle

I had just gotten out of the shower when the doorbell rang. My heart was beating with excitement. Tonight I was getting my man back!

I pulled the towel tightly around me, sprayed a little mango-scented mist at my neck and wrists, then moved to the door. This time it's going to work, I just know it, because I'm not letting anyone stand between us. That's a promise.

Swinging the door open, I found Ron waiting on the other side. His eyes traveled down to my towel-clad body and he smiled.

"Whassup?"

I struck a pose as I leaned against the door jamb. "Are you going to come in or you planning on standing out on my porch all night?"

Chuckling, he moved into the house. I pulled the door shut and moved to stand in front of Ron.

"Where's your daughter?" he asked.

"She doesn't live here anymore."

"That's too bad."

"No, it's not," I said and stepped forward until my thighs brushed against his. "Ron, I meant what I said. I am so sorry for not believing you when you tried to tell me the truth."

He looked unconvinced. "Are you now?"

"Yep."

"You ready to show me just how sorry you are?"

"Yes." I rose on my tiptoes and tried to kiss him but he pulled back.

"Yo, it's gonna take more than that to show me."

"What do you want?"

"Shit, you know what I want," he replied with that thug cockiness that I missed.

I smirked, then reached down for his zipper. "Yep, I know exactly what you need." As soon as his pants hit the floor, I dropped to my knees and removed his dick from his boxers. I had forgotten how big and beautiful it was. I eased it inside my mouth, sucking gently while stroking his length. I was determined for him to remember how good it used to be between us. Within seconds my head was bobbing back and forth as I deep-throated his length.

"Yeah, that's it. Take this dick."

I moved faster. Ron rocked back and forth, then grabbed the back of my head and guided me. It got to be too much and I started to gag, but I wasn't about to complain or stop because I was willing to do whatever it took to make Ron happy. To bring my man back home. I could feel his muscles tighten with every stroke. I sucked him continuously while using one hand to massage his balls.

He finally pushed my head away. "That's enough. I need to be inside you."

I rose.

"Come here."

As soon as I did, he snatched the towel away. Staring down at me, he stroked the length of his dick. "Move over to the chair."

Obediently, I moved and took a seat.

"Nope. Turn around. I want your ass in the air so I can see that pussy."

I assumed the doggy-style position, and before I could take a breath he slammed deep inside me. It was rough and hard and just the way I liked it until it got to be too much. He was banging me so hard I felt him all up in my stomach. "Ron, you're hurting me!"

Ron slapped me hard across the ass. "Take this dick! You know you like it." He smacked my ass again. "Tell me you like it."

By this time the walls of my kitty-cat had completely relaxed and I was coming all over the place. "*Oooh, baby! I like it.*"

"You love it."

"Yes, I love it!"

"You love me?"

Tears streamed from my eyes. "Yeah, baby! Yeah, baby. I love you so much. I never stopped loving you." It was so good and powerful that I started to bawl. Here I was making love with the man I loved. How sweet is that!

Ron plunged harder and it hurt so good. It wasn't long before I came hard, screaming his name at the top of my lungs.

"I'm about to come all in that pussy! Uuugh!" he grunted, then squirted hard inside me. He pulled out and collapsed on the floor, and I landed on top of him and held on to him tight. There was so much I wanted to say. I wanted to tell Ron how much I still loved him and how hard it had been these last several months without him. The fact that he had come home to me proved that he was hurting as much as I had been. Yep, Ron and I were going to be together forever. I lay there thinking about waking up to him every morning again.

After a while, I rose and moved to the bathroom next to the kitchen to grab a towel. Ron lay there on the floor while I cleaned him up.

"Want something to eat? I think I might have some Twinkies."

"Nah. I need to get home."

My face dropped. *Home. He's already home.* "Why don't you stay the night with me?"

He shook his head, avoiding eye contact, and reached for his pants. "Yo, I got some business to take care of. I'll be in touch."

I sat on the floor and watched as he got dressed and walked out my front door.

12

Renee

Landon and I went at it all night and after the third round I was quite satisfied. Damn, it had been a long time since I last had dick. I love my vibrator and it definitely does the job, but nothing can come close to a real dick and a warm body lying beside you afterward.

I was curled up against Landon dreaming my ass off when I felt something warm and wet. After our night, wetness was a given, but this felt unusually wet. I opened my eyes. It was a hissing sound that made me swing back the covers and jump out of the bed.

That nasty mothafucka was pissing in my bed!

I was stunned beyond words, because like catching my husband fucking another man, I never expected to witness something like this either. I couldn't get my lips to move. All I could do was watch Landon holding the base of his dick while he shot out pee like it was a water faucet. Get this, when he finally finished, he shook off his dick.

Hell nah!

That mothafucka must have been dreaming and thought

he was in the bathroom taking a piss. What took the cake was that washing his hands was obviously not a habit of his because as soon as he was done, instead of rubbing his hands together, his nasty ass rolled the fuck over and went back to sleep.

I reached for a pillow and started beating him upside his head. "Wake up! Landon, get the fuck up!"

It took a full minute to wake him out of his groggy state. "What? What's wrong?"

"What's wrong is that you pissed in my bed!"

Landon had the nerve to look confused. "Pissed?" Looking down, he noticed the wet spot, then mumbled, "Damn," and grabbed his dick.

"Look at that shit! You . . . you pissed all over me!"

"My bad," he replied like it was no big deal.

"Who the hell you think you are, R. Kelly?"

"I said I'm sorry," he said defensively as he got up and reached for his pants. His pissy ass wasn't even going to take a shower.

"Sorry ain't going to buy me a new mattress."

He had the nerve to laugh.

"I don't see shit that's funny."

"Come on, Renee, calm down. I'll buy you a new mattress."

"When?"

He had to think about it a moment. "When I get paid next Friday, I'll swing by and pick you up and we can go to the mattress store together."

I rolled my eyes because there wasn't shit else to say. I mean, what were we supposed to do at this point? Go back to bed? Move into the kitchen and I'd make us breakfast? *Hell nah!*

"Well, I'll give you a call tomorrow," he replied, signaling an end to our evening.

I started removing my expensive sheets from the bed so I could throw them funky things in the trash. Instead of offering to help, Landon reached for his keys and left. From the window, I watched him climb in his Tahoe and drive home, smelling like piss.

13

Danielle

After work on Monday, I headed over to Calvin's house. He had gotten back from his conference yesterday and was dying to see me. *What else is new?* Sometimes I felt smothered by the fact that he wanted to be with me all the time. But after screwing Ron Friday night, I felt so guilty, I owed it to him. Besides, it had been a long day at the hospital. Working as a labor and delivery nurse was no easy task. I had no intention of cooking anything and I was so hungry, I was tempted to stop at a fast food restaurant on the way, but Calvin, who was a wonderful cook, was preparing dinner.

Usually, I go home first and change out of my scrubs into a pair of jeans and a T-shirt, but it was only Calvin. No point in dressing up.

I pulled into his subdivision and drove up the drive of the first house on the left. A two-story, three-bedroom house with blue siding. I jumped out of my car and moved up to the door. Damn, it was cold this afternoon. I guess it could have been a lot worse. Like snow and ice.

"Danielle, you made it," Calvin said as soon as he spotted me standing there in his doorway. Before I could enter, he leaned down and gave me a big hug and then a kiss. "Damn, I missed you."

"I missed you, too," I murmured against his lips. "Now can you move so I can get out of the cold?" Not waiting for a response, I brushed him aside and hung my coat on a hook in the foyer. "Something smells good. What are you cooking?"

"It's a surprise. Please come have a seat."

He signaled for me to follow him into the living room. Soft jazz music was playing on satellite television. I took a seat on the couch and he sat beside me.

"How was your weekend?"

I should have known he would ask. "Dull like always," I lied. I still couldn't believe Ron hadn't called me yet. I felt a connection between us the other night and couldn't understand why he wouldn't just come home and stop playing games, because it was starting to get old. "You know how this little boring-ass town is. Nothing to do here but eat out and go to the movies."

"That sounds like a wonderful idea. How about we go and see a movie on Friday?"

"Maybe, depending on the way my week goes. I'll let you know." Ron was going to call, I was sure of that, and there was no way I was passing up a chance to be with him.

Calvin wrapped his arm around me and I leaned back against him. He always made me feel comfortable. I closed my eyes while he ran his fingers through my shoulder-length hair.

"Danielle, I would like to know where you see our relationship going."

I was glad he couldn't see me frown. "Going?"

He chuckled lightly. "Yes, Danielle. Going."

Nowhere, if Ron calls. And it better be soon. I was thinking about running by his mama's house on the way home to see if he was there. I don't know where he's living at now and didn't think to ask him the other night. *Stupid! Stupid!* Why didn't I get his home phone number? All I was thinking about was being with him; I never thought about how we were to keep in touch. "I don't know, Calvin. I've been enjoying our relationship. I like taking it one day at a time."

He pulled me closer. "I love you, Danny, and would love to spend the rest of my life with you if *we* decided that's what we want."

I frowned. Why now? Why couldn't he wait until I had a chance to see where things were heading with me and Ron first? Don't get me wrong, I care about Calvin a lot, really I do, but I know that I'm not ready for what he wants. Not as long as I think I have a chance with Ron. And I was certain I did. I could feel it in my gut. It was just a matter of time. Unfortunately, patience has never been one of my strong points.

"Can we just leave things the way they are . . . for now. I'm afraid if we try to rush things we're going to ruin everything that we have." I held my breath hoping that what I said had gotten through. I wasn't lying, really I wasn't. I just needed more time.

Calvin gave an impatient sigh, then kissed the top of my head. "Sure, Danny. We can take all the time you need."

I released a sigh of relief.

He patted my thigh. "Come on, let's eat."

I eagerly rose and followed him into the kitchen. I was more than ready to eat.

He made a fabulous meal of shrimp fettuccine, garlic

bread, and red wine. Calvin was a fabulous cook and I loved the way he got creative in the kitchen.

Halfway through the meal my cell phone chirped. I practically choked on a shrimp. I reached down for it and checked the ID. Damn, it was Renee! I put my phone down, smiled over at Calvin, then started eating again. We talked about his conference and Regina, his assistant, finding excuses to knock on his hotel room door late at night. That sneaky bitch had been trying to climb up on Calvin's dick. I teased him about it until he blushed. Regina was wasting her time, because Calvin's dick belongs to me.

After dinner I helped with the dishes and then we moved into the bedroom with our wineglasses.

"You staying the night?"

I usually do, but what if Ron came by? Nope. I needed to be home just in case. Because if he came by and I wasn't there, he wouldn't come back. "No, I've got nothing clean to put on in the morning and need to wash, but I can stay for a little while." I could tell he was disappointed and I felt a little guilty, but Calvin would never understand that I couldn't deny what I was feeling.

I moved over to the bed and he signaled for me to roll onto my back and started working his magic. Mmmm, he knew how much I loved getting a massage. I closed my eyes and enjoyed his magic fingers. That is, before my phone rang and I practically jumped from the bed, knocking Calvin over onto his butt. I fell on the floor on top of him.

"What the hell?"

I reached down for my phone while I tried to come up with an explanation. "I'm sorry. I heard my phone and thought I better get it." I looked down at the missed call. *Private.* Oh no! No, no, no! That was Ron. I know it. I just know it. I hit the Talk button and listened to my voice mail. My heart sank. There was none.

"Are you expecting something important?" I could tell he was pissed.

"Uh . . . yeah. My mom called earlier and said that Portia wasn't feeling well this morning and she was going to take her to the emergency room if she didn't start feeling better."

He looked pleased to hear that. "So does this mean that you and her are going to work things out?"

Hell no. If it wasn't for Portia, I would be at home right now with Ron lying between my legs. I rose from the floor, moved over to the end of the bed, and took a seat. I shrugged. "No, but regardless of what she's done, she's my daughter."

Rising, he stood over me. "Hopefully this baby will bring the two of you back together."

I doubt it. "Look, I need to get home." I'm sure Ron had tried calling me on my house phone as well. I couldn't wait to look at the Caller ID when I got there. I rose and leaned up against Calvin so he would know that I cared about him. "Baby, I'll make it up to you later, but I do need to go home and wash clothes and relax before tomorrow."

"I understand," he said between kisses. "Call me when you get home."

"I will." I kissed him one last time, then moved to the living room to retrieve my coat and purse. Calvin walked me to my SUV. I was ready to race home but he wanted to kiss and hug. Dammit, for all I know, Ron was pulling in my driveway at that very moment.

I gave him a deep kiss full of tongue and promises of more on another day, then hopped in my SUV and peeled out of the parking lot. Halfway down the road, I called home to check my answering machine. Dammit! No messages. *Okay, okay, don't get upset.* Ron had never been one to leave messages before, now was no different. He felt seeing his number on the Caller ID was sufficient.

"Nooo!" I squeezed the steering wheel. If he called it would say *Private* again. Damn.

I hurried home, hoping that he was waiting in the driveway. Hell, hopefully he still had his key. Or did I change the locks after my brother beat his ass? I couldn't remember. Nevertheless, he wasn't still mad because if he was, he wouldn't have come over the other night. Or would he? *No, no, no, don't start second-guessing yourself.* Not now. Not when I was so close to getting him back. Six months. I've waited six months for this day to come. And it was finally here.

I hurried onto my street and turned up the road. Dammit! No car in my yard, but then it dawned on me. He didn't have a car. I had taken the Chevy Impala I had purchased in his name when we split up. When Kee and his boys went to teach him a lesson, my brother made him sign over the title and hand over my keys.

I pulled in front of the house and left the car running while I went inside to check my Caller ID. Sure enough, another private caller. After checking my hair and reapplying my makeup, I hopped into my car and drove over to his mother's house. I know it might sound crazy, but I had to know if he had called me and the only way to find out was to go over and ask him. I was certain he was waiting for me to make the next move since I was the one who put him out in the first place.

Quickly, I drove down to the city certain that as soon as I pulled in front of the house he'd be ready to go home with me. I would definitely take the day off tomorrow and we'd spend it together. Maybe we could sleep in late and then we could have breakfast and then ... I had to giggle as I thought about all the possibilities. Tonight would be the start of a whole new beginning. I was sure of it.

I waited impatiently for the light to finally turn green, then I made a left onto Nita's street and pulled in front of her house in time to see Ron and another girl come out of the house. It was the same girl who drove the yellow Mustang, only this time she wasn't hiding behind the car and my mouth dropped.

The long leather coat could not hide her large, swollen stomach.

14
Renee

"Why orange and chocolate?" I asked.

Kayla reached for the container of shrimp fried rice and dumped some on her plate before answering. "Because those are the colors I've always wanted to have at my wedding."

"Whatever floats your boat," I said with a frown, then picked up the pen and added her color selection to the list.

"Hopefully our dresses are going to be chocolate, because I don't look good in orange," Danielle replied between chews.

"Yes. There is going to be orange trim on the dresses. The flower girl and my maid of honor are going to wear orange dresses."

"I still can't believe you chose Carol over me to be your maid of honor. I thought we were girls?"

Kayla looked over at me wearing a sympathetic look. "We are, but I didn't want to have to choose between the two of you so I decided it was safer to let my sister do it."

I could understand that, because if she had chosen Danielle over me I would have been highly upset.

I wrote Carol's name down. "Okay, how many bridesmaids, and I need all their names."

"Four. You, Danielle, my coworker Crystal, and Nadine."

"Who's gonna walk Nadine down the aisle, Jordan?"

Danielle slapped my arm. "Nae-Nae, shut up."

"What? I just asked." Hell, her dyke ass might not want to be linked with a man.

"I'm pairing her with my cousin Timmy."

Danielle's brow rose. "Didn't they used to mess around back in the day?"

"Oh shoot! I forgot about that. Never mind. Renee, scratch that. One of you will have to walk with him."

"Uh-uh, I'm not walking with his little sawed-off ass!" Danielle cried.

I reached for an egg roll and agreed. "Me neither."

Kayla pushed her plate away and sighed heavily. "Fine. He can walk with Crystal."

"Okay, so who's walking down the aisle with me?"

Kayla shrugged. "Probably one of Jermaine's cousins."

"And what about me?" Danielle asked.

"Another one of his cousins."

I gave her a curious look. "What do they look like? 'Cause inquiring minds wanted to know."

"What difference does it make?"

"It makes a lot of difference." I snorted rudely.

Kayla pursed her lips and gave me a hard stare. It's rare when my holier-than-thou friend gets mad. And right now she looked like she was seconds away from throwing both of us out of her house. "Renee, can't you for once think about someone other than yourself? This is *my* wedding."

"Girl, I know and I'm sorry, but can you do me one favor? Whatever mothafucka you have walking me down the aisle, just make sure he doesn't pee in the bed."

Danielle fell back onto the floor and started kicking her legs up in the air and I couldn't help but laugh even though the shit would have been a lot more funny if it had happened to someone else.

Kayla looked at Danielle, then turned to me with a puzzled look. "Pee in the bed? Oh Lord, do I even want to ask. What in the world are you talking about?"

"Landon spent the night with Renee and peed in her bed!" Danielle shrieked.

Kayla's eyes grew round. "What? Who's Landon?"

"This stinky mothafucka I went to high school with."

Danielle sucked her teeth. "You didn't think he was stinky when you saw him stroll into the club."

"Hell, how was I to know he peed in the bed."

Kayla looked mortified. "Ugh! He came to your house and peed? Oh my God! What did you do?"

"I put his stanky ass out! That's what I did."

"Kayla, he thought he was in the bathroom," Danielle added between chuckles.

"Yeah, he was holding his thang and had the nerve to shake it when he got done." I used my hands to demonstrate.

Danielle screamed and Kayla started laughing. Hell, I even gave a few chuckles before I started getting angry again. "That shit ain't funny. I haven't heard from his pissing ass since. I've gone to his job and even his house and I can never catch him."

"Kayla, you haven't heard the best part. Nae-Nae, go ahead and tell her what you made me help you do."

"Don't try to act like I *made* you. You were more than

happy to help." Danielle always tries to make it seem like I'm the only one that does all the crazy shit.

She rolled her eyes. "Whatever, ho, just tell the story."

I leaned forward against the coffee table. "Landon told me he would buy me a new mattress two weeks ago when he got paid. I waited all day for him to call me and then I started calling his ass but he refused to pick up. I called his cell phone, house phone, and even rode by his mama's house looking for him. Anyway, I waited until Wednesday and blocked my number before I called and he answered. I asked him where the hell was my money and that motha-fucka had the nerve to hang up on me. So you know a black bitch like me got mad!"

Kayla rolled her eyes as she reached for her orange soda. "Oh Lord, what did you do?"

Danielle jumped in. "Nae-Nae, let me finish telling it." How could I say no when she looked like she was about to pee her damn self?

"Go ahead."

Danielle crossed her legs and sat up straight on the floor. "Okay, this crazy girl gonna call me and tell me she's on her way over to pick me up. So I go outside and she pulled up in her uncle's raggedy-ass truck and told me to get in. I climb in and we go back to her house and pick up those mattresses she had lying in the garage. They reeked with pee." She turned up her nose.

Kayla interrupted with a heavy sigh. "What did y'all do?"

I sucked my teeth. "We took those mattresses to his apartment complex and left them in his front yard."

"No, you didn't," Kayla said, for some reason finding it hard to believe. I don't know why. She knows how I do.

"Uhhh, yes, we did."

Danielle nodded in confirmation.

Kayla shook her head and tried to act like she was disappointed, but I could see she was trying not to smile. "You are stupid."

"No, I'm not. Landon's the one who's stupid to think that I would just let that shit go." I exhaled, showing my frustration. "His pissy ass owes me eight hundred dollars."

"Kayla, girl, Nae-Nae wrote in big letters on the mattress, 'he who lives here, pees here'!"

"What!" Her eyes grew wide.

"Yep, we leaned them mattresses against the big tree in his yard for the whole damn neighborhood to see."

Kayla laughed out loud. "You are too stupid. Renee, what did he say?"

"He called me and had the nerve to be pissed. Saying he had run into some financial problems and he'd get me next payday."

Danielle snorted rudely. "Payday's tomorrow, and I bet you don't hear from his ass."

I rolled my eyes. "And I'm not going to let it go, either."

"We know," Kayla and Danielle answered at the same time.

I gave a dismissive wave. "Whatever. Let someone come over and pee in your bed and see how you feel."

"Asia used to pee in my bed all the time," Kayla said with a shrug.

"That's different. Hell, Quinton peed on himself until he was six, but that's my kid. If his grown ass was still peeing in the bed, then we'd have a problem."

"I think you should just leave it alone and let the Lord deal with him."

"Kayla, puh-leeze. That man owes me and he's gonna do right by me."

Danielle frowned. "You better leave him alone before he pees on you again."

Kayla cracked up laughing.

I rolled my eyes at both of them. "Enough about Landon's stinky ass. We've got a wedding to plan."

15

Danielle

On the way into work on Friday, I spotted Ron driving a brand-new Honda Accord. He pulled up beside me at the red light, looked my way, bobbed his head in acknowledgment, and before I managed to roll the window down, he pulled off. I couldn't believe that shit. Not a hello. Nothing. Why was he ignoring me? Two weeks. It had been two weeks since he had come to my house and fucked me, and not one phone call.

I climbed off the elevator and moved down the hall to Labor and Delivery mad and frustrated because it wasn't until I watched him peel away from the light and leave my ass in the dusk that realization hit me. Ron didn't love me. He couldn't, because he had done nothing short of using me. And it was time to face the honest truth: what Ron and I had ended long before I showed up on his doorstep begging him to come home.

I was moving down the hall ready to plow anyone in my way when I looked down at the end of the hall. I almost tripped when I spotted a brotha who was so fine he made you want to slap yo mama. I tried not to stare. He was wearing a white hospital coat, which meant he worked here. Damn, he could be a medical student or even a new resident. I knew fine when I saw it, and it was definitely him. The closer I got, the more I couldn't keep my eyes off him. He looked up from the woman he was talking to and our eyes met long enough for me to gasp. It was the guy I had met at Athena's. Chance. I looked into his big hazel eyes. He smiled, then licked his thick lips and I was sure I came in my panties. *Bitch, snap out of it! He's had your number for the last two weeks and ain't called you once.* He was definitely the last thing I needed, regardless of how wet he made my panties. I dropped my head and moved down the hall to the unit, clocked in, and went to listen to the morning report.

It wasn't until noon that I had an opportunity to sit down at the nurses' station and check my e-mails. While I waited for the computer to boot up, I checked my cell phone. I frowned. Four missed calls, and they were all from Mama. She had been blowing my phone up all morning, and the last thing I needed was to talk to her about Portia.

I logged in and noticed a message from someone I didn't know. I clicked on it and opened the e-mail.

Sexy, I saw you looking at me. Tell me a little more about yourself.

Heart pounding heavily with anticipation, I looked both ways before I raised my hands to the keys and typed a short paragraph, and hit Send. I couldn't believe it. He was feeling me. I was tempted to ask him why he hadn't called me, but maybe he didn't remember me from the other night.

My phone in my pocket vibrated. I looked down and felt a stir of guilt. It was Calvin.

"Hey."

"Whassup, baby? How's your day?"

"Could be better. I didn't get much sleep last night." Last night I camped out near Nita's house hoping to catch Ron coming or going but never did. Around midnight I finally gave up and headed home. Maybe he moved in with that girl. *What do you care? He doesn't love you anymore, remember?*

"Do you feel up to a movie tonight?"

Might as well. Ron was no longer a part of my life. Besides, it's Friday night. "Sure, baby. What time?"

"How about I pick you up at seven? That should give us plenty of time to eat and catch the nine-thirty show."

I hung up and started to feel excited about my evening with Calvin. Why in the world did I even think I wanted Ron when Calvin was everything I need in a man? Stable, financially secure. He's been with the university police department for the last fifteen years. Has a big house. A nice ride. And money in the bank. Calvin had more than Ron and the dozens of Rons before him. So why is it that I crave excitement and drama?

The phone at the desk rang and I picked it up.

"Hey, whassup?"

I almost dropped the phone. Without him even giving his name, I already knew it was Chance. "I'm fine. How about you?"

"I'm good. I saw you looking at me."

"You did?" Damn, I knew I had made it too obvious.

"Yep, 'cause I was looking at you, too."

Well, at least I wasn't the only one.

"How long you been working here?" he asked.

"Too long." I suddenly remembered something and asked with straight attitude, "How come you never called me?"

"I lost my phone."

"Yeah, right," I replied and snorted rudely.

"Serious. I wouldn't do you like that."

"Uh-huh." I wasn't totally convinced, but I'd let him slide for now.

"So what is it you like about me?"

Talk about stuck on himself. "Who said I liked anything about you?"

"I could tell," he replied with confidence. "So tell me."

I was cheesing so hard I'm sure it was obvious in my voice. "I think you're kinda cute."

"Kinda?" he asked, sounding offended.

"Yeah, kinda." He had to laugh and I joined in.

"You married?"

"Nope."

"Kids?"

I was tempted to say no. "Yep. One who lives wit her grandmother."

"I don't have any kids."

"You married?" It was my turn to interrogate.

"Not anymore. I was in the National Guard. While I was deployed in Iraq for eighteen months, my wife cheated on me."

"What?"

"Yep. And when I got back I moved into my own place."

"So what do you do?"

"I'm a veni-puncture technician. I draw blood."

"I know what a veni-puncture tech is. How long you been drawing blood?"

"For a while. I was a medic in the military and just retired last summer."

"That's whassup." Hallelujah, a man with a career. "What brought you back to this little town?"

"I got sick of St. Louis and wanted something slower paced."

Nothing wrong with that.

"Can I tell you something?" he asked.

"What?"

"You've got a fat ass."

I should have been offended but I wasn't. "You go from sounding educated to sounding all ghetto and shit."

"Yo, baby girl, I got to play the part at work. I have a degree in biology so I do have an edjumication."

I had to laugh at that.

"Yeah, but like I was saying, you do have a fat booty."

I was still laughing. "Oh, so you noticed?"

"Yep, and I liked everything I saw. You're sexy as hell."

"Thanks."

"I'd really like to take some time to get to know you. How about dinner tonight?"

"That would be—" I stopped short and groaned inwardly. I had already made plans with Calvin for the evening.

"Come on. I know you want to say yes."

"What gives you that idea?"

"Because you're feeling me and I'm feeling you."

He was right. I did want to say *hell yes*. Talking to him had brightened what had started out as a miserable day. And before I knew it, I heard myself saying, "Okay."

"Good. How about you give me your number again and I'll call you this evening. You're not going to stand me up, right?"

"No. I'm not. Just don't lose your phone this time." I gave him my number and hung up with a big smile on my face. *Damn, now I have to find a way to cancel my evening with Calvin.*

16

Renee

I was so proud of my daughter. We had driven through the neighborhood and not once did I have to yell at her to stop the car. *About damn time*. I have been working with Tamara for almost four months and was starting to think that we were never going to get to this point. Now I could see that my work here was almost done.

She pulled into the driveway and that feeling of uneasiness returned until she put the car in park.

"Don't worry, Mama, I'm not going to run into the garage again."

"Uh," I mumbled as I looked out at my new garage door. I think she must have fallen asleep at the wheel that day. By the time I'd realized she wasn't going to put her foot on the brake, she had already slammed into the garage door.

We went inside and I moved into the kitchen to make dinner while she went to her room to do her homework. Every day I picked her up from school and every day she drove us home. The hours worked perfectly for me and Tamara. Quinton had his own car—a big-ass Bonneville.

I reached inside the refrigerator for the ground beef because I was in the mood for spaghetti. While I was browning the meat, Danielle called.

"Remember that fine guy I met at the club?" She sounded too damn happy.

I had to dig through my memory bank for a second. "The dark-skinned one with a mouthful of gold teeth?"

"Yep, Chance."

"What about him?"

"I just found out today he works at the hospital."

"Where at?" Probably housekeeping. My girl has a thing for thugs and blue-collar workers.

"No, he doesn't work in housekeeping or food service. He draws blood."

"Really." That was definitely an improvement.

"I ran into him in the hallway and he called me at the nurses' station and asked me out to dinner tonight."

"Hell nah. And he's paying?" Hey, I gotta ask because she's usually the one who does.

"Yeah, he's taking me to Red Lobster."

"Go 'head, girl!"

"I know. I can't wait." I could hear the excitement in her voice.

"You know Calvin's gonna kick yo ass."

Danielle sighed heavily in the phone. "I'm ready to kick him to the curb."

"I thought you were feeling him." For the last several months, all Danielle talked about was Calvin and how good he was at sucking her toes and shit.

"I like him a lot, but he's boring. I wished he had a little thug in him."

Why am I not surprised? "Don't you think it's time your old ass started looking for something in your life besides drama?"

"Girl, I can't help it if I like a man that is a little rough around the edges."

"Yeah, I like my men like bread, brown and a little crisp around the edges, but damn, the mothafuckas you always pick are like burnt toast." For as long as I can remember Danielle has had a thing for thugs. Most of them are younger, unemployed, living at home with their mamas, and with at least one baby's mama. Now don't get me wrong. John was a damn bore and I like a little excitement in my life as well, but if I'm gonna be with a thug-ass nigga, then you best believe he better keep my pockets fat, 'cause I ain't giving this coochie up for free.

I opened the pack of spaghetti and put it in a pot of water. "So what you gonna do about Calvin?"

"I'm gonna try and cool things off for a while, but he's such a nice guy I don't want to hurt his feelings."

"You can't have it both ways. Just tell him you want to start seeing other people."

"That would have been okay if he hadn't just told me how much he loved me and then I told him the same."

My brow rose. "Do you?"

"I'm not sure."

I had to bite my tongue. "Then why the hell you tell him you did?"

"Because it sounded like the right thing to say at the time."

"I told you not to be playing with that man's emotions."

"You got a lot of nerve."

True, I do have a tendency to make a brotha think I

want him and then kick him to the curb, but we ain't talking about me or the bustas I fucked with. "Just tell him the truth."

"I can't do that."

"Then what he don't know won't hurt."

She paused. "I guess, but I got another idea."

"What?"

"Make a pass at him."

I almost dropped the Ragu sauce. "What?"

"You're starting to sound like a parrot."

"And you're starting to get on my nerves," I spat back. I couldn't have possibly heard her right. I was not about to make Calvin think I want his ass.

"I'm serious," she began with a hint of desperation. "I need a reason to end our relationship so I won't feel guilty."

"Aren't you jumping the gun? What if things don't work out with you and Chance?" Danielle did have a tendency to fall in love way too fast.

"It doesn't matter. I've been thinking about this for a while. I really like Calvin and might even love him, but he's ready to take our relationship to the next level and I'm not. At least not yet. You're the only one that can help me." I heard that pleading tone and didn't like it one bit.

"Why, because I used to fuck him?" My voice was dripping with sarcasm.

"Yeah, and you *did* want him back."

"That was before I knew you were screwing him." Hell, the last thing I wanted was her hand-me-downs. I dumped the Ragu in the skillet and stirred it into the beef.

"Come on."

Back in the day Calvin and I used to date, and when he started kicking it with Danielle I felt some type of way about it because her sneaky ass didn't tell me they were dating. When I found out I was pissed because friends have an unwritten rule not to mess with each other's exes. Come on. I used to ride that dick, and might I add, it was a nice long ride, but what makes her think I want her left-overs?

"You owe me," she finally said in her defense.

"How you figure that?"

She smacked her lips all in my car as she replied, "Do I have to remind you . . . Reverend Leroy Brown?"

I had to laugh at that one because she was right. Kayla had been messing with the Baptist minister for years, and I got tired of him treating her like shit so I videotaped him with this fag I knew he messed with. Un-fortunately, the whole thing became a circus act with me and Danielle right smack in the middle.

"Okay, you're right. I do owe you."

"Damn right."

I purposely blew out a heavy breath so she would know that I was not feeling her idea at all. "When do you want to do this?"

"Tomorrow night."

While I made dinner, we spent the next hour coming up with a plan. I got off the phone with a bad feeling. *Hopefully this isn't another episode to come back and bite me on my ass.*

I left the sauce simmering and moved into the family room and found that Tamara had left her shoes under the table. How many times I got to tell that girl to clean up behind herself? I moved down the hall to her room. Sec-onds after opening her door, I stood there shaking my head. Nasty mothafucka. It don't make no sense for a young woman to live like that. Clothes in piles all over the floor. Soda cans lining her headboard. Sheets and cov-ers hanging off the bed. I don't know where she got that from. Must be her father's side of the family. Her grand-mother had kept a cluttered house and when I met her father, his apartment was a pigpen.

"Tamara!"

"Yes?" she called from the basement where I guarantee she was on the computer.

"Get your butt up here and clean your room!"

"Mama, it is clean."

"No, it's not. Now get your ass up here!"

She came stumping down the hall and had the nerve to have an attitude. Hell, if anyone had a right to be mad, it was me.

I stood outside her room with my arms crossed. "You got homework?"

"I already did it."

"Good, then you can spend the rest of your evening cleaning your room."

"It's my room. I don't know why I have to clean it up," she argued.

"Because it's my house. That's why." One thing I can't stand is for a kid to argue with me.

She moved into her room and slammed the door. I ignored it because Tamara knows I would snatch her little ass up in a minute if I wanted to. Since I was making her clean up her room, I went to check on Quinton's. As usual, it was spotless. At eighteen, he was a neat freak. Had been since he was a kid. He was at work and wouldn't be home until after nine.

I went in the kitchen and almost broke my neck when I slid in a puddle. I reached for a mop and the smell hit me. Dog piss! Dammit, this was the third time this week.

"Nikki!" I called. I spotted my schnauzer in the living room, and as soon as she saw me she ran under the coffee table and lowered her head. "I'm not mad at you, baby.

Something must be wrong with you because I know you know better than to be peeing on my floor." I stroked her head as I spoke so she would know that I understood. I decided to make her an appointment with the vet first thing tomorrow. Maybe she had a bladder infection or something.

I patted her head one more time and was heading to the kitchen to finish dinner when I heard the doorbell. Before I got there, whoever it was leaned against the bell, ringing repeatedly.

First thing came to mind was one of the neighbor's kids playing games. I flung the door open and there stood our friendly neighborhood bag lady. I quickly hit the lock on the screen door.

"I don't mean no harm, but can you take me to the store to get some toilet paper? I'll give you five dollars."

She looked tired and sweaty, white spit was on her tongue and the sides of her mouth. It took everything I had not to get sick just looking at her. The way she was wagging her tongue, it was obvious she was cuckoo for Cocoa Puffs.

I quickly came up with an excuse. "I can't leave. The baby is asleep."

She nodded, then left to knock on the neighbor's door. I felt sorry for her but it was apparent she was going to be like a stray dog. And as I said before, as long as I helped her, her ass was going to keep coming back. But as I watched her walk up the street and head back home, I couldn't help but to think that could be my mother and what if everyone thought like I did.

I rushed into the bathroom and grabbed three rolls of toilet paper, then went to my purse, pulled out five dollars, and hurried up the street before she got too far. "Excuse me!" I called. "Miss, excuse me!"

She swung around and appeared surprised to see me.

"Here," I said and handed the bag and the money to her.

Her eyes got so wide you would have thought I told her my name was Ed McMahon and she had just won the Publisher's Clearing House Sweepstakes.

"Thank you," she said with tears in her eyes. "God's going to bless you."

I nodded and turned away before she could see the tears filling my own eyes. I'm a sucker for tears. *Damn, now she's never going to leave me alone.*

17

Danielle

I waited until I was sure Calvin was home before I called his house. He answered on the first ring.

"Hey, I was just getting ready to get dressed so that I can come and pick you up."

My heart was pounding rapidly. "Calvin, I don't feel good tonight. Can we do it tomorrow instead?"

He paused and I could tell he was disappointed. "Sure, tomorrow's fine. You need me to come over and bring you something?"

"No," I said with a sigh. "I've had a long, stressful day and didn't get much sleep last night. All I need is a hot bath and some sleep."

"I could come over and wash your back."

I groaned inwardly. Why couldn't he just take no for an answer? "No, because if you come over we're gonna have something else on our minds, and as much as I want you, baby, I'm just too tired."

"I understand," he said, although his voice said he really didn't. "Okay, then, tomorrow it is. Go get some rest."

"Thanks, Calvin. You're too good to me."

"Never that, baby. I love you."

I rolled my eyes at the ceiling and wanted to kick myself for getting in this mess in the first place. "I love you, too."

As soon as I hung up the phone, I dashed into my room and started weeding through my closet. *You got a date with a fine-ass nigga tonight!* I needed something sexy as hell to show Chance just what he was up against. I was no joke and wanted to make that loud and clear.

At the back of my closet, I located a pair of black jeans that I had never worn and paired it with a burgundy turtleneck sweater. I was ironing the outfit when my cell phone rang. I didn't recognize the number but something told me it was Chance.

"Hey, sexy, you ready to roll?"

I smiled. Chance sounded so good on the phone. "Almost."

"All right. Give me your address and I'll see you at eight." I gave him directions to my house, then hurried to get ready.

I was so looking forward to this evening that I probably was too anxious. But Chance was fine and something about him turned me on. He spelled b-a-d-b-o-y, and that was something every woman wanted in her life.

I rushed into the shower. While reaching for my washcloth, I allowed it to graze my left nipple and Calvin came to mind. His touch was always soft and gentle. But what I was dying for was something hard and rough, the way it used to be between me and Ron. I closed my eyes, feeling guilty that I was even thinking about screwing someone else when I already had what some would consider the perfect man.

But if you're not happy, how is he perfect?

I pushed Calvin from my mind. I wasn't going to think about him tonight. Instead, I allowed myself to think about Chance and the evening ahead. I stroked my clit and couldn't help but hope that maybe by this evening it would be his juicy lips I would feel grazing my pussy instead of my own hand. Since Ron's disappearing act, I had been riding my dildo on a regular. But no matter how many times I made myself come, it in no way compared to a big fat dick with a roughneck attached.

And Chance was just that.

I giggled happily because I knew I could have him tonight if I wanted. I quickly lathered my body and made a mental note to change my sheets before he arrived.

"I'm getting some dick tonight." I kept chanting that phrase while I got ready. I slipped into my Deréon jeans and smiled. The second I saw Beyoncé wearing them, I knew I had to have a pair. Turning side to side in the mirror, I admired how well they hugged my body. The sweater emphasized all my curves. Other than I didn't have enough breasts to fill it, it looked quite good. No problem. I reached inside my drawer and pulled out some bra inserts that changed my double As to Bs. Smiling in the mirror, I was more than pleased with the outcome. Just enough cleavage to draw attention to my narrow waist and perfect-size hips.

Moving over to my closet, I pulled out a short pair of black stiletto boots I had found while in St. Louis last spring. I looked damn good.

By eight, I was in the living room waiting when the doorbell rang. I opened it up and found Chance's fine ass standing on the other side. Whoever said clothes made the man wasn't lying. That brotha was wearing the hell out of a black Dickies outfit and some Timberland boots.

"Goddamn, you're fine! I'm gonna be the envy of every nigga in town tonight."

I grinned at the compliment. It was Friday night and I couldn't wait to be seen on his arm, either. Tonight tongues would be wagging and bitches would be hating.

"You ready to bounce?"

I nodded, then reached for my short leather jacket and purse off the couch and locked the door behind us. Chance helped me into a black Lincoln Navigator and I couldn't help but think, "This mothafucka is living large!" as he came around to the other side and climbed in. Music boomed from his speakers and the bass caused the SUV to vibrate.

"Yo ride is nice."

"Thanks, baby girl. Sit back and enjoy the ride."

Looking at Chance, I couldn't help but to think about riding something else. I discreetly looked out the corner of my eyes to check if I could see an imprint of his dick on the side of his leg and couldn't, but there was definitely a bulge at his crotch, which could be a good sign.

He leaned low in the seat and drove with one hand. Chance looked so fine sitting there, I felt my pussy pulse. And when he looked over and winked and gave me that sexy-ass smile showing off his grill, I about came on myself. Oh, hell yeah, I was getting some of that tonight. *Damn, I forgot to change my sheets!*

We pulled up to a small juke joint and as he drove through the parking lot, heads turned. I leaned back proud and had to keep from laughing when I saw a few haters turn and look my way and gasp when they saw me sitting on the passenger's side. I gave them a look that said, "Yeah, bitch, it's me. And this is my nigga." Our date had just started and I was already calling Chance mine.

Yep, you better believe I planned to do whatever it took to make that shit a fact.

He captured my eyes with his. "We not gonna stay long. I just need to holla at someone and then we can go and get something to eat."

I nodded like it was no big deal. Shit, I was glad to be out with everyone seeing who I was with. I hadn't but just met Chance and apparently he was someone special, because as we moved through the building brothas were giving him mad love.

He took me by the hand and guided me through the crowd to the VIP section and told me to have a seat at the bar while he went in back.

"Hey, Yo-Yo! Fix my girl here a drink," he yelled to the girl behind the bar. He disappeared in back. The barmaid moved over to me and I could tell she was sizing me up, hating.

"What can I get you?"

"Patrón and pineapple."

She rolled her eyes and went to fix my drink. I kept my gaze on her every move. The way she was looking at me, I wouldn't be surprised if she tried to spit in my glass.

When she returned, I told her thank you, then looked around the room while I sipped my drink. It wasn't even ten o'clock and the place was already packed. A toothless brotha tried to holla at me but I sent him on his way and made it clear I had a man. I smiled. *I have a man.* I like the sound of that.

"What you doing here?" said a familiar voice.

I cursed softly and swung around to find Ron standing behind me. As usual he smelled like weed. I rolled my eyes and tried to act like my heart wasn't pounding at seeing him again. "None of your damn business," I said with attitude.

He shrugged. "Yo, I just asked a question."

"You gave up that right when you played my ass that night. What? You had to run back home to that pregnant bitch?"

He glared down at me. "Hey, payback's a mothafucka."

"Whatever! I told you I was sorry."

He smirked. "Oh, you gon be sorry, that fo sho."

"What the hell's that supposed to mean?"

Before he could comment, I spotted Chance heading my way, and he didn't look too happy.

"Do we have a problem here?" he asked as he drew near.

Ron sized him up, then reached inside his pocket for a cigarette and smirked. "Nah, no problem."

"Then you need to quit trying to push up on my girl."

Ron gave a short laugh. "Nigga, you getting my leftovers," he said, then chuckled and rolled out.

"Whassup wit y'all?" Chance asked with a possessive gleam in his eyes.

"Nothing, not anymore," I assured him as I glared after Ron. I had a feeling he was up to something.

"Good, because I don't believe in sharing what's mine."

For some crazy-ass reason, knowing that he already considered me his turned me on. I forgot all about Ron and focused on the man in front of me.

Chance ordered himself a beer while I finished my drink. Out of nowhere some tall, light-skinned woman stepped in my man's path.

"What, Chance? You forget to call me last night?" She turned up her nose.

I could tell he was trying to ignore her. "Nah, I had things to do."

She glared at me evilly, then returned her attention to him. "What are you doing tonight?"

"Got plans."

"Change them and I'll make it worth your while."

She stepped all up in my man's face, blocking my view with her narrow behind. Oh no, she wasn't trying to disrespect me like that. Didn't she see me sitting here? I was itching to cuss her ass out but then I would be giving her the satisfaction of pissing me off. Instead, I eased off the stool, moved up to Chance, and wrapped a hand around his waist. "Boo, everything okay?"

He smiled down at me. "Yeah, baby girl, everything's straight."

"Baby girl? Baby girl?" the woman repeated with straight attitude. "Now you calling her baby girl? What's up wit that shit?"

Ignoring her, Chance finished his beer, then took my hand. "You ready to bounce?"

I nodded and we walked off. I could hear her girlfriend say, "Girl, no, you didn't let him play you like that."

Skinny rushed around and said loud over the thump of the music, "Girl, don't get excited 'cause the mothafucka can't eat no pussy!" She and her friends screamed with laughter.

I could tell Chance was trying to keep his cool, but that comment caused his jaw to clench. He swung around. "And if yo pussy didn't smell like Starkist Tuna, maybe I might not have minded eating it. I ain't never like fish and I wasn't about to start now." Whoever was ear hustling roared with laughter. That shut her ass up and we left out the way we came. Outside, Chance turned to me and tried to apologize.

"Baby girl, I'm sorry for that little episode. But that ho rubbed me the wrong way."

I squeezed his hand to show him I was on his side. "You had every right. If you want I'll go back in there and kick her ass."

He tossed his head back and laughed, and I was pleased to see his dimples reappear. "Nah, she ain't worth it." He took my hand and led me over to his SUV. Before opening the door, he leaned in and pressed his lips to mine. I looped my arms around his waist and deepened the kiss. When he moaned, I leaned forward and rubbed my pussy against him trying to feel what he was working with and was tickled pink to have at least felt *something*.

"Damn, girl, you make a nigga's dick hard."

"Ummm, really?" This was my chance. *Please let him have a big dick.* Oh, man. He had to have one. Otherwise, tonight would be one big disappointment.

"Let me see." I laughed. Chance grabbed my hand and guided it to where his dick was hanging. *Dayuuuuum!* He had a gigantic dinga-linga-linga. I was so happy, I released him and started *walking it out*. Cracking up, Chance held his stomach.

"Yo, baby girl, you're too much. Now get yo fine ass in," Chance added with a playful pat on my ass. I climbed in and he closed the door and moved around to the other side. A shiver raced up my arms. Chance felt good and he made me feel even better. I truly felt like a lucky woman this evening.

We rode to Red Lobster and had dinner. Chance ordered lobster tails for both of us. I have to say that the sweet, tender meat tasted better than crab legs. Afterward we went to see a Jackie Chan movie. During the entire movie, he held my hand. We then rode around and talked for what felt like forever. It was well past one in the morning when he finally pulled into my driveway. I knew it was late and I had to get up in five hours and do a Saturday morning shift, but I just wasn't ready for the evening to end.

"Tomorrow I have my nephew, but I'll give you a call when he settles down for the night."

I swung around on the seat so I could see his expression as he spoke. "How old's your nephew?"

A grin curled his succulent lips. "Five. I watch him once a week while my sister takes weekend classes."

"Where's his father?"

His expression hardened. "Bailey messed around on my sister. The woman had the nerve to start calling the house telling my sister they were sharing Bailey. Anyway, she kicked him out and is now trying to make it alone."

I simply nodded. I knew what that was like.

"I can put up with a lot of things, but sharing my pussy ain't one of them. Feel me?"

I nodded again. I definitely understood. "The last thing I want is to be sharing my dick." And now that I knew what he was working with, I definitely considered what he had as mine.

His hazel eyes came up to study my face. "I knew from the moment I first saw you, you was going to be mine."

I sat there grinning like a damn fool. *Sorry, Calvin, but you ain't getting this back. There's a new sheriff in town.*

I knew I should wait until we had a chance to really get to know each other before I invited him in, but like I said, I just wasn't ready for our evening together to end. Besides, Chance already made it clear that I was officially his woman. "You want to come in?" I held my breath.

His smile returned. "Most definitely."

I climbed out and grabbed my keys and we moved inside.

Chance strolled through the living room taking it all in. "Nice crib."

Glancing over my shoulder, I smiled. "Thanks. Go 'head and make yourself comfortable." I moved up to my room, hung my purse on the back of the door, and quickly slipped out of my jeans and turtleneck and headed to the drawer for something comfortable. I swung around and screamed when I ran right smack into Chance.

"Sorry, baby girl, didn't mean to scare you," he said while his eyes ran up and down my half-naked body. He didn't even try to hide his smile. "You said make myself comfortable. What better way than up here wit you?" he whispered, then leaned down and caught my bottom lip between his. Chance Garrett was a man who knew what he wanted and tonight that something was me. Now it was my job to make sure he kept coming back.

"Yeah . . . what better way," I whispered, trying to sound in control.

He scooped me up in his arms and carried me over to the bed, then reached up and unbuttoned his shirt. LL Cool J had nothing on him. He was ripped! Large biceps. Flat stomach. Chance knew I was checking him out because he gave me that cocky grin that I was sure getting used to. Next were his pants, and sure enough, the head of his dick was peeking at me from beneath his boxers. He moved beside me and unsnapped my bra. He removed it and to my embarrassment my bra inserts fell onto the floor. Chance glanced down with an amused look and I closed my eyes, wishing the floor would just swallow me up.

He chuckled and shook his head. "Come here, baby girl." I took a step forward and he cupped my breasts. "More than a mouthful is a waste." He captured one nipple between his teeth and I exhaled and fell back against the bed.

My hands started traveling along the muscles around his shoulders and back. This was like a dream, the way he was making me feel. My pussy was pulsing and juices were wetting my panties. I started rocking my hips because I needed him to touch me there. I reached over and stroked the head of his dick and felt it jerk and heard him moan.

"Damn, baby, that feels good," he moaned before his lips started traveling downward. I lifted my hips and allowed him to slide my panties down over my hips.

Burying my fingers in his curls, I held on while he worked his way down to my pussy. First he blew on it, then he licked my clit. *Oooh yeahhh*, that felt good. With my eyes closed I rocked into his mouth. I started coming and Chance licked every drop. *That bitch at the club was hating, because my man had mad skills!* It wasn't long before he had me dangling over the edge.

"I want to be inside you," he said, then rose and removed his boxers.

I spread my legs wide and crooked my finger, signaling for him to return. Chance positioned himself and slid inside. I felt so full, I cried out "Oooh!"

"You like this?" he asked.

"Yes," I answered.

"You want me to stop?"

"*Hell nooooooo*," I moaned.

He gave me a devilish grin. "Good, 'cause I'm about to tear this pussy up!"

He deepened his strokes and had me speaking in tongues. It was so good. It wasn't long before I was coming, and he came seconds after. When he was done, I was hoping that we could have lain there and cuddled.

"Baby girl, go get a towel."

I opened my eyes, hating to ruin the moment, and moved into the bathroom for a washcloth. I cleaned myself, then him.

Chance gave me that irresistible grin again. "Thanks, I can't lie here with cum all over my dick."

I nodded. So what if my man liked to be clean.

"Now grab a towel for the bed, 'cause you was coming all over the place and one side of the bed is wet," he joked.

I went and retrieved a bath towel and laid it beneath us.

"Now come on and lie down with your man," he ordered.

I loved the sound of that and slid beneath the covers with my head on his chest.

"Uh, baby girl, can you slide that towel over. It's still a little wet over here."

I was glad it was dark so that he couldn't see me rolling my eyes. Chance had a touch of obsessive compulsive disorder. After I shifted the towel, he lay back on it and looked pleased.

"That's better." He kissed me. "It's you and me, baby girl. Together we can rule the mothafuckin' world!"

I don't know what the hell he was talking about, but it sounded good. Curling my head on his chest, I started drifting to sleep when a rotten smell hit my nose. I sat up in the bed. "Did you just fart?"

Cracking up, Chance pinned me to the bed and covered my head with the covers while I kicked and screamed. I was truly feeling my new man even though his ass was funky.

18

Renee

I made dinner, then hurried over to Danielle's house so we could go over the details. She then headed out the door and I moved upstairs to change. My heart was beating with excitement. I don't know why, but I get off on doing crazy shit. We hadn't done anything this wild and crazy since we set Reverend Brown up last year.

I showered, dried off, and ten minutes later, I stood in front of her full-length mirror giving myself mad props.

Damn, I'm sexy.

I had on a short red skirt that I'd been dying to wear since I bought it in New York at a book conference back in November, and a black form-fitting shirt. On my feet were my come-fuck-me shoes—black rhinestone stilettos. No bra. No panties. I was ready for happy hour, or at least that's what I wanted Calvin to think.

At exactly seven o'clock the doorbell rang.

"It's showtime." I opened the door to find Calvin smiling, holding a bouquet of flowers.

I batted my eyelashes flirtatiously. "Ooh, for me! You shouldn't have."

He laughed. "I didn't. They're for Danny."

I gave him a playful pout. "Hey, you can't blame a girl for trying. Come on in." I shut the door behind him and swung around in time to catch him checking out my outfit. He gave me a nervous look.

"Where's Danny?"

"Uh . . . she . . . uh." I paused and pretended to clear my throat. *Get it together.* Otherwise my stuttering ass was about to blow it. "She had to go in and cover a shift, but she should be home around seven-thirty. I was on my way to happy hour and she asked me to come and open the door for you and keep you company until she gets here." *Okay, now your ass is rambling.*

Calvin nodded, accepting my excuse, and turned toward the living room.

I reached for the flowers. "Here, I'll take those. You want something to drink?"

He looked down at my outfit again, and I could see he was trying to decide if it was a good idea or not, being alone with me. I chuckled inwardly. I guess he doesn't trust himself around me, which was probably a good idea. "Yeah, a beer would be good."

I carried the flowers into the kitchen and sat them on the sink. I didn't know where she kept her vases. I poured myself Grey Goose and cranberry, then put a dab of vodka behind each ear for an added touch. Certain I was ready for the games to begin, I reached for a beer out of the refrigerator and headed back into the living room, making sure to appear off balance every other step.

Calvin took the can from my hand with his brow rose. "Are you okay?"

"Why would you say that?"

" 'Cause you act like you're drunk."

"Nah," I said as I took a seat on the couch. "Just got a lot on my mind."

Calvin popped the tab. "Like what?"

I allowed my lower lip to quiver and acted like I was trying to hold back tears. "I'm having man troubles. I met a guy who I really thought I had connected with and . . . and found out . . . he was married. I just don't have any luck. Six months ago, I caught my husband in the bed with another man."

He gave me a sympathetic smile. "Yeah, Danny told me about that."

"You know . . . it kinda messes with my womanhood that he'd rather have a man than me." I allowed a tear to fall. *Damn, I'm getting good at this shit.*

"I must not be doing something right." I slowly crossed and uncrossed my legs like Sharon Stone from *Basic Instinct* and could see his eyes taking it all in.

"Knowing you, I'm sure you were doing everything right," Calvin said with a reassuring smile.

I blinked my eyelashes trying to produce more tears and leaned in closer so he could see down in my shirt. Not that I got shit. I'm a member of the itty-bitty-titty committee, but hell, he's with Danielle and she's got less than I do.

"I love that man! I gave him some of my sweet kitty-cat whenever he wanted, yet that wasn't enough. Hell, I couldn't even keep you!"

He gave a short laugh. "Renee, you dumped me."

"Oh yeah. And that was a mistake I never forgot," I said in a rush. "You were a wonderful man. I just didn't appreciate you."

"Well, thanks." I started rubbing his leg and could tell he was starting to get a little uncomfortable because he squirmed on the couch. "When did you say Danny would get here?" He cleared his throat, then glanced down at his watch. "Uh, what time did she say she'd be home?"

"She didn't say." I slid closer. "Calvin, be honest with me. Did I satisfy you sexually?"

"Renee . . ." he warned with a scolding look.

"Puh-leeeeeze, Calvin. I have to know," I pleaded, then sat up straight on the couch. "Maybe since I have two kids my pussy ain't as tight as it should be. Do you think that's why my husband decided to trade in my worn-out shit for a tight booty hole?"

Shaking his head, Calvin was trying not to laugh. "No, Renee. I don't think that was it at all."

"Okay, then tell me something . . . when you were inside me, could you feel my walls tightening around you?"

"Renee. That was a long long time ago. Jesus!" He dragged a frustrated hand down his face. "What would Danny say if she knew you were asking me these questions?"

"I won't tell unless you tell," I cooed. "Now listen, because this is serious." Leaning back on the couch, I pulled up my skirt, spreading my thighs. Calvin wasn't a fag like John. He was a man. So he couldn't do anything but look. I had shaved Ms. Kitty bald this morning.

Calvin licked his lips. "Damn, you still got a pretty pussy."

"Thank you," I purred, then reached up and stroked my clit. "She's the girl for the job, or at least I thought." I slipped a finger inside and out, then brought it to my lips. "Mmmm, and she tastes good, too."

I saw movement down at his crotch and chuckled inwardly. Men ain't shit. Before Calvin could object, I rolled onto my knees and moved over to straddle his lap.

He was sweating. His eyes grew big and round. "Renee, you've had too much to drink."

"I know, but I just need a little attention. Danielle never needs to know." I ran light kisses along his ear and neck, then ground my hips against his length. "Please just touch me . . . let me know I am scxy . . . that you're attracted to me.

"Please, Calvin," I begged. "Touch me. Let me know you like what you see." I lifted my shirt over my head and my golden nipples were right in his face. He stared at them and moistened his lips. I leaned forward, making them impossible to resist. As soon as his lips closed down I arched against him. "*Yessssss!*" I moaned, then rolled my eyes and glanced over his head at the clock on the wall. Damn. I still had twenty minutes to kill.

I closed my eyes and allowed myself to enjoy the moment. I ain't had none since pissy Landon. So if I had to do this, I should at least get something out of the deal. Besides, from what I could remember, Calvin had skills even back then. We dated when he was in college, which is why I ended things—because he was a baby and at the time, I needed a man. But despite that he was good in bed and had skills.

I kissed him on the mouth and pushed my tongue between his lips, and he stopped resisting and kissed me back. Scope does it every time. He was such an amazing kisser. I don't know why Danielle messed with him in the first place if she had no intention of being with him.

I reached down and unfastened his belt. At first he resisted but that didn't last long. Like I said before, men ain't shit.

As soon as his zipper was down, I reached inside and released him. Oh boy, he wasn't the biggest but he definitely had enough to do the job. I rubbed and teased the head while I brought my mouth down to touch his again.

"This is so wrong," he said between groans.

"Then why aren't you stopping?" I asked between kisses.

"'Cause it feels too good."

Like I said . . . men ain't shit. A year ago, before he had even started kicking it with Danielle, I made a pass at Calvin and he turned me down, saying he doesn't give second chances. Now here we are on Danielle's couch with me straddling his lap while playing with his dick and he was loving it. *You hear me? Loving it!*

"Ooh, yeah!" he moaned.

So much for a challenge. I was starting to grow bored and decided it was time to get this show on the road. I pulled his sweatshirt over his head.

"Maybe we should keep our clothes on just in case Danielle comes home early."

"Shhh!" I put a fingertip to his lips, followed by my lips. "She ain't coming and when she does, she's going to knock because I put on the dead bolt."

"Good looking out."

I kissed a path down his chest and when I reached his belly button, I rubbed his tip along my cheek, then sniffed his crotch. Ugh! He smelled like pee and sweaty balls. *Damn, that's too bad.* If he'd been smelling fresh to death, he might have gotten a suck.

Calvin tried to guide me with his hands, but I pinned his arms to his sides and brushed the head of his dick against my breasts instead.

"Come on, Renee. Suck it." He was practically begging.

"You do me first."

I was just joking, but shit, he must have wanted me to

suck his dick bad because he flipped me onto my back and got to feasting on my snatch. Yeah, and the brotha had skills.

I was so into him, it took me a second or two to realize Danielle had come through the back door and was now standing at the middle of the room.

"What the hell?"

Damn! I was just about to come. Calvin jumped up from between my legs. I quickly got into character and sat up straight on the couch.

"Danny, I can explain."

Anger burned from her eyes. "Explain what? How my man's mouth just happened to land between your legs? Bitch, puh-leeze."

"Bitch?" Oh, she was taking this shit to the next level.

Calvin was trying to fix his pants and explain at the same time. "Danielle, I-I know there is no excuse for what just happened, but . . . but I'm sorry."

"You're right, there isn't. I loved you and this is how you treat me," she began between sobs. "Get the hell out of my house!"

I have to give it to my girl, the tears looked real. *Okay, it's time for my line.* "Danny, it isn't his fault. Blame me."

"You right, I blame yo slutty ass. What the hell you doing having my man eating yo stanky-ass pussy? You just couldn't stand that fact he didn't want you." She was taking this shit a little too seriously.

"Slutty? If I'm not mistaken, he does want me, otherwise he wouldn't have been sucking on my clit."

Danielle lunged at me. She started swinging and yelling. A black bitch like me started swinging back and we were two clawing, catfighting fools. She dug her nails in the side of my neck. *Hell nah!* I swung with my fist but Calvin stepped in and I got him in the chin.

"Crazy bitch!" I screamed when I wiped away blood.

"No, you're the one who's ate up. Both y'all get the fuck outta here!"

She didn't have to tell me again. Calvin's punk ass kept trying to reason with her but I reached for my shirt, slipped it over my head. It wasn't until I was outside walking to my car that I realized I was wearing Calvin's university police sweatshirt. I was too mad to go back inside.

What the hell was Danny's problem? We were supposed to have been playing, but she took that shit to the next level. She got life fucked up, scratching me on the neck!

I pressed the remote unlocking my car. I was about to get in when a black Expedition pulled up to the end of the driveway. *Who the fuck is that?* I paused, waiting for whoever was behind the wheel to either get out or roll down their windows and ask for directions. Nothing. I dropped my hand to my hip and glared across the yard with attitude. The windows were too dark for me to see who was behind the wheel. Okay, you know what? I ain't got time for games. I moved down the drive and before I reached it, the SUV pulled off down the road. I didn't have much time to wonder who that might have been when I heard loud shouting. Danielle was going off. The last thing I wanted to see was Calvin's face when he came out of the house. He was probably trying to find his sweatshirt.

I climbed in and looked at my neck in the rearview mirror and got mad all over again. "Ain't that a bitch!" This was her idea, not mine. So how the hell she gonna get mad? I pulled out the driveway and headed home.

My neck stung, and with each feeling of pain I wanted to turn back around and knock Danielle out.

Okay, maybe I was wrong for having her man going downtown, but hell, she didn't want his ass, and honestly I should be compensated for my time and energy so I got a little licky-lick, but instead of thanking me, her ass wants to be mad.

What-the-fuck-ever.

I didn't want to get involved in the first damn place.

I was so mad, I made a right at the next corner and headed toward Landon's apartment to see if his Tahoe was in the driveway. Of course that mothafucka wasn't home, but as I rode past I spotted Leslie's fat ass coming out the door to his building.

I blew my horn, then pulled up to the end of the driveway and lowered my window. "Tell your pissy-ass man to call me!" Before she could say a word, I rolled my window back up and pulled away. Despite everything, I tossed my head back and started laughing as I rode down the road and headed home. I know I pissed her the fuck off. A pissed-off woman and a pissy-ass man. Damn, they made an amazing couple. I had to chuckle at that one.

I pulled into my subdivision and spotted our friendly neighborhood bag lady standing in front of her mailbox. I didn't dare look in her direction because I was not in the mood for her begging and me feeling sorry for her ass.

I zoomed past and pulled in the driveway just as Quinton and some girl came out the front door. Hell nah! Call it Mother's instinct, but I hadn't met the girl and already didn't like her. She was dark chocolate and thick and had a ghetto hairdo with enough gel to hold it in place for the next six months.

Quinton looked over at me and I gave him the look. I

could tell by the expression on his face he was shocked to see me come home so soon. Good for his ass! 'Cause he knows he's not allowed to have company, especially not a girl, when I'm not at home.

"Hey, Mom." He walked around the car and kissed me on the cheek. He was trying to lay on the charm so I wouldn't embarrass his ass in front of his girl.

"Hello, and who is this?" I looked over at the girl standing near his car looking at me like I was trying to push up on her man or something.

"Mom, this is Alicia."

"Hey, whassup?" she asked, smacking on gum. She had long acrylic nails and three gold caps in her mouth.

I gave her a blue light special smile, then turned to my son and pursed my lips. "Where you off to?"

"I'm going to take her home and go over to my boy's house."

He knew I wanted to knock his slick ass out but I would deal with him later. I gave him a long look then moved into the house. I went straight down the hall to his room to check his bed. Uh-huh! Just like I expected. A big wet spot.

19

Danielle

I glared across the room at Calvin, who had the nerve to try to explain.

"Danny, listen. I was wrong, I admit it, but I don't think that's a reason to end our relationship."

"What?" I know I hadn't heard him right. "You were in my house on my couch with your head buried between Renee's legs but you don't think that's a reason to end our relationship? Come on!"

"I know and I'm sorry. I shouldn't have given in."

I turned the attitude up high, especially since he thought I was stupid enough to fall for that. "I'm getting sick just looking and listening to what you have to say. Get out!"

He grabbed my arm. "Please, Danny, we can work this out. It isn't like Renee and I don't go back. Hell, you know how she is."

"And that's supposed to make it right?" I jerked my arm loose and rolled my eyes over at him before disappearing in the kitchen. I was so mad, I wanted to spit fire.

I had been so worried about hurting his feelings when all along he had been more than willing to screw my best friend. There was no telling how many other women he was screwing.

"Why you walk away from me?"

" 'Cause I'm done talking. Now please leave."

"I love you. Doesn't that count for something?"

"Obviously not, because I wouldn't have caught you eating pussy."

He came up behind me and wrapped his arms around me. "I'm going to give you a few days to think."

I jerked free. "There ain't shit to think about! You tried to screw my *so-called* best friend and now it's over. Now get the fuck out before I call the police." Angry tears were streaming down my face. Damn, I didn't want him to see me crying.

I waited until I heard the door pull shut before I turned and moved back into the living room.

The evening hadn't turned out the way I planned. Renee was supposed to start crying, draw Calvin's attention and find a way for him to kiss her. I was then supposed to walk in on them and cause a big scene.

Well, you definitely did that.

That's because I had really been angry. No need for faking and trying my hardest not to hurt his feelings. Instead, he had hurt me by satisfying my best friend the same way he did me or better, I thought as I remembered the way Renee had been squirming beneath his tongue. Now that Renee opened the door on them, he closed the door on us. It was over, and I wasn't as happy about it as I thought I would be.

It made me so mad, I was tempted to go over to Renee's house and beat her ass. That long scratch across her neck would just have to do for now.

My cell phone played Robin Thicke's "Lost Without U." A smile curled my lips. That ring tone belongs to Chance.

"Whassup, baby girl?"

I chuckled. "Whassup with you?"

"Not a damn thang. Whadda you doing later tonight?"

"Nothing. Why? You want to hook up?"

"Yeah. I'll hit you back in a few."

I closed my phone and tossed it onto the couch. One chapter closed and another opened.

20
Renee

I waited another half hour and called Danielle. Calvin had to be gone by now. The phone rang and rang, then went to her voice mail.

Yep, the bitch was tripping, because any other time, the second that mothafucka walked out the door, she would have been calling me with all the details. We're best friends and that's what best friends do. *Fine, let her ass trip.*

I went into my office and decided it was time to get to work on my manuscript. I have a bad habit of procrastinating until the last minute, and then I'm stressed out trying to get done. Well, not this time. As soon as I outlined the next scene, of course the phone rang. The only reason why I answered it was because I thought it was Danielle calling.

"Renee, how could you?"

"Could I what?"

"Sleep with Calvin," Nadine stated frankly.

"I didn't sleep with Calvin."

"Well, you probably were only seconds away from it if Danny hadn't walked in when she did."

"She asked me to seduce his mothafuckin' ass!" I cried defensively.

"Yeah, come on to him. Not try to screw him."

"I can't help it if men can't resist me."

"I'm sure you didn't make it easy," Nadine replied sarcastically.

"Whatever. I faked tears and next thing I knew he was going down on me."

"And you just couldn't say no."

"Why would I do that? The whole idea was to get him to come on to me so that Danielle could walk in and go off."

"Yeah, but she was supposed to catch the two of you kissing. Not with your shirts off and his head down between your legs."

"What she do, call you the second she kicked his ass out of her house? Shit, I can't help it if he wanted a little licky-lick."

"No, your nasty behind wanted him to lick it," she corrected.

That bitch thinks she knows me. "Girl, puh-leeze." I snorted, even though I knew good and damn well Nadine wasn't going to fall for it.

"Renee, you know I know how your ass is."

"Well," I finally admitted, "how could I tell him to stop? Hell, that shit felt good as hell. Nadine, don't play, you wouldn't have stopped him, either."

"Yes, I would, because—"

"Oops, my bad. I forgot you don't do men."

There was a noticeable pause. "A tongue is a tongue. If he's good, I'd be willing to make an exception."

"What?" I couldn't believe my ears. My dyke-ass

friend would let a man eat her stanky-ass coochie? "You mean to tell me you're thinking about coming back over from the dark side?"

"I didn't say that," she quickly corrected. "I said if it's good, it doesn't matter what sex that tongue belongs to."

Hell nah! I couldn't believe my ears. Shit, maybe there's some hope for her yet. "The tongue was good. That brotha has mad skills, but then I already knew that. Remember, I messed with him long before Danny did."

"So is that what this is really all about?"

"Hell nah! I'll admit last year when they first started talking I was feeling some type of way about the whole thing with her going behind my back, but I've since gotten past that shit. I wasn't thinking about Calvin's tired ass until Danny asked me to do that stupid shit, and now she's got the nerve to be mad."

"She said you took the shit too far."

"Too far! Did that bitch tell you she scratched the shit out of me?" My question was met by silence. "No, I guess she didn't."

"You shouldn't have done what you done."

"And that gave her the right to scratch me?" I was too through. "Fuck her. She better be glad I didn't dot that eye."

"You owe her an apology."

"For what? Giving her the excuse she needed to end her relationship with Calvin? Hell, if she wasn't such a punk I would have never been in the middle of her shit in the first place. So if anyone's to blame, it's her." I was mad. Danny's ass was definitely stuck on stupid.

"If anyone should be mad, it's me. Hell, I was five seconds away from getting off when her ass came barging into the room. Shit, if it had been me, I would have at least waited until she got hers first."

"You should call her and apologize."

"I'll apologize when she tells me she's sorry for scratching my neck with her long-ass fingernails! Do you know she drew blood? Hell, I bled all over my shirt." Well, Calvin's shirt, if you want to get technical about it.

"She wouldn't have scratched you if you weren't with her man."

"Whose side are you on?"

Nadine chuckled. "I'm on nobody's side. I'm just trying to keep the peace."

"Girl, fuck Danny! I'm not about to kiss her ass. She'll get over it like she always does." Hell, it ain't like this is the first time the two of us have bumped heads.

"Whatever, we've got a wedding to plan and don't need this shit."

"Hey, as far as I'm concerned it's business as usual. Hell, I'm not about to change my number. She's the one tripping, not me. Anyway, enough about her. How's the baby making going?"

Nadine sighed heavily in my ear. "It's a long story."

"Shit, I ain't got nothing but time tonight."

"What? You don't have plans?"

"I was hoping a man was coming by to give me some, but I guess that's not happening, so I'm free."

Nadine had to laugh. "You want to go and have a drink at Tropical Liquors?"

Our favorite frozen drink spot. "Sounds like a plan."

"I'll meet you at eight."

On the way to meet Nadine, I stopped at the gas station at the corner to put some gas in my car. With gas prices it was cheaper to ride the bus. If we had better public transportation, I probably would. I finished pumping my gas when I spotted Landon's punk ass coming out of the convenience store.

"Landon!" I yelled. He turned and as soon as he noticed it was me, he looked away and started heading toward his Tahoe.

"Pissy! You hear me calling you!" I quickly moved across the parking lot trying to catch him before he climbed in his car. "Where's my goddamn mattress?"

He continued moving like he didn't hear me.

Oh, he heard me.

I sprinted over to him calling his name, but before I could even contemplate jumping on the hood of his SUV, he peeled off. I was so mad, I hurried back to my car and went after him and missed him at the light because the old lady in front of me was too scared to run a yellow light. I blew my horn and her wrinkled ass gave me the finger.

Damn!

I picked up my cell phone and retrieved his number from my contact list and started to dial but decided to block the call first.

"Hello?"

"You pissy ass—" *No, he didn't hang up on me.* I called Landon again but naturally he didn't answer, so I waited until his voice mail picked up. "Pissy, you need to be buying me a new mattress before I come to your job and embarrass your stankin' ass."

When I got to the restaurant I was even madder from thinking about it. I spotted Nadine at the back of the restaurant and headed over to where she was sitting.

"Sorry I'm late." I flopped down on the seat across from her.

"What's wrong with you?"

I shrugged out of my coat and rolled my eyes. "I ran into Landon's pissy ass."

Nadine started giggling.

"I saw him and tried to flag him down and he tried to

play me." I reached for the menu. "Hell, he heard me calling his name."

"Maybe he's embarrassed."

"He should be, pissing in the bed! What he needs to do is man up and buy me a new mattress."

Nadine shook her head. "I still can't believe he peed in your bed. I told my brother and he cracked up laughing." Her brother and Landon went way back.

"Tell Murray he needs to tell his boy to buy me some new mattresses or else I'm gonna fuck him up."

"Renee, shut up. You're not gonna do shit."

I rolled my eyes. In the years we've known each other, she obviously doesn't know what I'm capable of.

I gave her a dismissive wave. "Enough about me. Tell me what's up with the baby making."

"Jordan and I found a sperm donor."

"Cool, and when's the screwing begin?"

She dropped her head, avoiding eye contact. "It already started."

"Ooh, what's he look like?"

"Fine."

"Fine?" She had my full attention.

Her eyes grew real big. "Chocolate body, good hair, educated, you name it."

My brow rose. "And you noticed?"

"Oh yeah, I noticed, and that's the problem."

I couldn't believe what I was hearing. "Wait, I got to go and get a drink first, 'cause this shit is too good to hear without a buzz." I moved over to the bar and waited impatiently for a couple of college students to quit sampling the drinks and make a selection. When it was finally my turn, I quickly ordered two frozen Long Island iced teas and an order of nachos, then scurried back to our table before Nadine clammed up. She has always been a private person. Shit, she didn't even want to tell us she was a dyke and probably wouldn't have if it hadn't been for my sister Lisa, who died of cancer three years ago. So the fact she was even trying to share her feelings was enough to make my ass want to run.

That top twenty shit they was playing was loud as hell, so I moved to the chair beside Nadine so I wouldn't miss one word. "Okay, girl, go ahead and spill the beans about this man."

"Well," she began between chews, "the funny thing is I never think about being with a man. But ever since we . . . I can't seem to get him off my mind."

I took a sip. This was better than a movie. "Are you craving dick now?"

She dropped her head and took a deep breath before answering. "I already had it."

"What! Ooh, you need to back up and explain, because inquiring minds want to know."

Nadine then started confessing more shit than I needed to know. A ménage with her, Jordan, and the sperm donor. I almost fell out of my seat. "I didn't plan on participating, but Jordan wanted me in the room. Watching them turned me on, and the next thing I knew I was taking off my clothes and Jordan invited me over to join them. I wanted everything he was giving her." Nadine had to take a deep breath as she reminisced.

"Damn." I sat there chewing on chips, hanging on her every word. This was some freaky, deaky shit, and I was the queen of freaky so you know this shit had me turned on. "Shit, what's the brotha working with?"

Her eyes practically rolled inside her head. "Danny girl, that man is *huuung*! Ooh! And he can work it. He had me cumming all over the place."

"Hell nah!" Now why couldn't I meet someone like that?

"Renee, I can't stop thinking about him. Even when I'm with Jordan I'm thinking about him. I feel guilty as hell."

"Have you done anything to feel guilty about?"

"Yes. He and I met and had sex without Jordan."

My jaw dropped. "You're lying."

"No," she began. She placed her elbow on the table and rested her chin on her fist. Nadine looked like she was going to cry. "We've met at a hotel at least three times since that night with Jordan."

"Shit." I paused, raising an eyebrow before responding. "Maybe you aren't ready to commit yourself to a woman."

"Maybe," she said with uncertainty.

"Do what feels right." I couldn't believe I was saying this shit. "Life's too short to do otherwise. I like Jordan . . . but if you're thinking about getting dick on occasion, maybe the two of you need to talk. Maybe adding a little dick every now and then might be good for your relationship."

She frowned. "Jordan's not going for it. She was not at all happy about a man touching her. If she doesn't get pregnant this time, I don't think she'll go through it again." Nadine took a sip and shook her head like she was trying to rid herself of the thoughts. "Listen, I love Jordan. We are planning to start a family. I didn't exchange vows with her during the holidays for nothing."

"Then leave that fine-ass mothafucka alone."

Nadine took a deep breath. "I don't know if I can do that."

Damn, this was more serious than I thought. "Then

follow your heart. In your case, listen to your kitty-cat, 'cause the kitty don't lie."

"I thought it was the hips?"

I tossed a chip at her. "Bitch, you know what I mean." We both laughed and then Nadine changed the subject and started talking about nothing in particular. I think it was just to take her mind off of her sudden desire for dick.

"How's the driving lessons going?" she asked between sips.

"Much better. I need to find a little cheap car for Tamara."

"I'm selling that Honda I bought for Jay." Her son went off to school and ended up buying himself a new car.

"I thought it wasn't running?"

"It runs. It just won't stay started for some reason."

"So what the hell am I going to do with it?" I said with attitude. Why she trying to push her junk off on me?

"Hondas are good cars. I could get my boy Kenny to look at it."

I shrugged. "Depends on how much he's going to charge."

She pursed her lips and leaned closer. "Girl, he does really good work. But for Kenny all you got to do is let him rub your leg and he'll give you a discount."

"What?" I laughed.

Laughter shone in Nadine's eyes. "I'm serious. He's been trying to get me to go out with him for years."

"Is he cute?"

"Ugh! Not at all."

"Shit, for some free repairs he can be my type, for the day."

"Yuck! Glasses, goofy laugh. I'm sure you've seen him before. I think he's Kayla's cousin."

My eyes searched her face. "He got a woman?"

She nodded. "He lives in Boonville with her. They've been together a long time. Her name is Reese."

Reese? Reese? I shook my head. "I don't know her." Which was a good thing because already the wheels were turning. "What she look like?"

"Homely. He used to pop that head."

"What! You trying to hook me up with a woman beater?"

"That's what I heard. I don't know how true it is. He's got a daughter with Robin Hathaway."

The name sounded familiar but I really didn't have a clue. "I don't think I know her."

"Yes, you do. Robin rides around in the 700 series BMW and always has the blond weave in her hair."

"Oh yeah, she used to fuck with my cousin Neal. Straight gold digger."

She nodded. "Yep, that's her."

"Hook it up," I replied between sips. "Tell Kenny I'll take him to lunch if he gives me a good deal. Hell, if it's free I'll even let him lick my kitty." We cracked up laughing. "How much you want for the car?"

"Five hundred dollars?"

"Sold." I reached for my checkbook.

Monday afternoon, I left the veterinarian's office and started bawling. Nikki has diabetes. My first question was how in the world does a dog get diabetes? But just like people, it's all about diet. I started blaming myself. Nikki had already lost part of her eyesight for the disease going untreated for so long and would have to take insulin for the rest of her life. I was sitting in the examination room crying like a damn fool while Nikki lay across my lap wagging her tail and looking at me as if to say, "Bitch, what the hell's wrong with you?" The next thing out of the veterinarian's mouth was, "We can put her to sleep." I cussed his ass out then asked him would he kill one of his kids if they were diagnosed with diabetes? He grew red and knew he had hit a nerve with me. I guess he thought I couldn't afford it. Whatever! He quickly wrote me a prescription for insulin and needles and instructed me how to check her urine, then sent me on my way. I took my baby home, kissed and hugged and promised to take better care of her. I kept crying and blaming myself and promised to be a better mother.

I put Nikki in the kitchen and put up a baby gate, then rushed off to the pharmacy to fill her prescription. The doctor assured me that as soon as I started her insulin the frequent urinating would stop. I was waiting in the check-out line when I received a text from Nadine.

CALL 857-3212

Wondering where she was calling me from, I went ahead and called while I waited for the woman in front of me to make up her damn mind. I expected to hear Nadine's voice on the other end. It was a man instead.

"Hello?" I asked, wondering who I was speaking to.

"Hey, whassup? This is Ken."

Damn, Nadine moved fast. "Hey."

"Nadine told me you had a car you wanted me to look at."

His voice was country as hell. "Yeah, it's a 1990 Honda

she's selling. I'm going to go by and look at it later. Nadine said it won't stay started."

"I'll tow it to Boonville this weekend and take a look at it. Hondas are good cars. It's probably not too much."

"You gonna give me a good price?"

He chuckled. "Depends if I get to lick it."

No, she didn't tell him that.

"Boo, I don't let everybody lick it."

"Oh yeah?"

"Yeah. I reserve that for special people." I thought I was talking low but a tall man standing beside me turned and winked at me.

"So what's it going to take to be special?" he asked with laughter in his voice.

"I'll have to think about that one."

"You do that." There was a pause. "You married?"

"Well . . ." How do you tell someone you're still married to a fag?

"Be honest. I'm going to be straight up with you. My girl lives with me. We've been together for twelve years and we're getting married in May."

"Oh, okay, well, I'm going through a divorce. So you're committed and I'm not."

"I'm a man," he said with a chuckle. "I've always had another woman on the side."

"Oh really?"

"Yeah, I don't know why or if I'll ever change, but I always take care of my women."

"Really? You got it like that?"

"I work at FedEx in the evening and my body shop during the day. I own a small farm in Boonville that's paid for."

I was already adding the money I'd be saving in my head.

"Can you meet me for dinner tonight?" he asked, getting directly to the point.

I glanced down at my watch. It was almost three. "What time?"

"I take my dinner break around ten o'clock."

I pretended I was giving it some thought before I agreed. I hung up and reached for my wallet to pay for Nikki's prescriptions. Tonight, I had a seduction to plan. I chuckled. *By the time I'm done with him, Kenny Johnson is going to not only fix my car for free, but have it purring like a kitty-cat.*

21
Danielle

I walked into the house and released a heavy sigh of relief. The unit had been extremely busy all afternoon. Everybody wanted to have their babies. And as soon as we got one delivered, it was time for the next patient to start pushing. I barely had time to do charting into the computer when it was time for my three-thirty shift change.

After tossing my purse on the coffee table, I moved into the kitchen and removed from the refrigerator a meatloaf I had prepared before leaving for work. I turned the oven on and slid the glass pan inside. By the time I took a hot shower and changed into something comfortable, dinner should be ready.

I climbed the flight of stairs to my bedroom and quickly removed my clothes. I was sweaty and hot and feignin' for a shower. Damn! I should have known the phone would ring. I moved over toward the nightstand and glanced down at the Caller ID.

Double damn! It was my mother, Victoria.

"Hello, Mama, I was just getting ready to get in the shower."

"Guess what?" she said as if she didn't hear a word I had said, which was typical of my mother.

"What?"

"Portia's having a girl."

Despite everything my daughter has put me through, I couldn't help but feel a tinge of excitement. I was going to have a granddaughter.

"That's nice," I replied, although the words stuck in my throat. Now what? If my mama even thought for a second I was excited about the news, there was no telling what she would do.

"Aren't you excited? Portia made it clear that she didn't want to know what the sex of the baby was, but last night she was having labor pains and her father rushed her to the hospital."

"Is she okay?"

Her mother chuckled. "Why don't you call and ask her yourself?"

"No, thank you."

"Quit acting like you don't care," she scolded, then continued in a softer tone. "Yes, she's fine, but during all the excitement the nurse blurted out that her little girl was doing just fine. Portia called me the minute she got back in the house."

I pursed my lips and couldn't help to feel a bit of envy. My daughter was sharing her pregnancy with everyone but me.

Why do you even care?

"I think she would love to share her news with you, too."

"I'd rather not."

She breathed heavily in the phone. "When are you going to stop acting this way?"

"I'm not acting any kind of way. Just because she's having a little girl doesn't change the fact that I don't want to have anything to do with my daughter."

"Danielle, six months is long enough."

"Long enough for what? To forgive and forget? Mama, puh-leeze! I'll never forgive my daughter for what she has done to me."

"So what? Your man left you. Get over it. Men will come and go, but your children are forever."

I couldn't believe my mother had said that. I groaned. "Mama, can we talk about this later?"

"No, we cannot. We have put this off long enough."

So much for a shower. "Mama, I've said all I am going to say on the subject of my daughter and her accusing my man of sleeping with her."

"If you hadn't been dating a man younger than you, none of this would have ever happened."

"So it's my fault?" I was livid.

"Partially you are to blame. Your daughter is only sixteen. She's too young to consent."

Oh brother, here we go again. I've been hearing the same thing from Mama since she first discovered Portia was pregnant. "Her hot tail has been consenting for the last two years."

Victoria gave an impatient sigh. "Listen, let's leave the past in the past. What we need to worry about is my granddaughter's future."

"She's fine. Alvin has everything under control." Let him handle it. Now that my uptight and high-siddity ex-husband was married to a doctor, he thought he was better than everyone else.

Her mother snorted at the mention of her former son-in-law's name. "That man is so strict. Portia can't fart without asking for permission first."

"Good, that's exactly what her hot tail needs. She's pregnant, what the hell does she need to be running the streets for anyway? She needs to go sit down somewhere."

"Well, she only has nine weeks left, and then what?"

"Like I said, that's her father's problem, not mine."

"Don't you want to be a part of your granddaughter's life?"

"Yep. I'm just not interested in associating with her mother."

"Danielle, you really need to start going back to church. Would you like for me to have Reverend Jackson give you a call?"

Hell no. After that episode with Reverend Brown and all the sinning he had been doing, the last thing I needed was to put my faith in a minister. I believed in God and Jesus Christ, but anyone on earth was questionable. "No, Mama, I don't want to talk to him. I am fine. Really. Just not in the mood to deal with my daughter. I tell you what. If Portia decides she's ready to apologize for ruining my life, then I'll listen to what she has to say."

Mama was quiet. Good. She knew good and damn well Portia didn't think she had anything to apologize for, which was fine with her. The less I had to deal with her hot ass, the better.

"Mama, I got to go. I was just getting ready to get in the shower."

"Let's talk this weekend."

"Sure thing." I hung up before my mother could question me further, moved into the shower, and turned the water on full blast. Just like Mama to ruin my evening. All I had wanted to do was relax and enjoy a good meal while reading a mystery I had been dying to read. Now I would spend the rest of the evening thinking about Portia and the baby.

I climbed into the shower and pulled the curtain back and closed my eyes. Yes, I know Portia's a child and yes, I needed to be the bigger of the two, but I couldn't bring myself to do it. This was one time when sorry just wasn't enough. I had loved Ron with everything that I had, and now that relationship was over.

I ran a hand through my hair. I was having a bad day. That's all it was. Calvin had shown up on my job with flowers begging me to forgive him. I jumped into bitch mode and sent him stepping.

I know I broke his heart the other day, and I feel bad about it. Maybe I should have just asked him for some space instead of playing games with him, but after that stunt with him and Renee, I wasn't so sure anymore if he had ever really cared about me at all.

And Renee's trifling ass . . . I could just hit her in her mouth. I don't even know why I was surprised. She had always had a way of making things about her. She had fucked Kayla's man while they were in Jamaica, so I don't know why I even thought for a moment that this time things would have been different. Renee was all about herself. I asked her to do me one favor and she had to make it all about her.

I pushed the whole episode out of my mind before I was tempted to pick up the phone and cuss Renee's ass out. The only reason I haven't is that I have a new man in my life. Chance.

22

Renee

I purposely showed up five minutes late because I wanted to make an entrance. I parked on the side of the building so I'd have to walk across the parking lot. If Kenny was sitting anywhere near the window watching, he was definitely about to get an eyeful. I checked my makeup and cocked my black pageboy hat to the side and smiled at my reflection.

Damn, your ass is cute.

I chuckled and shut off my car. My cell phone rang before I could get out. *Damn, I'm already late.* I saw it was Kayla. Oh hell, Kenny could wait a few minutes more.

"Hey, want to go to the Martini Bar on Friday? Kim Massey's playing."

She's a rhythm and blues singer from the STL who we love. "Yeah, that sounds good."

"Cool. I'll holla at you on Friday."

I caught her before she could hang up. "Hey, Kayla. You know Kenny Johnson?" After all, she's from that podunk town.

"That's my cousin."

Nadine had suspected as much. I giggled. "Really? He's going to be working on a car for Tamara."

"Oh brother! And he's going to be all over you. Hot! You're just the way he likes his women."

"Really?" I found that bit of information intriguing. "I'm supposed to meet him for dinner in a few minutes. What's he look like?"

"You've seen him before. He's Marcus's brother."

Marcus was her first cousin, and he wasn't nothing to look at. Glasses, receding hairline.

"They look the same, only Marcus is older."

"Well, I'm already in the parking lot at Country Kitchen and getting ready to walk in the restaurant and meet him now."

"Oh boy! I can't wait to hear how your evening goes. He is going to be on you, probably ready to call out from work and go home with you."

We shared a laugh. "I'll call you tomorrow."

"Nope, you need to call or e-mail me tonight with all the details."

I agreed, then hung up the phone.

I check my lipstick one more time, and my nostrils to make sure there weren't any boogers lurking around, then I slowly climbed out of my car and sashayed toward the door in a pair of tight-ass Baby Phat jeans and matching jacket, rhinestone belt, black boots, and an off-the-shoulder black top that along with a padded bra made my boobs look perfect. While chewing gum, I moved like I had all the time in the world before I stepped through the door and glanced around for him.

Oh my goodness! I spotted him sitting at a booth in the corner, and it took everything I had not to laugh. Kenny's glasses were so big they were hanging on the end of his nose, and just as Nadine had warned, he had a big goofy-ass smile on his face. He rose and stood close to six feet. I noticed how skinny he was. "This is going to be easy," I mumbled under my breath. *Like taking candy from a baby.* "Hello."

"Whassup?" he greeted with a smile.

I took a seat on the bench across from him and he returned to his seat. Kenny was staring so hard I knew he liked what he saw. He wasn't ugly, in fact he was kinda cute in a goofy Urkel kinda way. And I do mean goofy.

His hair was thin and receding like his brother's. All he needed was a piece of tape in the middle of his glasses and he would have looked like a straight-up nerd. He was staring so hard his tongue was hanging out of his mouth. All I needed was for him to slobber and I knew I had his homely ass.

"What's wrong?" I finally asked. I already knew but needed to hear him say it.

"You're fine as hell."

"Thanks," I replied, grinning.

The waitress came and took our orders. He ordered a burger and fries and I ordered onion rings. That way he wouldn't try to kiss me.

"I probably don't look anything like you thought."

"Actually, you and your brother look alike."

"Oh yeah," he said, all country and shit. "Everybody always says that."

"Yes, except he's darker than you."

"I'm just an old country boy, that's all."

I smiled. Yep, he was definitely that.

"But country boys are supposed to be some of the best men."

My brow arched. "Oh yeah?"

"Yeah."

While we ate, he asked what I did for a living and I told him. He admitted he wasn't much of a reader, which I suspected as much. Then we talked about the people we both knew.

"I'm good friends with your cousin Kayla."

His face lit up. "Oh yeah? Did you tell her you were meeting me tonight?"

"Yep and she said, 'oh brother, you're his type.' "

"My cousin ain't lying," he said with a goofy laugh. "I wanted to ask you to stand up so I can see that big ass again."

Rolling my eyes, I pretended to be insulted. "You're just going to have to wait until we get done eating."

"Oh yeah?" *Damn, oh yeah, oh yeah, is that all he knows?*

"Yep, you're gonna have to wait."

He gave that goofy laugh again. "What are you doing the rest of the night?"

"Lie across my bed and watch TV."

He wet his lips. "I'm tempted to not go back to work and go home with you instead."

Freak. He was so desperate he couldn't even wait for an invitation. "Not tonight. I'm worn out."

"Maybe another time?"

I nodded and when we finished eating, I walked toward the register with him coming up behind me. I knew he was watching my ass, so I swayed just a little harder. *Oh yeah, this is going to be easy.*

After he paid, he walked me out to my car, then climbed in on the passenger's side.

"When do I get to see you again?"

I shrugged and looked out in front of me. "I guess whenever you're ready to pick the car up."

"I can get it on Friday, but I don't want to wait that long to see you again."

If he thinks he's getting some before he fixes my car, he better think again. "Just give me a call."

"Okay." He looked over the tops of his glasses at his watch. "I better get back to work." I could tell he was in no rush to leave. "I've got ten minutes to clock back in."

"Then you better get rolling."

He gave me a nervous laugh, then leaned over and kissed me. Mmmm, not bad for a country boy.

"I'll call you tomorrow."

I nodded. He climbed out and I watched him walk to his truck as I drove away. I was chuckling and reaching for my phone to call Kayla back with the details when someone behind me started flashing their lights. I stopped at that light and a truck pulled alongside me. When I saw who it was, I smiled and rolled down my window.

"Yes?"

Kenny stuck his head out of his big Ford truck. "What time you going to bed?"

"Around midnight."

"I'll call you in an hour to make sure you made it home okay."

I nodded just as the light turned green and pulled off. This was definitely going to be easy.

23

Renee

Kenny called me every morning and we shared dinner in the evening. We had a lot more in common than I ever imagined, and I was surprised because most men didn't like talking on the phone. I wanted so badly to pick up the phone and tell Danielle every detail. Because that's what best friends do—they gossip and talk about their men. Kayla and Nadine are cool, but Kayla's too religious and judgmental and Nadine doesn't understand normal relationships. Her relationship with her parents is dysfunctional. And her personal life . . . well . . . you get the idea. I wanted to share my experience with Danielle, but if her ass wants to stay mad then that's her problem.

Friday, I had been at the job for almost an hour when my personal line rang.

"Good morning."

I rolled around on my chair wearing a big grin. "Good morning to you. What are you doing up so early?" It was barely nine o'clock.

"I came to pick up your daughter's car. Have you had breakfast yet?"

"Nope. Was running late." At the exact moment I looked up at the doorway, Kenny stepped in holding piping hot coffee and a bag I was sure held cinnamon raisin biscuits. "Good morning."

"I thought I'd stop by and see you before I headed back to Boonville," he said as he returned his phone to his pocket and moved toward my desk.

"Thank you." I took the bag from him and peeked inside. Sure enough, hot biscuits were inside.

"I got somebody waiting in the car, but I wanted to drop by and see you before I headed back."

He was wearing his worn work clothes, yet he still looked good to me. I moved around my desk, shut my door, pushed him back against it, and gave him a kiss big enough to put something on his mind.

"I better go before I tell you to lock that door."

"And then what will you do?" I reached down and grabbed his crotch. Just as I thought, he was already rising to the occasion.

"Keep it up and you'll find out," he warned.

"Show me."

He gave me a nervous laugh, then reached for the handle. "I better go before I get you fired."

His heart was racing, so I knew I had him like I said. "I'll call you when I get off."

"What time you getting home?"

"Probably two."

"Anybody going to be home?"

"Nope."

He gave me a horny smile. "Meet me there."

"I'll let you know."

He nodded and gave me one final kiss and I watched him leave. I moved back to my desk and called Nadine on her cell. "Guess who just came to my job."

"Kenny?"

"Yep. He wants to meet me at my house after work."

"You know what he wants."

"I know. I'm trying to stall his ass until Tamara's car is done." I snorted.

"He just picked it up this morning. As slow as he is, it's going to be another two weeks. He probably knows that once the car is done you're through dealing with him."

I had to laugh at that. Probably so. He was trying to put off the inevitable as long as possible.

"Then I guess you better throw it on him so he'll be feigning for more."

"That's not a bad idea. Then I'm guaranteed to have my car fixed . . . for free. Okay, I'm going to let him come over. I guess I'll be pulling my handcuffs out of the drawer."

"Girl, don't tell me that, because I'm not going to be able to keep a straight face when I see him."

"You know how I do."

"I do, and that's the problem."

I hung up and called Kenny on his cell and invited him to my house.

I hurried through the rest of the afternoon and left an hour early to make sure the kids were gone. Quinton worked every Friday evening and Tamara was at her dad's. He lived in a country town about forty minutes away, and he and his new wife had a daughter that Tamara loved.

I put fresh sheets on my bed, hopped in the shower, and put on a pair of tight-ass shorts, a T-shirt, and a pair of silver stilettos. I found my handcuffs and flavored oil and put them on the side of my bed, out of plain sight. I had just sprayed a little perfume at my wrist when I heard the bell. *Showtime.* I took my time going to the door.

I opened the door halfway so he'd have to open it himself, then moved over to the window to pretend I was looking outside. I heard him hiss under his breath. "God-damn."

"Hey, you," I finally said as I turned to face him. He was slipping out of his shoes while his eyes were glued to me.

"Whadda you looking at?"

"You."

"Really?" Without saying anything further, I turned on my heels and didn't wait for him to follow me. Like a little puppy he was on my heels, and as soon as I closed the bedroom door, he was on me like a leech.

"Hold up. Wait a minute," I said as I pushed him back on the bed.

"Hell, I've waited long enough."

"Too bad." I slowly pulled my T-shirt away and stood in front of him in nothing but a thong. He sprang to his feet. I pressed a hand to his chest, halting him from touching me, then pulled his shirt over his head. Skinny. No muscles, and curly hairs on his chest. And a gut. He looked like a turtle.

Goodness, at forty-seven, he didn't have much of a body. Oh well, this was all about business.

"Lie back." Obediently he moved to the center of the bed and lay back against the pillow. As soon as he was settled, I straddled his waist and dropped my lips to his chest. He started laughing.

"I'm ticklish."

I frowned while he squirmed. How the hell was I supposed to turn him on if he couldn't sit still? Reaching over toward the side of the bed, I grabbed the handcuffs and hooked him to the bedpost before he knew what happened.

"Let my hands go," he demanded, then tried to pull his arms free. It was useless.

"Nope, you're moving too much and messing up my flow." I ran my tongue along his chest and across his belly, stopping to nibble at his belly button. He squirmed helplessly on the bed.

"Come on, I don't like being tied up."

"Too bad."

I reached for the fly of his pants and while I dragged my tongue across his gut—I mean abs, I released the button. As soon as his zipper was down, I kissed him one last time, then rose and gazed down into his eyes. "Let's see what we have in here." I motioned for him to raise his hips and lowered his pants and boxers. My mouth dropped and my knees buckled.

He was hung like a horse.

Oh. My. God. It had the prettiest head that I ever did see. All I could do was stare and lick my lips.

Kenny gazed up at me with pride. "I bet you didn't expect that."

I couldn't help but to chuckle along with him. "No, not at all." But it definitely made up for the gut and receding hairline. I wrapped my lips around the head and sucked.

"Damn, you do it just like a young girl."

I took that as a compliment. "You mean to tell me your woman doesn't slob on your knob?"

"Not like that," he managed between moans.

I loved knowing I was better at pleasing him than his old-ass woman could ever be. I reached over, grabbed the flavored oil and rubbed it along his length, put a drop on my tongue, then leaned down and kissed his lips.

"Mmmm, that tasted good. What is that?"

"Butterscotch."

I teased his length, then swallowed him in one gulp and then kissed him some more.

"Damn, that feels good."

"Of course it does. I aim to please." I nibbled, sucked, and teased some more, and within minutes he was bucking his hips.

"That's it, baby, I'm about to come!" he cried. I stroked him faster, and within seconds he shot all over my hand. "Aaagghh!" I milked him dry, then reached for a towel and cleaned up. I freed his hands, then lay beside him. "Damn, that was good."

"I aim to please."

"Oh yeah?" he said.

I chuckled. "Oh yeah."

24
Danielle

I lay across my bed in flannel pajamas reminiscing. After only one week, I knew I had to be in love. Or deeply in like. Our relationship was amazing. I felt like a schoolgirl. We had lunch together in the hospital cafeteria. Walked through the halls, holding hands and kissing. After work I rushed home to get ready to spend the evening with Chance. I had to look down to make sure my feet were on the ground, because I had to be floating or even flying through the sky. Every day I felt like calling someone and sharing what I was feeling. Kayla seemed to be the only one who understood, because she was in love. Still, when I talked to her last night, she warned me to be careful and to slow down.

Slow down for what? If it's right, it's right. And it definitely felt like the real thing. Pounding heart. Dry mouth. Giggly and silly. Yep, sounds like love to me. I couldn't stop smiling. Even now my smile had a smile. I've only thought about Ron once today, and Calvin hadn't even crossed my mind until I was about to pick up the phone to call Renee and remembered she and I weren't speaking.

"Bitch!" I mumbled to myself. How long was it going to take her to call me and apologize? After all, she was in the wrong, not me. She had no business letting Calvin lick her pussy. It didn't matter that I didn't want him anymore. This was one time when she stepped over the line.

I remembered all the years we hung out. We never needed to compete because there was always a man for her and a different man for me. I'm tall, skinny, with shoulder-length hair and a light brown complexion. Renee is thick, with a clear caramel complexion and short honey blond hair. We're both cuties and getting a man has never been a problem for us. But we've always had an unwritten rule—never fuck with the other's exes. Now don't get me wrong. Maybe I shouldn't have started messing with Calvin in the first place. But their relationship was almost fifteen years ago and *she* dumped *him*. Besides, she told me she didn't care that I was seeing him. Okay . . . maybe it was after she found out I was already seeing him. But I told her I had no problem ending the relationship if it bothered her, and Renee assured me it did not. Yet the second I gave her permission to make a pass at Calvin, she took it to the next level.

Sighing heavily, I rolled onto my side and reached for the remote control. I wasn't going to waste another second thinking about Renee, no matter how much I missed her.

Besides, I didn't need her. I had Chance.

Remembering I had forgotten to get the mail, I climbed off the bed and moved downstairs and out the door. It was freezing, and without my coat, I was shivering by the time I made it back into the house.

A cup of hot chocolate was just what I needed. I

moved into the kitchen and popped a mug of hot water into the microwave. While it warmed, I thumbed through the mail. Bills. Electric. Gas. Macy's credit card. I frowned at the last piece. A small pink envelope was addressed to me with no return address. I quickly tore it open and removed a small sheet of paper that was typed in all caps.

BE CAREFUL OF THE COMPANY YOU KEEP.

My brow rose. What the hell did that mean? I flipped it over looking for a sender, and there wasn't one. The postmark on the envelope showed that it had been mailed right here in Columbia. "Okay, someone's playing games."

I wasn't about to waste any more energy wondering who sent me the note. It was probably some kind of sales scam. I tossed it aside and moved to the pantry to get a package of hot chocolate.

My phone rang. I reached over and picked up the receiver.

"Hey, baby girl, how about Chinese tonight?"

I exhaled at the sound of Chance's voice. "That sounds wonderful."

"Go ahead and order from Lo Mein and I'll pick it up on my way over. Just make sure you get some pork fried rice and egg rolls."

"Okay."

"Did I tell you how fine you was looking today?"

Seductively, I replied, "Yeah, but go 'head and tell me again."

We laughed, then talked a bit more before I hung up and danced over to the drawer to retrieve the yellow pages. As soon as I had the order placed, I dashed off to the bathroom to brush my teeth and gargle.

"My man is coming over," I sang as I danced to my bedroom. I reached for my mango peach spray and pulled the elastic on my sweatpants and sprayed my freshly trimmed pussy. "I can't wait for Chance to taste my mango-scented kitty." I pulled my hair up in a ponytail because Chance loves when I wear my hair up. He says it makes me look young and so damn sexy. I brushed on cinnamon-flavored lip gloss and a little eyeliner and mascara. I've never been big on makeup. All I needed was enough to emphasize and draw attention to my slanted little eyes. I've been told I have the kind of eyes that make a man want to take me straight to bed. Ha-ha! And that is exactly where I want to be.

I moved downstairs, tossed a log in the fireplace, and started a fire. I needed the mood to be just right.

"Wine! We need wine!" I screamed, then hurried into the refrigerator and released a sigh of relief when I found a bottle of white Zinfandel I had bought weeks ago and never gotten around to drinking. "We will be drinking it tonight." I removed it, stuck it in a bucket and filled it with ice, reached for two flutes, and headed into the living room.

When the doorbell finally rang, I practically ran to the door. "Girl, quit it!" I scolded, then took a deep breath before opening.

"Hey." Chance kissed me. "Damn, baby girl, you smell good."

Uh-huh, wait until he smells my kitty. I grinned in response, then moved aside so he could enter. He put the bag of Chinese food on the coffee table, removed his coat and tossed it on my recliner, then wrapped his arms around me and tackled me onto the couch. "Damn, I missed you, girl. It's only been a couple of hours and I miss you." He pressed his lips to mine, then stared down into my eyes. "You're my baby girl, right?"

My heart was pounding like crazy. "Yes," I whispered.

"Good. Because now that I've got you, I ain't letting you go."

I kissed him. "Good, 'cause I ain't going nowhere." He rose with me hanging on with my legs wrapped around his waist. Chance kissed me once more, then patted me playfully on the butt, and I dropped my legs to the floor and released him.

"I'm starving."

I winked. "So am I, but it's not for food."

"Don't you worry. Ima take care of you. Now give yo man another kiss."

I loved the way that sounded. *My man.* Yes, he is.

I grabbed two plastic plates and we dug in. Chance was an expert at removing the cork from the bottle, which was good because I always made a mess and had pieces floating in my wine. Chance talked about his ten years with the National Guard. And his failed marriage.

I reached for an egg roll. "How did you find out?"

"She told me."

I choked. "What? She told you?"

He chewed his orange chicken before answering. "Yep. I called home to check on her and she had the nerve to tell me she had a new man and not to come home."

My eyes grew large. "That is fucked up. She could have at least waited until you got home."

"Exactly. I was going crazy. Here I was out protecting our country, can't do shit but sit around and think about my wife fucking another nigga in my house."

"Damn." That's all I could manage with a mouthful of rice.

"Yeah. It was fucked up."

I pulled a knee to my chest and leaned back against the couch. I suddenly felt like a fat pig. "What happened when you got home?"

"What you think happened? I put her ass out!" We laughed and then he continued. "Don't you know she had the nerve to tell me they had broken up and she wanted to give our marriage a second chance."

I shook my head. Some women are so stupid.

"Anyway, the next woman I commit to, it's forever. My parents are still together, so I want the same. Come here." As soon as I was on his lap, he wrapped an arm around me and continued. "I don't share. If you're not interested in something serious then you need to let me know now, 'cause I'm really feeling you, girl."

Nodding, I said, "I'm feeling you, too, Chance."

"That's what I needed to hear."

He kissed me and I felt like the luckiest girl in the world. I had a man who actually wanted a commitment. I wanted to freeze this feeling for as long as I could.

Chance carried me over near the fire and lowered me down onto the carpet. He pulled my sweatshirt over my head, removed my bra and sucked one nipple and then the other. *Oh yeah*. By the time he reached my navel, I was sliding my pants down over my hips along with my panties.

"Slow down, baby girl." He chuckled. "We got all night."

"I can't help myself when I'm wit you."

He rose and started unbuttoning his shirt. "Baby, we've got plenty of time because I'm not going anywhere."

I watched him undress, admiring him. He spent hours in the gym and his body was proof of that. He slipped off his boxers and his big black snake sprang forward. "Damn, I'm a lucky woman."

"It's all you, baby girl."

"And don't you forget it." I spread my legs wide. He

lowered on top of me and I kissed his lips while he positioned himself and entered me with one push. "Y*esss!*" I rocked my hips back and forth and met each of his deep, penetrating strokes. I can't believe we were fucking in front of the fireplace. How romantic is that?

"Damn, yo pussy is good," he panted. "With that heat on my ass I'm going to come fast, but I promise to take you up to your room for round two."

"You promise?"

"Yeah, baby," he moaned. "Tell me whose pussy it is."

"Yours, Chance. All yours." I moved fast and pleaded for him to take all of it, deeper and deeper still. "It's yours, baby."

"And don't you forget it." He wrapped his hand around my neck and squeezed. "You promise not to give my pussy up?"

I clawed at his hand and struggled for a breath, but he pounded harder while repeatedly asking me to promise not to share his shit. His hands tightened around my neck. I was feeling a combination of pleasure and pain that I'd never felt before. I was dangling on the edge. And just as I thought I was going to pass out from a lack of oxygen to the brain, Chance came hard. He loosened his grip and I came right along with him just as air entered my lungs. Oooh, it was an exciting feeling. I had never experienced anything like that before in my life. And wasn't sure if I wanted to again.

25

Renee

I moved into the bathroom and decided a long, hot bubble bath was in order. I turned on the water, not too hot, then pulled off my work clothes and tossed them onto the floor. As soon as the tub filled, I climbed in and leaned my head back against the pillow.

Kenny asked me to join him for dinner at nine. I went over and we drove up the street to Sonic and sat in my car, talking and chomping on cheeseburgers and fries. He never lets me pay for anything, and I was so attracted to that quality about him. Even before it was time for him to return to work, he slipped off a fifty and told me to put it in my tank for my time. A smile curled my lips. I couldn't wait until morning so I could see his goofy smile. Can you believe that shit?

My cell phone rang. I didn't recognize the phone number and thought it might have been John's worrisome ass if it hadn't been a St. Louis number.

"Hello?"

"Nae-Nae, it's me."

I groaned inwardly at the sound of my brother Andre's voice. "Hey, whassup?"

He gave a nervous laugh. "I should be asking you that. I haven't heard from you in . . . in a long time."

"I've been busy."

"I was hoping you could come to my house for Dad's birthday. Jorja is making dinner."

My stepfather's birthday was next month. "I don't know. I'll have to check my schedule."

"Come on. Make time."

"I don't know. I've got a book due and I'm not sure I'm going to make my May deadline."

"You said that last year."

He was right. Andre had invited me to spend Christmas with him and his family along with Paul and his new wife. I had planned to come, then changed my mind at the last minute, deciding I just wasn't up to being fake all evening.

"I'll try, but I won't promise you anything."

There was a long pause. "Nae-Nae . . . he's sick."

"So?" I tried to sound like I didn't care. And wish in my heart I didn't. "What's wrong with him?"

"He has colon cancer."

I felt a lump rise to my throat. Not another. My sister had died almost three years ago from complications only hours after having surgery for her ovarian cancer. My life hadn't been the same since. Lisa and I had always been close even though she stayed in my ass. I couldn't stand it then. Now I would do anything in the world to hear her nagging one more time.

"It's spread. He's going to have surgery next month but would like to spend some time with us before then.

Please, Renee, he wants a chance for the two of you to talk."

Shit, he never cared about talking to me before. "I'll get back with you. How's my niece and nephew?"

"They're doing good. Why don't you come down for yourself and see?"

"I will. I promise. Look, I got to go. I'll call you in a few days."

"You do that. Otherwise, I'm calling you."

I ended the call, then sank lower in the tub and closed my eyes. The last thing I wanted to do was to think about Paul. I hated him and that's the way I wanted it to stay. Ever since Lisa passed, Paul had been trying to get Andre to talk to me about giving him a chance to make things right between us. I wasn't hearing it and ignored every effort. The last time I spoke to Paul was the afternoon I caught John in bed with Shemar. He had called to invite me to his home for Thanksgiving.

When Paul pissed me off, I always called Danielle. One thing I could say about my girl is that no matter what, she was always there for me when I needed her. This last week with her not talking to me has been hard. I pulled an angry leg to my chest. *Danielle needs to quit trippin' and call me.* Hell, I called her several times and she ignored every last one of my attempts. Shit, I'm not about to beg. I'll admit I was wrong for letting Calvin lick it. But what's done is done. We've been through worse. So it was time to get past the dumb shit and move on.

My cell phone rang. I looked down and it was a Philadelphia pay phone. I frowned because I don't know anyone who lived in Philadelphia.

"Hello?"

"Renee, please don't hang up!"

"John, what the hell you doing calling me from Philadelphia?"

"It was the only way I could get you to answer."

That fool drove an hour just to make a phone call. "I don't have shit to say to you." Before he could say anything further, I ended the call. I had enough problems. The last thing I wanted to do was to talk to his faggot ass. But even as I said that, a part of me couldn't help but wonder what was so important he drove all the way to Philadelphia to call me about it.

"Call his cell phone and find out," I said out loud.

Nah, I'll pass. If it's that important he'll call me again. And even then, maybe I'll answer. Maybe I won't.

26
Danielle

Wednesday was the day from hell. One bitchy mother after another, whining and complaining. I was so sick of cleaning bedpans and checking incisions I was ready to scream. Luckily, the day was almost over.

"Danielle, you have a call on line one!"

"Thanks, Jennifer," I replied to the girl behind the reception desk as I moved away from the medicine drawer and over to the nurses' triage station to take the call. "Hello, this is Danielle."

"Hello, this is Ms. Evans at Hickman High School."

My eyes immediately rolled to the top of my head. The last thing I wanted to deal with today was my daughter. "I'm sorry, but you need to call Portia's father at—"

She cut me off. "I'm not calling about Portia. I'm calling about Tamara Martin."

"Tamara? What's wrong with Tamara?" And why were they calling me about Renee's daughter?

"There was an incident in the cafeteria at lunchtime, and as you know the school strictly enforces no fighting."

"Fighting?" My brow rose with skepticism. Tamara was one of the sweetest kids I knew. So many times I wished my daughter was more like her.

"Yes, she was in a fight, and unfortunately we have to suspend her for the rest of the week. We tried reaching her mother and didn't have any luck. Your name was listed as an emergency contact."

I glanced over at the clock on the wall. I was getting off in thirty minutes anyway. "All right, I'll be there as soon as I can to pick her up."

I hung up and was thinking about Tamara as I moved back to the medicine cart. Renee was always available on either one of her phones. I frowned. There was no telling what she was doing. *Probably meeting Calvin at her house.* I knew that I was bitter, but damn, what she did was inexcusable.

I went down the hall to give one of my patients their afternoon medicine and spotted Chance at the end of the hall, talking to this narrow-behind nursing student. By the way she was smiling up at him, he was either flirting or saying something that was so good it had her hanging on to every word. I have straight attitude. Jealousy bubbled up inside of me that I tried to keep at bay, but Chance did say he was *supposed* to be my man. At least that's what I thought he had said, although since Chinese at my house, I hadn't seen him and all my calls gone unanswered. Now seeing him on our floor pissed me off. He'd been here all day yet he hadn't bothered to contact me. Before I left today, I was going to find out why.

I stood there pretending to be looking for clean linens on the cart at the end of the hall, but the whole time I was watching them. He tossed his head back at something funny she said and she placed a hand on his arm. Hell to the no. I was not going to let him get away with dissing me like that. After all, I was supposed to be his woman. I had given up Calvin for a chance with him. *Uh-uh*. He wasn't about to play me, especially not with that snaggle-tooth heifer he was talking to.

To make sure he saw me standing there, I moved to the center of the hall with my hand propped at my hip, and as soon as Chance noticed me, he ended the conversation and headed my way.

"Hey, baby girl. Damn, you look sexy. Whassup?" He smiled flirtatiously.

I rolled my eyes. "I should be asking you that. What were the two of you talking about?" I know I sounded jealous, but so what.

"Business, baby," Chance said with that sexy gold-tooth smile and almost made me forget I was supposed to be angry with him. He reached up and caressed my cheek. "It's about the business of making money."

I didn't believe a word of it. "What kind of money?"

"Damn, baby girl, give your man a break," he replied angrily.

Boy, that had a wonderful ring to it. "My man? How you my man and I haven't seen you since Friday? It's now Wednesday. Usually I at least run into you at work, but that hasn't happened either. So where you been?"

"Damn, baby, get off these nuts! The less you know the better. Just be assured yo man is holding it down in these streets."

I didn't have to have a college degree to know what holding it down means. He was hustling. I wasn't even surprised. In fact, I expected as much. On a technician's salary, the Navigator, expensive clothes, and pocket full of money should have spoken words all on their own. But instead of being turned off by the idea, I was more attracted to Chance than ever. He was a true soldier and I was proud to know he was mine. *Bitches, stand back!*

My mind was already working. "What are you doing tonight? I could fix us some steaks." It would mean going to the store, but I had a strong feeling that Chance was definitely worth it.

"You ain't said nothing but the word. What time you want me over?"

"How's six?"

He hesitated. "I got to go to court this evening."

"For what?"

"You don't want to know."

"Try me." I was indignant.

"My license is suspended, so I ain't supposed to be driving except to work and home."

"How did you get your license suspended?"

"Long story ain't even worth getting into, but the skinny of it is that the reason you haven't heard from me is because I got arrested for driving. A while back I let my insurance lapse and had a car accident and had my license revoked. Anyway, my boy Dre, who's always got my back, came and bailed me this morning."

I laced my fingers with his and breathed a sigh of relief. For a moment there, I had thought he was lying. "Next time, call me. If I'm your girl, then that's what girls do."

"That's what I'm talking about! Having a damn good woman in my corner." He was grinning and seemed pleased I considered us a couple. He would soon learn that there ain't nothing I won't do for my man. Renee calls it being stupid. I consider it having my man's back. But what does she know? That's why she can't keep a man.

"I better go and clock out. I'll see you tonight." He moved down the hall and I watched him move, shaking my head. Damn, my baby is fine!

I was moving to my patient's room when I noticed that nursing student staring as well. I moved up to her and glared down at her. "That's *my* man and I play for keeps."

She had the nerve to roll her eyes and toss her long acrylic nails in my face. "Whatever."

No, she didn't. *Oh, I got her whatever*. "Since you seem to have a lot of free time on your hands, Mrs. Carson in 713 needs an enema." Her smirk turned into a frown and it took everything I had not to laugh. She was a student nurse, so she had no choice but to do as I said.

With a wink, I moved into my patient's room and suddenly remembered I had to go and get Tamara.

Thirty minutes later I was pulling away from the hospital heading to the school, grinning like crazy because I was spending the evening with my man. Mrs. Danielle Garrett. That had a wonderful ring to it, or maybe Brooks-Garrett. Yeah, that way I could hold on to my identity.

"Maybe Kayla won't be the only one walking down the aisle this year," I mumbled to myself. Wouldn't that be exciting? Kayla and I getting married. Nadine hopefully having a baby with Jordan. And Renee getting a divorce. I had to smile at that one, because my girl has always had the world at her fingertips. Now she was struggling to keep from falling to the bottom.

Damn, I don't know why I was thinking so badly about Renee. Regardless of how crazy she is, one thing she's always had is my back. And I love her for it. She just pissed me off so damn bad. I was ready to go to her house and hold her down until she apologized. Now that I had Chance, there was no reason for the two of us to be mad over a man neither of us was with. *Or at least I hope she isn't with Calvin.* Nah, he wouldn't be blowing up my phone and coming to my job if he was.

I pulled into the school parking lot, parked in a visitor's parking spot, and hurried inside. Hickman High School was huge but I didn't need directions. I had been in this place so many times for my daughter it wasn't funny. Her hypochondriac ass always had one excuse after another as to why she needed to come home. I had to take a deep breath because just thinking about the roller-coaster ride she put me through, I was starting to get angry again. *Just thinking about my man will keep a smile on my face.*

Sliding my purse farther on my shoulder, I moved down the hall hoping that Renee hadn't arrived and I had come all this way for nothing. Tamara was my goddaughter and I would do anything for her even if I wasn't speaking to her mother at the moment.

I turned at the corner and just as I was about to step inside the office, I spotted Portia standing in front of a row of lockers at the end of the hall with her best friend Celina. I froze in my spot and knew the exact moment she spotted me because her eyelids flew open. While we stood there staring at each other, I eyed her from head to toe. I hadn't seen her since I dropped by my parents' house two months ago and saw her sitting on the couch reading a book. Portia had ignored me and I had done the same.

Her face had grown rounder. Her thick black hair was longer and the ponytail made her look so young, too young to be an expectant mother. Her stomach was large. I wanted to run across and get my baby. Portia had always been a little on the thick side, so pregnancy hadn't changed her much.

I don't know how long I would have continued to stand there if the bell hadn't rung. Celina slammed her locker shut and turned and headed in the other direction. Portia gave me one final look, then went to catch up with her friend. My heart sank, but what did I expect? An apology this late in the game? As far as Portia was concerned, she didn't owe me anything. And I'd be damned wasting another second thinking about it.

Snapping out of it, I stepped into the office and spotted the secretary behind the desk reading a book. I had to clear my throat twice to get her attention.

"May I help you?" she finally asked.

"Danielle Brooks to pick up Tamara Martin."

"One moment, please." She punched a button on the phone, announced my arrival, then hung up the receiver. "Mr. Peterson is the last office on the left."

I groaned because I really wasn't in the mood for a lecture from the principal's big football head. Victor Peterson attended high school with me back in the day and was a pain in the ass even then. Angrily, I moved down the hall. I was anxious to get to the store so that I could fix my man his steak. Now I was going to have to rush.

I stepped through the double glass doors and found two big cornbread-fed girls sitting on the bench outside his office with their heads hung low.

I hope good and damn well these aren't the girls

Tamara got into it with. Both of them looked like they needed to start pushing their chairs away from the table a little sooner.

I knocked once on the door, and as soon as I was summoned, I stepped in. Mr. Peterson was sitting behind his desk with Tamara sitting in the chair across from him. She had a busted top lip.

"Tammy, you okay?" I asked with a concerned look.

She nodded and I moved over and examined her closer. She didn't look okay, but I would worry about that later.

"Ms. Brooks, so good to see you again."

I don't know why he sat there and said that lie. He rose and reached his hand across the desk. I shook it, then took a seat in the chair beside Tamara.

"What happened?" I looked from her to the principal.

"Apparently there was a little altercation in the lunch room this afternoon. The two girls sitting outside the office and Tamara got into a squabble that resulted in fists being thrown."

Tamara glared over at him. "She shouldn't have stuck her foot out and tripped me!"

Mr. Peterson gave a skeptical look. "Unfortunately, we have rules, and you should have come to us to handle it."

Tamara drew back on the chair. "And look like a punk? You've lost your mind." She emphasized this with a roll of the eyes.

I agreed. She would never be able to hold her head up again.

Tamara turned to me. "Aunt Danny, they've been picking on me all school year. I tried to be nice but today was the last straw. As soon as I got off the floor, I punched one of them in the mouth. Then her sister gonna jump in it!"

I looked from her to Mr. Peterson, who gave her a long

look, then folded his hands on the table and turned his focus to me. "It's really a shame that it had to come to this. Tamara is an honor roll student, but the school district has established a no-tolerance policy for fighting."

"But y'all wasn't doing anything! I kept telling you them big girls were messing with me."

"And I called and talked to their mother."

It was time for me to intervene. "Well, Mr. Peterson, obviously that didn't help."

He shook his fat head. "I'm really sorry."

I just bet his sorry ass was. "So now what?"

"All three girls will be suspended for the rest of the week and can return on Monday."

"Let me get this straight. You're suspending her for defending herself."

"Rules are rules."

"And rules can be made to be broken."

He cleared his throat and I could tell he was getting a little agitated. "We just can't tolerate that kind of behavior in this school."

Tamara swung around and faced me. "Aunt Danny, because of fighting I'm getting dropped from National Honor Society."

I remembered Tamara calling me and how excited she was when she was asked to be a member of an organization that was predominantly white. "What's one got to do with the other? She's still an honor student."

"Students in the organization set an example for the rest of the students. Students that are caught fighting are not positive role models."

I rose from the chair and slammed my hands on the desk. "That's a bunch of BS. So just because she got into a fight she is no longer deemed worthy of being part of an honors organization."

"I'm sorry."

"Not half as sorry as you're gonna be when her mother gets here."

As if she had been standing outside the door waiting for her cue, Renee stepped into the office. She looked from her daughter to the fat man across the desk and pursed her lips. "What the hell is going on in here?"

27

Renee

I had dropped my phone in the damn toilet. Can you believe that shit? Yep, exactly. In a toilet full of shit.

It was hooked to the side of my jeans. When I raised them and turned around to flush, my phone fell off and into the toilet. By the time I fished that damn thing out it had already suffered water damage. I went down to the phone company only for them to tell me it wasn't covered by my insurance, so I had to buy a new one that cost me almost three hundred dollars. I wanted to scream. By the time I got home and got the message that Tamara had been suspended, it was already an hour old.

I glared over at Victor's buck-tooth ass. I remembered when I was seventeen. Victor had a mad crush on me back then. And I was curious what it was like to be kissed by a white boy. I let him but he kept scraping my tongue with those big-ass teeth of his.

"I asked a question. What is going on in here?" I glared across the desk. Obviously, Victor had no idea Tamara was my daughter because he looked like he was ready to pee on his big ass. By now, you know I have no sympathy for mothafuckas that pee on themselves.

Danielle blurted out. "Nae-Nae, he got the nerve to suspend Tamara for a fight she didn't even start, and that's not the worst of it. She's been removed from National Honor Society."

My girl Danielle, I should have known she'd have my back. She looked like she was about to tear him a new asshole. And that was good, because I was going to help her dig it.

"Victor, you know good and damn well Tamara is no troublemaker."

Nervously, he adjusted his collar. "I realize that, Renee, but rules are rules."

"And rules are made to be broken. That shit ain't fair and you know it. Look at my daughter's face." I rushed over and cupped her chin. I took in every scratch, every bruise, getting angrier by the second. "Which one of those big Amazons hit my daughter?"

"Both of them, Mama! They were trying to double-team me."

"What?" I looked over at Victor and rolled my eyes. "Didn't I tell you two weeks ago my daughter was having a problem?"

He leaned back in the chair. "Yes, and I addressed your concerns with their mother."

"Obviously your *addressing* didn't work, *otherwise* her face wouldn't be looking like this. Y'all supposed to be protecting my daughter. I mean . . . come on. Who's supposed to pay these medical bills?"

His brow rose. "You don't have health care?"

"You damn right I have health care. I'm not some project ho. But just because I have insurance doesn't mean I have to pay for this. Your school should be held accountable."

He gave a short laugh. "Come on, Renee, you're being ridiculous."

"No, I'm not. In fact, I think you're still holding a grudge because I wouldn't date your big-headed ass."

"Mama," Tamara whined under her breath, then sank low in her chair. My daughter was embarrassed by my behavior, but so what. She better be glad someone was trying to take up for her.

"Renee, I think this discussion is inappropriate."

Danny started laughing. "Actually I think it's quite amusing, especially since he's been trying to hit on me for months. Maybe that's why I got called to the office all the time." She turned to me. "Renee, correct me if I'm wrong, but doesn't that sound like sexual harassment to you? He wouldn't even drop one of Portia's detentions until I came to the office to meet with him."

"Yep, sounds like harassment to me." I glared over at him, daring him to say something.

He took a deep breath and I could tell he was trying to choose his words carefully. "Listen, you both are blowing this out of proportion. I am suspending Tamara and dropping her from the organization for participating in a fight. When Danika tripped her, if she had just come to me instead of hitting her in the nose, none of this would have happened."

I rolled my eyes to the ceiling, wanting to make it loud and clear I had straight attitude. I could tell the exact moment Victor knew I was about to blow, because his pale ass turned beet red.

"Okay, so let me get this straight," I said loud and indignant. "If a kid is getting beat up by another student, they are supposed to just act like a punk and get their butt kicked in front of the whole school?"

"Well, I . . ."

"But that's just what you said. So if my daughter receives bodily injuries or even worse, is killed behind some BS, the school would be liable, right?"

He mumbled something that wasn't understandable.

"You gonna have to speak up, because it sounded to me like you said no."

He cleared his throat. "Renee, you're putting words in my mouth."

"Then you need to man up and explain."

Victor sat up straighter in the chair. Men, black or white, hated when you call them a punk. "I'm sorry, Renee. But the school cannot be held accountable for the behavior of their students."

"Oh, but you're going to be liable for any damages that happen to my daughter." I swung around and faced Tamara. "Princess, are you all right?"

She looked nervous as hell. "Yes." I gave her the look and she quickly started shaking her head. "No."

I leaned in and took a closer look. "I'm no doctor, but it looks to me like you might need some stitches in your top lip and you're holding your neck funny. We might need to get that looked at. Danny, you're a nurse. What do you think?"

Danielle chimed in. "I think she might need to be checked for a concussion."

I nodded in agreement, then moved to lean over, resting my palms on his desk. "And I'm sending all those bills to the school, and don't even think about not paying them because I'll slap a lawsuit on the school district and get the NAACP involved."

Tamara pleaded with her eyes for me to shut up and

quit embarrassing her. *Whatever*. That girl should be glad Danny and I were taking up for her.

"Renee, I-I don't think we . . . we have to take it that far," he said, stumbling over his words. "I think I can make an exception and let Tamara continue to be a member of that National Honor Society."

"Wise decision. When can she return to school?"

"She can return on Monday."

Danielle rose from her seat. "And what about homework? Because up until this point my goddaughter has been an honor roll student, and this event in no way had better affect her academically!"

"I know that's right." I gave Danielle a high five.

I could tell he was intimidated at having two black women leaning over his desk because he reared back in his chair. Any farther and he would fall back onto his big ass.

"You can pick her homework up every evening or I can ask the teachers to e-mail you."

"E-mail would be more convenient," I replied roughly.

I turned toward the door. "Come on, Tamara, let's get out of here."

She scrambled out of the seat, anxious to get out of the office and home as quickly as possible. I still don't get what she's embarrassed about.

As we stepped out of the office I almost ran right into the two Amazons' mama and could see that they both got it honest. Big Bertha was at least six feet with a pair of boobs that almost put my eye out.

She turned to the daughter on the right. "Is this the girl that got y'all suspended?"

Grinning, the nappy-headed one to her left nodded, then looked over at me as if to say, "Ooh, you fin to get it!"

I reared back. "Correction, *your daughters* got my girl suspended over some BS. What you need to do is teach them some home training."

"They get plenty of home training!" she barked back.

"Obviously not, because if they did they would have had sense enough not to double-team my daughter."

"Uh-uh, Mommy, I jumped in to help Kiandra," the fattest one insisted.

Tamara smacked her lips. "I wouldn't have hit her if you hadna tried to trip me."

I chuckled. If she jumped in, then that meant Tamara was beating that ass! *You go, girl.* I straightened my face and glared. "It sounds like your girls started the whole thing."

"Nah, they finished it," she slurred, sending spit flying across at me and Tamara. We both wiped our faces in disgust.

Danielle moved forward. "Damn, if we needed a shower, we would go home and take one."

"I know that's right. Keep them gorillas away from my daughter, otherwise I'm coming for yo ass."

She glared at us and we glared back.

Mr. Peterson finally got off the phone and hurried to escort the family of Amazons into his office. "Sorry for the delay, Mrs. Tolliver. Please come on in."

She pushed her girls into the office and it wasn't until she brushed past me that I noticed the back of her dress was bunched inside a pair of holey-ass grandma panties. I bumped Danielle in the arm and signaled with my head for her to look. We both started laughing.

Mrs. Tolliver swung around angrily. "What's so funny?"

"You."

"And those holey-ass drawers you're wearing,"

Danielle added, then grabbed my hand as we both ran out of the room cracking up.

"Did you see their faces?" Them four-eyed girls and Mr. Peterson were all stuttering when they realized her big booty was on wide display. I was too through.

"Gosh, y'all are so embarrassing!" Tamara groaned when we reached my car.

"Girl, you need to be glad you got us in your corner."

"Why do y'all always have to be so loud?"

Danielle moved over and gave her a hug. "Poor Little Tammy," she began in a baby voice. "You know I'm going to make sure no one messes with my little girl."

"I know that's right. Now stick your lip in and let's go and get some ice cream," I ordered with a playful pat to the head.

Danielle agreed, then hopped in her car and followed us over.

We each ordered a sundae with everything on it. After Tamara gobbled hers down, she excused herself and went to the bathroom.

"You think she's going to be okay?" Danielle asked.

"Yeah, she's a soldier just like her mother. You know Tamara is all about appearances. She was more embarrassed having me come down than she was getting jumped by them two girls."

"Yeah."

There was a momentary silence while she took another bite of her ice cream. Even though my head was down I could feel her staring at me.

"You know I'm still pissed at you."

I raised my head from my bowl and met her eyes. I tried to look innocent but Danny wasn't going for it. I could see the hurt and disappointment. I expected it, but it didn't make it any easier to deal with. "Yeah, I know, and you have every reason to be."

"That shit was grimy, Renee."

"I know and I'm sorry." There, I said it. And just so you know, I don't say sorry too often. "I was just trying to help you out but things got a little carried away."

"A little? Calvin was having a little afternoon snack when I walked in."

"Actually it was a feast," I teased.

"Ho, shut up," she barked although I could tell she was struggling to keep a straight face.

I was laughing, then got serious quick. "Danny, I'm sorry really. I really didn't know you were feeling Calvin like that. If I had known, I never would have even went there with him."

Danielle gave me a skeptical look. I'll admit that in the past I've done some scandalous shit, but I have never *intentionally* slept with a man if I knew he was involved with one of my girls, and that's on the real.

"Don't you remember screwing Kayla's man?" Danielle asked as if she could read my mind.

"Because I thought she didn't want him," I cried defensively.

She took another spoonful of her ice cream although her eyes never strayed far from mine. "I'll admit it was partially my fault. I should have never asked you to get involved in the first place. I should have just been up front with Calvin. Instead, the shit blew up in my face." Pondering, she chewed on the spoon. "I didn't realize how much he meant to me until I saw him with you."

"Are you sure you don't just want him so that no one else can have him?"

She shook her head. "No, that isn't it at all. I really do care about him a lot."

"Okay, so what's stopping you from working things out? He really loves you. That man has been blowing up my phone. You need to take him out of his misery."

"Chance is my man now."

"And . . . ?"

"And I really like him because he keeps it real."

"But . . . ?"

Danielle pursed her lips together thoughtfully. "No buts. The relationship is still new but I'm crazy about him. I get turned on the second I see him."

I pointed a finger at her. "Remember I used to feel like that about Bryant, and it took me a month before I figured out his ass was psycho."

"Chance is also a fabulous lover."

"You already screwed him?" I asked incredulously.

She rolled her eyes. "Don't act like you don't screw on the first date."

I had to laugh because she had me on that one.

"We've been dating for the last two weeks."

"And what's he working with?"

She licked her lips. "Oh, he has a hell of a package on him."

My eyes grew round with interest. "Shit, it sounds to me like you have a winner."

"I think so, and that's what's scary. He seems almost too good."

I finished the last of my ice cream. "Have you looked his ass up yet on Intelius?"

She shook her head then looked uncomfortable. "No, not yet."

"What the hell you waiting on?"

She shrugged. "I'm scared to look. I don't want to ruin things. Things are so perfect. Looking him up means

I don't trust him. He hasn't done anything yet to make me doubt my trust."

I told you my girl was stuck on stupid. As a practice, anytime we meet a guy we first go online and look him up. Anyone who's been to court for anything, including a traffic ticket, will be listed. You'd be surprised how many convicts I've met in the club and ran home to look their asses up and found out they just got out of jail for rape. Hell to the no. You better believe I looked Kenny up.

"What's his last name? I'll look him up."

She hesitated. "Garrett."

"And how do you spell his first name?"

"I guess it's C-h-a-n-c-e."

I nodded. "Got it."

She shook her head. "I can't believe you're going to look his name up in the computer."

"Yep. You know I am, and I'll call you later with a status report."

She looked like she wanted to say something else but changed her mind and ate her ice cream instead.

I pointed my spoon at her. "I'm seeing someone now."

"Who?" she asked impatiently.

"Kenny Johnson."

"Kenny! Skinny Kenny?"

I was offended. "He's not that skinny."

She burst out laughing. "Girl, puh-leeze. Kenny's skinny with glasses and looks goofy as hell."

She was hating on my man. "I think he's cute."

"Ugh!"

"Shut up!"

"So what's up with y'all? I mean how serious is it?" she asked, then started cracking up.

"It's new," I said, trying not to sound too excited. "He's working on a car that I bought from Nadine."

"Now one thing about Kenny, he's good with cars." She paused, then frowned. "Isn't he living with Reese?"

I nodded. "You know her?"

"Yep. Ugly, but then he ain't nothing to look at, either."

"Girl, quit hating on my man."

"Your man?" She was staring at me like I'd lost my mind.

"Bitch, you know what I mean. We're just friends right now."

She gave me a skeptical smirk. "I know Kenny, and he's gonna try and get in them drawers before he fixes that car."

I thought about how true that statement was, but I wasn't about to admit it. "Girl, we talk on the phone all the time. He seems like he's a sweetheart."

"He is. He used to date this one girl I worked with and she said he takes care of his women."

Good, because that was one criterion I had for the men I dated, they needed to have a job and not be stingy with their money.

"What's he going to do about Reese?"

"What do you mean?"

"Girl, I heard they are getting married. You know he's going to try and dump her for you."

I smiled because the thought had crossed my mind. "Hey, that's on him," I said with a shrug.

Danielle shook her head. "Wouldn't that be something if he did? Don't hurt him," she teased.

Tamara finally made her way out of the bathroom and I turned up my nose as I rose. "I hope you washed your hands."

"Yes, I washed my hands," she groaned and moved out to the car.

Danielle nudged me in the side. "Quit embarrassing that girl."

"Shoot, I just wanted to make sure her stinky behind washed her hands before she touched my car."

28

Danielle

I was barely home an hour when Chance came knocking at my door. Dammit, I'd been having so much fun I forgot all about fixing him dinner. As soon as I opened the door he pushed inside and started looking around the room. "Where you been?"

I had to turn around at that because I was sure my daddy wasn't in the room. "I went out for ice cream with my girl and her daughter."

He gave a laugh and flicked his nose with his thumb like he didn't believe me. "You sure you weren't with yo otha nigga?"

I rolled my eyes and flopped back on the couch so I could catch the end of my program.

"What, cat got your tongue?"

"Nope. I'm just not answering." I tried to keep a straight face. I love when a man is jealous.

Chance took a seat beside me on the couch and rested a hand on my knees. I just continued to sit there popping my gum. "That's okay if you're seeing someone else, just tell me."

I jerked my head around. "I'm not fucking anyone but you."

"I told you I wasn't sharing."

"Would you just shut up!" Damn, it was cute for the first thirty seconds, but now he was getting on my nerves.

Chance started laughing, pushed me back onto the cushions, and started tickling me under my armpits.

"Stop!" I screamed. "Dammit, I said stop!"

"Nope. Not until you tell me you're still my boo."

"Yes, yes! I'm still your boo."

He stopped and climbed on top of me. "That's more like it." His tongue slid between my lips in and out, mating with mine. Then his lips moved to trail along my cheek where he whispered, "Don't ever leave me."

"I won't, baby." I hungrily kissed him back, stuck my hands beneath his shirt, and pulled it over his head. My lips moved across his shoulders and traveled to his flat nipples, which I licked and nibbled until he was moaning. I reached for his belt buckle, unfastened his pants, and reached inside for my prize and squeezed.

"Damn, baby, that feels good."

"I know what would feel even better."

"What?"

"You, being inside me," I cooed close to his ear.

Chance rose from the couch and I quickly removed my clothes, then moved back over to the couch. Chance frowned. He took my hand and pulled me up beside him, then kissed my lips. "Come on, baby girl. We don't want to mess up the upholstery. Let's take this to the bedroom."

I felt a twinge of disappointment because it took away

the spontaneity that comes with trying something new. "How about we fuck on the kitchen counter?"

He gave me a look of disgust. "Near the food? Hell nah! Now come on, I'm horny as hell." He took me by the hand and we raced up to my room and fell on the bed together. Chance removed his clothes and rolled on top again. "You are so beautiful," he whispered as he started kissing me again. I could feel his beautiful dick pulsing against my inner thigh and my pussy clenched with excitement. That belonged to me. His lips traveled downward and my nipples tingled as they waited for the contact.

"Aaah, that feels so good." There were no words to explain the way I felt by the time he slid inside my body. Chance started slow, then built up his strokes until they were long and deep. His entire body slammed against me and I locked my ankles around his waist and held on for the ride. "Baby, I'm about to come. Eeeaaahhh!" I had no control. My hips were rocking hard and I arched off the bed and knew the exact moment he came because he shot so hard inside me I felt its impact following a hot, wet feeling. He grunted inside my mouth and stroked hard while I squeezed my thighs tightly together and milked him for everything he had. With one final breath, he collapsed on top of me, then rolled over.

"Uhhh, Danielle . . ." I heard him say then his voice purposely trailed off.

Knowing the routine by now, I rose from the bed and moved into the bathroom to get two towels. One to wipe him off and the other one for us to lie on. Chance smiled, pleased that I knew what he liked without him having to tell me. As soon as I was done I snuggled my head under his arm, resting into his chest. A smile was on my face. "Tell me something about you that I don't already know."

"Like what?" he asked, sounding like he was suspicious.

"I don't know . . . anything."

"Okay, well, let me think a second." He was quiet but I could tell he was thinking. "I like lying in bed watching Lifetime on Sundays."

"Are you serious?" I couldn't believe that shit. A man was actually admitting to watching those crazy-ass movies. "So do I."

"I guess we know how to spend a Sunday together."

I grinned. "I guess we do."

"Your turn. Tell me something about you."

"I'm thinking about getting breast implants."

"Why? I love your body the way it is, especially your breasts."

I squirmed uncomfortably. "I don't. I never have. I've just learned to live with it, but I've never accepted having such little breasts. I've been saving up for the last three years to get the surgery done."

"Damn, that deep. I guess I need to be honest with you." He drew a deep sigh and I braced myself for what he was about to say. Damn, Renee was right. I should have checked his ass out on the Internet.

"What?" I asked impatiently.

"Okay, here goes . . . I'm thinking about getting a dick implant for this little-ass dick I got."

I raised up and stared at him. He tried to keep a straight face. I tossed a pillow at his head and he broke down with laughter. "Be serious!"

Chance embraced me and kissed my lips. I don't know what I expected to hear, but it definitely wasn't that. I held on tight, loving everything there was about this man, wanting to know anything and everything there was to know.

"Have you ever been arrested?" I asked.

"What black man hasn't?"

I had to laugh at that because it was true. "What were you arrested for?"

"Stupid stuff. Never anything that I had to serve time for. What about you?"

"Yep. Writing bad checks."

"No shit?"

I sighed, hating to even bring up that time in my life. "Yeah, my husband and I had split up and I was struggling trying to raise Portia with almost no help. I started writing checks to buy food and got myself in a mess. I had checks bouncing all over town. The prosecuting attorney's office only gives you thirty days, and I couldn't pay them all in time so I was arrested. I only had to stay in jail overnight, thank God, but it was long enough for me to know I never ever wanted to set foot in there again."

He pulled me into the circle of his arms and dropped his lips to the top of my head. "Jail ain't no place for a woman. Especially not my woman."

I lay there and drifted off to sleep. *I don't think I have anything to worry about.*

29

Renee

I went home, logged onto my computer, and clicked on Intellus. It took me a while to find Chance Garrett's name. Something with the way his name was loaded. So I scrolled through all of the Garretts until I came across Chance. There was only one. He lived right smack in the hood. *Aggravated assault. Ex parte. Child support payments.* "What the hell?"

I reached for the phone and called Danielle's cell phone, but she didn't answer. I'd try again in the morning. For the time being I sent her a text message. LEAVE THAT CRAZY MOFO ALONE.

My office phone rang. I reached over and grabbed it.

"Hello?"

Silence.

"Hello?" I said with a little more attitude.

"Bitch!"

I took the phone away from my ear, looked at it before bringing it against my mouth again. "Excuse me?"

"You heard me. *Bitch,*" she sneered.

"I got your—" Oh no, she didn't hang up on me. I flipped over the receiver and quickly checked the Caller ID. Dammit. The call had been blocked. I was so angry I slammed down the phone. Who the hell was calling me? I could think of dozens of people who couldn't stand me for various reasons, but no one recent I had pissed off besides Landon. Speaking of piss . . . I reached for the phone and dialed his number and wasn't at all surprised that he didn't answer. "Listen, you pissy bitch, you better call me this evening, otherwise I'm coming to your job tomorrow!" Once again I slammed the phone.

After a while I decided to push my anger aside and get to work. I had a book due and a new scene to write. I turned on Destiny's Child, "Cater 2 U," and started outlining the next chapter. An hour into my work, I heard a knock on my office door.

"Mama, there's some man at the door to see you!"

A man. I sprang from my chair and moved out of my office and down the hall to the front door to find Calvin waiting on the porch. "I got it."

Tamara hurried back to her room. I opened the door. "Come on in out of the cold."

"Thanks." He moved inside. His hands were deep in his pockets and he looked like he had the weight of the world on his shoulders. The bags underneath his eyes meant he hadn't been sleeping much.

"Please, have a seat." I moved over to the couch and waited for him to take the wingback chair across from me. "Whassup?"

He leaned forward, resting his elbows on his knees. "I want to know what happened that evening."

I gave him a silly smirk. "You need me to spell it out for you?"

Calvin shook his head and gave me a look that said,

quit playing games. "I want to know why you made a pass at me."

"I . . . I was feeling vulnerable and needed a man to make me feel good." Damn, I hated lying to this man.

He pursed his lips. "I think you did that on purpose to break us up. The question is why?"

"You are a grown-ass man. I can't make you do anything you don't want to do," I said with straight attitude. No way was he going to put all the blame on me.

Calvin dragged a hand across his face and blew out a heavy breath. "I know, and I'm beating myself up. Hell, I'm a man and we are known to be weak."

"That's for sure," I teased.

"Listen, I know this might be hard for you to believe after everything that happened between us, but I love Danielle."

I could tell he was sincere, which only made me feel worse about what happened between us. "I'm sorry, Calvin. Really I am."

"If you're sorry then you'll help me get her back."

Oh no! The last time I got involved, she and I stopped talking. I wasn't about to go through that shit again. "I'd rather not. She just started talking to me again."

He blew air between his teeth. "I think she's seeing someone else, and what happened the other day just gave her the excuse she needed."

Damn, he was smarter than I thought.

"What do you want me to do?" Part of me felt that I owed Calvin. It wasn't his fault that he was a weak man and couldn't resist tasting this caramel kitty over here.

"Can you please talk to her? I've been to her job. I've called all of her numbers, but she refused to speak to me." He was pleading with those sexy brown eyes of his for me to help bring them back together.

"Damn, for a minute there I thought you had dropped by to see if we could finish where we left off the other evening," I teased.

"Renee . . ." he warned.

I tossed my hands up. "I'm just playing. Damn, can't you take a joke?"

Calvin reached inside his pocket, pulled out a small black box, and opened it. "Does this look like I'm joking?"

My mouth flew open. That sucker was huge. The carats had carats. "Oh. My. God! You bought that for Danielle's crazy ass?" I slid off the couch and moved in for a closer look.

"Yes. I was waiting for the right time to propose to her."

I took the ring from the box and slipped it on my finger. It was a little too small for my finger, but nothing a jeweler couldn't fix. "Damn, I didn't know y'all were that serious."

"I love her, Renee."

My eyes narrowed. "Then answer this question. Why was you eating my damn pussy? 'Cause inquiring minds want to know."

He had to think about that one a minute before answering. "I really don't know."

"Probably because that bitch is too pretty to resist," I mumbled.

Calvin shook his head, then started laughing. "Renee, you are too much."

"I'm just keeping it real." I put the ring in the box and he slipped it back into his coat pocket. "I'll try to talk to her but I can't make any promises."

He nodded and looked at least hopeful that I was willing to help. "I appreciate that. Just don't mention the ring. I want that to be a surprise. That's if she'll still have me."

I doubted that, the way this Chance guy had her nose all wide open. However, she did say that she hadn't realized how much she really cared about Calvin until she saw him with me. So maybe there was hope after all, but then Danielle ain't the brightest Skittle at the end of the rainbow.

"Thanks, I'll call you in a couple of days."

"All right." I walked him to the door then watched him leave. *Hopefully after I tell Danielle what I saw on Intelius, she'll leave that fool alone.*

I was about to close the door when I noticed a black SUV pull away from in front of my house. It wasn't until I was heading back to my office that I remembered it was the same vehicle that had pulled up beside me at Danielle's. I hurried back to the door to see if the SUV had returned. It hadn't. I returned to my office but spent the rest of the evening wondering who had been sitting behind the wheel.

30

Renee

It was lunchtime and I was on my way home from work when I realized I still hadn't heard from Danielle's crazy ass. She should be eating, so I hit her on her cell phone.

"Hey, what's up?"

"You. I was wondering if you was still alive."

Danielle got all serious and shit. "What do you mean?"

"Did you get my text message last night?"

"What text?"

"I told you to leave that crazy fool alone. I looked Chance up on Intelius and he has assault charges and some chick put an ex parte on him."

"What!"

I chuckled. "Yep. That mothafucka is ca-ra-zy!"

"Maybe it was all a misunderstanding."

"Understanding my ass. Girl, he's even been sued for back child support payments."

"Child support? Now I know you're lying 'cause Chance don't have no kids."

"Well, I guess you better tell the mother of his child

that, because he's been sued and she granted back child support in the amount of six thousand dollars. That wouldn't have happened if it wasn't true."

She was quiet. Too quiet.

"You still there?"

"Uh-uh. Girl, I'm fin to call him now."

I knew that was her way of getting off the phone. I hung up and rode home, waiting for her to call me back. Hopefully she kicked his ass to the curb or threatened to get her brother to beat his ass. Kee ain't no joke. When Portia was running around crying wolf and claiming that Ron was the father of her baby, oh, you better believe Kee whupped that ass! I thought the shit was funny because Ron might be fine as hell, but messing with a teenager is nothing to be playing with. But once we found out Portia's ass was lying, I couldn't blame Danielle for putting my godchild out.

I made a left and headed to the *Columbia Daily Tribune*.

"May I help you?" asked an attractive woman sitting behind the reception desk.

"Yes, is Landon Lawson in today?"

"Yes, he's in the workroom." She pointed to the door at my far left.

I strolled down the hallway carrying my purse and a brown paper bag and pushed through the door. There were probably a dozen other workers in there as well, eating their lunch. As soon as Landon spotted me he froze and the sandwich dropped from his hand. "Renee."

"Well, hello, Landon, sweetheart. How are you this morning?"

"Fine," he mumbled.

I dropped my bag on the table. "Sweetie, you were in such a rush you forgot these this morning and I thought I better bring them to you," I replied in a sweet potato pie voice. I then reached into my bag and removed a box of Depends and sat it on the table.

Landon jumped back like it was a dead rat. "What do I need those for?"

A couple of his coworkers started laughing.

"Don't be ashamed. You know you have a bladder problem." I glanced over at the women in front of the copy machine. "Just last month, he peed in my bed. Ain't that right, boo? Don't be ashamed." I patted him lightly on the back.

"She lying," he insisted and looked around the room for someone who believed he was innocent.

"Man, you do run to the bathroom quite a bit," one guy in the corner teased.

"I know that's right." Another cackled and then the others joined in.

Landon turned red and glared over in my direction.

"I'll see you later." I smiled, turned on the heels of my expensive shoes, and left the building. I had barely made it out to the parking lot when my phone rang. Would you believe it was Landon? Now what made him decide to call me? I chuckled and retrieved the call. "Yes, pissy? What can I do for you?"

"That's fucked up! How you gonna come to my job and embarrass me like that?"

"It wasn't like I didn't warn you," I replied calmly.

"But you didn't have to do that. I told you I would buy you some new mattresses."

"When? When it's convenient for you? I don't think so. I'll see your ass in court." I hung up on him before he had a chance to say anything else and headed straight to the courthouse. Landon pissed on the wrong woman.

31

Danielle

Leave it to Renee to make me look like a fool. I bet the second she walked in the house, she raced to the computer and logged onto the Boone County Courthouse Web site so she could get the dirt on my man. When what she needs to worry about is that little shrimp cocktail of a man she's screwing. Damn! She's my girl and all, but sometimes I can't stand her. If I thought she had looked up Chance's info because she was looking out for me that would be one thing, but I know she was just trying to be nosey. Shit! There is probably another Chance Garrett in Boone County. And who's to say I even spelled his name right. I was just guessing.

Nevertheless, I couldn't face him and made sure I stayed busy all day. For lunch I ate what one of the patients left on her tray. After giving report, I took the stairs to the parking garage, hopped in my car, and peeled off before Chance could catch me.

I went into the house and hopped in the shower, trying not to think about what Renee discovered, but I couldn't get it off my mind so I went online myself to confirm the information. To my disappointment, there was only one Chance Garrett in the database, and it was the psycho Renee had told me about. I couldn't stop thinking *this is the same man I planned a future with. The same man I gave up Calvin for.*

Around seven, my house phone rang. It was a private call and my heart started pounding because I thought it might be Ron.

"Whassup, baby girl, why haven't you called me?"

Damn, it was Chance. The last thing I wanted to do was discuss what I had discovered over the phone. What I needed to say needed to be said in person. "We need to talk. I asked you last night if there was anything you needed to tell me, and you said no, but I've heard otherwise."

He hesitated and I could feel his frown. "I don't like the sound of that. I'll be over in a second."

That second turned into almost two hours before I heard his beats coming down the street. He knocked twice before I opened it and let him in.

"Damn, you look good." He greeted me with a crooked smile and a searing kiss. It felt so good being in his arms that I almost forgot what I was angry about. Not to mention he looked good in a fitted Rams cap and matching jersey. He moved over to the couch and took a seat across from me. "Baby girl, tell your man what's bothering you."

He looked so concerned, I almost felt guilty even bringing it up. "I looked your name up on Intelius."

He looked confused. "And what did you find?"

"A hit-and-run and an ex parte."

He swiped a hand across his face and gave a defeated sigh. "Yeah, you're right."

I couldn't believe his ass was admitting to it.

"But can yo man explain?"

I nodded, then leaned back in the chair with my lips pursed so he would know that it better be good.

"My ex-girlfriend Yolanda and I had gotten into it one night. She was yelling and acting a damn fool so I told her 'yo, I'm fin to bounce.' I went out to my car and hopped in, and that fool came running out the house in her pajamas acting a damn fool. She started banging on my glass 'cause I wouldn't roll down the window. I told her to move so I could leave and she wouldn't, then she had the nerve to grab hold of my car as I tried to pull away. She fell flat on her ass in the driveway. But then the neighbors came out and found her lying there, and I bounced because there was a warrant out on me for failure to appear and if I stuck around, I sho nuff was going to jail. Next thing I know they got a warrant out on me for hit-and-run."

He sat there staring, waiting for me to say something. Did he honestly expect me to believe that lame-ass story.

"I know it sounds like I'm lyin' but I swear I'm telling you the truth. We going to court next month and I want you there just so you'll know yo man is telling the truth."

I rocked my leg and didn't say anything for a long time. Maybe he was telling the truth. After all, I wasn't there. Wasn't he supposed to be innocent until proven guilty? "What about you owing back child support?"

He dropped his head, and when he looked up at me again tears clouded my man's eyes. I felt so guilty because whatever he was about to say appeared to be quite painful.

"Baby, I told you I didn't have any shorties because I don't. Wait a minute, let me finish. I had met this girl name Charlise and we just started kicking it when she told me she was pregnant and the baby's daddy didn't want to have anything to do with her. I really liked her and hung in there with her. I took care of her, and when she went in labor I told her I would give her baby a name and I signed the birth certificate. Later she dumped my ass for another nigga, then had the nerve to put child support on me even though she knows good and damn well that a baby ain't mine! I've been trying to get a blood test for three years, yet she comes up with one excuse after another. Telling folks I'm wrong for wanting her son to get stuck with a needle just so I can prove something that is already in writing. As far as the state is concerned, since I signed that birth certificate, Trenton is legally my responsibility until I prove otherwise."

Damn, he was good.

"I really loved that kid like he was my own, but what she's trying to do—that bitch is grimy."

He wiped his eyes and I could tell he was fighting tears. That last thing I wanted to see was a grown man cry. "Baby girl, anything you want to know about me, all you have to do is ask. You don't need to ask nobody and you definitely don't need to be going on the computer looking. Hell, I ain't got shit to hide."

"Uh-huh," I mumbled, not sure how to respond.

He rose. "Look, I came over here not to argue but to give you this." He reached inside his pocket, pulled out a vanilla envelope, and handed it to me.

I took it and glanced at him suspiciously. "What is it? A warrant for your arrest?"

He gave me a sexy smirk. "I see you got jokes. Just open it."

I looked inside and removed a gift certificate that was for a one-hour body massage at HANDS ON MASSAGE.

"I heard you saying you could use a massage, and

since I don't have skills in the department I thought I'd treat my baby to the best."

I didn't know what to say because no one, I mean no one had ever done anything that nice for me. "Thank you."

He dropped down on his knees in front of me and took my hand. "I love you, baby girl." He leaned in to kiss me at the same time I felt him slip something on my finger. I looked down and noticed the sparkling cocktail ring on my finger. There were so many stones my hand was heavy.

"Oh my God!"

"I take it you like it."

I was speechless. "I-I do. I-I don't know what to say."

"Saying you like it would be a start."

"I love it! I really love it."

"Good, because I love you. I know you probably think it's too soon. This ring is simply my promise to be yo man and to take care of my girl the way she deserves to be treated. That's if you still want me in your life."

I sprang into his arms. "I love you, too."

He kissed me and held me tight. "That's my girl."

As far as I was concerned, Renee needed to learn to mind her own business.

32

Renee

By Friday, I decided I had strung Kenny along long enough. It had been a week since I had given a blow job. Besides, I was horny as hell. As soon as nine o'clock came I called him at the shop. "Hey you."

"Hey, what you doing?" He sounded happy to hear from me.

"Thinking about you," I cooed.

"Oh yeah, what are you thinking?"

I lowered my voice just in case one of the professors came down the hall. "I'm thinking about riding some dick this afternoon. You think you're up for the job?"

"Hell, yeah. I'm up for it. What time?"

"Meet me at home at noon." That would give me three hours before the kids came home.

"I'll be there."

He arrived right on schedule. As soon as we were in the room, in one swift motion he flipped me over onto my back.

"What are you doing?" I laughed.

"I'm taking control this time." He reached for a condom, slid it on. Kenny was acting like he hadn't had pussy in years. He pushed inside and was so big that I started breathing heavily while my body stretched to accommodate him. "Damn, your pussy is tight."

"Does it hurt?"

"Nah, that shit feels good."

"And so do you." Oh, but did I feel full.

He got me this time but the next, I'm going to be in control.

After Kenny left, I made my weekly Wal-Mart run. I hadn't been there twenty minutes and my cart was already full. I was in the meat department when Danielle called. I hadn't heard from her since I told her what I had found on Intelius.

"Guess what?"

I was afraid to ask but I did. "What?"

"Chance bought me a ring."

Her voice was dripping with excitement so I tried to hold back the sarcasm. "Really? What *kind* of ring?"

"A promise to love me ring."

"Love!" I shouted. "Since when did the two of you decide you're in love?"

"Last night."

I could feel her smiling all the way through the phone. *This I've got to see.* "You at home?"

"Yep. I just got back from the jewelry store. I went to see if I could get my ring sized without them keeping it and they told me no. So I bought one of those bands that you can slide on your finger to hold your ring in place. Nae-Nae, wait till you see it."

"I'll be over as soon as I finish shopping."

I hung up and quickly decided on a family pack of center cut chops. Price really wasn't a factor since I was spending money that Kenny had given me. That's one thing I can say about my boo, he keeps my pockets lined.

I moved down the aisle for some cornstarch because I learned from my grandmother how to make real gravy. Forget all that fake stuff. As I was turning down the next aisle, I noticed that big Amazon woman from Portia's high school staring at me. When she noticed me looking her way, she quickly dropped her head and looked the other way. I glanced over at the cornstarch and when I turned again, I caught her staring once more. I made a show of looking down at my clothes. Hell, I knew I was looking good in blue jeans and suede knee-length boots. My form-fitting sweater emphasized my small waist. After making sure that everything was intact, I stared her butt down until she turned and went the other way. I was tempted to still go over to her and ask her fat ass what the hell she was looking at but I needed to get out of the store and over to Danielle's as soon as possible.

As soon as I stepped inside Danielle's house, she held out her hand and I examined the huge cluster of diamonds on her finger. The stones were shiny like polished glass. "And you think it's real?" I asked, looking up at her.

She looked offended. "Why wouldn't it be?"

My brow rose. "Why would it be?"

She snatched her hand back and placed it on her hip. "Because Chance gave it to me. Do you really think he would go to all that trouble to buy me a cheap ring?"

"Girl, you know good and damn well men will do whatever it takes to get some ass."

She frowned and I knew I had pissed her off. "He was already getting the ass."

Trying to lighten the mood, I laughed, then moved over

to her couch and flopped down on the cushions. "Yeah, and he knew you had caught his ass in a lie and he was trying to butter you up and he did just that."

"Shut up."

"Whatever." She hates to hear the truth. "Well, at least tell me that while you were at the jewelry store, you had someone examine the stones."

"I was at Wal-Mart's jewelry counter."

Okay, that answered that. I reached for the new *Essence* magazine that I had been tempted to buy in the grocery store and was glad that I hadn't. I told you Danielle was stuck on stupid. If she wants to believe that ring is real then she can go right ahead. The first thing my ass would have done was run to a jeweler and have those stones looked at.

"Calvin stopped by my house the other day," I said off-handedly as I flipped to the next page.

Danielle swung around and gave me an evil look.

"No, bitch. It was nothing like that. He wants you back."

She really liked him because she was grinning from ear to ear. "Is he still mad about what we did?"

I shook my head. "He doesn't know what *we* did and I'd like to keep it that way. No. He told me to tell you he's sorry and that he loves you."

She nibbled on her bottom lip, then dropped her head and tried to avoid eye contact. "Tell him I've got a new man."

"Uh-uh, I'm not telling him anything. I promised to give his message and that's where it ends."

"He's been e-mailing me and sending me cards and flowers."

My eyes grew large. "And you haven't said anything?"

She shrugged. "Because I'm with Chance now."

Whatever. "I don't know why the hell you need another thug when you have a nice man who wants nothing more than to settle down with you."

She rolled her eyes at me. "You are one to talk. John was the nicest man I've ever known, but you were never happy with him."

I gave a strangled laugh. "John's a fag."

"I'm talking about before you found out about that. Besides, I don't think he's a fag. He's just on the down-low like all the others. I really don't think he expected you to find out that he liked to get a little booty every now and then."

"Whatever. John and Calvin are in two different categories."

"Well, it doesn't matter. I'm with Chance now. He completes me."

I wasn't even going to respond to that comment. Ron completed her as well.

"He gave me a gift card for a massage, and you know how much that shit cost."

I looked up from the magazine. "Where at?"

She rose, walked over to the kitchen counter and picked up the gift certificate, and handed it to me. HANDS ON MASSAGE.

I looked it over, and sure enough he had gotten her a one-hour body massage. I was impressed. "Oh shit. I heard this place was nice."

"I know." She beamed with pride.

Okay, maybe she got me on that one, but something was fishy with Chance's ass, and it wouldn't be long before I started seeing that dog's fleas.

"Look, I got to go. Kenny's coming over and I'm cooking tonight."

She smiled. "It must be getting serious between y'all."

"Girl, I'm just trying to show him I'm just as good in the kitchen as I am in bed."

"You slept with him?"

I was grinning so I know it was written all over my face. "Yep, this afternoon."

"How was it?"

"*Giiirrrrl*, it was so good! Quick, but good."

She gave me a look of disbelief. "Kenny?"

I nodded. "He's got a dick on him."

"Kenny?"

"Yes, bitch, Kenny."

She fell back against the couch. "Hell nah! Kenny Johnson got a dick on him. Well, they do say that skinny men are packing."

"Well, I don't know about all the rest but my man has it going on."

I told her I'd call her tomorrow and headed out to my car and noticed I had left my cell phone on the seat. I looked down and saw I had one new text message. I scrolled through and what I read made me gasp. "Hell nah."

STAY AWAY FROM MY MAN, BITCH!

33

Danielle

I sighed while expert fingers kneaded my flesh across my shoulder blades, over my funny bone, and then down along my spine. I haven't felt this relaxed in weeks.

"Hmmm, that feels good, Carlos," I moaned.

"Thank you, Danielle." He skimmed my sides and then smoothed back toward my neck. After moving along my bra line down toward my waist, his hands left and were replaced by a warm blanket. "I'll be right back. I've got a fabulous new eucalyptus and lemon massage oil I want to try on you."

"That sounds wonderful."

"It is. Just keep your eyes closed and enjoy the music," Carlos urged, then exited the room.

The acoustic sounds of India.Arie floated through my veins. Any second now and I'd be fast asleep. Coming here was a fabulous idea, I thought with a sigh.

I folded my arms beneath my head and closed my eyes.

The knob turned and the door opened, signaling Carlos's return. I heard him set a bottle on the table beside me, and movement as he returned to stand next to me. He removed the blanket from my back, then lowered the sheet even farther below my waist. Seconds later, warm oil dribbled onto my skin.

"*Aaaaah,*" I moaned.

He massaged the warm liquid along my spine. His strong hands kneaded and squeezed as he moved downward. When he traveled back toward my shoulders, a thumb grazed the side of my breast. I flinched at the intimate touch. The shock of pleasure was enough to threaten my composure. Heat filled my cheeks and desire settled at my stomach. Since when did a massage turn me on?

Again, Carlos's fingers traveled along the sides of my breasts, and I had to bite my lower lip to keep from moaning out loud. Oh, but his hands felt good. They were strong and rough and reminded me of Calvin during foreplay. Whenever his fingers slid across my skin, any tension after a long, hard day was quickly replaced with arousal.

Like I'm feeling now.

Shifting slightly, I squeezed my thighs together and tried to simmer some of the heat I was feeling down between my legs. This was not the time to be horny. Yet my kitty-cat was purring and yearned to be stroked.

Girl, get it together.

I forced myself to take a deep breath and focus not on my sexual needs, but instead on the masculine hands massaging my lower back. However, when his fingers traveled below my waist, creeping toward my inner thighs, a disturbing response began to stir in the pit of my stomach. My instincts were on red alert. *Danger, Will Robinson!* Something told me he was not going to stop until his fingertips slid along my most intimate part. I held my breath while my brain screamed, *What kind of day spa is this?* Obviously, the kind where a massage included a little somethin' somethin'.

And, bitch, you're enjoying every second of it.

I refused to acknowledge what I was feeling. Instead, I raised my head and was about to cuss his ass out when his hands slipped between my legs, guiding them apart. All I could do was hold my breath while strong fingers caressed my slick folds. A moan escaped my lips and my head rolled to the side in delight. I couldn't stop him. I didn't want to stop him, not even when one of his fingers found my opening and plunged inside. "Ohhh," I gasped. My breath caught in my throat, cutting off any ability to form words or even coherent thoughts. Heat pooled and throbbed between my thighs, wetting me shamelessly. A powerful surge of wanting hit me and I wanted so badly for it to be Calvin. I rocked my hips toward his fingers ready to beg him to—

Snap out of it!

Realization finally sank in. Slamming my legs shut, I swung around, facing him. "What the fuck are you—!" My demand died on my lips.

Familiar hazel eyes stared down at me.

Oh. My. God. I swallowed hard with relief. My body wasn't yearning for the touch of a stranger. My body, as well as my heart, had known the man standing before me for the last three weeks. Tall and fine with smooth milk chocolate skin that simply melted in your mouth like a Hershey's Kiss.

Chance studied me for so long, I flinched.

"You asked what am I doing?" Chance asked as he lowered his hands to my thighs again, causing heat to resume. "Take a guess. What do you think I'm doing?"

Our eyes locked for several intense moments until my thighs clenched. I knew that look. It was the look he got just before playing my body like a musical instrument. "I-I don't know."

"I came to remind you who yo man is. Do you have a problem with that?"

I stared up into his handsome face while my heart slammed against my rib cage with excitement. "No, not at all."

"Good," he replied, then eased my thighs apart and stood between them. "What I'm getting ready to do now is touch you here," he began as his fingers slid across my pussy. "And here," he continued as his thumb grazed my clit.

"*Ohhh*." I bit my lip to keep from crying out and risk someone hearing us, which was no easy task. Chance's finger slipped between my wet lips, moving in and out in slow, determined strokes. Leaning back with my feet planted firmly on the table, I spread my legs wider, opening wantonly for his touch. "*Yeeesss*," I panted.

His fingertips teased and probed, reminding me how much I loved him being inside me. I love his aggressive, this-is-my-pussy dominant behavior. Another moan escaped my lips as a familiar surge of pleasure flowed through my body. Suddenly, I wanted him to take all that I had to give. I rocked my hips toward him, encouraging Chance to stroke me hard and deep.

"Did you know it was me and not Carlos touching you?" he asked.

"I knew . . . *oh* . . . I knew." Telltale evidence of my arousal was now slick on the inside of my thighs.

"Liar," he snarled. "I told you I ain't sharing my pussy with no one."

At his tone, I opened my eyes expecting to see anger. Instead, I saw a look of satisfaction. I gazed through half-mast lids while his finger continued to probe my body. It was difficult to think when all I wanted was him, inside me. My breath hissed between my teeth. "You know the only person *this* belongs to is you."

Chance let out a low groan. "How I know that? You looked like you were about to give some to Carlos."

Hell to the no. Why would I do that when I had some-one like him? My head thrashed to the side. "I-I'm sorry, baby. I won't give your pussy to anyone else." I was prac-tically pleading.

"You promise?" he asked before lowering his mouth, kissing me for the briefest moment.

"I promise. Never, baby. Never," I chanted as I rocked my hips. "Never."

Chance lowered the table, and I stifled a groan when his fingers left my swollen lips to swirl in my short-cropped pubic hair.

"Oh, yeeesss," I whimpered softly. He slid his fingers along the entrance to my kitty-cat again and I had to stop myself from crying aloud.

"You're wet, baby girl."

My knees started shaking as he inserted one long fin-ger inside me, drawing out another whimper. While his finger moved slowly inside, his thumb continued to caress my clit. Breathing excitedly, I bucked against his hand so his fingers slid deeper inside.

My head rolled to the side, then my eyes opened, and I suddenly remembered where I was. What the hell was I doing, letting Chance finger fuck me in a public place? Carlos was bound to return at any moment.

When his strokes deepened, my eyelids fell shut again, and any fear of being caught was the furthest thing from my mind. With my pussy leading the way, I couldn't have asked him to stop even if I had wanted him to.

And I did not.

Within seconds, I was hanging from a cliff, trying to hold on. I withered, cried out, and raised my hips higher to meet his thrusts, demanding release.

"I love this, Danielle. I love you," he said hoarsely.

"Me, too, baby. Me, too."

He shoved another finger in and drove harder. I massaged his fingers with warmth and wetness, and was more than ready for something thick, chocolate, and no less than ten inches. I was ready to tremble beneath his hard thrusts, to cry out his name in delight.

"Damn, that feels *sooo* good!" I moaned.

His callused thumb was still stroking my clit. Rocking my hips back and forth, I was able to feel his finger against my spot. A climax was so close, I could taste it. But before I could take myself over the edge, he removed his hand. I protested with a loud moan. "Fuck, Chance. Quit playing!"

Chance chuckled. "Patience, baby. You waited this long. I think you can wait a little longer," he told me with a cocky grin.

Damn him! He purposely held me dangling from a thread just shy of an orgasm.

He trailed his fingers up over my belly, leaving behind a path of heat. His hand reached my breasts and I muffled a sob at the light friction that caused my nipples to pucker. They became so tight the only thing that could soothe them was a warm, wet tongue. Only he lowered his head, instead, and captured my mouth. Our tongues tangled in a heated dance so sensual my body ignited. There was nothing gentle about his kiss; it was so intense and possessive it made my head spin.

With him standing between my legs, leaning over me, his jeans rubbed against my clit and I gasped and came up off the table. I never knew my body could feel like this, tight, aching, and yearning. As much as I enjoyed fore-play, I was eager for a stiff, hard ride on his ten-inch dick.

"Please, Chance. I need to feel you inside me—*now*." Playing with my pussy was not enough.

Pulling back, he looked down into my eyes and said, "Not yet, baby girl."

I was on the verge of screaming. He was torturing me and wouldn't give me an inch until he was good and damn ready, even if I felt like I was gonna lose my mind.

I glided my hand beneath his shirt. His muscles con-tracted with every touch. His heart throbbed against my palm. Oh, how I loved this man!

He flicked his tongue across my nipple before his lips touched me and I shuddered. Sucking and nibbling one, and pinching the other with his fingers, he wasn't even trying to be gentle. I moaned with delight while he sucked greedily.

"Please!" I cried. I hadn't had any in two days and that had been much too long.

Chance ignored me, drawing out my torment, and con-tinued to draw circles around my nipples. His fingers slid down to the apex of my body with lazy intent, playing with my belly button, then settling between my legs to nudge at my clitoris again. On contact, I quaked against his fingers. He rubbed and teased until he had me trem-bling wildly. Within seconds, I was crying out his name and practically speaking in tongues. I was about to come and then he stopped.

"We don't have much time before Carlos comes back," Chance murmured as he rose.

The pulse between my thighs had me squirming on the

table. I didn't need much time. As horny as I was, I'd take whatever the fuck I could get.

With his eyes glued to mine, he pulled off his shirt, then reached down for his belt buckle and unfastened his jeans. His muscled arms flexed with the movement and sweat glistened down the hard ridges of his massive chest. My pussy clenched with anticipation. As soon as his boxers were off, Chance pulled me to the end of the table and positioned himself between my trembling thighs. His dick pressed against me and my legs drooped wider, naturally.

"You planned this." It was a statement.

Locking eyes, he watched my expression. "I did," he said with a heart-stopping grin I loved so much. "Now tell me what you want."

"You."

Chance rubbed against my wet folds. "Where do you want me?"

"There . . . oh, right there." I moaned and lifted my hips, trying to guide him where I needed to feel him most, only he pulled back. I whimpered, and for the first time felt powerless.

"Please, Chance," I pleaded.

"Please what?" he asked. His swollen head brushed against my clit, sending a bolt of heat shooting through my veins.

I was out of my mind with lust. "Fuck me, dammit!"

"Only if you promise to be mine forever," he said, then stilled, trapping me between explosive pleasure and further torment.

With a sound of desperation, I wrapped my legs around his waist. "I promise, now . . . *please* . . . I need to feel you inside of me."

Chance thrust his hips forward and my body stretched

to accommodate him. When he finally drove the full length of his dick inside me, I gave a cry of pleasure. I forgot all about the rest of the world and focused on him and only him. His strokes lengthened, each time sliding all the way out then driving back in hard. Groaning, I rocked my hips and met him, my needy body taking him fully.

"*Yeeesss*, that feels *sooo* good," I gasped into his mouth.

Tremors took over my body. Chance swallowed my cries and deepened his strokes, hammering into me hard and fast. His grip at my hips tightened and his breathing became ragged. I fought for my breath as he kept up the pace. Within seconds, his dick bucked and I knew he was about to come.

I tightened, my breath caught. He groaned while I whimpered. He came and on his final surge, my lips parted and a sob spilled from the back of my throat. "*Yeeeeeessss!*"

Chance finally collapsed on top of me. While holding him close, I listened to his deep breathing and felt his heart pounding next to mine. I felt so complete. My fingers stroked the taut muscles of his back. Light kisses rained his neck. I could have stayed like this for hours. I sighed and heard a knock at the door.

I stiffened. "Did you remember to lock the door?" I asked barely above a whisper.

Chance chuckled. "Yes, baby. I remembered." He kissed my mouth, then withdrew and rose and reached for a towel. "Now we better get out of here before we get my frat brother in trouble."

"Frat brother? Carlos?" When he nodded, I slid off the table and swatted him playfully on the ass. "I'm going to get you back for this," I said with a laugh.

In one fluid motion, Chance snaked an arm around me and pulled me close. "I look forward to it," he whispered and seared my mouth with a powerful kiss. "I told you before, it's just me and you, baby girl."

I was scheduled to work second shift today, something I didn't do too often unless of course like today we were short-staffed. Today I was feeling too good to let it get me down. I would just have to wait and see Chance when I got off at midnight.

On the ride to work, I was all smiles. Ron and I had done some freaky things before, but never anything quite as naughty and exhilarating as what had just occurred, and the best part about it was I had enjoyed every penetrating second.

Thoughts of Chance stroking me the way I had grown accustomed to filtered through my mind. My kitty-cat clenched, forcing me to squeeze my thighs together.

How I loved this man.

I arrived at the hospital feeling more relaxed than ever. At dinnertime, I grabbed a burger and fries and moved to a table in the corner of the cafeteria. I hadn't seen Chance since the massage parlor but I was hoping he would come by when I got off at ten.

While chewing on a cold french fry, I glanced up and spotted Alvin heading in my direction. Shit! What the hell did he want? I pretended like I hadn't seen him and concentrated on my book. I read the same sentence twice, but anything was better than trying to hold a conversation with my ex.

"Hey," he said and flopped down in the chair across from me.

"Whassup?" I replied with a nod, then reached for my burger. As long as I had food in my mouth I didn't have to worry about holding a conversation.

"I came over here so I could talk to you."

"About what?" As if I didn't have a clue.

"What do you think? Our daughter."

"What's her problem now? Is she not going to school?"

He nodded. "Oh no. She hasn't skipped class once. In fact, her grades have been really good."

"That's a first."

"Danielle, she is really trying."

I shot him a twisted smile. "Good, then your parenting skills are working."

"Why don't you give her a chance? She really wants to make amends."

"I don't think so." I bit into my burger and waited for him to respond. I've known Alvin long enough to know something was on his mind.

"My wife and I are having a hard time coping with a teenager in the house. I don't know if I told you this or not but Bonnie can't have kids, so with Portia staying with us and about to have a baby . . . it's been really hard on my wife." He paused and scratched his head. "After the baby's born, she can't stay with us any longer."

"Why not?"

"Because it's too hard for Bonnie."

"I don't see why. This baby could become the baby she's always wanted."

He ran an impatient hand across his thick dark curls and I briefly remembered how I used to love to run my fingers through them while he rested his head on my chest and slowly drifted off to sleep. Damn, that was a long time ago. Now I couldn't even think about kissing his uppity ass.

"Danielle, she's your daughter and it—"

I cut him off. "My daughter? Oh, so *now* she's my daughter."

"That's not what I meant."

"Well, that's what you said and I don't appreciate it. I'm the one who's been raising her these last sixteen years while you breeze in for a weekend here and there acting like Santa Claus."

"That's not true. I've been there for my daughter all these years."

"Yeah, when it was convenient for you."

"I've been there for her for the last six months, so that should count for something."

"Yeah, but now you're ready to hand her back to me."

"I can't handle it. Okay? Is that what you want to hear? I can't handle being a full-time father. And I definitely am not ready to handle two of them. It's already a strain on my marriage."

I hoped the hell he wasn't expecting me to feel sorry for him. "Who's first in your life, your daughter or your woman?"

"Don't judge me, because I clearly remember when you first found out Portia was pregnant, you choosing that thug over my daughter."

I swallowed and looked away because part of what he said was true, but I'll be damned if I'd admit it. "That thug you like to keep reminding me of and I aren't together anymore because I believed my daughter."

"And knowing you, the second you found out she was lying you went running back to him."

It took everything I had to keep a straight face because I was not going to let him think he knew me as well as he thinks. "I've moved on."

He gave a cross between a snort and a laugh. "When can she move back home with you?"

"She can't."

"Then I hope you have some other options because she can't stay with me."

"You are one helluva father, turning your back on your own daughter."

"And you better not hold your breath waiting to receive any mother of the year awards, because you failed your daughter. You were too busy running after some little boy."

"Fuck you, Alvin."

"Nah, never again." He rose from the chair. "Get that room ready because Portia's coming home."

I gave him a long, evil look because he was not going to get the better of me today. I've been dealing with his shit for years and had enough.

"And if she comes home you better believe I'm taking you back to court!"

He swung around. "For what?"

"An increase in my child support payments." He suddenly looked sick and I smiled. "I haven't asked for an increase in five years, and if Portia's coming home then I guess we'll need more money. Don't worry, we'll put it to good use." I finished with a chuckle.

"I'll be in touch," he mumbled.

"And so will my lawyer."

I watched him walk away in highwater navy slacks and wondered what I ever saw in his tight ass.

Thanks to Alvin the rest of my evening had been ruined. I couldn't seem to get anything right. I tried calling Chance, hoping that hearing his voice would brighten the rest of my evening, but he didn't answer his cell phone.

It was after midnight when I finally gave report and headed out to my Durango. It wasn't until I climbed inside that I noticed a note on my windshield. I waited until I had closed the door and started the engine before I read it.

BE CAREFUL OF THE COMPANY YOU KEEP.

What the hell? "Who keeps sending me this shit?" I stared down at the note and tried to come up with possibilities and couldn't think of anyone. Not one single person.

34

Renee

"I'm in love."

We were at El Maguey's for happy hour minus Kayla, who was having dinner with her future in-laws. As soon as Danielle strolled in with that wide grin on her face, I should have known something was up.

Nadine and I gave Danny a funny look at her confession. "You're in love? Did you ever look Chance up on the Internet?"

She gave me an evil look. "Yes," she finally said and reached for the salsa.

"And? I'm listening." I sipped on my margarita and waited.

Reluctantly, Danielle went into a big spiel about Chance standing in as a father for someone else's baby. I kept my comment to myself but when she told me about a woman chasing him down the driveway and he speeding away while she lay on the gravel, I couldn't hold back and fell out laughing.

"Come on, Danny. You don't really believe that, do you?"

"Why wouldn't I?"

Nadine and I looked at each other and were both thinking the same thing. Stuck on stupid. "Because it even sounds like a lie. This woman grabbed on to his car as he peeled off and fell flat on her face, so now he's being charged with hit-and-run and battery. Come on. I don't believe that for a second."

Nadine gave a skeptical look. "Danny, I have to agree. It does sound a little fishy."

"Well, I know women like that who throw themselves at a man's car. Hell, my cousin Jackie did that and I don't put anything past her," she said in a rush of words.

Nadine took a bite of her sandwich. "Maybe so, but it sounds to me like you better watch your back with him."

"Shit . . . her back?" I snorted. "You need to start sleeping with one eye open."

Nadine started laughing and I had to join in. Danielle gave us a look that said she didn't see anything funny and threw a hand in the air.

"Regardless of what y'all think, I love him and plan to stand by my man."

I simply shook my head. "Danny, I don't think you know what love is."

"You got a lot of nerve! You're messing with a soon-to-be married man."

"Yeah, but at least he's been up front with me."

"How do you know that? Kenny talks about how he wished he never proposed. How do you know he isn't just telling you what he thinks you want to hear?"

"He might be, but he's never said to me he was going to leave her."

"But you wish he would."

"Of course. I'm crazy about his skinny ass, but I also know it is what it is. I have no expectations except that he takes care of my needs and puts money in my pockets."

Nadine laughed. "I know that right."

"What I'm saying is that I enjoy it for what it is, and if it blossoms into more, then fine. If it doesn't, then I'm prepared."

The waiter came and took our orders. We all decided to have the shrimp and beef fajitas. When he moved to the next table, Nadine clapped her palms together.

"Well, I've got good news. Jordan's pregnant."

"That's wonderful!" We both screamed then both raised our glasses and clicked them against hers.

"How far along is she?" I asked.

"Not sure yet. She just took a pregnancy test this morning."

"That is great," Danielle replied.

Nadine smiled. "Yeah, she's very excited and so am I."

I looked at her out the corner of my eyes. "Are you still involved with you-know-who?"

She looked uncomfortable and dropped her eyes to her salad. "Yeah."

Danielle looked from me to her. "Who are we talking about?"

"The sperm donor."

Danielle really looked confused.

"Jordan's baby's father and the man who Nadine's been screwing on the DL."

Nadine kicked me under the table.

"Ow! What you do that for?"

Danielle couldn't believe her ears. All three of us screamed and started cracking up like a bunch of teenagers. While we ate, Nadine told Danielle about the secret relationship she was having and how she was torn with her feelings.

"Girl, he sounds fine as hell. I think I would be torn as well."

I nodded in agreement. "You can't have it both ways. Me and John tried that and you see where it got us. You need to decide who you're going to be with."

Nadine thought about her answer while she finished chewing a chip. "I'm planning to end the relationship. Dick is just not worth losing love for."

My brow rose. "Hmmm, I don't know if I can agree with that, because good dick is hard to find."

We gave high fives and all laughed at my remark. My phone vibrated and I glanced down, saw it was a blocked call, and ignored it. It was either John's worrisome ass or my mystery caller.

Danielle noticed. "Screening your calls?"

"Yep. Someone's been calling to say, 'bitch, stay away from my man.' "

"You are lying!"

I took a sip. "Nope, and I have no idea who it could be."

"Girl, Reese probably found out about you."

"I asked Kenny, but he said if she knew she would have said something to him about it by now."

"Who else's man are you messing with?"

"No one."

"You was messing with Landon."

Nadine started laughing. "Pissy little Landon."

"Shut up. I took his ass a bag of Depends to work."

Danielle almost fell out of her chair. "You are lying!"

"No, I'm not. I also went down to small claims court and filed a claim."

Nadine intervened. "You're taking him to court for a pissy mattress?"

"Yep."

Danielle was laughing so hard now she had tears in her eyes. "I can't believe this shit!"

"You better believe it."

"That's why Leslie is calling your phone."

I hadn't thought about it, but maybe it was Leslie. After all, I did catch her ass coming out of his house one afternoon.

"I bet you it's Leslie's ass."

"You might be right. It sounded like something her crazy ass would do."

We pigged out on food, then I headed toward Landon's house. I was almost convinced that Leslie might be the one who's been calling me since she always acts psycho when she gets a man. I turned down his street and rode past his duplex and sure enough, Leslie's Dodge Neon with the license plates LH was pulled in his driveway behind his Tahoe. They were back together. *I guess she doesn't mind him peeing on her*, I thought with a chuckle, then turned left at the corner and headed home.

I got there and saw that both Quinton and Tamara's cars were in the driveway. I pulled in, then got out and walked into the living room. They were watching a scary movie and Alicia was sitting on the couch with Quinton and Tamara was lying on her stomach on the floor, eyes glued to the screen.

"Hey, Mama," she said over her shoulder.

"Hello," I mumbled, then looked at Quinton and his little girlfriend. They were holding hands.

"Hey, Mom!"

"Hello, Mrs. Moore."

I waved and moved into the kitchen, trying to keep my opinions to myself. Quinton is eighteen years old and I know it's time for me to accept that he is no longer a child. He's a man and a man with needs so he's going to have women in his face. Especially as fine as he was. I just wished it was someone other than that hoochie, but whatever! I'm sure they don't like that I'm no longer with John, but so what?

I found my mail on the counter, thumbed through the stack of bills, and found a white envelope with no return address. Inside was a personal check for one thousand dollars from Pissy Landon Lawson. I smiled.

Maybe now the phone calls will stop.

35

Renee

I had to get Kenny back. I couldn't hold my head up high as Renee Moore without letting him know who was really running things. Last Friday I was so mesmerized by his dick that he had me speaking in tongues, but it was time to show him who was running things.

Quinton and Tamara were both working, so the stage was set. When Kenny stepped into my house, I was standing in the living room waiting. Immediately, his gaze traveled to the lacy black teddy hugging my thick frame.

"You're late," I scolded before taking his hand and guiding him to the bedroom. Once there, I began unbuttoning his shirt.

"I thought you had a staff meeting this afternoon?" he asked while stealing a quick kiss.

"Canceled," I replied.

Kenny bent his head to nibble at my earlobe. "What about the kids?"

"At work." I freed the last button, then pulled back and

gazed up at him. "Why? Are you trying to come up with an excuse to leave?"

Shaking his head, Kenny held up his hands in surrender. "Not at all."

"Good, then quit stalling," I purred and reached for his belt buckle. "I cleared my schedule so I could spend some quality time with my man."

"Really?" he asked between kisses. "So I'm your man now?"

"Yep." Standing on tiptoe, I touched my lips to his one more time. "Now that you're here, do you have any idea what I plan to do to you?" I asked with a wicked smile.

"No, but I can't wait to find out."

I slid my fingers through the opening in his shirt. "First, I'm going to take your clothes off." I paused and with a flick of my wrist, his shirt fell from his shoulders onto the floor. "Then I'm going to rub warming oil *all* over your body." I pulled his belt free, then leaned into him so my breasts brushed against the fine hairs on his chest.

Kenny cleared his throat. "I like the sound of that."

I smiled, pleased to hear the catch in his voice. "And that's only the beginning."

"The beginning?"

Nodding, I smoothed my palms over his nipples, feeling them turn hard and erect. Oh yeah, I was going to enjoy getting him back. I rose onto my toes and captured one between my teeth, nibbled and sucked, then ran my tongue over to the other. "But there is one condition."

"What's that?" He looked almost as if he was afraid to ask.

"You're not allowed to touch me unless I say so."

"I think I can handle that," Kenny said.

I didn't miss the hint of uncertainty in his voice, or the obvious erection straining against his zipper. "We'll see about that." I released the zipper and his jeans fell down around his ankles. I brushed my hand slowly across the front of his silk boxers. My fingers passed lightly over his rock-hard shaft, causing his knees to shake and his breath to come in slow pants.

"What's wrong, baby?" I asked as if I didn't know what I was doing to him.

"Nothing," he replied, although the erection pulsing against my hand told me otherwise.

I slid his boxers over his hips and onto the floor. While Kenny kicked them away, I drew back slightly and looked down at him, standing at attention.

All nine glorious inches.

Ignoring the familiar spike of desire spreading through my every nerve, I smiled. "For a man who just got some yesterday, you sure are"—I stroked the head of his penis lightly—"hard."

"It's what you do to me, boo," Kenny managed between gritted teeth.

"You got a nice dick."

He chuckled. "Reese calls it her hot dog."

"Hot dog?" I started laughing.

"That sounds country, doesn't it?"

"Yep, country as hell." *Wait until I tell Danielle.*

Placing a hand at his chest, I pushed him back onto the bed. "Lie down."

Obediently, Kenny scooted up to the headboard and leaned back.

Still holding his gaze, I slid the teddy off my shoulders and it slithered to the floor around my feet.

Kenny's gaze was enough to arouse me completely.

As his eyes moved down my body, I could feel the heat of his gaze. My nipples hardened. My kitty-cat clenched. I took a deep breath and noticed I wasn't the only one aroused. His hard dick thrust toward me with uncontrollable need. Feeling increasingly confident by his reaction, I continued my slow seduction.

"You see something you like?"

"You know I do," he groaned.

"Which parts?" Taunting him further, I reached up and squeezed my breasts. "These, perhaps?"

"Yes, definitely those."

Under his watchful eyes, I flicked a thumb over one hard nipple, then the other, and sucked in a breath at the intensity. Finding my own pleasure was something I enjoyed doing, but having him watching was sweet torture.

After I tugged and squeezed at my nipples some more, I slid my hand lower. Kenny's eyes followed my fingers as they slid past my belly button, through my pubic hair, and dipped between the soft folds of my sweet pussy. Sucking in a sharp breath, he reached down, grabbed the base of his dick, and began stroking his length.

Yes! A feeling of victory swept through me. Smiling, I continued touching myself.

A muscle at his jaw twitched.

Lust glittered in the depths of his eyes. The only part of him that moved was his hand along his delectably swollen penis.

His breathing had become shallow and I chuckled inwardly. Physical evidence proved he was quickly losing control. His dick bucked for attention, but I resisted the urge to touch him.

Suck him.

Straddle his lap and ride him.

Swallowing, I forced myself to look away. As much as I wanted that dick buried inside me, I couldn't give in. Not yet.

I'm going to get you back.

Yep, I was definitely in the driver's seat and, oh, what a ride I had in store for him.

I moved through the folds of my pussy, stroking and coaxing creamy moisture, then inserted one finger, then two, in a firm, smooth motion. All the while I watched the uncontrollable thrust of his erection, the chocolate tip pointing in my direction. Kenny's reaction while I played with myself was sending me toward an orgasm.

I moved to my clit, using my thumb, and had to take a calming breath when wetness slid down my inner thigh. My control was quickly diminishing, the ache becoming unbearable.

"Do you like this part?" I asked, then removed my fingers from my kitty-cat and licked them one at a time.

Kenny made a sound that was a cross between a growl and a groan. "You know I do." He was fisting his dick in one hand, stroking the stiff shaft, its head gleaming with a creamy drop of semen. Kenny crooked his finger. "Come here, Renee."

His order sounded like a plea. Anticipation seeped through my veins.

I forced a frown. "I know your mama raised you better than that. I didn't hear the magic word."

"Please."

"I'm sorry, I didn't hear that. You're gonna have to speak up," I said, cupping my ear.

"Please come here—*now*!"

"Much better." I moved onto the foot of the bed and crawled slowly toward him. As soon as I was close enough, he reached for me.

I halted. "What did I tell you? No touching."

A curse fell from his lips before he lowered his arms to his sides.

Straddling his legs, I reached over and removed a bottle of butter rum massage oil from the side table and poured the liquid across his groin area.

While licking my lips, I stared down at his dick, then leaned forward and inhaled his scent. *Damn, he smells good enough to eat.* I rubbed my nose along his inner thigh, then opened my mouth and slid my tongue across his balls. *Delicious.*

"Hell yes!" he hissed. "Suck me."

I wrapped my hand around the base, then slid my fingers along the hard surface with lazy intent, paying a little extra attention to the tip. He pulsed in my hand.

Lowering my head, I darted out my pink tongue and traced the head. His legs trembled. As he groaned, I continued to lick the length, loving the taste of him on my tongue. I captured a drop of precum and swallowed. "Mmmm, you taste good," I cooed, then took his dick between my lips and sucked. Kenny delved his hands through my hair and cried out. Before he could catch his breath, I drew him deeper into my mouth then looked up, making sure I had his attention.

Oh yeah. He's definitely watching.

"I love watching my dick slide in and out of your pretty mouth," he groaned, eyes glazed, mouth opened.

Kenny raised a hand to cup my breast and I felt it from my nipples all the way down to the slick nub of my clit. Stifling a groan, I pushed his hand back down, then took him deeper into my mouth. My rhythm was consistent while my eyes never left him. Beneath my tongue, I could feel his tension building, and he held onto my shoulders until he no longer had the strength to do so. His panting grew louder. Pulling back slightly, I rolled my tongue over the head, then sucked, taking him just to the edge of release.

"Damn, that feels good," he groaned, then shuddered. Certain he was seconds away from coming in my mouth, I released him. Startled, Kenny opened his eyes and groaned again.

"Patience, baby. You waited this long, a few more minutes won't hurt."

"Like hell! I've waited long enough." He grabbed me by the arms and pulled me up so I straddled his hips. The thrust of his erection rubbed against my inner thigh as if begging for me to let him come inside.

My body burned with arousal. I reached for his hands and forced them above his head, then wiggled my hips suggestively. "Now what would you like me to do?" I whispered.

"Ride me," he panted.

I wanted to drag the torment out, but I wasn't going to deny myself any longer. I had started a fire that only his dick could put out.

I locked my eyes with his, watching his expression while I lowered onto his length, easing him inside. My cry mingled with his moan. Kenny's grip at my waist tightened. I felt him throbbing and I clenched my walls, tightly surrounding him, then lifted my hips. Kenny bucked his body upward against me. Closing my eyes, I set a hard pace.

"Can I touch you now?"

"*Yeeesss!*" I moaned.

"Good." He drove hard inside me.

"Oh, that feels *sooo* good," I wailed as my head rolled back.

My breath caught when he dipped his head to catch

one pebble-hard nipple between his lips. Pleasure rushed to every part of my body. My lips parted and each quick thrust drew a harsh breath. *Oh, it doesn't get any better than this.* I was panting and trembling. All the while, Kenny kept thrusting into me, holding me steadily by my hips.

I wrapped my arms around his shoulders and clung to him while my body shuddered. The rhythm he set was too good. I rode him, meeting his thrust with equal passion and kissing him as deeply as he was penetrating my body. His face showed the strain and I knew he was trying to hold on, waiting for me to find release first. Knowing what it would take, he moved one of his hands down to my clit where he firmly stroked the sensitive flesh with his thumb. A ragged cry burst from my lips.

"You like that?" he asked, hot breath fanning my lips.

I nodded with a moan, then my body stiffened and my vaginal walls clenched him like a vise. "Yeeesss, yeeesss!" I exploded and Kenny followed, letting out a roar of pleasure as he pumped wildly into my body, filling me with his semen.

With a groan, I sank forward and rested my head on his shoulder while I tried to catch my breath. "Damn, baby," I panted.

Kenny shifted slightly onto his side so he could stare deep into my eyes. "It's better here than it is at home. I could get used to this."

That is the plan.

36

Danielle

I slowly rolled out of bed the next morning and jumped in the shower. I was so tired I was tempted to call in to work and stay my narrow ass at home, but if I did that I would have to listen to Chance's mouth, and I really wasn't in the mood to listen to all that jealous talk. Especially since things had been going so well between us.

As soon as the water turned warm, I climbed in. It usually took hot water beating across my back to get me going. While I stood there with my eyes still closed, I couldn't help but think about Calvin. When he was here, he made it his business to give me a back rub, especially after a long day of caring for patients. Thinking about him caused my heart to lurch. I hated to say it, but I missed him. I mean I really, really missed having him in my life. He had been a bright spot. And as much as I loved Chance and the things he does for me, and as much as he reminded me of Ron in bed, he just hadn't filled the void that I felt now that Calvin was gone.

Damn. I don't know why I was thinking about this

now, especially since it was over with me and Calvin. I already dumped him once for Ron, so I know he's not thinking about my ass anymore. And it's not like Chance's not a good man, because he is. He keeps money in my pocket. Knows how to suck a sistah's toes, but I miss cuddling and lying in the bed holding each other while we're discussing our dreams. All Chance can talk about is playing the lottery on Saturday, hoping he'll win that thirty million so that he will be sitting pretty and buy himself a fat ride. I sighed. It was so sad I could have laughed. My boo-boo just needed a woman like me to motivate his ass to look toward the future and think bigger than a Lincoln Navigator on twenty-sixes.

Not sure how much time I'd wasted, I reached for my washcloth and quickly washed up, then climbed out and grabbed for a large towel. When I stepped into my bedroom, I saw Chance holding my cell phone to his ear. Hell to the no!

Dropping my hands to my waist, I waited for him to flip it closed and return it to my nightstand before I cleared my throat. As soon as he noticed me standing there, he turned around and frowned.

"You had a call," he informed me.

My brow rose. Who the hell told him he could answer my phone? "Who was it?"

"Some cat named Calvin."

I gasped. "Calvin? What did he say?"

He reached for his pants and slipped them on while he spoke. "He asked for you and I told him you were in the shower."

I was still trying to digest what he said when he walked across to me and planted a kiss on my cheek, then walked into the bathroom like it was no big deal. Oh, but it was definitely a big deal.

"Um, what made you decide to answer my phone?"

Reaching for the toothpaste, he paused and swung around, giving me a crazy-ass look. "'Cause I'm yo man, that's why."

He looked like he was waiting for me to say the wrong thing so that he could go off on me. Like I said, I wasn't in the mood and didn't have the energy so I didn't say anything. Calvin never tried to answer my phone. I respected his privacy and he respected mine.

"Ain't I yo man?"

"Well, yeah," I began. "But what would you say if I answered your phone?"

"You my girl. So you can do that." He started brushing his teeth and I stood there stunned. I couldn't believe this.

"Did Calvin tell you what he wanted?" I tried to ask like it was no big deal.

"Nah, he just said to tell you he called," he said with toothpaste running down his chin.

Shaking my head, I turned and headed back into the bedroom.

"Yo, baby girl. If we gonna do this, you need to tell them otha cats you got a man now and they need to lose yo number."

I swung around with attitude. "Lose my number? What, I can't have male friends?"

"What you need them for when you got me?" he asked with a grin, then wiped his mouth, came over and scooped me off the floor, and carried me back to the bed, kicking and screaming. I couldn't help but laugh because Chance could be so silly and always made it hard for me to stay mad at him.

"Baby, I'm feeling you and I'm in here for the long haul, but you've got to be willing to help make this thang work, and that means cutting them otha cats loose."

I gazed up into his sexy brown eyes and my body started talking nasty to me. "I do want things to work."

"Then that means it's me and you. I don't need no otha woman when I got this sexy thang here, and hopefully I'm all the man you need."

Oh, he was definitely keeping me satisfied. Sex was not an issue. "You're all the man I need, boo."

"Good, then you can tell Calvin to lose yo number. I don't believe in sharing. I've been telling all them fe- males at work that you my girl and all. And some of them been hatin' but hey, I'm all about being exclusive."

I could just imagine which females had been smiling all up in my man's face. It made me feel good knowing he had chosen me. "Make sure you let them know you're my man."

"I'm glad to hear that," he said with a smile, then glanced over at the clock. "Look, I gotta get to work."

I watched him put on his shoes and frowned. "Aren't you gonna take a shower first?"

"Nah, baby, I'm wearing you to work today." Leaning down, he kissed me. "I get to smell you all mothafuckin' day." He kissed me once more and headed for the door.

I was grinning. As long as he smelled like me, I didn't have to worry about him being up under some other woman at work today. And that's just the way I liked it.

37

Renee

It wasn't long before I found myself falling for Kenny, which I thought was crazy since he is absolutely nothing like the men I am used to dating. And maybe that's the reason I was attracted to him, because he was absolutely different from John.

We have been dating for a month. I've used every trick in the book to keep that man coming and he was doing just that—cumming. I kept on making sure he saw what he had with me so that he could think about what he'd be giving up when he married Reese.

One night I lay in bed and had to laugh. This relationship felt like something out of the popular eighties movie, *Revenge of the Nerds*.

I was happy. Kenny was a man who believed in taking care of his woman. Every Friday he left money on my nightstand. If I mentioned I needed something, he took care of it. It was a great feeling. Good sex was the icing on the cake. The only thing standing in the way was Reese's tired-looking ass. I couldn't understand how he could be marrying her if he spent the majority of his nights with me.

One evening while lying in his arms, I asked him.

"I don't know," he said following a deep breath. "My family says I'm crazy. We've been living together for so long, so what's the point of ruining a good thing."

"So why are you?"

He rolled onto his back and signaled for me to rest my head on his chest before he continued. "We attended her cousin's wedding and she asked me when we were going to get married. We had been drinking and I guess I got caught up in the moment because any other time she asked me that, I told her why ruin a good thing, but that time I told her to go ahead and set a date. The next day her best friend had dragged me to the jewelry store to find her a ring."

"Do you love her?"

"Yeah. She's a good girl who's put up with a lot of my shit for years. More than any woman should have to put up with."

Sounded to me like she was stuck on stupid.

"They don't offer medical insurance at her job, and I feel after all this time she deserves it."

"Sounds more like obligation than love."

Kenny heaved a heavy sigh. "Maybe. I do love her, but if I had known I would meet you I would have never agreed."

I was quiet for a long time. "If you could change anything, what would it be?"

"Sleeping with Reese's sister."

"What!" I sat up straight on the bed. Did he say *sister*?

"You can't tell anyone, especially Kayla."

I shook my head. "I won't."

He gestured for me to lay my head on his chest before

he began. "Baby, I used to be a really bad boy. A real bad boy. It was about four years ago. Her sister stayed over. Reese went to work and I was moving down the hall and I saw her sister lying there butt naked. Next thing I knew I was in the bed screwing her."

I couldn't believe he was telling me this.

"Her sister ended up telling Reese, trying to break us up. It took us a while to rebuild our relationship after that."

Reese must be desperate to forgive a man who fucked her own sister. Damn!

He wrapped his arms around me. "I try to be honest with you. When I get married I want you to know that nothing is going to change."

"Nothing?"

He kissed the top of my head. "Nothing except her last name."

I had to smile at his attempt to reassure me. "We can just enjoy each other until then."

He lifted off the pillow and stared down at me. "Oh, so it's over once I get married?"

I shrugged. "I've never been one to mess with a married man."

Kenny rolled me onto my back. "Then I guess I better keep making it good to you so you won't want to leave me."

I'd be happier if you'd just go ahead and leave her.

Long after we got done making love and Kenny left for home, I lay in bed thinking about him. My cell phone beeped, and I looked over on my nightstand. Smiled when I saw it was him. He never called the house at night because he didn't want to disturb my kids.

"Hey."

"Hey, I wanted to say something." He sighed as if what he was about to say was difficult.

"What?"

"I love you," he said in a rush. "I've always had a hard time saying those words, but I just had to tell you."

Oh. My. God. "I love you, too." I hung up the phone with a big exhale, then I lay on my back staring at the ceiling and decided I was going to do whatever it took to break him and Reese up. I know it sounds selfish, but it's a dog-eat-dog world, and it's obvious he is only settling. Why have second best when you can have a dime piece like me, that's what I plan to make him see. Closing my eyes, I started making a mental list of everything it was going to take. Renee Moore planned to get her man, and what Renee wants, Renee gets.

"Kenny told you he loved you?" Kayla repeated with a look of disbelief.

"Yep."

"Hell nah!" Danielle screamed. She and I had met at Kayla's house to work on the wedding arrangements. Planning a wedding was too much damn work.

"Yep, he told me yesterday," I said, hugging my knees to my chest. "I think I'm crazy about him as well."

"Hell nah! You? Crazy about Kenny's country ass?"

"Yep, me, and quit talking about my man," I said with attitude. She got a lot of nerve with her man and all his charges.

Kayla shook her head. "Please don't tell me anything else. Next thing I know he'll be canceling his wedding."

I took a sip. "Good."

"No, that's not good. Reese's excited and she would be

heartbroken." Kayla gave me a long, scolding look. "Why can't you just sleep with him like you do with all the others and leave him alone, because as soon as he calls off the wedding and decides to be with you, you're going to dump him like you always do."

"Right," Danielle cosigned.

I rolled my eyes because those two think they know me. "I would never intentionally break them up."

"Uh-oh. I heard a however."

I smiled. "However, I ain't got nothing to do with what Kenny decides to do. If for some reason he decides marrying Reese is a big mistake, then that's on him."

Kayla pursed her lips. "And I'm sure you're going to do everything in your power to make that happen."

I laughed. "Hey, I'm just going to be me. I can't help it if he can't get enough of this sweet kitty-cat."

"And then what? The two of y'all going to live happily ever after?"

I shrugged. "Maybe."

"Hell nah!"

I rolled my eyes in Danielle's direction. "Girl, if you don't shut up with that *hell nah*, you sound like a damn parrot."

"I don't know what else to say because I'm like Kayla, you don't really want Kenny's skinny ass."

"Actually, he has a nice ass."

"Ugh!" Kayla put her hands over her ears.

"And a big dick."

"She's too much." Danielle shook her head.

"I'm just keeping it real."

"Can we talk about something other than my cousin's body parts? Just remember if he cheats on her, he will cheat on you, too."

Danielle nodded. "That's true, because men ain't shit."

"And if you had him, what would you do with him?"

"What do you mean, what would I do?"

Kayla leaned forward, I guess to make sure that I heard every word. "Kenny's not moving to Columbia. Kenny's a country boy. He lives on a farm up the road from his mother, who makes his meals and washes his clothes."

"That's 'cause Reese doesn't cook."

"Uh-uh, that's because his mother has spoiled his behind and he won't eat anybody's cooking but my aunt Pat's." Kayla shook her head. "She's got all three of her sons so spoiled no woman with any sense would want to be bothered. Kenny doesn't even know how to turn on a washing machine."

Okay, she was lying now. "I don't believe that."

"Ask him."

"I will, and I bet if I cook this weekend he'll come over and eat."

"Probably will, but he'll need to be back home in time for his mother's cooking. Trust me, I know."

Danielle finished chewing and interrupted. "Enough about Kenny's turtle-looking ass! We're supposed to be planning Kayla's wedding."

I was glad to change the subject because I'm tired of them dogging out my man.

38

Danielle

It was Wednesday night. Chance had been over every night for the last four weeks. I know he was my man, and it was wonderful for him to want to spend all his time with me, but I was itching for a chance to fart without him right behind me sniffing it.

I made dinner, then we moved to my room where he screwed my brains out, then we spent the rest of the evening watching television. Chance got up to fix us something to drink and I curled deeper into the sheets. His cell phone vibrated. I started to ignore it, but then thought better of it. Chance said he had nothing to hide, so I reached over and answered it.

"Hello?"

"Is Jaycee there?" someone asked with attitude.

My brow rose a fraction. "Jaycee?"

"That's what I said."

No, she ain't trying to get smart. "You have the wrong number."

She sucked her teeth. "Wrong number? This is the same number I called last week."

"Sorry, but this is my man's phone and his name ain't Jaycee." I ended the call and five or ten seconds later the phone rang again. "Hello?"

"Is Jaycee there?"

Now I had an attitude. "I just told you there is no one here by that name."

She mumbled something under her breath, then hung up. I was returning the phone to the nightstand when Chance walked back into the room. He almost dropped his water when he saw me with his phone.

"Yo, baby girl, whadda you doing?"

"I was answering your phone. But it was a wrong number. Some chick was looking for Jay-Z or C."

He frowned, then started laughing. "Jay-Z? They most definitely had the wrong number. Hell, I wish I was that nigga. Although I have to say my woman is finer than his," he teased.

I had to smile at that one. He took a seat and handed me a bottle of water and opened his. He was quiet, so I knew he was thinking about something.

"Yo, baby girl, check this out."

The look on his face said that whatever he was about to say was serious. "What?" I moved and took a seat beside him.

"Yo man is trying to hold it down in these streets, and I don't want you to have no part of that."

I could understand that.

"I don't want you answering my phone. Most of them calls is business. My clients hear a strange voice on the phone, they might be tempted to hang up." He must have looked at the pissed-off expression on my face because he pushed on. "Like that female that just called. She was probably one of my customers. She heard your voice and gave you a fake name to try to cover it up."

He did have a point.

"You understand, baby." He stared at me until I nodded. "If I wasn't using that phone for business, you could answer it all day long and it wouldn't matter to me."

"It sounds to me like you need two phones, then."

"You right. How about you get me a phone on your plan? Then I'll have one for business and one for personal and you can answer the personal one all day long. I'll even let you put the message on my phone."

I grinned. Yep, that was exactly what I planned to do to let all them hos know that Chance was my man.

His phone vibrated. I glanced over in time to see if it was that same bitch calling. He reached for it. "Speak to me." Whatever she said caused him to smile. "Chill out, that was my girl. Hold up a moment." He covered the phone and stared over at me. "See, didn't I tell you? It's just business, baby. Yo man trying to hold it down. Ima go take this in the other room."

I nodded and watched him leave the room. I felt proud knowing he was in high demand. If he was really doing the damn thing like he said he was, then I think a shopping trip this weekend was in order.

39
Renee

It's been a long week, but I made sure I saw Kenny every night. I'd been pulling out the stops to get him. I spent so much time at the adult store buying flavored oils, costumes, and sex toys. I did everything to show him what life with me would be like.

I called him one morning and instructed him to be at my house at five. No ifs, ands, or buts. A smile curled my lips when I pulled into my driveway to find him already there.

"You're late," he greeted with a wink.

"And you're early."

We hurried into my house and as soon as the door was shut he pinned me on the wall and we got busy right on the wall in my living room. Afterward we moved into the bedroom.

I could tell something was bothering him. "Baby, what's on your mind?"

He hesitated. "I'm just thinking about this wedding. I

know I'm making a big mistake, but there's nothing I can do about that now."

Yes, there is, but I kept that comment to myself.

While he took a quick nap before he began his night shift at FedEx, I went into the living room and retrieved our clothes before the kids came home and saw them. I was no longer keeping our relationship a secret from them. Kenny had come over last week and taken me and the kids out for ice cream. We have so much fun together, and he has even said being with me is nothing like being with Reese. I still can't figure out why he feels obligated to marry her, but I guess it's kind of like me feeling sorry for John for so many years. Too nice to hurt her feelings.

I glanced over at the clock and noticed that it was almost three. Time to get up and send Ken down the road. Even though the kids knew we were seeing each other, I didn't want them to catch us in bed. I was a freak, but what I did behind closed doors was my business.

I planted a kiss on his cheek. "Get up."

"Is it that time already?" he asked in a groggy voice.

"Yep." I moved into the bathroom, lathered a towel, carried it back into the room, and washed him up. As soon as he was dressed I followed him down the hall toward the door and ran right smack into Quinton and his hot-ass girlfriend coming through the door.

Ken jumped and looked like he'd seen a ghost.

Alicia dropped a hand to her waist and smirked. "Daddy? What you doing here?"

Daddy! Hell nah!

"I'm visiting a friend." He tried to laugh, but his nervousness rang loud and clear. "What are you doing here?"

She touched Quinton's arm and smiled. "This is my boyfriend."

"Oh yeah?" Kenny looked amused, but not as tickled

as his daughter. The smirk rang loud and clear on her face that she was up to no good.

"Well, I was getting ready to leave." He moved to the door to put his work boots on while his daughter stood there with her hands at her waist, looking from him to me and back.

"What's going on with y'all two?"

He frowned. "Don't worry about what I'm doing."

She and Quinton were both grinning like fools.

Quinton swung his book bag over his shoulder. "Mom, we're going to the family room to do homework."

I rolled my eyes. "You know how I feel about company on a school night." My son was pushing his luck with this little girl.

"Mom, just for a little while, then I'll take her home. She's going to help me with some math problems."

Quinton knows I hate being put on the spot. He should have called and asked me before bringing that hot-ass girl in my house. But the frown on Kenny's face stopped me from saying what I wanted to say. I followed him out to his truck.

"What's wrong?" I asked.

Kenny brushed a hand across his receding hairline. "I wish I had known my daughter was dating your son."

"I didn't know," I replied, then studied his eyes. "You think she's going to tell on you?"

He opened the door to his truck and took a seat. "Alicia has a big mouth. As long as I give her what she wants she won't say nothing, but the moment I piss her off she'll go to Reese and blab her mouth."

I tried to hide a smirk. His daughter was the excuse I needed to get Reese out of the picture. It would be so easy to piss her off, then chances were she would run back to her future stepmother and mention that I was fucking her daddy. But I could tell by the look on his face he was worried.

"Do her and Reese get along?"

"Not really. But Alicia talks to Reese when she wants something."

"I guess you'll have to pay her off."

"Yeah, I guess." He sighed. "I better go."

I tried to cheer him up. "Maybe you should call her and tell her not to say anything."

He shook his head. "If I do that she'll definitely run her mouth. Just don't say anything to her."

As much as I didn't want to, I would respect his wishes. I waited until he had gone around the corner before I went back in the house. I headed straight to the family room in time to catch the two of them kissing.

"Uh-uh, y'all need to go on somewhere with that."

"Mom," he groaned. "I'm eighteen."

"And from what Ken tells me, his daughter is only sixteen. I don't want or need any problems. The two of you need to go up to the kitchen table to work on homework, and then you need to take her home so we can have dinner."

Alicia turned up her nose and pouted as she followed my son into the other room. As far as I was concerned, I couldn't care less who her daddy was, her hot ass could go home.

That evening I waited until Quinton got back home for dinner. When he stepped into the kitchen I turned and pointed the spatula at him. "This is the last time I'm going to tell you not to bring that fast-tail girl to my house."

He looked as if he had no idea what I was pissed off about. "Mama, but that's Kenny's daughter."

"And that's supposed to make it right. He ain't even raised that girl."

He mumbled something that sounded like, "Uh-uh."

I waited until I put the chicken on the table before I asked, "What did Alicia say about her daddy being here?"

He smirked as if he knew a secret. "She thought it was funny. She told me her daddy was engaged to get married next month. Is that true?"

I took a moment to speak. "Yeah, but he ain't married yet." And as far as I was concerned, he never would be.

40

Danielle

I got off work on Wednesday, and when I called Mama and found out she had made collard greens, I turned off Providence Road and made a left. There was nothing like a good Southern meal.

I was halfway there when I glanced down at my phone and saw Chance's number flash across my screen. I wasn't up to dealing with him today and ignored him.

His jealousy was starting to be a problem. Two days ago, he saw me in the hallway talking to one of the residents assigned to our floor. The second Dr. Kemp walked away, he came up and took me by my arm and led me into the supply closet.

"Chance, what are you doing?" I asked, then yanked my arm free.

"Are you fucking him?" he demanded.

"What? What are you talking about?"

"Bitch, don't play with me! You heard what I said." His eyes were small and I could tell he was dead serious.

"No, I'm not fucking him."

"Then why you all up in that mothafucka's face?"

"Because we were discussing a patient."

"Yeah, right." Before I realized what he was doing, he slipped his hand inside my panties and rubbed.

I pushed his hand away. "What the hell are you doing?"

He brought his fingers to his mouth. "Why's your pussy wet?"

"What? I don't have time for this shit!" I tried to push past him, but he grabbed me by the arm.

"Didn't I tell you I don't share my pussy with no one?"

"I don't have time for this bullshit!" He pressed his lips to mine, silencing me, then slid his fingers back inside my panties and this time slipped them inside my mouth.

"Taste that? That's my pussy you're tasting. See how good that tastes? That's why I don't want no otha mothafucka hitting it. You feel me?" He stroked my clit with each word. I couldn't do anything but agree.

"Yes, baby. I'm not giving it to anyone but you."

"You better not be lying," he whispered near my ear, then released me and left the closet, leaving the door wide open behind him. I got myself together, then moved to my patient's room.

Ever since, I've been finding him lurking in the corners, watching me. Even after the end of his shift he was still there somewhere close by and once I got home, I was barely in the door when he was pulling in the driveway. At night he wanted to fuck, and if I refused because I was tired, he swore up and down I was giving it away to another nigga. I was starting to think something was wrong with my man. I loved him, and that was one of the reasons why I was trying to stick it out and make it work. The other was, of course, the sex. Damn, I'm a slave to his dick.

I parked in my parents' driveway and used my key to get in and found my daddy sitting in the living room in his favorite recliner watching the evening news.

"Hey, Daddy."

"Well, hello, pumpkin."

I gave him a hug and kissed his wrinkled cheek. "You bowling tonight?"

Daddy nodded. "Yep, we have a tournament tonight."

My dad had been part of a bowling team for the last five years. I think it gives him something to look forward to each and every week. He had just celebrated his sixty-third birthday and was starting to slow down. I took in his curly salt-and-pepper curls and the pot belly that he'd gained over the years and noticed that Daddy was starting to look his age.

"Daddy, you okay?"

He gave me a strange look. "Feel better than I have in years."

I gave him another hug. "I love you." I haven't told him that in a while.

"I love you, too, pumpkin."

I finally released my daddy and headed toward the kitchen of the home I had grown up in. Mama was pulling a pan of homemade cornbread out of the oven.

"Hey, sunshine. Glad you could come and join us. Is your friend coming for dinner, too?"

Hell to the no. That was the last thing I needed. He was wearing my nerves and I definitely was looking for one evening without him trying to smell my pussy. "No, he had to work," I lied.

I heard movement upstairs and gave my mother a strange look. "Mama, who's upstairs?"

She looked away, so I knew what she was going to say before she said it. "I let Portia move in with us."

"What?" I can't believe Alvin came over here and conned Mama into taking his problem off his hands.

"Alvin came by and we talked."

"But he was supposed to keep her, not put that burden on you."

"I was the one that said I wanted her staying with me. His wife ain't the nicest woman in the world, and my granddaughter shouldn't be somewhere she isn't wanted." She wiped her hands and gave me a warm smile. "This way I can help her when the baby is born. She only has four more weeks to go."

I wasn't going to admit it, but the baby being there in the house with Mama meant I would get a chance to see my grandbaby anytime I wanted.

Mama removed her apron. "Let me show you something."

"Mama, I don't feel like talking to Portia."

"Quit being stubborn and come up and see."

I released a heavy sigh and followed her up the stairs. We moved down the hall, where there were four bedrooms. My room now belonged to Portia. The door was shut but you could hear her music. My mom opened the door to my older sister's old room and stepped aside so I could enter first. I gasped.

The room had been painted yellow. Clouds had been stenciled on the ceiling. Gold carpet was on the floor, and teddy bears was the décor. My eyes filled with tears. "Who did this?"

"Your uncle Charles did it for me. He took your old baby furniture and refinished it for me as well."

I walked over and fingered a little brown bear that was inside the crib.

"That used to be your bed."

I knew it was nothing like the cheap shit they sell in

the stores today. There was a solid wood matching dresser, changing table, and a rocking chair.

"I've been planning to ask Portia to live here ever since we found out she was pregnant. Taking care of a baby will give me something to live for."

"Mama, quit talking stupid. You're not about to die." I hated when she talked like that.

She shrugged. "Not yet. But one day. In the meantime, I got to help my granddaughter."

I heard a door open down the hall, and seconds later, Portia peeked her head in the door. She gave me a shy wave.

"Hi, Mama."

"Hello," I said and almost choked. I looked at my little girl with her big swollen stomach and felt my heart melting. "What do you think of the baby's room?"

Portia smiled. "It's really nice. Uncle Charles and Grandma did a good job."

"Yes, they did."

There was a long silence as we each waited for the other to make the next move. Mama decided to step in.

"Why don't we all go down and have dinner like a family?" She was smiling, pleased to know that we were at least speaking.

I nodded and followed Portia down the stairs. Together we set the table. The doorbell rang. Before Daddy could get off the couch, I went to answer it.

On the other side of the door stood a short honey-colored woman with a ghetto fabulous hairdo. A tall boy was standing behind her with his head hung low.

"Does Portia live here?"

I gave her a suspicious look. "I'm her mother, and yes, she does."

She turned and grabbed the boy by his arm and pulled

him up to the door. "This here is Demetrius and supposedly he's her baby's daddy."

He looked like this was the last place he wanted to be. What Portia wrote in her diary was true. He wasn't much to look at. He had an extra-wide nose, thick lips, and was light skinned with a severe case of teenage acne. Hopefully my granddaughter will take after our side of the family.

"Why don't you both come in?"

She nodded and practically shoved her son through the door. "Forgive my manners. I'm Toni Carlson, and this here is my son Demetrius."

I took her proffered hand, then turned to her son. "Hello, Demetrius. I hope you're ready to be a father."

He nodded. "Yes, ma'am."

His mother glared at him, then propped a hand at her slim waist. "He better be. He had no business out there in the first place making no babies, but since he did he's gonna get a job and help take care of his responsibilities. Won't be no deadbeat daddies living in my house." She popped him upside his head.

"Ow! Mama, I said I was going to take care of her."

"Damn skippy."

I smiled. I'd just met Toni and I already liked her style. "I think we're going to get along just fine."

She nodded. "I'm glad to hear that. Now where's your daughter? I want to meet her. If she's anywhere as pretty as her mama, I'm gonna have me a beautiful little grandbaby."

We can only hope so. "We're just getting ready to sit down and have some collard greens and fried chicken. The two of you are more than welcome to join us."

She licked her thick lips the way a dog does when he sees a chicken bone. "I don't want to put you out of your way, but I do love me some collard greens!"

I signaled for them to follow me into the kitchen. As soon as Portia saw Demetrius her eyes grew round.

"Mama, Daddy, this is Demetrius and his mother, Toni Carlson. He's the baby's daddy."

She and my dad rose and shook hands.

"So nice to meet you. Young man, you know you got a baby to take care of, right?"

He nodded. "Yes, ma'am."

"Good. Well, welcome to the family." Mama embraced him. As soon as she released him, he moved around to where Portia was standing.

"Why you been avoiding my calls?" he asked.

Portia shrugged and avoided eye contact. "I don't know."

"Well, she won't be avoiding him no more because we got diapers to buy!" I said with a rude snort.

"I know that's right!" Toni said and gave me a high five.

Mama reached for two more plates. "Y'all have a seat. There's plenty for everyone."

We all took a place at the table, and by the end of the meal Demetrius and Portia were talking and he was rubbing her belly. I couldn't help but smile. Even though my daughter and I had yet to talk, I had a good feeling that everything was going to be all right.

41

Renee

After Alicia caught her dad at my house, Kenny slowed our relationship down and didn't come by as much as before. I was hurt because that told me he was afraid of losing Reese, and she meant more to him than he had admitted. I was still so pissed at Quinton for the whole thing that we barely spoke. I'm sure he couldn't wait to leave for college in the fall, and if I had this kinda shit to look forward to, then neither could I.

I was at work one morning calculating the expenses for the month, hoping that Kenny would drop by and bring breakfast. He hadn't done that all week, and it worried me that maybe I was losing him. I'm not going to lie and fake the funk. That shit hurt because I put myself out there emotionally and that is just something that I don't do.

My cell phone rang and I grabbed it, hoping it was Kenny calling to at least say good morning.

"Mama!" Tamara shrieked. "I was sleeping so good, and guess who knocked on the door at eight o'clock this morning?" I forgot my kids didn't have school today.

"Who?"

"That lady."

"The bag lady?" Dammit, here we go again. I thought she had gotten the hint by now. "What did she want?"

Of course Tamara went into animated details. "I opened the door and she was standing there and she said 'Forgive me. I know I've worn out my welcome.'"

"What did she want?" I asked impatiently. If I waited on Tamara it would be another thirty minutes before she finally got to the point.

"She asked for sanitary napkins."

"Sanitary napkins?" Hell nah! I tried not to laugh but couldn't help myself. "Did you give her some?"

"No. Mama, I was so mad I told her no and slammed the door shut."

I couldn't blame Tamara, but at the same time I felt sorry for the woman. "Tamara, you should have given them to her."

"Mama, I didn't mean to be mean, but she made me so mad! If I gave them to her she would be back."

"Yeah, but if she's asking for sanitary napkins then she must really need them." I hate to think of that woman having to use a dish rag.

She groaned. "I know, Mom, but she woke me up."

"Well, if she comes back, go ahead and give her a box."

I could hear the frustration in her voice. "Okay."

I hung up, disturbed by the situation and surprised at Tamara. She is usually such a softy that she doesn't know how to say no. I finished up the last figures, then with nothing else to do, I pulled out my disk and started working on my manuscript. I was so engrossed with the erotic tale that the afternoon passed by quickly, which was a good thing because it took my mind off Kenny.

By the time I had locked up my office and was heading out to my car, Tamara called back.

"Mama, my conscience was bothering me. I got up and walked around the block and gave her a box. She said 'bless you, child.' "

"I hope you didn't give her the pads with the wings." Hell, I paid five dollars a box for those.

"No, I gave her those generic ones at the back of the closet."

"Good." I think I deserve at least one blessing for that.

I climbed into my car and headed to Office Depot. I noticed I had a missed call and retrieved it. It was Calvin. He sounded pitiful as shit.

I moved into the store and headed over to the copy paper while I called him back.

"University Police, may I help you?"

"Sergeant Cambridge, please."

"Who's calling?" the woman asked like she was screening his calls.

I decided to be funny. "His boo, that's who."

She mumbled something under her breath, then put the call on hold. A few seconds later, he picked up.

"Hello?"

I couldn't help but laugh. Calvin sounded anxious as hell. His secretary must have told him his boo was on the phone.

"Calvin, it's me, Renee." I couldn't help it. I started laughing.

I heard him sigh. I didn't even have to see his face to know he was pissed off.

"You need to quit playing. That's what got me in this mess in the first place."

"I'm sorry!" I said with a rush of laughter, then

quickly shut up and got serious. "I'm really sorry. Whas-sup?" I grabbed a box of paper and headed to the register.

"I was wondering if you have spoken to Danielle yet. I had flowers delivered to her job the other day, but she didn't even bother to call and thank me."

He was so desperate he was starting to sound pathetic. No wonder Danielle didn't want him back.

"I talked to her but she's seeing someone else."

There was a long pause and I'm sure my comment played a major role. "Do you think it's serious?"

As far as Danielle was concerned, yes, but from what I have seen and heard so far, I guarantee she's setting herself up for disappointment. "No, not at all. I think it's her way of coping with what happened between y'all." I hated lying to him, but the truth was something he really didn't want to hear.

"I appreciate you at least trying."

"I'll keep doing that. I feel like it's partially my fault, so I'm going to do whatever I can to get the two of you back together."

"Thanks," he said, although his voice sounded like he was giving up hope.

We hung up and I put my pride aside and decided to call Kenny. I was disappointed when he didn't answer. *Girl, just forget about him. He's about to get married anyway.* It was easier said than done. Kenny had a piece of my heart that I wasn't sure I was going to get back anytime soon.

I made it home and moved to my office. It was time to sit down and start paying some bills. I picked up the stack and thumbed through my bank statements and noticed a letter from my bank.

"God dammit!" I screamed when I opened it and saw

the check from Landon had been returned for insufficient funds. Stupid me had dropped my case at small claims court the same afternoon I had deposited the check. Now I was going to have to start over again. I reached for the phone and called his stupid ass and cussed out his answering machine, then slammed down the phone. I was definitely having a bad day. I moved from my office up to my room and decided to do some kickboxing to ease some of the frustration. Nothing was going right today.

I slipped on my gym clothes and my Reeboks, then stuck in the video just as my cell phone rang. I rushed to it, hoping it was Kenny. "Hello?"

"Bitch! Quit calling my man!"

What the . . . I glanced down at the Caller ID that said *blocked.* "Who is this?"

"You heard what I said." The phone went dead.

I immediately hit Star 67 even though I knew good and damn well there was no way to trace the call. My mind started racing, trying to come up with possibilities. Hell, I wasn't messing with anyone but Kenny, so it had to be Reese's ass.

I stabbed the keys and dialed his phone again.

"Yeah?" he asked in a sleepy voice.

"Uh, your woman just called me," I said with attitude.

"What?" He was suddenly wide awake.

"I *saaaaid*, your woman just called my phone."

"What did she say?"

"She said, 'Bitch, quit calling my man.' "

There was a pause. "How do you know it was Reese?"

"Who the hell else is going to be calling me?"

"I don't know. It might be one of your other niggas."

Ugh! Men could make me so sick with the bullshit. "Whatever. It was Reese. She had to get my number from your phone."

"I don't know how she would do that. I always hide my phone when I'm at home."

"Then she got it from your phone bill. Whatever! Just tell the bitch not to call me again!"

I hung up because he had pissed me off. How does he know she didn't call me? I don't know who else it could be. Kenny's the only man I'm fucking. Let me catch that bitch on the street. Because it's on.

I was mad the rest of the evening. At nine I left to pick Tamara up from work. I pulled up in front of Wal-Mart and thank goodness Tamara had her behind at the curb waiting. I hate when she makes me wait for her to come outside.

I moved over and got on the passenger's side.

"Mom, I don't feel like driving today. My stomach hurts," she whined.

"Girl, too bad. I'm sick of picking you up all the time. You need to learn how to drive whether you feel good or not."

She pouted over to the car and climbed in behind the wheel.

"And straighten your face. You're too old to be acting like that." I was in a bitchy mood and knew I was taking it out on her, but I couldn't get myself out of this funk.

I put on my seat belt and waited for her to put hers on as well, then she put the car in drive. She put her signal on and waited for a woman and a little girl to cross before she made a right and pulled out onto the street. After a few minutes I started to relax on the seat. Tamara was doing a really good job.

"I think you'll be ready to take your test next week."

Her eyes widened. "You really think so?"

"Yep. You'll never know unless you try."

She looked pleased. As soon as the light turned green she started moving again and brought us safely into traffic.

"Mama, I was in line and a woman came through buying a bunch of fake flowers. She said she was making a flower arrangement for her friend who was getting married next month in Boonville. I told her my mama's boyfriend lived in Boonville and was getting married next month, too," she replied, smiling. "Small world, huh?"

My eye snapped to her gullible ass. "Girl, don't be announcing in public that I have a boyfriend. Kenny has a fiancée. For all you know that could have been one of her relatives."

She gave me an innocent look. "I didn't say his name."

"It doesn't matter. You shouldn't have said anything at all." Sometimes I think my daughter needs a seat on that short yellow bus. Doesn't she know what messing around with someone else's man means? I was quiet the rest of the journey. I got home, checked my messages on the answering machine hoping for a call from Kenny. There were two. One was a telemarketer. The second gave me chills.

"You stupid bitch! Didn't I tell you to stay away from my man!" she screamed, then hung up. This shit was really starting to piss me off.

42

Renee

Kee slipped the slim jim in against the window and wiggled. I glanced around nervously, hoping no one came out and saw what we were doing. Hopefully, it wouldn't take more than fifteen minutes.

"Do you think he has an alarm?" Danielle was standing near the steps with her hands tucked in her jacket, shivering.

"Nah, I remember him locking his car and not setting an alarm."

"Hurry up, Kee!" she cried. "Damn, it's cold out here."

"Yo, hold the fuck up! Y'all crazy-ass mothafucka got a nigga out here breaking into someone's vehicle and then got the nerve to try and rush me?"

"Would you be quiet before someone hears us!" I said in a loud whisper. I moved around the SUV and looked up at the window on the left. The last thing I needed was for Landon to know we were out here breaking into his Tahoe. At least not until we were done.

"Got it," Kee announced, then removed the slim jim

and opened the door on the driver's side. "Aw'ight. Give me my money 'cause I'm out."

I reached into my pocket, pulled out a fifty, and put it in his hand. "Thanks, Kee." I rose on my tiptoes and kissed his bearded cheek.

"Nae-Nae, when you gon' quit playing and let me take you out?"

I smiled and patted him playfully on the cheek. Danielle's older brother was tall and skinny with shoulder-length locks and a platinum grill that was a turn-off, but despite that, he was a cutie. But I've known him since he used to eat boogers, and he was too much like family for me to imagine fucking with him.

"Sorry, big brother. I told you before you can't handle all this."

"What the fuck eva! I ain't no little boy."

"Kee, shut up and go before you get us all arrested!" Danielle said with a shove.

"Yeah, all right. I'm out." He moved down the sidewalk to his Explorer parked at the end of the block behind Danielle's Durango.

"Come on, Nae-Nae, it's after midnight. I want to get this shit over with before we get caught."

"Yeah, yeah." I reached for a spray bottle I had sat in the grass and moved back over to the Tahoe. "Just keep watch while I do this."

I reached in my jacket pockets, removed a pair of rubber gloves, and slipped them on my hands, then opened the driver's side door and leaned inside.

Danielle's teeth chattered. "I can't believe you're doing this."

"Payback's a bitch." I turned the nozzle on the bottle, started spraying all over the interior of his Tahoe, and chuckled.

"You're stupid." Danielle cupped her mouth and started laughing.

I looked over my shoulder. "Nah, Landon's the one who's stupid. I warned him not to fuck with me."

Since Landon had no intention of paying me back, I took matters in my own hands, and thanks to my diabetic dog, I had the perfect payback. The last few days, whenever I collected urine to dip, I saved it in a milk jug until I had just enough.

I saturated the insides of his windows, then started spraying the dashboard.

Danny turned up her nose. "That shit stinks! I can smell it way over here."

"It ain't shit. It's piss," I joked.

"Whatever, bitch. It smells like a grown-ass man who's been drinking all night."

"That's the idea. I bet Landon won't piss in another woman's bed and play her ass again," I replied and had to laugh as I sprayed his cloth seats. Oh, he was going to be hot.

"Renee, hurry up. I'm cold."

Danielle was starting to get on my nerves. "Damn, I'm moving as fast as I can." I shut the door and started on the backseat. There was no way Landon would ever be able to get this smell out of his Tahoe. I took the top off the bottle and even poured some on the floor in the back, making sure it soaked in through the carpet. I was trying to not rush because I didn't want to get piss on me, but I sprayed my face a couple of times. The smell was nauseating.

I heard Danielle gasp. "Renee! Here comes a car."

Quickly, I shut the door, dropped the bottle on the ground, and moved around to the side while Danielle rushed over to the porch and made it look like she was just coming out the building. A Dodge Neon pulled in be-hind his vehicle. It was Leslie. She turned off her car, got out, and slammed the door, then looked at me and Danielle.

"What are you doing standing next to my man's Tahoe?"

No, she wasn't trying to act all tough and shit. That bitch picked the wrong day to be fucking with me. "We ain't thinking about your man. We were upstairs visiting someone."

She glared at me like she didn't believe us. "No, you weren't. The only other person who lives here is two gay white men. I bet you were knocking on Landon's door."

"Puh-leeze, the last person I want to see is *your* man."

Danielle and I moved down the driveway and she jumped back, frowned, and sniffed, "What's that smell?"

I snorted rudely. "You should be used to it. You smell it every time you crawl up in bed with that pissy-ass man of yours."

As I passed Leslie, she propped a hand at her waist and glared at me like she was putting some fear in my heart. "We need to get something straight."

"Uh-oh." Danielle was laughing and shivering at the same time. "I'm going to go and get my truck," she called over her shoulder.

"Yeah, okay." Ignoring Leslie, I slipped the gloves off my hands, turned them inside out, and stuffed them in my back pocket. They were going in the trash the second I got home. "What is it that you *need* to get straight?" I purposely articulated each word.

"I've seen your phone number on my man's Caller ID. Quit begging. Landon doesn't want you."

I had to laugh at her big ass. "What the hell do I want

with a man that still pisses in the bed?" I pushed past her and headed down the driveway.

"Quit calling my man!"

I froze. Okay, let me rewind this shit. Did she just say what I think she said? Oh, hell yeah. It was the same message I'd had on my cell phone.

I turned around and moved to stand in front of her. "Bitch, you been calling my phone?"

"Who you calling a bitch?" she spat, trying to act all big and bold and shit.

"You."

Leslie moved all in my face like she dared me to hit her ugly ass.

I heard a horn blow. Danielle had backed up to the end of the driveway. "Come on, Renee. Let's go!"

"You better go before you get hurt," she hissed.

I acted like I was leaving, then swung around and punched that bitch right smack in the mouth.

Leslie fell back, then quickly recovered and came charging at me. The two of us were some swinging and scratching fools. I'll give it to Leslie, the bitch had heart, but I was fueled by my anger from her man pissing in my bed and her calling and playing on my damn phone. I hit her hard in the jaw, then grabbed a handful of that fake-ass weave and swung her around. She hit her car and slid down onto the ground. I started kicking her.

"Don't call my phone again!"

Danielle jumped out of the SUV and raced up to me screaming, "Renee, enough!"

I leaned over and tried to catch my breath. "Fuck that bitch."

She grabbed my arm and started pulling on me. "Come on, let's go before you get arrested."

Just then the door to the complex swung open and

Landon came rushing out in sweatpants and a T-shirt. "What the hell's going on?"

"Your bitch needs you," I spat.

He moved around the SUV, then came over beside Leslie and helped her to her feet. "Baby, you okay?"

"Get your hands off me!" she screamed, then shrugged his arm away and stomped her feet all the way to the front door.

Landon glared at me. "What happened here?"

I pulled away from Danielle and gave him a dismissive wave. "Yo woman can tell you about it later. By the way, your check was returned."

"Uh, yeah . . . about that . . ."

"Don't even worry about it because we're even now." I reached for the spray bottle, took off the top, and just as he turned to head up the drive I called after him. "Landon?"

He swung around. "What now?"

"Catch." I tossed the open bottle at him, spilling the rest of the pee on his face and T-shirt.

Danielle screamed and grabbed my arm. We ran and hopped in her Durango and peeled off. I couldn't stop laughing. Neither could she.

"Your ass is crazy! He might try to sue you for damages."

"No, he won't," I said confidently. "Because if he does, I'll have him prosecuted for passing bad checks."

We kept on laughing. When Danny got to the corner she swung in my direction and turned up her nose. "Yo ass stinks!"

I smiled. "Yeah, I know. But it was worth it."

43

Renee

We met Kayla at the bridal shop and did fittings for our dresses. I'll have to admit that chocolate and orange ain't a bad combination. The form-fitting chocolate gown with the orange trim accented my small waist and big behind and took attention away from my itty-bitty titties. But I had just the right bra at home to add that extra cleavage that I needed. When Kayla stepped out in her long A-line dress, all three of us gasped.

"Oh my, girl, you're wearing the hell out of that dress!" I exclaimed.

"You really think so?" she asked with that same insecurity that had its grasp on her for years.

Danielle rose and stood beside her in front of the mirror. "Yes, you look so beautiful."

Nadine whistled. "Wait until Jermaine sees you in that dress."

We all stood in front of the mirror at our reflection with Kayla. I got misty-eyed as I remembered us in this same exact pose when we were all teenagers trying on clothes to go to some party we were having down at the community center. The only one missing from this picture was my big sister Lisa.

Kayla was the first to break the silence. "I never thought I'd see this day."

"I don't know why not," Nadine scolded and draped an arm around her waist. "You are the only one of us with any sense."

I had to cosign that. "I know that's right."

"I've waited all my life for this moment." Her bottom lip quivered and I knew if one of us didn't say something funny she was about to cry. And then we all would be crying.

"And a good thing, too, otherwise you'd be like Renee's crazy ass, married three times," Danielle teased.

I bumped my hip against hers. "Whatever. I believe in going for the moment. You never know unless you try."

Nadine's brow rose. "Yeah, but how many times do you have to try before you get it right?"

I stepped away from the group and took a seat in the dressing room. "I'm not trying anymore. I think single life is just meant for me." But even as I said that I couldn't help but think about Kenny and wish things could be different. However, chances were that if I could have had it, I wouldn't have wanted his skinny ass at all. "Let's get out of these dresses and go have some lunch."

I moved behind the partition and reached for the zipper, but Kayla continued to stand in front of the mirror. I couldn't blame her. She was beautiful and deserved everything that was happening to her.

Last year when Kayla was accused of murder, Jermaine, one of the academic advisors at the medical school where she was employed, had supported her through the entire ordeal and eventually confessed his love for her.

"Hey, Kayla."

She swung around.

"You can't marry Jermaine unless you get that dress altered. It can't get altered if you don't take it off," I teased.

Smiling, she wiped away the tears. "I see you've got jokes."

"Always." We shared a smile, then she moved into her dressing room.

We all changed clothes and went down the street to eat at the St. Louis Bread Company. I grabbed a bowl of soup and a small salad and found a large table in the back away from the door and the crowd. I was finishing up my soup when I noticed a man walking into the building.

"Danielle, isn't that Chance over there?"

Her head snapped around and I noticed her frown before she quickly painted on a smile. "What's he doing here?"

"Stalking your ass," I mumbled under my breath. Danielle looked over and glared at me.

Kayla appeared eager to meet him. "Invite him over."

Danielle raised her hand and signaled him over. Chance didn't even look surprised to see her. I told you he was a stalker.

He was wearing the hell out of a pair of jeans, a navy blue Sean John sweater, and a fresh pair of Timberlands. I ain't gonna lie, Chance is fine in a thuggish kinda way. He's just too damn possessive for my taste. I'd be damned if some man would be checking my cell phone.

"Hello," he said, flashing his pearly whites, marred by two gold teeth.

"Everybody, this is Chance Garrett. Chance, you met Renee, and that's Kayla, my friend who's getting married."

"Congratulations," he said as he shook her hand.

"Thanks," Kayla said happily.

"Oh, and that's Nadine coming our way now."

"Hello, I . . ." As Nadine drew closer to the table his voice trailed off. And we all noticed the stern look on her face.

"Hello, Jaycee. Fuck any dykes lately?"

Jaycee. Oh. My. God. The dude who impregnated Jordan. The same dude she'd been fucking. Oh, this was about to get good.

Confused, Kayla looked from one to the other. "Jaycee? Who's Jaycee?"

Nadine took a seat with her eyes still glued to Chance's, giving him a chance to explain. She was better than me because I would have just busted his ass out. All his slick ass could do was stand there and stutter. I couldn't help it. I had to instigate.

"Jaycee? Isn't that the name of Jordan's sperm donor?" I looked at Nadine. She gave me a look that said *stay out of this*.

Chance finally found his voice and gave a nervous laugh. "You . . . you got me confused with someone else. But look, baby girl, I've got to go. I'll holla at you back at the crib."

I jumped up and blocked his path. "Uh-uh, where do you think you're going?"

He glared at me, then tried to soften his expression. As far as I was concerned he wasn't going anywhere.

"Look, I've got things to do."

"Like what?" I folded my arms across my chest and waited. "Danny, you better check yo man."

Nadine's eyes narrowed dangerously. "For what? She gonna still be with his trifling ass tomorrow."

"You don't know what I'm going to do!" Danielle

turned to Chance, who stood there looking amused by the whole thing. As soon as he saw Danielle cut her eyes, his face dropped. "Are you the father of Jordan's baby?" she demanded to know.

Chance looked from Nadine to Danielle. Both looked like they were ready to strangle his ass. Hell, even Kayla looked like she was ready to land a few licks if the need arose.

"Baby girl, we're in a public place and don't need to be putting our business out in these streets," he replied in a sweet, innocent voice.

"Hey!" His slick ass pissed me off, so I threw a cherry tomato and got him right smack in the eye. "My girl asked you a question. It's either yes or no." He looked like he was ready to punch me. I mean mugged him, daring him to even try.

"Like I said, we'll talk about this when you get home." He leaned over and kissed Danielle on the lips. "Baby girl, I'll see you back at the house." Luckily, he stepped around me because I was all set to throw a salt shaker at his head.

I swung around. "You just gonna let him walk out of here!"

Danielle lowered into her chair and mumbled, "He's right. We'll talk when I get home."

I flopped back down in my chair. "That lying motha-fucka ain't gonna tell you the truth!"

"What truth? His name isn't Jaycee. It's Chance."

I was tempted to throw a cherry tomato at her ass. "Danny, your man is probably lying."

Nadine angrily stabbed her salad. "There's no *probably* about it. He is lying."

Danielle glared across at her. "Why would he lie?"

I butted my way into the conversation. "Because he

doesn't want you to know he's donating sperm to dykes."
Everyone at the table turned and glared at me. I rolled my
eyes and reached for my soda. I was just trying to help.

"Danielle, I know who the father of Jordan's baby is. I
was there when . . . when he and Jordan met and hooked
up." Nadine turned so red in the face, she dropped her
head and reached for her sandwich.

What Nadine wasn't saying was that she fucked him,
too, but that was something she had told me in confidence
so my lips were sealed . . . for at least the next five minutes or so.

Danielle tried to act like it was no big deal and ate her
sandwich. "Well, I'll talk to him about it when I get
home."

"Who's going with me to look at flower arrangements?" Kayla asked, trying to change the subject. I don't
blame her. This was supposed to be her day and it had
been ruined by Chance a.k.a Jaycee, the dyke baby
maker.

I huffed. "Girl, I'll go with you."

We each ate our food. Nadine finally tossed her sandwich on the plate and pushed her chair away from the
table. "I forgot I have an appointment downtown. Kayla,
have fun. I'll talk to some of you later." We mumbled our
good-byes and watched her leave.

She was barely out the building when Danielle finally
spoke. "Nadine is so full of shit. Chance is not the guy
Jordan's pregnant by."

I waved my hand in the air. "Correction. He wasn't
messing with her; he was *depositing* sperm."

Danielle pursed her lips. "Whatever the case may be, it
wasn't my man."

I started laughing at her because she's stuck on stupid.
Kayla gave me a look that said *leave it alone* but I couldn't

do that. "Danny, Nadine's too much of a lady to say this, but remember when she was telling you about the man she was fucking on the DL? Well, she was talking about Chance."

"What?"

I nodded. "That's how she knows who he is. Hell, she probably can describe his dick if you ask her." I told them everything Nadine had told me in more detail than either of their asses cared to hear.

"I think I'm about to be sick." Danielle raced off to the bathroom, almost knocking over a woman with a wide cardboard ass.

Kayla shook her head. "Can we ever get past the drama and start acting like women who are over thirty?"

I gave her an innocent look. "What? What did I do now? I just told her the truth about her man."

I could tell the entire episode had Kayla upset. "Where did Danny meet him?"

"At the club."

She blew air between her teeth. "Figures."

"He also works at the hospital. Mr. Fuck-a-Dyke has been practically living with Danielle for the past month." I kept looking over at the door waiting for her to come out.

"I really don't think Danielle needs this right now. She has been going through so much. That whole episode with her daughter, and then you messing with Calvin." Kayla shook her head.

I was starting to get pissed off. "I wasn't messing with him! Danny asked me to set up his simple ass."

"Whatever the case may be, she's been through a lot."

"She's been through a lot? What about me? I'm the woman who caught her husband fucking another man in the ass!"

Kayla's expression became apologetic. "You're right. I forgot about that."

She forgot because everyone always feels sorry for everyone but me. Can't I be the victim sometimes? Damn!

"I guess I better go and get Daniellc." Kayla wiped her mouth with her napkin and started to get up from her chair.

"Here she comes now." I watched her walk back to our table with a painted-on smile. She wasn't fooling anyone. "You okay?" I asked.

"I'm fine." She nodded, reached for her purse, and swung it over her arm. "Look, I'll talk to you later." She turned and walked out the door, but not before I saw the tears stream down her face.

44

Danielle

It took everything I had to hold my head high when Nadine called my man out like that. *Jaycee*. I guess they're his initials. JC Garrett, just like OJ Simpson and TK Carter, which means his first name starts with J and Chance is his middle name. No wonder I had a hard time finding him on Intelius. Ain't that a bitch. I remembered the time I had answered that fool's phone and the woman on the other line had asked for Jaycee. Like a dummy, I told her she had the wrong number. No wonder she got an attitude. She knew more about Chance than I did.

Damn, you're so pathetic.

It was bad enough Chance was screwing a dyke, but to know that he had been servicing two of them at the same time was enough to send my ass over the deep end. I was so humiliated all I could do was run to the bathroom and try to hide. When I finally came out the last thing I wanted was to discuss my problem. And I most definitely did not feel like hearing Renee telling me "I told you so." I know my friends only wanted to help, but I needed to be alone to think and feel sorry for myself.

I got out of the restaurant as fast as I could, then drove around for an hour, crying my eyes out while trying to get my head together before I made it home.

My life is fucked up. Here I was with a daughter who accused the man I loved of sleeping with her. The man who loved me, I dumped, and now I found another man who I love only to discover he's been fucking me and a pair of dykes at the same damn time. It pissed me off because Chance would have a fit if I had been fucking someone else, yet he'd been giving my dick away to two other women! That's what I get for playing around on Calvin. He was such a good man, yet I was too stupid to appreciate him. *Why, Lord? Why is it that I always have to have drama in my life to feel satisfied?*

The longer I drove around, the angrier I got, until I was more than ready to confront Chance. I pulled up to the house to find his car parked in the garage, which meant I had to leave mine in the driveway. I slammed the car door shut and moved into the house, where the smell of food hit my nose. I stepped into the kitchen to find Chance fixing dinner. As soon as I spotted him in front of the stove, my mouth dropped.

He was wearing nothing but a pair of Timberland boots.

He glanced over his shoulder and smiled. "Hey, baby girl. I've got Shake'n Bake pork chops in the oven."

I tried not to look at his tight ass as I confronted him. "Don't play with me. I want to know who Jaycee is."

He swung around and all I could do was look down. It was hard to be mad at someone when ten inches was staring right smack at you.

I forced my eyes to his face. "Who's Jaycee?" I repeated. I could tell he started to lie, but the expression on my face must have told him that was not a good idea.

"Baby girl, come, have a seat."

Reluctantly, I walked over to the kitchen table. Chance moved in the chair across from me with his legs wide open and his dick staring right at me.

"My name is Joshua Chance Garrett III. I've been donating to a sperm bank since college."

My eyes snapped to his face again. Uh-uh, no, he wasn't about to tell me another lie. "Jordan didn't get your sperm from a sperm bank."

"I know. I was getting to that." He leaned back in the chair, reached down, and stroked his meat. I started licking my lips.

"Yo, quit looking at my dick!" he scolded but I could see humor burning at the back of his eyes.

I rolled my neck as I spoke. "If you don't want me to look then go put some clothes on yo naked ass," I snapped. "Now either quit stalling or get the hell outta my house."

Chance released a heavy breath, then reached over and cupped my hand. "I grew up with two women. One who I had always thought was my auntie until I asked my mother one day why the two of them slept in the same bed. That's when I found out my mom was a dyke. She told me she and Auntie Mamie wanted a shorty so bad. They couldn't afford to go to a fertility clinic so they ran an ad, looking for a disease-free donor for a small fee. And that is how I was conceived. I grew up around my mom's friends, mostly dykes, who wanted to have babies. Some of them used to joke about how fine I was and that one day I could make a lot of money helping females like them have babies. I thought about that when I went to college and decided that it was a helluva way to fund my education."

I didn't answer right away because I couldn't get my eyes off his dick. When I finally did, I rolled my eyes. "What does that have to do with the price of tea in China?" When his brow bunched with confusion, I gave an impatient breath. "Why did you sleep with Nadine?"

Chance slid his chair closer to me. "So that she could feel like she was part of the whole conception process. I wanted both women to experience what it was like being with me so I had them share the intimacy together. It's business, baby girl, nothing else. I swear to God I'm not lying."

For some strange reason that shit made sense to me. Or maybe it was because he was sitting so close and I saw that black snake move.

"There is nothing going on with me and either of those women. I was paid to do a job, that's all. It's not like I'm the first person to do something like that. It happens all the time."

I gave him a long, skeptical look. "I never heard of it before. I just wish it had been with someone other than one of my best friends."

"I didn't know. I swear to you. But it doesn't matter. I love you, boo. I don't need no one else. Especially not no dykes."

I had to smile at that one.

I shook my head. "I don't know. Nadine was pretty upset."

He frowned. "Yo, it's not my fault she wanted to read more into it than it really was!"

"I got the impression it was more than a job. The two of you met and screwed when Jordan wasn't even around."

He took my hands in his. "Baby, I was doing a job. I'm paid *well* to do a job." He gave me that sexy panty-dropping grin of his. "She was the one paying for my services, and I wanted to make sure she got her money's worth. Sure, I might have hustled her into giving me a big tip, but like I said, it's strictly business."

"She's my friend and I don't turn my back on my friends."

I could tell he was growing tired of this discussion. "That's cool she's your friend. Just remember who your man is and that I love you and plan to spend the rest of my life with yo sexy ass. If you need me to holla at ya girl, I will. I'll admit I was wrong for pretending I didn't know who she was at the restaurant, but I just didn't want you to find out that way." He was using that seductive voice of his that he knew always made me weak. I struggled for strength. There was no way I could make this easy for him.

I twisted up my mouth. "How many other times have you done this?"

"In the clinic? Dozens of times. But through an ad, this makes my fourth."

"How much did you get paid?"

"Ten grand."

That wasn't anywhere near enough to end a friendship over. But it was definitely enough to go shopping.

"I used the money to put a down payment on something special for my baby girl. But I can't tell you just yet what it is." He held my hand and started rubbing the second to last finger on my left hand. *A wedding ring! Hell yeah, he paid down on a ring.* I couldn't help but feel excited at the idea.

"Well, if you're going to be with me then you have to give that business up," I demanded with a pout.

He smoothed an uneasy hand across his hair. "Baby, you don't understand. I'm too high in demand to stop. I've got three new clients. How do you think I pay for my Navigator and afford to keep you looking nice? Weren't you happy when your man lined your pockets last week with enough to go shopping in St. Louis with your girls?"

Last week he broke me off fifteen hundred dollars. Renee and I spent the weekend shopping until my feet started to hurt.

"I can't do those types of things if I give up my job. If you still want to go to Miami next month, I have to keep my job."

I frowned. "You sound like a gigolo."

"Hey, and this gigolo is getting paid!" He took my hand and lowered it onto his dick. "This here is a strong, black working man!"

I snatched my hand away and he howled with laughter. I couldn't help but join in. "You're stupid."

"Nah, baby, just keeping it real, but hey, if you can't handle it, then me and Frank are out." He rose from the chair with his hard dick in his hand and made a show of getting up and moving over to the stove. "Let me get these pork chops out and then I'll be on my way." He then got real quiet.

Dammit, Chance had a way of twisting the shit around and making me feel guilty. And Lord knows I wanted to believe that what he said about him and Nadine being just business. She was the fool for making more of the shit than it really was. I was embarrassed and pissed off by the way I found out, but I can't just throw away a good thing. He's right. He's a hustler and a damn good one. I have to accept all or nothing with him. Chance is everything to me. I don't want to lose him. Do I like the idea of sharing my dick with everyone else? Hell nah! But if they're all being tested for diseases first and it's just a bunch of dykes who are more interested in licking pussy than getting dicked down, then why should I be trippin'? Especially if Chance keeps my pockets fat and he does things like making me dinner butt-ass naked. I stared at his ass and my lips curved in a smile. Besides, he had all but admitted he plans to marry me. He can keep doing what he do, for now. Once we're married, I wasn't going to have him doing that mess anymore. The only one who would enjoy that dick would be me.

Chance studied my face. "Well, what's it gonna be?" He sounded impatient. Like time is money or some shit. "Are we cool now?"

"Yeah, I guess. *For now.* Later you're going to have to make it up to me." He wasn't completely out of the water yet. It was going to take a couple of licks on my clit to get back in my good graces, and some money to get my hair and nails done.

"No doubt, baby girl. I plan on doing a whole lot of making up." He strolled over and stopped right in front of me, then took my hand and put it on his dick. He had grown hard enough to slam a ball out of the park. "Hope you're ready to touch them toes."

45

Renee

I was home dozing off while watching a late-night movie when the phone rang. I ignored it because I had a pretty good idea who was calling, again. A glance at the Caller ID confirmed I was right. Danielle. She refused to tell me what happened when I called her earlier, and now that it was convenient for her, she wanted to call me back. I guarantee Chance told her some lame-ass story to get her to believe him. So now she wants to call me to throw it back in my face. As far as I'm concerned, I'm staying out of it. If she wants to believe that sorry mothafucka, then so be it. I know she better not come running to me when the shit hits the fan. She wants to believe him, then she can deal with the consequences. If she had any sense, she would take Calvin back.

The next morning I went to work, but after an hour my head was hurting so bad I decided to just go home for the day. It was the end of April and school was called off due to an electrical problem. Usually when the kids were home I tried to stay as far away as possible, but the thought of going home and curling underneath my covers was too good to pass up.

I was halfway home when I decided to give Kenny a call just so he wouldn't wake me up after I had fallen asleep. Nothing pissed me off more than to be disturbed when I was dreaming good. And after a dose of medicine that's exactly what I would be doing.

"Hello?" he said, sounding like he was still in bed.

"I thought you were going to the shop this morning." Sometimes I think Kenny is lazy as hell.

"I started to but the bed felt so good this morning, I decided to just lie here."

"I can definitely understand. My head is killing me so I'm on my way back home to bed."

"Who you got meeting you? That other nigga?"

"Whatever." He could be so ignorant at times. I don't know why I even bothered calling him.

"That's okay, just tell me the truth."

"Kenny, the kids are at home. How much entertaining do you expect me to be doing?"

"I come over when your kids are there."

"That's you. They know who you are. I don't make it a habit of having a bunch of men running in and out of my house." Hell, why do that when I can just meet them at the nearest hotel?

"How I even know you're going home? Why you call me from your cell phone?"

"You are really talking stupid."

"Yeah, you right. I don't have no right to ask," he said and waited for a response.

I was already tired of this conversation. "I'll call you when I get home." I hung up and groaned. I can't stand a jealous-ass man. Never have. Never will. Some women think that shit is cute. Well, I don't.

Now my head was really pounding, and I felt relieved when I finally pulled my car into the garage next to Quinton's. The second they heard school was canceled this morning, they both jumped back into bed and went back to sleep. Which was fine with me, otherwise they'd be wanting me to make them pancakes or something and I wasn't feeling up to doing anything but taking a nap.

I moved into the quiet house and went straight to the bathroom to pee. Once there, I noticed that Quinton had taken a shower and as usual had left the bathroom a mess. I frowned. He kept his room clean, but the bathroom was another story all together. As soon as I washed my hands I moved down the hall to his bedroom and knocked.

He didn't answer.

I turned the knob and found that the door was locked. So I started banging on the door. "Quinton, get your butt up!" I heard mumbling on the other side. Two voices, and one was female. Hell nah! Reaching over the trim of the door, I grabbed the small key and stuck it through the lock. As soon as the knob turned, I barged into the room. The television was on and Quinton was lying in the bed.

"What's going on in here?" I demanded to know because something smelled fishy, and I mean that literally. Whoever was in his room needed a douche.

He rubbed his eyes and tried to act like he was just waking up. "Huh? What are you talking about? I was asleep."

I pursed my lips and gave him a long look, then dropped down and looked under his bed. He sprang up and the covers fell low and I could tell he didn't have any clothes on.

"Mom, what are you doing?" Panic was apparent in his face. He quickly reached for his boxers.

"Looking for the girl you're screwing." I rose to my

feet, moved over to the closet, and flung the door open. Crunched down in the corner was Alicia. She looked scared to death. And needed to be.

"Get dressed and go home!" I managed between gritted teeth. I wanted to cuss her ass out but decided to save that for Quinton. She stepped out, wearing one of Quinton's shirts, pouting with straight attitude like I'd done something to her. "Don't ever come over here and disrespect my house like this again!"

Quinton tried to take up for his girl. "Mama, it isn't her fault. I invited her over."

"And she came knowing good and damn well she couldn't do that same shit at her house."

She sucked her teeth. "Actually, my mother doesn't mind if I have company in my room."

"Then that's *your* mama, because I don't allow it in my house and Quinton knows it. Now both y'all, get dressed." I moved out the room and down the hall to mine, where I called Kenny and woke him up again.

"You made it home."

"Yep. And guess what I walked in on? Your daughter and my son fucking in my house."

"What!"

"Yep."

He was quiet. "That's because her mother lets her do whatever she wants."

"Well, she won't do *whatever* she wants over here. Do you want to talk to her?"

He was quiet. What the hell did he have to think about? "Nah. She'll just get pissed and then run home to tell Reese on me."

Did I hear him right? "Is that all you care about?"

"Listen, babe, I just don't need that kind of drama right now. I'm getting married in two weeks."

"Then you need to quit fucking around!" I slammed the phone down because now I was pissed off. So much for getting some sleep.

By the time I moved back down the hall, I heard Quinton's car pulling out of the driveway. I walked over to the window and glanced out in time to see Alicia mean mugging me. I stuck up my middle finger, then turned and went to the bathroom to find some ibuprofen. My head was pounding.

I took a nap and when I woke up around five, I headed to the store. I didn't have any missed calls, so Kenny hadn't even bothered to try and call me back. I was hurt beyond words. I obviously did not mean as much to him as I thought I had. That's what I get for giving my heart to a mothafucka.

On my way back home, I reached for my phone and called Kayla. I just needed someone to just listen to me without passing judgment. Maybe she might throw in a scripture or two to help me come to terms with what was going on.

"Hello?"

"Hey, girl. Where you at?"

"I'm at Wal-Mart in the jewelry department talking to Reese about her wedding."

I hit my brakes. "Is she still there?"

"Uh-huh, standing a few feet away." Her voice was low so that she wouldn't be overheard. "I can't believe I'm telling you this."

I hit a U-turn. "Neither can I, but I'm glad you did. I'll be there in a few." I pushed my foot on the gas and went as fast as I thought I could get away with. A couple of weeks ago Kenny had shown me a picture of Reese, but nothing would be like seeing her in person.

Five minutes later I was jumping out of my car and

making my way into Wal-Mart. I dialed Kayla back. "Where is she now?"

"I don't know. She said she was going over to the cosmetics department."

"As ugly as everyone says she is, I doubt makeup can help."

Kayla breathed heavily in the phone. I know she was regretting even telling me.

"What's she wearing?"

"She's wearing navy blue capris and a white sparkle T-shirt."

I moved into the store and headed to the cosmetics department, scanning each aisle as fast as I could, looking both ways. I reached the end and was in the pet department. "I don't see her."

"She's here unless she left."

I started walking down the main aisle and moved past each of the checkout lanes hoping to see her.

"She can't be too far. All she was talking about was her wedding and all of her arrangements. I wouldn't have even told you, but she's having a bridal shower and didn't even bother inviting me. I thought she and I were friends."

"I guess not. Or maybe she knows that I'm fucking her fiancé and that we are friends."

"I doubt that. She would have confronted me. She's like that. A whole lot of talk."

I moved to the other side of the store where the groceries are and found Kayla and her daughter Asia in the bread aisle. I hung up my phone and moved over to her cart.

"Hey, Asia." I gave her a hug. "How's school?"

"Good," she answered with a shy smile. She's a pretty

girl. Tall with pretty light brown skin and long jet-black hair. She's only ten but looks every bit of thirteen.

I hugged her once more, then turned my attention to Kayla. "Where's she at?" I mumbled so Asia wouldn't know who we were talking about.

She shrugged. "She was just here. Maybe she left. She did talk about going to Tropical Liquors for a drink afterward."

I huffed out a frustrated breath and reached for a loaf of bread. I was sure we could use some at home. I glanced over her shoulder and my eyes grew round. "Is that her over there?"

Kayla turned around and tried to act like she was grabbing a pack of bagels. "Yep, that's her."

Before she could stop me, I walked in Reese's direction so I could get a closer look. She was standing in the meat department examining the lunch meat. As soon as I saw her pick up a pack of hot dogs, I started cracking up laughing. She turned and looked in my direction. *Ugh* was right. She looked like she'd had a hard life. She was close to fifty and looked every bit of it. She had big round eyes and high cheekbones that, like her breasts, were starting to sag. I moved closer and could tell that she once had severe acne because it left black spots and craters in her face. I wouldn't call her skinny or fat, but she did have a tire around her middle section that you just couldn't stuff in a pair of capri pants.

I moved over just so I would have a chance to see if she recognized me. Up close and personal. I reached over and grabbed a pack of bacon and looked up to find her staring at me.

"Aren't you the writer, Caeramel?" Reese asked.

The shit I write I have to pen under a pseudonym. "Yep, that's me," I said, trying to be polite.

"I thought so. I read your last book *Feignin'*. It was really good."

I couldn't help but grin at the compliment. "Well, thanks. I have a new book coming out at Christmastime called *A Delight Before Christmas*."

"I'll have to grab a copy. Well, keep up the good work." Her smile was genuine.

"Thanks," I said and watched her head over to the milk.

As soon as she wasn't looking, I turned and headed back down the bread aisle. Kayla's eyes were wide as saucers. I know she was dying to know what the two of us were talking about. I didn't want Reese to know we knew each other if the shit ever hit the fan, so I called Kayla on my phone and told her to meet me in the photo department. She must have run because she beat me there.

"Oh my God! What were the two of you talking about?"

I looked around to make sure Reese wasn't around because people have a way of popping up on you. "She was complimenting me on my book."

"Man, do you think she knows?"

I thought about it for a second, then shook my head. "Nope, or she doesn't know that Renee Moore and Caeramel are the same person."

"Maybe that's it. She's looking for Renee." She started laughing. "Wouldn't that be something when she finds out?"

I snapped my fingers. "No, come to think of it, she would know it was me because when I ignore those blocked calls, my voice mail picks up and it says Renee Moore loud and clear."

"Then maybe it isn't her calling you."

"Maybe not." If not, then who?

I reached for a roll of film. "Have you spoken to Nadine?"

Kayla nodded. "Briefly this morning. She's still pretty pissed off about that whole thing."

I nodded. Her feelings were quite understandable. "I'm gonna give her a call tomorrow."

Asia looked like she was anxious to get home, and I was ready to get out of the store myself. I said good-bye and moved to the register to pay for my stuff. I saw Reese once more. She waved and headed to the door. I stood there trying to figure it out. If it wasn't Reese and it wasn't Leslie, then who could it be?

It wasn't until that night after I had given up expecting a call from Kenny and had climbed under the covers that my cell phone vibrated. I grabbed it hoping it was him. It was a text message.

BITCH THIS IS UR LAST WARNING.

46

Danielle

As soon as I spotted Renee pulling into the parking lot, I grabbed my purse, hopped out of my SUV, and climbed in on the passenger's side. Rhianna was coming through the speakers, and while listening to the song "Umbrella" I started to relax.

"Why am I picking you up in Walgreens parking lot?"

I dropped my eyes and pretended that I was looking for something in my purse. "Because I told Chance I was going over to my mother's house."

Renee gave me that look and I knew she was about to start running her damn mouth. Why can't she just shut up sometimes?

"Danny, you're a grown-ass woman messing with some jealous mothafucka. Girl, tell that fool you got a daddy at home."

I leaned back in the seat and closed my eyes. I don't know what's worse, Chance's jealousy or Renee's mouth. "Girl, sometimes it's easier just to not even go there with him. Chance went through a lot with his last girlfriend. He was crazy about Jaclyn. She messed around on him so much he said he almost went crazy when he found out. Now it takes a lot for him to trust women."

"Sounds like too much work to me."

"I'll admit that I'm starting to get tired of his insecurities, but I'm hoping that he'll start trusting me more and more."

"Whatever," Renee mumbled, obviously unconvinced.

I can see why it's hard for her to understand. Renee has never had patience for anybody. With her you get one chance, and once you fuck that up there's no turning back. I, on the other hand, know that we all make mistakes, some more than others, and I'll have to admit that what I thought was cute has started to wear my damn nerves.

A couple of days after that incident at the restaurant, I met Kayla to look at flower arrangements. Chance called my phone every five minutes wanting to know what I was doing and who I was with, then he wanted to know when I was planning to be home. When I got home, I hopped in the shower and came back into the room in time to catch his crazy ass smelling my damn panties. When I asked, he said he wanted to make sure I hadn't been fucking nobody. What the hell?

My friends seldom called anymore because he always answered the phone, and when they did he asked them too many damn questions. Anytime I went anywhere he wanted to go or insisted I take his SUV. I know the only reason was that he has *OnStar* and wants to be able to know my whereabouts. My friends think I'm crazy and I'm starting to agree. Yet every time I was ready to put his ass out of my house, Chance knew exactly what to do to make me forgive him. I couldn't stay mad at him. He's just too damn sexy, and the sex is something I don't know if I can go without. Like I said before, I guess I'm a slave to his dick.

When Renee insisted that I ride down to Jefferson City with her to a get-together her cousin was having, I was tempted to say no just to keep from hearing his mouth. But since Chance had to work at the hospital tonight, I decided to go ahead and sneak out and be back before he returned.

"That bitch called me again last night."

I swung around on the seat and stared at her pissed-off expression.

"What did Kenny have to say about it?"

Renee pursed her lips with displeasure. "He said it wasn't Reese. That if she knew about me, he would know about it by now because she would be going off."

"Whatever, I heard that she ain't doing anything to jeopardize her wedding. She's probably trying to wait until after they get married."

"That's what I told him, but he insists she would still say something."

"Reese's messing around her damn self, so there is no telling. Shit, she might not care that she's sharing her *hot dog,*" I teased and we started laughing.

"Shit, if it ain't Reese calling me then I don't know who else it could be."

"Who else are you screwing?"

She took her eyes off the road long enough to roll them at me. "Fuck you, Danny. I'm not messing with nobody else."

Whatever, I love Renee, but her ass can be a straight ho when she wants to.

"Did I tell you I met Reese a couple of days ago?"

"You did?"

Renee nodded. "Kayla was at Wal-Mart and she told me Reese was there."

"I can't believe Kayla told you that."

"Right, but she did, and you know I hurried over there so I could see her. That bitch is homely as hell."

"I told you. Did she know who you were?"

Renee shook her head. "Nope. I wanted to see if she knew who I was. If she did she definitely played it off well. But I doubt she could do that much acting. She was asking me about my books and shit. I don't think she's the one who's been calling me."

"Damn, then who's calling you?"

She pulled onto the interstate and shrugged one shoulder. "Shit, for all I know it might be yo ass calling me for letting Calvin lick my damn pussy," she teased.

"Bitch, whatever." I couldn't help but laugh at that one even though that shit was still a sore subject with me. I'd been thinking about him a lot lately. "It might be She-mar's gay ass."

Renee suddenly looked over at me. "Girl, you might be right. John is still blowing up my phone. Shemar might be afraid he's losing his man."

I exploded with laughter and it felt good. The last few days I haven't had a lot to laugh about.

"Why don't you just see what it is that John wants?"

"I e-mailed him yesterday and told him not to bother trying to contact me again, any further contact should be through his lawyer, and that he needed to be getting one so we can get this divorce on the road. He never e-mailed me back."

John was really a nice guy. Too bad he liked booty. "John's hoping the two of you can work things out."

"What-the-fuck-ever."

The rest of the ride we talked about her son Quinton and Kenny's daughter screwing in her house. Hell nah! But what does she expect? Quinton is a teenage boy and that's just what they do. "Now think about it, Renee. When we were in high school, how many times did you sneak over to a brotha's house while his mama was still at work?"

She thought about it for a moment, then burst out laughing. "Too many damn times!"

"Okay then." We laughed and talked about the shit we used to do back in the day while we drove to her cousin's house.

When we got there, cars lined both sides of the street.

"What did you say was going on today?"

"My cousin Clarice, her daughter just passed her bar exam so she's having a celebration."

I nodded. I knew mostly all of her family. Most of them were crazy so I was surprised to hear that someone had actually gone to law school.

We got out and moved up the driveway. We walked through the door and the house was filled with people. Music was pounding from the back of the house. Cigarette smoke flooded the air. All the way, I stopped and said hello to quite a few people that I knew from the neighborhood.

"Danielle, this is my cousin Clarice."

I smiled over at the beautiful tall woman. "Wow! You don't look old enough to have a daughter in law school."

"Ooh, Nae-Nae! I like your friend already," she said,

completely flattered by my compliment. "The food's in the back. Danielle, make yourself at home."

I nodded and Renee grabbed two wine coolers from the refrigerator and we headed to the back where everyone was dancing. She introduced me to her cousin Jasmine, who looked barely out of high school, let alone law school. I congratulated her and she hugged me like we've been friends for years.

Two of Renee's cousins were doing the soldier boy and I stood back and watched. Three drinks and two hours later, Renee and I were out there trying to do it our damn selves. I was having so much fun hanging out with her crazy-ass family.

Jasmine came over and whispered something in Renee's ear. She nodded, then turned to me.

"Come on, I want you to meet someone."

I hoped she wasn't trying to hook me up with another one of her cousins. They had been sweating me since I arrived. Some of them were fine as hell, but I already had one man driving me crazy.

Renee moved through the large house and climbed the stairs.

"Where are we going?"

"Just follow me."

I couldn't help but be suspicious as I followed her down the hall to the last room on the left. Two of her teenage cousins were sitting on the floor watching television. One had a little boy on their lap. There was several little kids sleeping on a large king-size bed. They must be the designated babysitters while the grown folks partied.

Renee held out her hands. "Come here, Trenton."

The little boy looked up and raised his hands in the air,

and Renee lifted him off the floor and turned to face me. "This is Chance's son."

I gazed down at his darling little face and gasped. He looked just like Chance. I had no idea what his baby pictures looked like, but I had a strong feeling they looked just like Trenton. He had the same hazel eyes and curly good hair, and that small protruding nose was unmistakable. Renee was right. Trenton was Chance's son.

A tall redbone woman stepped into the room and Trenton held out his arms. She took him in her arms, kissed his forehead, then turned to Renee.

"Whassup, Renee?"

"Hey Charlise. This is my girl Danielle."

She looked my way and nodded an acknowledgment. "You the girl messing with Chance?"

"Yes."

"You need to tell that bitch-ass nigga he needs to send me some money before I tell the courts where he works. I'm tired of playing games," she said rather frankly, then rolled her eyes and moved out the room.

I looked over at Renee, ready to kill her. "I'm ready to go." I turned down the hall and took the stairs two at a time. It was another few minutes before Renee came out. As soon as she opened the doors to her Lexus, I climbed in and waited until we were back on the highway before I spoke.

"Why the hell you didn't tell me that before you took me all the way out there and embarrassed me?"

"I didn't find out until yesterday. I was talking to my cousin Clarice and she was babysitting Trenton while her daughter and Charlise went to the mall. It wasn't until then that I suddenly remembered why Chance looked so

familiar to me. I had met him over at my aunt's once back
when he and Charlise was kicking it."

"I can't believe that shit."

"I'm sorry but I knew if I told you, you wouldn't believe it until you saw Trenton with your own eyes." For
once, Renee sounded sincere.

She was right. I wouldn't have believed it. I leaned my
head back against the headrest and closed my eyes and
thought about all the lies he'd been telling me. Was I that
desperate for a man that I would believe anything he said?
I was starting to think so. There was no telling how many
other secrets he was hiding.

"Someone's been leaving me notes."

Renee took her eyes off the road. "What kind of
notes?"

"Be careful of the company you keep."

"What the hell is that supposed to mean?"

I shrugged. "I don't know."

"Why didn't you mention this before?"

"Because I was hoping that it would stop, but it hasn't,"
I replied with feelings of despair.

"When was the last time you received one?"

"Last week. Someone came to the nurses' station and
left an envelope with the unit secretary. I ran to the elevator and tried to see who it was, but I missed them. But
Janice said it was a black female wearing dark shades."

"Damn, you got drama like I do. Someone's calling my
phone and you got messages. Maybe it's the same person
and we can both whup her ass."

I had to laugh. Renee does have a way of cheering you
up when you need it.

"When did the notes start?"

"After I started dating Chance."

"Then there is your connection."

I inhaled deeply. She was probably right. Somebody was trying to tell me something.

"You sure you don't want me to follow you home?" Renee asked when we pulled into the Walgreens parking lot.

I shook my head. "Nah, I can handle it." I hopped into my Durango and drove home, ready to confront Chance.

I made it home around midnight to find him in the living room waiting for me.

He rose. "Com'ere."

I moved over to him thinking he was about to give me a kiss and instead he slid his finger inside the crotch of my underwear and rubbed my pussy. He pulled it out, then sniffed his fingers and released me.

"Just checking," he said, then lowered back on the couch. "Where the fuck you been all evening?"

I can't believe he just smelled my damn pussy. What the fuck is wrong with this man?

"Danielle, where the fuck you been?" he repeated.

I looked at him and rolled my eyes. "Out."

"Out? What the hell you mean out? I've been calling you for the last hour."

"I know. I was too busy talking to Charlise." His face turned pale. Before he could answer I turned on my heel and headed up to my room.

He followed. "What lies was she telling you?"

"She didn't have to tell me anything. I had a chance to meet *your* son."

"I told you I don't have a son! I'm so sick of Charlise lying on me."

"And I'm tired of your lies."

"I'm not lying."

"I saw that little boy with my own eyes. You could have

given birth to him, he looks so much like you." I took a deep breath. It was late and I wasn't in the mood for him. "I need some time alone to think."

"What the hell do you mean you need some time alone? I'm yo man. We spend our time together."

I lowered on the bed. This was not going as easily as I had planned. "Chance, I can't take the jealousy and the panty sniffing and the pussy rubbing. This relationship has gotten so out of control and I think we need a break from each other."

"We can work this out," he pleaded.

I shook my head and couldn't believe what I was saying. "I don't think that we can."

"What the fuck!" he shouted, then slammed his fist at my mirror, breaking the glass.

I was so shocked I couldn't speak. He really was crazy. "What you do that for?" I yelled, then moved over to assess the damage. He pushed me down onto the bed.

"Listen to me and listen good. Don't you ever tell me again what we will and will not do! I told you before, you belong to me, and that is never going to change."

I looked at the broken mirror and then at the blood on his hand. I had gotten myself into a mess. I moved over to the phone and started dialing.

"Who the hell are you calling?"

"The police, and I advise you to be gone before they get here."

As soon as he realized I was serious, he changed his tone. "Danielle, baby, I didn't mean to break the mirror. But we can work this out, I know it." He pleaded with his eyes.

I placed the phone to my ear. "There is nothing to work out. Now get out."

He was bleeding all over the place but he didn't notice.

He was now crying. Nothing bothered me more than to see a man cry, but with Chance I didn't feel the slightest bit moved.

"I need you to send a police car to my house," I said as soon as someone picked up.

"Okay, okay, I'll leave, but just remember I'm never going to be too far away."

I didn't hang up the phone until I was sure he was out of my life for good.

47

Renee

I had just made it back to my desk when my office phone rang. I smiled when the Caller ID showed Kenny's office phone number. Finally!

"Hey, boo-boo."

There was a short pause. "Who's this?"

As soon as I heard the female's voice, I sat up on my chair. Oh hell nah. Kenny's fiancée!

"How you going to ask who this is when you called me?"

Reese breathed heavily in the receiver, and I could tell I'd pissed her off. So what?

"This is Reese. I wanted to know who this is calling my *fiancé*?"

"As you can see from his phone log, your man calls me."

"Why is he calling you?"

"That's something you need to ask Kenny."

"Bitch, I'm asking you!"

Oh no, that wench didn't call me a bitch. I started

laughing. "Reese, if you must know, I'm borrowing your man."

"Borrowing? Don't you know we're getting married this weekend?"

"I know. Don't worry. I don't want him. I'm just borrowing him."

"Excuse me?"

"I'm sorry. That was probably too advanced for a country girl like you, so let me simplify it for you. I'm borrowing your *hot dog*."

"You're talking a lot of shit on the phone!"

"Oh, you're the one who called me."

"'Cause I'm trying to find out who the fuck you are."

"It's not that hard." I reached for my fingernail file. "I don't know what the big deal is. Don't worry. I don't want him because I'll be damned if a mothafucka is gonna wake my ass up at three a.m. to make him some Kool-Aid and scratch his fuckin' back."

There was a pause. "Then why are you fucking with him?"

"Shit, because the dick . . . oops, I mean, the *hot dog* is good." I started laughing. "Why you care anyway?"

"'Cause I got twelve years invested in our relationship."

"Then why you calling me?"

"Because I want to let you know that I'm here to stay."

"So I've heard. In other words, I can keep on fucking him because it's not going to make a difference."

"It's gonna make a big difference."

"Big difference how? You gonna stop giving him some? Okay, that's fine 'cause that just means he'll be at my house five nights a week instead of three."

"Whatever."

"Come on, Reese. It is what it is. You might be where he's at, but I'm where he wants to be." I had to laugh 'cause I stole that shit from Lil' Kim. "You live in his house. He supports you *and* your boys. Kenny's been messing around on you for years and it hasn't mattered, so what's one more time before he ties the knot?"

"He ain't leaving me for you."

"And you ain't leaving him? Have some respect for yourself. The mothafucka told me he fucked your baby sister, yet you still plan to marry him. What the fuck's up with that? That just tells me how stupid you are. You know what, Reese, do me a favor, when Kenny gets up, tell him to call me." I hung up because I was through talking to her. I couldn't believe I had almost felt sorry for her stupid ass.

As I prepared a report I thought about Reese and realized that even as stupid as she was, we were in almost similar situations. I too depended on a man to provide for my needs and was afraid to leave because I didn't want to get out on my own and try to survive. Only I woke up and had sense enough to leave when I found out my husband was fucking someone else.

She didn't, and the way Reese acted, she never would.

I called Kenny and told him I needed to see him immediately. By the time I got off work, he was in my driveway. We went inside and he kissed me, then we moved to my room. I hung up my purse while he took a seat on the bed.

"What's up?" I could tell the suspense was killing him.

"Reese called me at work today."

That negro looked like he had just seen a ghost. "What did she say?"

"She called me from the number in your shop, so she must have seen your phone bill."

"Shit! What did you say to her?"

I slipped off my shoes. "The truth. I'm just borrowing her hot dog." I was joking, but he didn't see anything funny.

"Why didn't you lie?"

"For what? The bitch is stupid. It ain't like it's really going to make a difference. Just threaten to cancel the wedding and she'll shut up."

He scratched his head. "I guess. I just wish you told her I was working on your car or something."

He was starting to piss me off. Was he really that worried about her?

"I don't want to hurt her. Reese's a good girl and hasn't done nothing to me."

I took a seat beside him on the bed and put an arm around him. "I'm sure she'll look past it."

His cell phone vibrated and he looked down at it again. I know it was Reese calling him.

"I better go."

"Go? But you just got here."

He looked down, avoiding eye contact. "Yeah, I need to get home and talk to my fiancée."

Fiancée? "Oh, so it's like that now?"

Kenny swiped a hand down his face. "Renee, I was honest with you from the beginning. I'm getting married this weekend. We needed to cool it for a while. At least until after we get married."

I pursed my lips with attitude. "I told you I wasn't messing with you after you tied the knot, but since I love you I guess I'll have to think about it."

Kenny nodded and looked so sad I had to bite my lip to

keep from jumping up from the bed and telling him I changed my mind.

"Well, I'll call you in a few days." He turned and walked out of the room.

"You do that," I mumbled and listened as the front door closed behind him, crushing my heart in two.

48

Danielle

Chance was stalking me. At work. At home. I was so sick of him and his lies and his excuses. Rumor had it he was now living with some white woman. I thought it would bother me, but I didn't care. Which told me I never really loved his trifling ass in the first place.

Friday I went on a shopping spree. I couldn't help myself. I went to Babies"R"Us and practically bought out the store. Next I went to Baby Gap and bought my granddaughter all kinds of hip outfits. I even found her a pair of Nike tennis shoes at Foot Locker.

After I maxed out my credit card, I headed over to my mom's to drop off all my goodies. I stepped inside with my arms loaded down and Portia came down the stairs.

She gave me a curious look. "Mama, what you been buying?"

"Stuff for my grandbaby." I was so excited. "Here, come help me."

Together we unloaded my trunk, carried everything up to the baby's room, and started putting it away.

"Where're your grandparents?"

She turned and looked over at me. "Grandpa had another bowling tournament and Grandma went to cheer him on."

I smiled. My parents have been married almost forty-five years and they still loved each other. I hoped to be like them someday.

Portia picked up a brown teddy bear I'd bought and took a seat over in the rocking chair cradling him to her chest. I looked over and grinned. "That's going to be your daughter in a few days."

She nodded and started crying. "Mama."

I stopped folding baby clothes and swung around, leaning against the dresser drawers. "Yes?"

Her lips quivered. "I'm so . . . so sorry for everything that I did. I-I was wrong for breaking you and Ron up and . . . and accusing him of sleeping with me. It was childish and uncalled for. I hope you can forgive me someday." She wiped her tears with the teddy bear.

I looked down at my baby girl and my heart flooded with tears. "Sweetheart, you're already forgiven."

She sprang from the chair and wrapped her arms around me, and I hugged her back. My life felt more complete now with her back in my life than it ever had with Chance or Ron. I felt movement and drew back with a look of surprise.

"Did the baby just move?"

Portia wiped her eyes and nodded. "Yep, she's doing a lot of that lately."

I placed my hand on her stomach in time to feel her kick again. "Wow! I think we got a fighter on our hands." I had a feeling she was going to be just like all the other women in our family.

As we finished putting the baby clothes away, Portia

and I really talked. She and Demetrius were back together and trying to do everything they could to make their relationship work. That's all you can ask of a couple of teenagers.

I hung around until my parents returned, then headed out the door. I had one more thing I had to do before I could sleep well tonight.

Fifteen minutes later, I pulled up at Nadine and Jordan's house. They'd had the two-story home built late last year in an exclusive neighborhood where mostly doctors and lawyers lived.

I knocked and Jordan came to the door. This beautiful woman with flawless peanut butter skin was a wonderful balance to my workaholic friend.

"Hey, come on in!" She moved aside so I could enter.

"Congratulations on the baby," I said with a hug.

"Thank you." Happiness was quite apparent on her face. "Go on back. Nadine's in her office."

I nodded, then moved down the spacious foyer to an office on the other side of a large kitchen.

"I see you're still working hard as usual."

At the sound of my voice Nadine looked up and scowled. "Yeah, I'm working on a divorce for one of my clients. Her husband has been hiding his assets for years."

"Men ain't shit."

She gave me a smirk. "You're right about that."

Nadine closed the file and I took a seat on a leather couch she kept in the corner of the room.

"I brought a peace offering." I held up a bottle of Riesling wine.

"Let me go get some glasses." Nadine rose. She was dressed comfortably in sweats and furry house shoes. She went into the kitchen and came back holding two flutes that had been engraved with the date of her commitment ceremony with Jordan last winter.

I waited until she opened the bottle and poured us both a glass before I spoke.

"Nadine, I am really sorry about the whole mess with Chance," I said in a low whisper. The last thing I needed was for Jordan to hear.

She gave a dismissive wave. "Don't worry about it. Shit happens."

I wasn't letting myself off the hook that easy. "No, it shouldn't have happened. Not with friends. You and I have been girls for years, and the second you tried to act like he didn't know you, I should have cut his ass then." I swallowed the lump in my throat. "I hope you can forgive me."

"Forgiven." Nadine took a sip. "I've been in enough relationships to know that the heart wants what the heart wants and there is nothing that anyone can do about that. I'm just glad you came to your senses. Renee says he's been acting like a possessive nut."

I rolled my eyes, then brought the flute to my lips. "That's an understatement. He's been begging and everything. It's crazy because Calvin is doing the same thing, only with him it doesn't seem nutty."

Her eyes shone with humor. "What you be doing to these men?"

I had to laugh at that one. "You know what's crazy? Both of them have slept with one of my best friends. Now what's the chances of that?"

She shook her head. "One in a million."

I had to drink to that.

49

Renee

I went out of town the day before Kenny's wedding. The best way to deal with it was sitting on a beach in Miami where I had a lot of time to think about him and what I was feeling. I loved that man. Can you believe that shit? I had given my heart to a married man. There was no future between us, but that didn't change what I was feeling at all. I didn't answer my phone the entire weekend, but Danielle called me Saturday evening to let me know Kenny had gone through with it. Reese was now Mrs. Reese Johnson.

I got back on Monday, and Kenny must have known because he started calling me. He's got life fucked up if he thinks he's about to get some of this that soon. I told him I would think about if I still wanted to fuck with him, and I meant that.

On my way home from work on Friday, Kayla caught me in the car.

"Girl, I hope you're sitting down."

"Yep. I'm in the car driving."

"Okay, listen to this."

"I'm listening," I replied impatiently.

"I spoke to Kenny today."

"How was the wedding?"

"Nice. They looked very happy."

That wasn't at all what I wanted to hear. "That's nice."

"Anyway, I called him today because I needed him to look at my car."

"Uh-huh." Hurry up and get to the point.

"And he told me he didn't know when he could look at it because he was on vacation."

"Vacation? That should give him more time to work in the shop."

"Girl, let me finish."

Damn, I wished she would hurry up.

"Anyway, he told me that he wouldn't be in Columbia no time soon because Reese was tripping."

"Why's she trippin'?"

"Apparently two weeks before the wedding, she and Christa, that's her best friend."

"Yeah, I know who she is."

"Well, she happened to be at the Wal-Mart buying flowers when she mentioned her friend was getting married."

I already knew where this was going but tried not to laugh as I waited for her to finish.

"When she mentioned going to a wedding in Boonville, *your* daughter told her 'my mama's boyfriend is also getting married in Boonville.' "

"Girl, she's lying. Tamara did tell me that she was running her mouth, but it wasn't Reese in line. She said it was a dark-skin girl with long, dark hair and we both know it wasn't Reese's bumpy-faced ass because she would have remembered the bumps."

"Girl, you're probably right. It was probably Christa who was at the store."

"Anyway, I asked Kenny if he called you and he said, 'Nah, she doesn't want to be bothered with me anymore,' " Kayla said breathlessly.

"Girl, he'll be all right."

"I told him I was calling you and he said to tell you that he wasn't mad at you or Tamara."

"Girl, I could care less if he's mad. Tell him to send Reese my way. I got something for her ass."

"She ain't stepping to you."

"She better not." I chuckled. "So he won't work on your car. Ha! She must have his ass on lockdown. I should call him and ask him to come over just to see if he'll come."

"You need to quit."

I hung up laughing.

The next morning, I waited until I knew Reese had left for work before I called him. Kenny answered on the second ring.

"Hey."

"Congratulations, boo-boo."

He laughed and I could tell he was glad to hear from me. "I told you ain't nothing changed but her last name."

Uh-huh, and that's why your ass can't leave the house, but I didn't want him to know that I knew. "I should be home by one. Can you come over?"

He hesitated for about five seconds before he started chuckling nervously. "I thought you didn't want to see me anymore after I married Reese."

I did say that, and if the bitch hadn't called me I would

have been true to my word. "Listen, do you want some of this or not?"

"I'll be over."

After work, I hurried home and went in the bathroom to prepare. I was determined to show him he had made a terrible mistake marrying her.

I showered and changed into something a little more revealing. A black negligee that I've been dying to model just for him. I sprayed on a little perfume even though he had asked me not to so he wouldn't go home smelling like a woman. I slipped on a pair of high heels and moved to the mirror to fix my hair and makeup. The doorbell rang, startling me. Damn, he was fast! I opened the door and found the UPS man.

"Ma'am, I have a package for you." I could see he was taking it all in. I pulled my satin robe closed, then took the clipboard and signed my name, and he handed me a small package that I noticed was from my editor. I glanced up and noticed that black Expedition parked across the street from my house. *What the hell?* I didn't even care that I was wearing a short robe with very little underneath. Hell, I didn't even care if the neighbors saw me. I stormed out of the house and across the street madder than a big dog. I was determined to know who the hell was calling me and stalking my house. Halfway down the driveway, I picked up a big brick and started to run.

"Hey, bitch! Yeah I'm fucking yo man. Now what?" I yelled. By the time I reached the end of the drive, the Expedition pulled off. I hurled that brick down the street and just missed the back bumper by a fraction.

I was huffing and puffing and screaming "mothafuckas" when I noticed my sixty-five-year-old neighbor grinning over at me. I looked down; my robe was open and one boob was hanging out. "Fuck!" I fixed my clothes and started up the drive just as Kenny pulled into the driveway. In this outfit my neighbor knew good and well what was about to pop off. Dammit! I told you I'm an undercover freak.

"What are you doing outside dressed like that?" he asked as he climbed out of his truck.

I was tired of playing games. "What kind of car does Reese drive?"

"Why?"

"Because I asked you a fucking question, that's why!" I was shouting and drawing attention to myself, but I didn't give a fuck.

He gave me a weird look. "She drives an Expedition."

I froze. "What color?"

"Burgundy."

I took a deep breath and then started laughing uncontrollably. I was so ready to beat Reese's ass and it wasn't even her.

He stepped closer to me. "Are you okay?"

"No, I'm not okay, but it ain't nothing that a little dick can't cure." I turned on the heels of my stilettos and signaled him to follow me inside.

I closed the door behind him and dropped my robe to the floor. I swayed away, making the cheeks of my ass, which were hanging out the back of my nightie, bounce.

"Damn, where you get that at?"

I tossed a smile over one shoulder. "I bought it with the money you gave me."

As soon as we reached my room, I kicked the door shut and helped shed his clothes.

"What were you doing outside?"

"I'll tell you later. Right now I need you inside me." I led him over to the bed. I didn't need any foreplay, just a dick inside me. I removed a condom from my nightstand and slid it on, then lowered onto my back and spread my legs.

"You in a rush?"

"Yes," I said, barely above a whisper. "I want all of you deep inside me, now."

Kenny settled between my legs, lifted them over his shoulders, and drove in hard. "Yessss," I cried. It had been almost two weeks since I last had some. He sent his whole length inside my pulsing kitty and I felt his balls rub against my wet lips.

He pulled out and sank into me again. "Damn, this pussy good." He rocked, withdrew, and despite my protest kept pulling out, then sliding all the way in again.

"Oh, it's so good. So damn good," I cooed. I dropped my legs and let them fall wide open, giving him plenty of room. I reached down and wrapped my hand around the base of his dick and guided him deeper. His breathing became ragged. My hips rose faster and faster to meet his thrusts. My tongue licked one nipple and then the other the way he liked it.

"You're gonna make me come," he warned.

"Then we'll come together." He pounded into me, gripping my hips and driving even harder. I lifted off the bed and met his thrusts. "Kenny, yeahhhhh, baby, I'm fin to come!" I screamed as I came hard, releasing weeks of pent-up frustration.

He threw his head back and slammed the final thrust home, coming hard. "Fuckkk!" he said. A few more strokes and I squeezed hard and milked him of everything he had left.

He held me and I wrapped my arms around him, enjoying a few stolen minutes together because I knew it would have to end soon.

"I missed you," he whispered against my ear.

"Really now?" There was no way I was going to let him know how miserable I have been without him.

We lay there for about thirty minutes before his cell phone started popping off. He groaned and rolled over. "That's her. I guess I better get out of here." He gave me a kiss on the lips, then rose and moved into the bathroom to clean up.

Reluctantly, I got up as well. My phone rang and I reached over and grabbed it.

"Bitch, stay away from my man!"

Okay, I'm mad again. "Bitch, I would if I knew who your man was. Either step to me like a woman or quit calling my fucking phone!" I slammed the phone down and Kenny came rushing out of the bathroom.

"What's wrong?"

"Some bitch is still calling my phone telling me to stay away from her man."

He looked nervous. "You don't know who it is?"

"If I did I would have solved this problem a long time ago."

I grabbed a pair of shorts and slipped them on while he got dressed. My mind was working overtime.

"You must be fucking someone else if their woman is calling you."

I glared over at his country ass. "Whatever, Kenny." I reached for a T-shirt, slipped it over my head, and grabbed my flip-flops.

"Come on, tell me. Who else are you screwing?"

I was so sick of him. "How in the world can your married ass question what I do?"

He shrugged. "I just asked."

"Then don't ask unless you really want an answer." I stormed out of the room, and by the time he made it to the living room I had the door open, waiting for him to go.

"I'll call you later once you cool down," he said, then brushed past me.

"Don't bother." I slammed the door behind him.

50

Renee

I carried a bouquet of spring flowers out to the cemetery. It was a beautiful day. I had always loved May. One reason being the weather was perfect enough that you didn't have to run the heat or the air conditioner. The second reason why May was so special was that it was Lisa's birthday.

I moved over to her gravesite and stared down at it. LISA RAE MILLER. LOVING SISTER, FRIEND, AND WIFE.

I lowered onto the grass and placed the flowers in a plastic vase that I had brought the year before. "Hey, sis. So much has happened since I last came to visit. Can you believe it? Kayla is getting married this summer. I am so happy for her. Danielle's daughter is due any day now. Can you believe it? Danielle's messing with some nut and me and John are getting a divorce." I pulled my feet to my chest and talked to my sister for over an hour before I said good-bye. My eyes were red by the time I made it home. I pulled into the driveway and noticed a 300C parked at the curb. I went ahead and pushed the garage door down and moved inside. As soon as I walked in and dropped my purse on the counter, I heard the doorbell. I hurried to answer it and gasped at the person standing on my front porch.

"Hey, Renee," John said.

"What are you doing here?" *I can't believe his down-low ass had the nerve to pop up at my door.*

"I knew you would be in town this weekend because you wouldn't miss your sister's birthday."

His fat ass was already pissing me off. "I asked why are you here?"

Not waiting for an invitation, John pushed past me and entered my house. "I need to talk to you and you've been ignoring all my calls, so I didn't have a choice."

"No shit. I don't have shit to talk to you about."

"Yes, we do."

I closed the door and swung around. "John, what the hell do you want?"

"We need to talk," he said, moved over to the couch, and took a seat.

"You should have thought about that before you decided to dip in someone else's ass."

"Can we let that go for a moment?"

"How am I going to let it just slide? That was some grimy shit. You had me fucking yo bitch. What the fuck? I've put up with all of your sexual issues over the years."

He leaned forward. "What issues?"

"Your dick half worked. And all you wanted to do was play with my damn nipples. No matter how often I told you to stop, it didn't matter. You still tweaked and tweaked and fucking tweaked! I thought I was going to lose my damn mind, but nooo, 'he's a good man' everyone said, especially Lisa, she insisted that I stay with you. So I did, and look what the fuck it got me."

I could tell I was starting to piss him off, and that is something that rarely ever happened. "I didn't come here for this."

"Then tell me. What the hell it is that is so damn important that you had to come all the way down here?"

"I'm HIV positive."

"You're what?" Oh hell no. I know I didn't hear him right. Did that booty bandit just tell me that he was HIV positive? My anger suddenly fizzled like a helium balloon. "I'm sorry to hear that."

"Renee, you need to go and get tested."

I got defensive. "For what? I'm not fucking another man, you are."

He took a deep breath. "Shemar doesn't have it."

It took me a few moments to register what he was saying. "I know good and damn well you're not trying to say you got it from me."

I could tell he was trying to choose his words carefully. "Where else would I have gotten it?"

I sprung from the couch and aimed blow after blow at his face. "I ain't gave you shit! You sick fucker!" I screamed.

He grabbed my hands and pulled me down beside him. "I didn't come here to argue. I just wanted to tell you so that you could get tested as well."

"Ain't shit wrong with me!"

Tears ran down his cheeks. "Please go get tested," he pleaded.

"Get the hell out of my house!"

51

Renee

I was scared.

All I could do was think about all the men that I'd been with and those few times that I gave in to the moment and let the feeling dictate my behavior. Five times in the last three years. There was three times that I could remember that I didn't even bother using a condom, and they were with men that to this day I couldn't stand. Two were while vacationing in Jamaica. Landon. The rest while swinging with my husband. What in the hell was I thinking? I knew the consequences and the risk. I had read the pamphlets. Saw the statistics. HIV in black women was rising, and we can't blame it all on down-low brothers. There's also making bad choices. And I had made plenty, but fucking without a condom was even worse.

Please, Lord. Let me be all right.

It was the Memorial Day weekend, and I was so glad Tamara was with her dad and Quinton went to St. Louis with his friends. I know Alicia went with them, but I'm through trying to fight him. I know I can't dictate who he sees. Besides, I have bigger problems.

I lay awake most of the night thinking about my life and wanted so badly to call my friends for inspiration, but I just couldn't bring myself to share this news with anyone. I didn't want anyone to know, at least not until I got my test results.

I prayed and read a couple of scriptures from my Bible. It's a shame that we only call on the Lord when we really need Him. I know that, but I need Him now. If Lisa was alive, she would have told me to think of all of the things I have to be thankful for. Friends. Kids. A career. My sister fought cancer for years and eventually lost the fight, but not once did she let her illness control her life. She was a fighter. I remember once when she told me, "I'm not about to let this condition dictate the future of my life. Ovarian cancer is what I have, not who I am."

That night I was sleeping soundly in my bed when the doorbell rang. I looked over at the clock and saw it was almost three o'clock.

Who the hell is ringing my doorbell at this time of the morning?

I got up and looked in the window and saw it was the neighborhood bag lady. Her eyes were wide and she looked like she hadn't taken her medicine in a couple of days.

"What do you want?" I didn't mean to yell, but it was too damn early in the morning for her begging.

"My mother had a stroke and I need money to go see her before she dies!"

I groaned. "I don't have any money." I think I had four dollars in my purse.

"I have to see her before she dies," she pleaded.

"How much you need?"

"Twenty-two dollars."

There was no way I was giving this woman that much money. I was starting to think that maybe she was on crack. I shook my head. "I'm sorry, but I don't have it."

"Oh no!" She started crying.

My heart started to bleed, but I just couldn't be giving her that much money. Something was wrong with that woman. She was either on drugs or mentally ill. "You've got to stop going to people's houses begging. It's just too early in the morning. Please go home before someone calls the police." She nodded with tears in her eyes and headed home.

I went back to my bed and couldn't go back to sleep because she was heavy on my mind. It was a relief to have something else to think about other than my HIV test.

I got up and took a shower and was at work before eight. I was glad there was a report for me to type because it gave me something to do other than sit and think about my problems.

I left around one and went over to the health department to get my testing done, then headed to the grocery store and to pick up Tamara from her dad's. I was taking her to get her driver's license today.

She passed her test and I was so happy for her. Her car was sitting in the garage waiting on her.

As we pulled into the subdivision I spotted the bag lady sitting on her porch. As soon as we passed, she rose from her seat.

"Shit, I bet she's on her way to our house," I mumbled under my breath.

"Mama, she's worrisome."

We started unloading the car as fast as we could because any second I would see her coming around the corner. Sure enough, as I reached for the gallon of milk, I spotted her coming toward the cul-de-sac. I carried the milk in the house.

"Mama, you want me to talk to her?"

"No." I shook my head. "I got her." We moved to get the last of the stuff out of the trunk. Tamara started laughing when she drew near. I stuck my head in the car and started laughing too, then forced myself to stop and think of what excuse I was going to come up with now.

The woman moved up my driveway and I looked over at her long face. "Hello."

"She died! My mama died!" Her shoulders slouched and she started crying hard. "I didn't even get to talk to her before she died. I tried to get to her but I couldn't."

I never felt so bad in my life. I just knew there was no way I could deny this woman the twenty-two dollars she needed to go and see her mother before she was buried.

I sighed. "What's your name?"

"Hattie. Hattie Woods," she said between sniffles.

"Where is your mom, Hattie?" I asked like I had just found a child who had been wandering around a store lost and crying because she couldn't find her mother.

"She's in St. Louis. I need to catch the Greyhound."

I could tell Tamara was touched as well. "Mama, you want me to call Greyhound?"

I nodded. "Yeah, go find the phone book." I reached for the last bag. "Hattie, come on in."

"You want me to help with your bags?"

I shook my head. "No, this is the last one." We walked into the house together, and I told her to have a seat on the couch while we found the phone book.

"I'm so sorry to bother you, but I just want to get to

see my mama. I've got a little money but not enough to get down there and eat on."

"Do you have any family?" I asked as I sat on the loveseat across from her.

"I have two brothers. They're married with their own families."

"Can't they send you the money?"

She started crying again. "They said they don't have any money to be sending me."

I pursed my lips trying to keep my anger at bay. I felt so sorry for this pitiful woman.

"I am schizophrenic, so I take medicine."

I had figured as much. "You can't keep wandering the streets of this neighborhood begging. You're going to end up in jail or worse."

She nodded like an obedient child.

Tamara brought me the phone book, and I looked up the phone number to Greyhound and dialed. As I listened to the recording I shared the information.

"The bus cost thirty dollars and ninety-three cents."

She nodded.

"There is one leaving at nine twenty-five tomorrow morning."

She nodded fast. "I've got to be on the bus. I got to see my mama."

I was quiet trying to think what to do. "Okay, how much do you still need?"

"I need twenty-two dollars. That way I can eat while I'm there."

Tamara came back carrying a box of Kleenex. A good thing because Hattie was snotting all over the place.

"Do you have any friends in Columbia?"

She shook her head and tried to keep her tears from

resurfacing. "If I had friends I would have borrowed the money from them."

"How long have you been in Columbia?"

She blew her nose before answering. "Five months. I was so tired of St. Louis I thought this would be a nice place to start over."

I gave her a comforting smile. "Maybe you need to think about going back home. You're struggling so hard here."

She nodded. "I might take your advice. It's been hard for me to make ends meet. I don't have enough food or money."

I remembered the time she had asked for food and money and I had turned her away and felt sick to my stomach.

She blew her nose and started crying some more. "All I wanted to do was go and see my mama but I couldn't make it!" she cried.

I felt so bad because if I had given her the money she might have made it in time to say good-bye. I tried to think of something to say. I've never been the most sensitive person in the world.

"When was the last time you spoke to your mother?"

She dabbed her eyes with the Kleenex. "Last Friday. And she was fine. She didn't complain about anything."

"That's how you need to remember her. We're all on this earth for a short period of time. When God says it's our time, it's our time. Just think, she's in a better place right now."

She nodded.

"Remember she loved you and hold that dear to your heart."

Hattie started crying again.

"Let me take you home and then I'll run and get some money for you." I rose and moved around to where she was sitting on the couch.

"Thank you. Nobody else wants to help me, but you always do."

She rose and was still bawling.

My heart broke. "Come here." I moved forward and embraced her. Tamara was standing to the side in awe. I guess she wasn't used to seeing this side of me. I couldn't help it, but this woman could be my mother.

"Now quit crying. I'm going to get you to your mama." I pulled back. "Do you have a ride to the bus station?"

She nodded. "My neighbor Melody will take me."

"You sure? Because I leave at seven and I can drop you off."

She shook her head. "She'll take me. I'm going to be there at eight o'clock even if I have to walk. I'm not missing that bus."

I gave her a weak smile, trying my damndest not to cry right along with her. "Come on, let's go." I draped an arm around her shoulders and showed her to the door. We climbed into my car and I drove her around the block to her duplex.

"You want to come in?" she asked.

"I'll come in when I get back with your money."

"Okay. I will give you your money back when I get my check on the first."

I patted her arm touched by the gesture. "Don't worry about it. Keep your money."

"You're so kind. My caseworker took me today to go and get my medicines and she tried to help me get the money. She took me to the voluntary action center, but they said I have already used up all my resources with them helping me with my utilities."

I kept my comment to myself, but if her caseworker was any kind of woman she would have just taken her own money and bought the ticket her damn self. "Don't worry. I'll be back with your money in a few minutes."

Hattie nodded, then climbed out of the car. I waited until she was inside before I pulled off and headed to the bank. I had barely made it to the corner when the tears started running down my face. It was so sad. I thought about all the times I had turned that poor woman away.

I picked up the phone and called Kayla. She immediately sensed something was wrong. "Renee, what's wrong with you?"

"Girl, I'm sitting in my car crying about this woman up the street."

"The one who begs all the time?"

I had told her about the money and sanitary napkins. "Yeah, she is so pitiful. I had a chance to really talk to her and she's no more crazy than my mom. She's just a nice woman who has a mental illness." I told her everything that had happened in the last twenty-four hours and kept having to stop and start over because I was crying so hard. All she wanted was to see her mother before she had died, and no one would help her. What had the world become? Suddenly me having HIV wasn't anywhere near as important as helping this woman.

"It's a shame," Kayla said with a sigh of despair.

"Yeah, I'm on my way to the bank to get her thirty dollars to buy her ticket."

"That's nice of you."

"Anyway, I didn't want anything, I just needed a shoulder to cry on."

"Anytime."

I hung up and made myself stop crying. *You're helping her now.*

A few minutes later I was back at her duplex and found Hattie sitting out on the porch waiting. As soon as she saw me, she rose and opened the door.

"Come on in."

I stepped into her apartment. It was so poor I had to make myself not cry. There was a beat-up couch and a coffee table in the living room.

"You can have anything you want," she said, offering me any of her worldly possessions for my kindness. There was no way I could take anything from this woman even if she did have anything of value.

"I started packing this morning." She signaled for me to follow her into her room. We moved through the kitchen. Dirty dishes were piled high in the sink. Canned goods with generic labels were on a small wooden kitchen table that had no chairs.

I stepped into her room and saw the twin-size bed and the small black-and-white television on top of a dresser that was missing a couple of drawers. In the middle of the floor was a suitcase that was almost full, and next to it was a large black garbage bag.

"You're taking that bag with you?"

She looked concerned. "Yeah, I don't have anything else. My suitcase is almost full."

I was thinking about maybe giving her one of mine. "Is someone picking you up from the bus station?"

She nodded. "My brother will."

She looked like she was waiting anxiously for something. Oh shit! I hadn't given her the money yet. I reached into my pocket and pulled out thirty-three dollars and handed it to her.

Her eyes grew large. "Oh thank You, Jesus! Thank You. Now I can eat! Now I can eat and won't have to ask my family for nothing!" She raised her palms toward the ceiling and said a silent prayer. I wish my kids got that excited when I gave them their allowance.

"I don't know how I'll ever repay you."

"Don't worry about it. You just get down there and see your mother." We moved back into the living room. "Please call me if you need anything."

"You've done more than enough. I won't call unless I just have to."

She handed me a disconnection notice from the electric company to write my number on. I knew what it was because I had one just like it at home. Mine was because I had been too lazy to mail the check. Hers was because she didn't have the money to pay it.

"Write your number big so I can see it."

I wrote my name and phone number in big block letters and had her read it for me. She saw it just fine.

"Do you think you're coming back?"

She shrugged. "I don't know. I'm going to take all my clothes and see what happens when I get there. There's nothing important here so I can just leave it."

"You got all your medicines?"

"Yes." She rose and moved to the kitchen. "Come see."

I followed her back into the kitchen and found six different bottles on the table. I glanced down at several that I knew my mama took. "You're diabetic?"

She nodded, then moved to the refrigerator and showed me her insulin.

"My dog's diabetic."

She found that funny. I laughed with her, then moved back into the living room.

"You know, my mom is schizophrenic, so I understand. You remind me so much of her."

"What's her name?"

"Bernice Brown."

Her eyes lit up. "I know her."

"You do?" She'd only been here five months, so there was no way she knew my mother.

"Yeah, I know her. I just saw her."

My mind was racing and I wasn't sure what to believe. After all, this woman was crazy. "When . . . when did you see my mother?"

"I just saw her a couple of weeks ago."

My knees buckled. My mother had been missing for years, yet this crazy woman said she just saw her. "Where did you see her at?"

"At the center."

"What center?"

"At Nyra Recreational Center. The van picks me up every Wednesday. We do crafts and have classes on taking control of our mental illnesses."

My heart was pounding rapidly. I wasn't sure if she was telling the truth or not.

"You look like her, except she has a bigger gap between her two front teeth."

She *did* know my mother. Bernice was known for her wide, gappy smile.

"When . . . when was the last time you . . . uh . . . saw my mother?" I was so nervous I couldn't even talk straight.

"Let me see. I think it was probably three weeks ago. Once a month we have a birthday bash at the community center in honor of everybody who has birthdays that month. And your mom was there because I remember her standing up and being recognized for her birthday."

Ohmygoodness. I couldn't breathe. It was June. My mama was born in May. I tried my damndest not to get overly excited because all I would do was set myself up for disappointment.

"When does the center meet?"

"Every day, but I go on Wednesdays. We have crafts and they make us lunch and have other activities."

I nodded, then rose. I desperately needed to be alone so that I could think. "Hattie, if you need anything else, please call me."

"Thank you so much. I'm going to finish packing tonight and have Melody drop me off at eight o'clock. I'll call you to let you know that I made it safely."

"I'd like that." I hugged her again, then headed out the door and climbed in my car. I only lived around the block, but it felt like eternity. I was shaking so hard I don't know how I managed to drive at all. By the time I pulled into my driveway my teeth were chattering. I couldn't believe it. I had found my mother.

I went in the room, buried myself in a pillow and cried like a baby.

52

Renee

I got up on Monday and called the clinic. I was shaking so hard I didn't know what to do. I gave her my name and number and waited for the nurse to return to the phone.

"Ms. Moore?"

"Yes?" I croaked.

"You'll need to come in and retake the test."

"What? Why?" I could barely get the words out.

"Something was wrong with the specimen we took. You'll have to come back in."

What the fuck? I've been agonizing now for the last five days just so this bitch could tell me I've got to go through the bullshit again? Hell nah!

"When would you like to come back in?"

I suddenly became sick with another thought. What if the test had come back, and instead of telling me my results were positive, this was their way of double-checking before breaking the bad news? Oh. My. God.

I dropped the phone and barely made it to the bathroom before I started throwing up. I heard someone at the door and tried to ignore it, but whoever was out on the porch was insistent because they kept right on ringing my damn doorbell. I moved to the window and spotted Danielle.

Surprisingly, I was glad to see her. Anything to take my mind off shit.

"What's wrong with you?" she asked only seconds after stepping inside my house.

"I'm about to lose my mind," I said, then collapsed to my knees and started bawling. I just couldn't hold it any longer. Danielle rushed to my side.

"Girl, what the hell is wrong with you?"

"John . . . has . . . H . . . I . . . V," I cried hysterically.

"What? When did you . . ." Her voice trailed off and I knew I'd caught her off guard. "Jesus! That DL shit done caught up with him."

My chest was starting to hurt. "He . . . he didn't get it from Shemar."

"Then who . . ." Her voice trailed off again and I knew it had registered, the most likely suspect—me.

I reached for a tissue and wiped my nose, then forced myself to calm down and take a deep breath. "Me. Maybe. I don't know. I went down last week and took the test, but something happened with the blood so I've got to go back and take it again."

"Oh, Nae-Nae, why didn't you tell me? I would have gone down there with you." She stroked my back.

I gave a defeated shrug. "I was too embarrassed to say anything. I just wanted the ordeal done and over with. Now I got to go back down to the clinic tomorrow."

"Fine, then I'm going with you and taking the test. Hell, it's been a year since I've been tested. Might as well get it over with."

I pulled my legs up to my chest. "Danny, this is so unreal. I never thought something like this could happen to me."

"None of us do. We put our lives at risk each and every time we lay down with a man. It's a damn shame. I just never really thought about it until now."

I shook my head. "I've been a ho for years, so this would have to be God's way of getting back at me for my wicked ways."

"He wouldn't do that," she stated firmly. "Everything is going to be fine, watch and see."

"I hope so."

"Quit worrying. What we need is a girls' night to take your mind off things. How about a slumber party?"

I gave her a weak smile. "That sounds like fun. We haven't done that in months."

"Then a slumber party it is." She moved to the phone to call my girls.

I got rid of my kids for the evening and waited for the girls to arrive. I pushed back all the furniture in the living room and got the blender ready for margaritas.

I put my sister's picture on the table. Lisa was the glue that always held us together. So if we're having a get-together, her presence and wisdom were definitely needed. I wished she was here because one thing my big sister always did was find a way to cheer me up. *Damn, now I'm crying again!* I brushed the tears away, then moved into the kitchen to find the popcorn.

The doorbell rang and they filed in one after another with hugs and words of wisdom. Danielle had definitely made sure they all knew what I was up against.

Kayla gave me a big hug. "Renee, I'm going down there with you tomorrow and take that test."

"Me, too," Nadine chimed in.

"We're all going to take that test. There is no reason you need to go through this alone." Danielle poured ice into the blender and frowned. "Let me get my hands on John's ass and I'll kill him myself, putting you through this shit."

I shook my head. "If I got it, then he got it from me."

"Well, we're not going to worry about that now, are we?" Nadine took my hand and smiled. "I've got some good news."

I sighed with relief. "Thank God! Because we can sho use it."

"Jordan's having twins."

We all screamed with excitement.

Kayla clapped her hands. "That is wonderful! I can't wait to hold them. I know they're going to be beautiful."

I looked over at Danielle and smirked. "Of course they are. Their daddy is one fine mothafucka."

Danielle rolled her eyes. "That crazy bastard. I hope you don't plan to let him be a part of the baby's life. Hell, he doesn't take care of the son he has."

Nadine removed the glasses from the top shelf and shook her head. "No way. That was part of the contract agreement."

"Good," Danielle said with a sigh of relief.

I poured the tequila in and added the mix. "Is he still stalking you?"

"Girl, yeah. I went and got an ex parte but I still see him popping up all the time. That's one I'll never be able to get rid of."

"You can if you really want to."

"That's the problem. I think about Calvin all the time, yet I miss Chance. I don't understand it."

I do. She's stuck on stupid. That fool is crazy. "Can't

nobody tell you when enough is enough. You have to decide that on your own. I just hope it's before he pops that head." I turned to her. "Are you still receiving those notes?"

"Yep. I got one last week."

Kayla gave us a puzzled look. "What notes?"

Danielle briefly told them about the notes she had been receiving.

Kayla turned to me. "Are you still getting the calls?"

I shook my head. "I haven't received one in almost a week now."

"Maybe whoever it was got the hint."

"I sure hope so." But I wasn't going to get my hopes up.

Danielle turned on the blender. I got the straws from the pantry and put them in the glasses. As soon as she had them all full, we carried our drinks into the family room and flopped down on our sleeping bags.

"Well, we have a month before Kayla's wedding and Portia's due any day now. Here's to new families," Danielle said and we all clicked our glasses together.

"Speaking of families, how are you and Portia getting along?" Nadine asked between sips.

"Fine, actually. I think we're going to be able to get past all that and start over."

Kayla smiled. "I'm glad to hear that."

"So am I, because I can't wait to hold that little baby," I said.

Danielle beamed with pride. "Neither can I. It's funny. I was so upset when I first found out she was pregnant, but now I'm so excited I don't know what to do."

"That's the way it works sometimes. Quinton and Kenny's daughter are still together, so I guess I don't have any choice but to learn to accept her ass."

"We can't pick the girls our sons choose," Nadine said from experience. Her son was dating a girl who had recently been arrested for shoplifting.

I scowled at the thought. "Yeah, I know, but it doesn't mean we have to like it."

"No, but if you want to have any kind of relationship with him then you're going to have to get over it. One day she might have kids, and I know you want a relationship with your grandbabies."

I had to smile at that. "I think I'll be a wonderful grandmother."

"Just remember that Kenny and Reese will be the grandparents as well," Danielle teased.

I tossed a throw pillow at her. "Thanks a lot."

We all started laughing and for the rest of the night I forgot all about my problems.

53

Renee

Three days later, I couldn't stop watching the clock. Another hour and I could finally call for my results.

I dropped down on the floor beside my bed and said one final prayer. "Lord, please forgive me for my wicked ways. I promise if You give me a second chance I'll make You proud." I choked back tears in my throat. "Lisa, please talk to Him for me." The last half hour I'd worried myself so sick that I had to throw up. I've been doing that a lot lately.

The results meant the start or end of my life. I was losing my mind, and the sooner it was over the better.

"I'm not about to let this condition dictate the future of my life. It's what I have, not who I am."

At two, I finally reached for the phone and was shaking so bad it took three tries before I was able to dial the correct number. When she answered, I gave her my PIN number and waited while she went to retrieve my file. I said one final prayer and had just finished when she got back on the line.

"Ms. Moore?"

"Yes?" I croaked.

"Your results were negative."

Negative. "Oh God! Thank You!" I didn't hear anything else after that.

I finally had my life back again. I dropped to my knees and cried tears of joy. "Thank You, Lord. Thank You."

I sat there for the longest time, feeling so good. Thinking about all the years I put my life in someone else's hands and how stupid I had been.

Never again.

This was the start of a new beginning for me. *I am going to stand by my word and start making smart choices.*

I'll admit I love Kenny. He's a sweet, considerate man, but I know that he is not the man for me. All that sneaking around with someone else's man is for the birds. Reese can have his skinny ass. I'll be damned if I'm getting up in the middle of the night to make his ass some Kool-Aid or even rub his damn back and stroke his receding hairline. No, that shit would start to get on my damn nerves after a while. I care about him, but now that my eyes are wide open, I know for a fact I don't need a man to be happy. All those days of being in love with the idea of being in love—they are behind me. I have so many possibilities. Happiness is what we make it, and I was already planning some private *me* time. I need to learn to be happy with myself before I can be happy sharing my life with someone else.

Rolling onto my back, I folded my arms behind my head and stared up at the ceiling. Everything was going to be okay.

The phone rang and I was tempted to ignore it and just continue to enjoy the moment, but whoever was calling was persistent because they called right back. I reached over and dug for my cell phone at the bottom of my purse and saw it was Danielle.

"Girl, get your ass to the hospital. Portia's in labor."

I almost had two accidents trying to get to the hospital. Why is it whenever you're in a rush everybody wants to take their sweet-ass time? I had road rage. I yelled "Get the fuck out the way!" out the window so many times I was surprised I didn't burst a blood vessel. The hospital wasn't any better. I circled around the parking lot three times before someone in a Nissan Altima pulled out.

I raced through the hospital and waited impatiently for the elevator, which finally arrived, and this familiar-looking woman rode up with me. It wasn't until we got to the seventh floor that I realized the woman was the same lady that I got into it with at Tamara's school. I looked up and caught her staring at me from the tops of her eyes.

"Can I help you with something?"

She had the nerve to look around like she had no idea who I was talking to. "Nope."

"Then quit looking at me. I know I look good." I got off the elevator and swayed my ass down the hall like I was the shit. Hell, I had a lot to feel good about.

I turned at the corner and was surprised to see Calvin.

"What are you doing here?"

He gave me a small smile. "My mom is in the hospital."

"Is she okay?"

He nodded. "She fell and fractured her hip, but I think she's going to survive."

"Good." I touched his arm, trying to offer some comfort.

"What are you doing here?"

"Portia's in labor."

His eyes grew round with excitement. "Danielle here?"

He still had it bad for my girl. "Yep. Why don't you come down and say hi?"

He was a little reluctant, so I took his hand and led the way. We passed that crazy-ass woman. She was standing at the end of the hall watching. Calvin noticed her also and shook his head.

"You know her?"

He looked uncomfortable. "Yeah, you can say that. Her name is Regina Tolliver. She's the administrative assistant in my department. I made the mistake of dating her."

"What? You must have been desperate."

"Nah. She is a really nice woman, just a little clingy. Our second date she wanted me to see the wedding dress she planned to wear."

"Hell nah!" I was still laughing as we went down to Labor and Delivery. The nurse at the station said Portia was in room 712. Calvin decided to hang out in the waiting room. I stepped into the room and Danny's mom Victoria was there, and Danny. Portia was in the bed breathing through a contraction. As soon as it eased, I went over and wiped the sweat from her brow.

"I hear someone is about to be a mother?"

She gave me a weak grin and closed her eyes. I moved and hugged Victoria, who had always been like a mother to me.

"I'm going to get a soda. Try to help Danielle relax." She grabbed her purse and moved down the hall.

Danielle did look like she was about to pull her hair

out. You would think after working as a labor and delivery nurse for years, she would be used to this shit.

"Girl, go smoke a joint or something."

I managed to get a laugh out of her. "This shit is crazy. My baby is having a baby."

"I know." The monitor read she was about to have another contraction. The two of us helped her breathe through it, then Portia closed her eyes again.

"Where's her baby's daddy?"

"He went to a basketball tournament. I just got in touch with his mother, and she is driving down to Springfield to get him."

Good. I think every man should see what women go through bringing a child into the world.

Danielle was pacing nervously around the room. "How long is it gonna take before the anesthesiologist gets here?"

"What she getting, an epidural?"

"Yep, and the rate they're going, it will be too late by the time they get here."

"Why don't you go check and on your way back stop by the waiting room? Someone's here to see you."

Danielle's brow rose. "Who?"

"Calvin."

I saw the way her eyes grew round with excitement before she left the room. I don't care what that girl says, she wants Calvin back. Now she just needs to get rid of that psycho.

54

Danielle

After one of the nurses assured me that someone was on their way up to ease my daughter's pain, I walked down to the waiting room and found Calvin sitting and watching television.

"Hey, you."

"Hey, yourself." He rose and walked over to me and I found myself meeting him halfway.

It had been three months since I had last seen him, and I couldn't stop looking at him. He looked so good. "What are you doing here?"

"My mom is in the hospital."

While he told me what was going on I couldn't take my eyes off him. Why did I ever let him go?

"Doctor thinks she'll be home before the weekend."

I nodded. "Good. Make sure you tell her I said hello."

"I will." I'd had dinner with his parents once and adored the couple.

We just stood there staring and grinning at each other.

"Ready to be a grandmother?" he teased.

"Don't have much of a choice, now do I?"

"No, but hopefully this means you and Portia have put aside your differences."

"I think we have."

"Good." He took my hand in his. I took a step closer, just wanting to be near him.

"Well, I better go because I'm working the night shift this week and need to get some rest. I'll drop by tomorrow and check on Portia."

"She would like that." *And so would I.*

I watched him leave and knew then I was going to do whatever it took to get Calvin back.

As I walked back to the room, I looked down at my cell phone, which I had put on vibrate, and noticed that I had five missed calls. All of them were from Chance. Psycho. I knew I better call him back or he'd never stop.

"Why the fuck you haven't been answering your phone?"

"Because I'm at the hospital with Portia. She's in labor."

"I hope you ain't with some other nigga."

I rolled my eyes. Did he not hear what I said? "I just said my daughter was in labor."

"You must think I'm stupid. You and your daughter don't even speak to each other."

"I had a change of heart. She is my daughter."

"And I'm your man and I need you to quit playing games."

He is crazy. I put an ex parte on him yet he still thinks he's my man. I don't know why I never noticed before how selfish Chance was. All he cared about was himself. "Chance, my daughter needs me. You and I are over."

"Oh, so it's like that?"

"Yeah, it's like that. Leave me the hell alone, otherwise I'm going to have my brother pay you a visit."

That time, he actually hung up on me.

Portia's labor was long. She had finally gotten her epidural but it seemed to slow down her delivery. By midnight I sent Mama home after I promised to call her the moment her great-granddaughter was born. Portia had dilated seven centimeters by the time Demetrius got there. He and his mother and Renee and I took turns helping Portia breathe, and finally at four a.m. Etienne Charice Carlson was born, all six pounds and twelve ounces.

I couldn't stop looking at my granddaughter. She was so beautiful to me with a head full of curly hair. She looked like Portia.

"Congratulations, Grandma, I'm going home to bed." Renee gave me a big hug, went over and kissed Portia, and exited the room.

While Demetrius and his mother stood and watched the nurses take the baby's vital signs, I moved over to Portia and stroked her forehead.

"How's my baby?" she whispered.

"Fine."

"What's she look like?"

Leaning down, I kissed her forehead. "She's beautiful, just like you. I'm so proud of you."

She started crying. "Mama, I'm so glad you're no longer mad at me."

"That's in the past, baby. It's time for us to move on and raise that little girl together."

"I love you, Mama."

"I love you, too." Tears were now running down my face, but they were tears of joy.

It was after eight when I got home. I immediately climbed under the covers and was just dozing off when the phone started ringing. It didn't take a rocket scientist to know it was Chance.

"Quit calling me!"

"Ms. Danielle Brooks?" I heard a woman say just as I was about to slam the phone down.

"Yes, who's calling?"

"This is Dr. Teresa Weber at the health department."

I was suddenly wide awake. "What can I do for you?"

"I need for you to come in and talk to us."

"About what?" My heart started pounding heavily.

There was a slight hesitation, but it was just enough to make me drop to the floor.

"I'm sorry to be the bearer of bad news . . . but you tested positive for HIV."

55

Danielle

My heart literally stopped beating. There was no way in hell she said what I thought she said.

"Excuse me?"

"I'm so sorry, Ms. Brooks."

"You've got my results confused with someone else, because there is no way I was HIV positive."

"I'd really like to start you on a medication regime right away. When can you come in?"

"Did I stutter? I said I am not HIV positive!"

"I can understand your frustration."

Oh, so now she wants to patronize me. "No, *you* can't understand. There is some kind of mistake." Yeah, that's it. "You got my lab confused with someone else's." Yep, it happens all the time.

"No. It was your specimen. We've already retested it, but we'd be more than happy to do it again. If you would like to come back in—"

"Damn right I will, because I just got tested last year and my results were fine. As soon as I get my results back

I'm suing y'all mothafuckas." I slammed the phone down. This wasn't happening. I was breathing so hard I was hyperventilating. *This can't be happening. In fact, I know it isn't. My daughter will be coming home tomorrow with my grandbaby and we're going to start rebuilding our relationship.* I had a granddaughter to help raise, and this was not at all happening.

I walked into the living room and started blowing up balloons. To hell with sleep. My mom and dad were picking Portia up tomorrow and I needed to go over and decorate the house for their homecoming.

I reached for the scissors and my hand was shaking so bad I couldn't even cut the streamers. I dropped to my knees and the tears began to flow.

"Why?" I screamed. "Dammit, why? I know I've done a lot of things in my life, but I never expected to be punished like this!" My problems were only beginning, because now I had to figure out who infected me so I could save his life as well.

56

Renee

I arrived at Danielle's with a trunk filled with gifts. My goddaughter's baby was beautiful. I had gone to the baby store and gotten a little carried away. But I love babies as long as they're not mine.

I removed the bags from my trunk and moved up the driveway. Kayla's car was on the street. The door was open and I walked in to find Kayla on the floor rocking Danielle in her arms. I dropped my bags.

"What's wrong?"

Kayla looked over at me and shook her head. "I don't know. I can't get Danielle to stop crying long enough to tell me."

I moved over to where the two of them were sitting and had a seat. "Danny, honey, is something wrong with Portia or the baby?" I was so afraid of what she might say.

She shook her head and kept on crying. She was scaring me. I don't remember the last time she cried this hard.

"Danny, you got to tell us what's wrong so we can help you."

Kayla agreed as she rubbed Danielle's back soothingly while trying to get her to calm down.

Danielle started screaming at the top of her lungs. Kayla tried to shake her. I walked up to her and slapped her hard.

"Danny, snap out of it!" She dropped to the floor and was bawling like crazy. I moved over to her and held her in my arms. "Danny, you're scaring me. Please tell us what's wrong."

She tried to stop crying long enough to tell us. "I got H . . . II . . . IV."

"What?" I looked over at Kayla and we were both stunned. *Dear God, when I asked You to make my test negative, I didn't mean for You to give it to my best friend.*

Danielle struggled free and rose. Her chest was heaving hard. "I'm a nurse, dammit! I know 'bout condoms and venereal diseases. I work on a floor with women who have to have caesarean sections because they have herpes on their damn pussies. I know all about HIV and how it's contracted. Yet my stupid ass put my life in a hand of some worthless-ass nigga. I trusted him."

Kayla tried her best to make it better. "It's not your fault."

"Yes, it is! I fucked up. I knew the risks. I could have said no or went and reached for a condom in my drawer, but I didn't. Now look at me. I've got HIV! HIV! My life is ruined." She collapsed on the floor and started bawling again.

I ran over to her and held her close. This could have been me. I could have HIV, but instead it was my best friend. Her pain is my pain.

"Why, Nae-Nae?" she wailed. "*Whyyyyyy!*"

"I don't know, Danny. I really don't. Things happen for a reason."

She started screaming and beating me against the chest.

"Go ahead and let it out. Once you do that we can all work on saving your life. Because you're not going anywhere. You hear me? Nowhere!" I was crying and snotting right along with her.

Danielle finally wore herself out. Kayla came over and said a prayer, and afterward the three of us cried together. I was feeling everything she was going through because a couple of days ago that had been me. Scared and worried if I was going to live long enough to see my grandchildren.

I called her parents and told Victoria we'd be late getting to her house. She was concerned and tried to ask questions, but I told her Danielle would tell her later.

The doorbell rang. I knew it was Nadine and Jordan. Right now was not the time for sharing with anyone outside our circle. Kayla went out, and while she talked to them, I continued to hold my best friend until she didn't have any tears left.

"Nae, wha . . . wha . . . what am I going to do?" she heaved.

"You're going to live."

57

Danielle

I finally got myself together enough to go over to my parents'. Portia and the baby came home, and for the next couple of hours I forgot all about what the doctor said and enjoyed the most important people in the world to me. It was a wonderful evening. I felt good until Portia went up to rest and took the baby with her. It was then I realized I just might not be around long enough to watch her grow up.

Renee and Kayla sat on the couch and held my hands while I broke the news to my parents. My mom broke down and started crying, and my father tried his hardest to hold himself together. I had the two of them promise not to tell Portia. I wanted to wait and tell her when I thought she was ready.

I don't remember saying good-bye or Renee driving back to my house. All I could think about was what the doctor had told me. *You tested positive for HIV*.

Kayla carried in a cup of hot tea that she promised would make me feel better. I laughed when she said that.

Yeah, right. It's going to take my HIV away. But I took it anyway and sipped while I was thinking.

Renee walked back into the room to tell me Nadine was on her way over.

I sat up straight on the couch. "I've got to inform all my partners."

Renee scowled as she took a seat beside me. "There is plenty of time for that later."

I shook my head. "No, I've got to tell Ron, Chance, and Calvin."

"Shit, for all we know one of them mothafuckas is how you contracted the shit."

"It doesn't matter. I still have to tell them." I put the mug down. "Kayla, hand me my phone."

She gave me a skeptical look. "Danny, can't you wait a couple of days?"

"No! They could be infecting someone else right now. I could never live with myself if that happened. I have to tell them I'm infected and there's a chance that they might have it, too!"

She nodded and handed me the cordless phone. I just wanted to get this ordeal over. I called Calvin and got his voice mail. I spoke to Nita and told her how vital it was I spoke to Ron. She said she would give him the message, but I know I'll have to track him down myself. Chance was the only one who answered.

"I knew you would come to your senses. Baby girl, I'll be right over."

I hung up the phone and finished my tea.

Kayla squeezed my hand. "Etienne is beautiful."

I was proud. "She is, isn't she?"

"And with all of these godmothers she's going to be spoiled rotten!" Renee added with a laugh.

The three of us talked until Nadine arrived and they let

me break the news to her in private. She and I cried together. I guess I must be getting used to the idea, because I didn't cry as much—or maybe I'm just all cried out for the day.

The doorbell rang and I knew it was Chance. Nadine went in the kitchen with the others so I could break the news to him in private. I took a deep breath, then moved over to the door and opened it.

"Whassup, baby girl?" He flashed that sexy grin, then pulled me into a bear hug. It felt so good to be held by him. Maybe, just maybe, since he loves me so much, he'll stick by me and see me through my illness.

Feeling hopeful, I took his hand and had him follow me over to the couch where we took a seat.

"Okay, hold up . . . Let me talk first." Chance got down on his knee in front of me and took my hand.

"Chance, please—"

He cut me off. "No, baby girl, let yo man speak." He took a deep breath. "I know I've been acting a fool and not being honest with you about my life, and I'm sorry. I'm really sorry. I promise to do better. I know I be acting jealous and shit, but that's because I can't imagine sharing what I have with you. What I'm trying to say is if you give me a second chance, I promise to be a better man. Hell, I'll even take counseling. All I ask is that we do this together as man and wife," he pleaded.

Tears flooded my eyes because I knew that wasn't easy for him to do. "Chance, please, get up and have a seat." He looked confused as he moved beside me. "I need to tell you something."

He really looked at me for the first time since he entered my house. I'm sure my eyes were red and swollen shut. "What, baby girl? You're scaring me."

I took his hands in mine and dropped my head. "Chance, I got a call from the doctor yesterday."

"Yeah?"

I exhaled deeply. *Don't cry, just breathe.* "I'm HIV positive."

He sat still for so long, I thought maybe he stopped breathing. Tears started streaming down his face. *Oh my goodness, he does love me.* Tears flooded my eyes and I wiped them away. "Baby, say something."

Then his face changed. I've seen that rage and anger before. I knew what was coming next, but I was too stunned to move.

"You stupid bitch!" He drew back and punched me in the head, and I fell onto the floor. "How the hell you gonna put my life at risk like that? I need this dick to make my money, and now you're taking that shit away!" He started kicking me in the stomach and head, and I screamed and rolled up in a fetal position. I couldn't fight and didn't want to because I deserved what was happening to me. He kicked me again and would have kept on if the girls hadn't come running into the room screaming. I heard a thump and he fell onto the floor. I looked up and Renee was holding my iron skillet.

"You stupid mothafucka!" she screamed and kept on hitting him until Kayla and Nadine pulled her away. "Don't nobody fuck with my sistahs!" Renee lowered onto the couch and flung that skillet, and it hit him again over the head.

"I'm calling the police!" Nadine ran over and grabbed the receiver.

Kayla rushed to my side. "You okay?"

My eye was swollen. I touched my mouth and wiped blood away and started shaking my head. I'll never be okay again.

* * *

The police came and took our statements. Since I had an ex parte on Chance, I didn't mention I asked him over. He was just starting to regain consciousness when they took him away. Kayla, Nadine, and Renee stuck around another few hours before I was able to finally get rid of them. They were my good friends, but I wanted to be alone so I could think.

I had to let Ron know my results. Even though he had dogged me out that night, it was the least I could do, especially after everything I put him through with Portia. I called his mother and left another message for him to call me. She must have heard the despair in my voice because she finally promised to go and get him for me.

While I waited, I took in the bruises on my face. I deserved every one. They weren't enough for all of the one-night stands I've had. While standing at the mirror, I felt different. On the outside I was the same person, minus the bruises and the black eye, but on the inside I had changed. Mostly it was the way I now felt about myself. Right now, it was overwhelming emptiness.

It was after five when my cell phone rang. I ran over and noticed the number had been blocked.

"Whassup, you called?" It was Ron. *Oh shit! Oh shit! Oh shit! Oh shit! Oh shit!*

"Ron . . . I'm HIV positive."

Silence. Dead silence.

"Ron, did you hear what I said?"

It sounded like he was smoking a cigarette. "Yeah, I heard."

"You heard?" How could he possibly be so calm? Unless . . . *Oh dear God!*

"Did you get the notes I left you? Ya know . . . be careful of the company you keep?"

I could barely speak. "Yes."

"Welcome to AIDS, *bi-aaatchhh*!" he shrieked and started laughing before the phone went dead.

I dropped the phone. My knees gave out and I sank onto the floor, too stunned for words. I must have sat there an hour before the tears started again, and they didn't stop until the sun rose the next morning. By then I ran out of tears, which was a good thing because I was so tired. I went to sleep and kept on sleeping. I heard knocks at the door and I ignored them. I was living on a tropical island with my daughter and Etienne and we were so happy. I was HIV free.

Someone was in my house. I could hear them but I ignored all the voices—Renee, Kayla, Mama—and just kept on sleeping. The only thing that finally got me up was that I had to pee, bad. I rose and felt every bruise on my body as I carried myself to the bathroom to relieve myself. I didn't dare look in the mirror. Instead I washed my face and brushed my teeth, then moved back to my room. There was a knock at my door.

"Come in," I mumbled. I wished they would all just go and leave me alone.

"Hey, you."

I turned my head to look at Calvin standing in the doorway. "Hi."

He strolled into the room. "My God! What happened to you?" He rushed to my side and helped me back down onto the bed. "Look at me, Danielle. What's going on with you? I had to work a double yesterday. As soon as I got your message I rushed over."

I stared up into his handsome face and prayed that I hadn't infected this wonderful man. *Please, Lord. Not Calvin.* The tears started again. I didn't know I had any left.

"Baby, please tell me what's wrong," he pleaded.

I took his hands in mine and prayed that the girls got upstairs in time to save me from another beating. Then again, maybe I deserved to die.

"Calvin . . . I'm so sorry. I . . . I . . . I'm HIV positive."

His eyes grew large. "What?"

My bottom lip quivered. "I'm so so sorry. I just found out and wanted to tell you right away so you could get tested."

He raked a hand across his face and rose, then moved over to stare out the window.

"Y-you have every right to hate me. I-I've put you through more than any man should have to go through. And I'm sorry. I truly am sorry. Go ahead and hate me."

He swung around so fast, I jumped. "Would you be quiet!" He returned to his seat. "How could I ever hate you? I love you, Danielle. I've been in love with you for almost a year, and you being HIV positive is not going to change that." He paused to take a deep breath.

"But I put you at risk."

"When we first started dating, did you know you were HIV positive?"

I wiped my cheek and shook my head. "No."

"Then you didn't put my life at risk. I did that myself, and if I've been infected then that is something I will have to deal with. The only thing that matters right now is how you are feeling."

I started crying hard again. I didn't deserve his friendship.

"Danielle, I love you. I want to be your husband in sickness and in health. If you'll have me."

I started shaking my head. "I couldn't do that to you."

"The only thing you can do is break my heart by saying no." He dropped down on his knees, reached into his pocket, and pulled out a small black box and opened it. My eyes were blurry from tears so I couldn't see anything but sparkle.

"Danielle Brooks, will you marry me? Together we can conquer anything."

I looked up at the door and saw Renee, Danielle, Nadine, Portia, and Mama holding my grandbaby. All were standing there nodding.

I returned my attention to Calvin, who was trying to be strong and not cry, but a single tear rolled down his cheek. It was then that I realized how much I loved him as well. And I planned to spend the rest of my life showing him.

"Yes, I'll marry you." I dropped into his arms and he cradled me close.

My family started screaming and clapping as I sealed my decision with a kiss. I knew it wasn't going to be easy, but with all of them surrounding me, I was going to survive.

58
Renee

Wednesday I went to Nyra Recreational Center looking for my mother. I hung around all day until one of the workers came up to see if she could help me. I guess since I'm not crazy I stuck out like a sore thumb.

"Can I help you?" she asked.

I looked into her kind chocolate face. "I was trying to see if my mother was here."

"Who's your mother?" Her badge said program director.

"Bernice Brown."

She frowned. "That name doesn't sound familiar, but I can check our database."

I sat around watching the mentally ill playing Ping-Pong and doing arts and crafts activities at a nearby table.

"I'm sorry, but we haven't had anyone by that name. I checked the computer. Every participant has to register to attend our services here and they have to sign in during each and every visit."

"What about Hattie Woods?"

He eyes lit up with recognition. "Oh yeah, Hattie is a regular here. Although we haven't seen her in two weeks."

"That's because her mother died and she went to St. Louis for her funeral."

Her brow rose. "Hattie's mother died when she was a kid. It was a traumatic experience because Hattie was spending the summer with her grandmother when she passed away. By the time she got home her mother had already been buried."

All hope swept from my body.

"Schizophrenics have moments when they believe something is happening that really isn't. If she told you her mother had just died then she was reliving that time in her life. It's really sad because they sound so convincing. Unless you know better, you believe them."

I left the building and felt like crying. I had gotten my hopes up. Despite everything I do and say, I really did want to see my mama again, but it didn't seem like that was going to happen until she was ready to come back home.

I drove home and spotted Hattie walking up the street. She stopped and waved when she saw me. "Hey, Hattie. What are you doing here?"

She was smiling and seemed agitated. "I just got back."

"Oh really?"

"Yeah, they did a cremation. When I get my check I'm going to pay you back."

I shook my head. "You don't have to."

"But I want to," she said in an animated voice. "I never saw my mother look like that before. She had on a white dress and a band around her hair that looked like a halo."

I gave her a sad smile and didn't even mention that a

few seconds ago she said her mother had been cremated. "Well, I'm glad you're back."

"Me, too," she said, then waved and moved down the street. I looked in my rearview mirror and realized she didn't even have on shoes.

I drove on home and went inside my empty house. The kids wouldn't be home for hours. I had taken off work because I really believed I was going to see my mama. I reached for my photo albums in the cabinet, pulled one out, and started flipping through it, looking at her pictures and remembering the happier times. Tears started running down my face and I reached for a tissue on the coffee table and wiped my face. Mama was out there somewhere. Hopefully, someday I'll find her, and when I do, I'm going to welcome her with open arms.

My cell phone vibrated in my pocket. I reached for it, and when I saw it was John I got mad all over again.

"Hello?"

"Renee, this is John. Did you go and take your test?"

"Yep. And guess what, mothafucka, ain't shit wrong with me."

"What?" He seemed stunned by my response.

"Do I have to spell it out to your gay ass? I don't have HIV!" There was a long silence. It was so long I thought he had hung up. "Are you still there?"

"Yeah, I'm just thinking, that's all. If I didn't get it from you or Shemar, I must have contracted it from Carl."

"Who the hell is Carl?"

"A man I met online last year. Sorry about that." He hung up just as I was ready to cuss his ass out. He put me through that shit for nothing. Gay-ass mothafucka! First thing tomorrow I am getting a lawyer and divorcing his ass.

My life was starting over. I hadn't heard from Kenny.

I'm sure he's going to call me once things die down for him at home. And when he does, I plan to tell him it's over. I never felt good about messing around with a married man, and I shouldn't have ever started something that I didn't believe in, but at least I still had a chance to correct my mistake.

I put the books away. I was going by Danielle's later to see how she was doing. My heart went out to her, but now that she had Calvin back in her life, I had a good feeling that she was going to fight HIV with everything she had.

The doorbell rang. I moved to the door and looked through the peephole. What the hell? It was Regina Tolliver. The stalker who worked with Calvin. "Can I help you?"

"I need to talk to you for a moment."

I don't know what we could possibly have to say to each other, but I opened the door anyway and let her in. She stepped into my living room and started walking around like she owned the house. "You've got a nice place."

"What can I do for you?" I asked in a curt tone. I hoped her Amazon daughters weren't picking on Tamara again.

She swung around. "You know I work for the university police with Calvin?"

I nodded. "Yeah, he told me. But what's that got to do with me?"

She heaved a heavy breath. "I'm in love with him, but he swears he's in love with someone else."

"He is."

Regina pursed her thick lips. "I know, and that's a problem."

"What are you talking about?" I snapped.

"I mean, I've warned you to stay away from my man

but you don't seem to be listening, so I thought I'd come and tell you personally."

My radar went off. *This* was the bitch who'd been calling my phone.

"I asked you to quit calling my man."

"What?" *She really thinks I want Calvin.* "Honey, you got me confused. I don't want Calvin." I took a seat on the couch and gestured for her to sit as well. She didn't seem interested.

"Why are you lying? I've seen the two of you together."

I can't believe this shit. She's been harassing the wrong woman. "Girl, you've seen us talking, that's it."

"You're lying! I saw you coming out the house wearing his university sweatshirt."

Sweatshirt? Oh shit! That day I set him up at Danielle's, I came out wearing his shirt and a black Expedition was parked at the curb.

"I saw him coming to your house. You called the office and asked to speak to your boo. And at the hospital the other day your hands were all over him."

I couldn't help it, I started laughing. "Regina, you got it all wrong."

"No, I got it right." She glared at me.

"Bitch, it's time for you to go." I rose and gestured toward the door. It was then I noticed she was holding a small twenty-two in her hand. She raised it and pointed it at me. "I called you private but you ignored me. Then the other day I was in his office and saw the ring he had bought you and I knew I had to do something soon."

I shook my head. "He's seeing another woman. Not me."

"I'm his woman, not you! The only person he should love is me!"

Okay, let me try another approach. "You're right. He is your man and I'm going to go and call him right now and tell him to come over." I moved toward the phone and heard the gun click.

"Bitch, don't you dare move."

Shit, she didn't have to tell me twice. I froze and swung around with my hands in the air. "Regina, please, don't do anything stupid that you'll later regret."

"The only person who's going to have regrets is you. You want to take my man from me and I'm not having it!"

I lowered onto the couch, keeping my eyes on the gun. "Please don't kill me. I have children and family who love me," I pleaded.

"What about the man I love! Huh? What about me?"

"You can have him."

"You're just saying that so I won't shoot you." She laughed and pointed the gun at my head.

"No, it's true! It's true. You can walk out of here right now and I won't tell a soul."

"Liar!"

She was getting more agitated by the second, and the last thing I needed was for that crazy bitch to shoot my ass.

"Get down on your knees."

"Please, you don't want to do this," I pleaded.

"Now!"

I dropped down and tears started flowing because I was no longer sure I could calm her crazy ass down. I had just been given my life back and now it was about to be taken away from me again. "Please, Regina. I am truly sorry. I never realized how much you really loved him."

"I was planning to have a baby for him but I got fired this morning. Now he no longer wants me and everything is ruined. You ruined everything!"

I was shaking so hard my teeth chattered. All I wanted to do was pick up the phone and tell my kids one last time how much I loved them. The thought of never seeing them again had me so upset I peed on myself.

"I plan to shoot you in the head, then I can act like I just came over and found you like that."

I tried to stall. "Won't work. They'll find trace evidence of gunpowder on your hands."

Regina scowled and started pacing the length of the room. "Damn. You're right." She nibbled on her lips, then grinned. "Then I guess you'll have to shoot yourself."

She was cuckoo for Cocoa Puffs if she really thought I was going to kill myself. "You'll have to kill me yourself."

Laughter danced in her eyes. "No problem."

I jumped out of the way just as Regina pulled the trigger. I screamed and felt a burn at the side of my head and another at my arm, then everything went black.

59

Renee

I glanced down at my lap again at my directions, making sure I was heading the right way. My brother had moved to a new house and had invited us over for Thanksgiving weekend.

Lisa would be so proud of me.

In the last five months my life had changed so much. Quinton got a full athletic scholarship to play football for Purdue. I was so proud of him, but it was hard to get used to my son not being around. Tamara was on the honor roll again. She had started her senior year and was still a member of the National Honor Society. I couldn't complain. Both my kids were doing the damn thang.

"Mama, I think that's his house over there."

I stopped in front of a brown two-story house with a wraparound porch and put the car in park. My heart was pounding. I was so nervous.

Tamara turned to me wearing a strange look. "Mama, are we getting out?"

I wanted so badly to tell her no and put my car back in

drive and peel away from my brother's house, but I had made a promise, both to my sister and to God, that I would see this day through, and I was going to do just that.

Even if it killed me.

"Yes, we're getting out." I turned the car off. I opened the door and slowly pulled myself out of the vehicle.

"Mama, you need help?"

I shook my head. I refused to be a victim. The last five months had been a rough, long ride.

Regina had shot me in the face and arm. The main nerve in my face was damaged so the muscles on the left side of my face sag and I can't close my eye. The second bullet hit the upper left arm, so I've lost all mobility. It's totally useless. I just thank God it wasn't my right arm, otherwise I would have had to retrain myself to write. Typing with one hand was bad enough. My voice recognition software no longer worked because I slurred when I spoke and most times I slobbered as well. Despite my handicap, life was good. I had a strong support group.

Kayla is happily married to Jermaine. Nadine and Jordan are the mothers of twins, Tristan and Trinity. Danielle is taking her medicines, receiving counseling, and learning how to be a survivor. She and Calvin will be tying the knot next month and I'm her matron of honor. Calvin didn't contract the virus. Thank God! Nobody has seen Chance, not even his baby's mama. A week after Danielle discovered she was HIV positive, Ron was found floating face up in the Missouri River. All of us suspected Kee of the murder, especially after the way he went off when he found out who had infected his baby sister. But none of us would ever breathe a word of it. As far as we're concerned, he was with us that night.

"Mama, Uncle Andre's house is pretty."

I returned my mind to the present and stared up at my brother's house. It was true. Big, spacious, with over an acre of land, and high maintenance. Little brother was doing quite well, but then I wasn't surprised. I had a house twice that size while I was still married to John. Now I had something that money couldn't buy, a peace of mind and a promising future. Something that months ago was quite uncertain.

There was a Cadillac in the driveway that I knew belonged to my daddy. He'd been buying them for as long as I could remember. In front of it was Janet's sports car. She worked as a Mary Kay consultant and being that her vehicle was pink, she was quite good.

Tamara rang the doorbell and by the time I managed to reach the wide porch, my sister-in-law had come to the door to answer it.

"Hello," she greeted with a wide smile and hugs for both me and Tamara. I returned the hug. She had always been nice to me. "I'm so glad you made it."

I released her, then smiled. "I'm glad to be here," I said, then swiped my mouth with the rag I carried around. The last thing I wanted to do was drool all over her house.

She opened the door wide, then took the cake from Tamara and signaled us to follow her down a wide hallway to the family room where the family was waiting. There was loud voices and laughter. My nephew raced down the hall and I managed to lift him with one arm and gave him a big wet kiss before his spoiled behind wiggled free of my hold and hurried to find his daddy.

Taking a deep breath, I moved into the room to find my brother sitting on the couch and my father sitting in the chair across from him. As soon as I saw him I gasped. Paul looked nothing like the man I last saw at Lisa's funeral. But that had been almost four years ago. He was thin, very thin. With a smile on his face, he rose and moved toward me. I could tell that he was moving much slower. His hair, what little he had, had all turned gray and his eyes looked tired and his cheeks sunken. It took all I had not to cry. Chemo was taking its toll on him.

Andre told me that while I was in a coma, Daddy sat there in my room, reading and talking to me. I don't remember any of that but I was glad to know he really did care about me. It was then that I realized I needed to forgive him and give our relationship a chance.

"I'm glad you came," Paul said and then he hugged me.

As soon as he wrapped his arms around me, the tears began to fall and I couldn't get them to stop. Before long I could feel his thin body shaking as he cried along with me. It felt so good.

When he finally pulled away, I looked up into his watery eyes and knew then that from that point on everything—kids, friends, family, and my relationship with my stepfather—was going to be all right.

From *Exposed*
by Naomi Chase

In stores now!

Chapter 1

"Tamia! Baby, get up."

Jolted awake by her boyfriend's frantic voice, Tamia Luke opened her eyes and stared at his dark, handsome face. "What time is it?"

"After seven," Brandon replied.

"*Shit!*" Tamia threw back the covers and sprang out of bed, naked breasts bouncing. "What happened? Why didn't the alarm clock go off?"

"The power must have gone out when it rained last night."

"Shit," Tamia repeated, bending over to retrieve her discarded clothing from the floor. "I can't be late for work. Especially not tod— *Ow!*" she yelped as Brandon slapped her soundly on the ass.

He grinned, dimples flashing in his cheeks. "*That's* for keeping me up late."

Tamia laughed. "I didn't hear you complaining last night, Negro!" she called as Brandon ducked inside the large master bathroom, a blur of mahogany stretched over lean, taut muscles. "And hurry up so you can take me home!"

Brandon's response was muffled by the sound of running water.

If they hadn't been in such a rush, Tamia would have joined him in the shower for round two of what they'd started last night. After attending a cocktail party at a ritzy downtown hotel, Brandon had invited her back to his place to spend the night. They'd doused themselves with a bottle of champagne, then licked, sucked, and fucked each other until they collapsed from sheer exhaustion. They probably would have overslept even if last night's storm *hadn't* knocked out the electricity.

Grinning slyly to herself, Tamia hurriedly tugged on her bra and panties and the black Christian Lacroix dress she'd worn to the cocktail party. Leaving Brandon to his shower, she headed out of the bedroom and made her way to the kitchen. It was a large, ultramodern room with gleaming granite countertops, black-lacquered cabinets, and stainless steel appliances. It was as immaculate as the rest of Brandon's plush condo, thanks to the cleaning lady who came like clockwork twice a week.

Tamia got busy brewing a pot of gourmet coffee, though she knew Brandon usually stopped at Starbucks on his way to the office. It was the thought that counted. If she'd had more time, she would have whipped up some eggs, bacon, and grits, though she knew Brandon often grabbed breakfast with a colleague at the prestigious law firm where he worked. Again, it was all about taking care of her man. Which was why she'd blown off her friends last night to accompany Brandon to some social mixer he'd forgotten all about until the last minute. And she hadn't batted an eye when he'd sheepishly asked her to pick up his tux from the dry cleaner. Tamia would have gone anywhere and done anything he'd asked of her.

Because she was on a mission to become Mrs. Brandon Chambers.

Oh, she knew she had her work cut out for her. Truth be told, Brandon was more interested in making partner at his law firm than getting married. Although Tamia frequently spent the night at his place, she was barely allowed to keep a toothbrush there. And after seven months of dating, she had yet to meet his parents, one of the most powerful political couples in Texas. Whenever she hinted at being introduced to them, Brandon always told her that his folks could be very intimidating, so he didn't want to scare her off.

What he didn't realize was that Tamia didn't scare very easily. So she'd be a good little wifey for as long as it took to convince him to put a ring on her finger.

Smiling at the thought, she poured steaming coffee into two fancy paper cups and snapped on the lids just as Brandon strode purposefully into the kitchen. He was impeccably dressed in a dark pin-striped suit that accentuated his tall, athletic build.

"Ready to go?" he asked.

"Been ready." Tamia straightened his tie, admiring his smooth chocolate skin, midnight eyes, and boyishly sexy smile. Brandon was the total package: fine as hell, rich, smart, and successful. He was going places, and she had no intention of being left behind.

"Here. I made you some coffee."

Accepting the cup from her, he took a long sip and let out an appreciative groan. "Damn, baby, you make the best brew. What would I do without you?"

Tamia smiled privately. *If I play my cards right, you'll never have to find out.*

* * *

Twenty minutes later, they turned off the main road and into a lushly landscaped development located in the shadow of Houston's Galleria. Brandon was on his Black-Berry, assuring his secretary that he wouldn't be late for a scheduled deposition that morning. So he didn't notice the way Tamia's hands clenched in her lap as they passed another car on the narrow street, nor did he hear the small sigh of relief that seeped past her lips.

He pulled up to a one-story stucco house situated on a perfectly manicured lawn. Tamia's red Honda Accord was parked in the driveway.

Grabbing her purse, she leaned over to kiss Brandon. "Have a good day."

He smiled. "You, too. Don't be late for work."

"If I am, I'll just *blame it on the rain,*" she said, crooning the old Milli Vanilli song.

Brandon laughed as she climbed out of his Maybach.

Although he was in a hurry, he waited until she'd reached the front door before he pulled off with a wave.

Tamia inserted her key in the lock, stepped inside the cool interior of the house, and closed the door. But she didn't move beyond the foyer. Staring anxiously at her watch, she waited until three minutes had ticked by. Then, opening the door, she poked her head outside and glanced up and down the tree-lined street, watching as cars backed out of driveways and joined the flow of other vehicles headed to various workplaces.

As Tamia locked the house and hurried to her own car, her cell phone rang. She fumbled it out of her purse and answered with a breathless, "Girl, that was close!"

"I know," Shanell Jasper agreed. "I was running late this morning. And so are you! What happened?"

Tamia grimaced, sliding behind the wheel of her car. "The power went out last night, so we overslept."

"Uh-oh. You've got that client meeting at nine. Are you going to be late?"

"I hope not." Tamia glanced at her watch, mentally calculating how long it would take her to get home, shower and change, and make it to the office on time. If only she'd had the foresight to leave a change of clothes at Shanell's place last night. But everything had been so rushed. After picking up Brandon's tux from the dry cleaner, dropping it off at his condo, and hurrying home to get dressed for the cocktail party, she'd reached Shanell's house just minutes before Brandon arrived to pick her up.

"How long do you think you can keep this up?" Shanell asked.

Tamia pulled onto the main road. "What?"

Shanell snorted. "You know damn well what I'm talking about. This crazy charade of yours, lying to Brandon about where you live and using my house as your cover. How long can you keep this shit up?"

"However long it takes."

"And what if it takes that man, like, five years to propose?" Shanell paused. "Or what if he never does?"

"He will," Tamia said resolutely.

Before Shanell attempted to sow more seeds of doubt in her mind, Tamia told her that she'd see her at the office, then ended the call.

She knew her coworker meant well, and God knows Shanell had every right to voice her concerns since she was doing Tamia such a huge favor. But Shanell didn't understand what was truly at stake here. She had no clue what it was like to grow up on the wrong side of the tracks and dare to aspire to greater things. The crumbling shotgun house Tamia still called home was a world away from the lavish River Oaks estate where Brandon had been raised. He wouldn't be caught dead dating someone from Houston's notorious Third Ward—no matter how smart, successful, and educated Tamia now was. So showing him where she *really* lived was out of the question.

Sure, she felt a pang of guilt every time she lied to him or had to inconvenience her coworker. But she was compensating Shanell for her trouble. And once she and Brandon were married, Tamia would spend the rest of her life proving to him that he'd made the right decision.

From *Suspicions*
by Sasha Campbell

In stores May 2011

1

Tiffany

"*Guuuurrrrrrrl,* I met this dude from Jamaica last weekend. Trust and believe me when I tell you, he was a straight up Mandingo!"

"Peaches, sit still before I burn your ear!" Damn! How was I supposed to style her hair if she kept moving? Besides, I don't know what made her think I wanted to listen to her talking about getting some from a dude she barely knew.

"Oops, my bad!" Peaches chuckled. "It's just not often that I find a man with some good dick."

"Ooh! I know that's right," cackled some toothpick with a jacked-up weave, sitting in the chair beside her. "I ain't had a man with anything worth talking about in a long time. They either can't get it up or when they do, it ain't worth my time."

While everyone on the salon floor started talking about men's private parts, I simply pursed my lips and kept on flat ironing Peaches' hair. I don't know why my clients always think I wanted to hear about their sex lives.

"Shhhh-shhhh! I don't know if y'all know this or not, but . . . Tiffany don't know nothing about getting laid."

I grabbed a comb and pointed it at Debra, ready to cuss

her behind every which way, but decided not to waste my breath. She's the newest stylist at *Situations* and unfortunately my booth happened to be right next to hers, which meant she had eavesdropped on one too many of my conversations. In fact, it was a bad habit I was determined to break. "Debra, nobody asked you to be spreading my personal business," I mumbled. What she needed to be worried about was that no-good baby daddy of hers.

Debra gave an innocent look then had the nerve to wave her hand like she was dismissing me. "I don't know why you getting mad. You should be proud to let everyone know you're not getting none."

"Not getting none?" Peaches' head snapped in my direction, her bubble eyes big as saucers. "What's up with that?"

Now all eyes were on me. Damn, why she all up in my business? "I'm just not out there trying to give it up to everybody." I wasn't yelling, but I had definitely raised my voice.

Debra started laughing. "Everybody? Hell, you haven't given it to anybody."

I gave her a nasty look. With God as my witness, before long, she and I were going to have it out. "Some of us were raised to hold onto our virginity for the right man while others weren't." I don't know why I was even trying to explain to a bunch of chicks who wouldn't understand that some of us didn't believe in giving it up to every Tom, Dick, and Jerry they come across.

"Okay . . . lemme get this straight. You saying *you're* a virgin?" Peaches asked for clarification and swung her seat all the way around so she could look at me dead in my mouth. Thanks to Debra, they were all trying to get in my business.

"Did I stutter? I'm saving myself for the right man," I

replied with a mean glare. "Now turn around." I was done discussing my personal life. Unfortunately, Peaches wasn't finished yet.

"Hold up, Tif. What about that cutie pie who picked you up the last time I was here?"

I glanced around to see if anyone else was listening. The last thing I wanted was one of these trifling females in the salon to try and push up on my man. "What about him?" I said with attitude.

"I *know* you gotta be getting some of that." She said like she'd caught me in a lie. *"Sheee-it,* I would."

"Puhleeze," Debra cackled. "Tiffany ain't gave him shit!"

"You lying?" Peaches' mouth was hanging open then all of a suddenly she and Debra looked each other and burst out laughing. "Dayuumn, Tiffany. I ain't mad atcha!" I was seconds away from telling Peaches to get the hell out my chair because I didn't give a damn if she believed me or not, but she was one of my best clients and times were hard.

The skinny chick sitting in Debra's chair threw her hands up in surrender. "Hell naw! I heard it all."

The conversation wasn't anything new to me. My girls had always thought it strange that I was twenty-seven and still a virgin. All of them couldn't wait to fall in love and have sex while I had the willpower they didn't have to say no. I won't say it had always been easy but it was either wait or deal with Ruby Dee. My mother was one woman you didn't want to mess with. If she said keep your legs closed then you better do it. Her fist was the only chastity belt I had ever needed.

I glanced around the floor then took a deep breath before I said, "Why is it if a woman says she's a virgin, she has to be lying?"

"Damn, Tiffany, it's not like it's a bad thing. It's just, well . . . almost unheard of," Debra said on the defense.

When Peaches finally stopped laughing, she said, "Also, there is this thing called *being horny*. Hell, I lost my virginity when I was fourteen."

And that's why she had four kids. I reached for a brush. "So what? Everybody ain't like you. My mother taught me that what I have is precious and I needed to make a man earn the privilege after he makes me his wife." I probably sounded like I thought I was all that, but so what? Women needed to have more respect for themselves.

Debra sucked her bucked-teeth like a horse. "I know that's right, girl! Make those niggas beg for it." That wasn't at all what I meant, but I doubt Debra would know the difference.

That anorexic-looking chick with the jacked-up weave had the nerve to give her two cents. "You a better woman than me, because there ain't no way in hell I would marry a man before I knew what he was working with. I think about all those women back in the day, who couldn't have sex until after they got married only to find out that not only couldn't her husband fuck, but his dick wasn't even circumcised."

"Ugh!" Peaches was laughing so hard, she practically fell from my chair. "I couldn't even imagine. Call me a ho if you wanna, but to me it's just like sampling a piece of meat in the deli. I need to know what I'm getting before I spend my money!" She flinched. "Ouch!"

"That's what you get for moving. I told you to sit still," I replied and tried to keep a straight face. That's what she gets for being all up in my business.

Now everybody wanted to get in the conversation. They were now shouting back and forth across the room with the chicks sitting in the waiting area. I half listened as I worked on my client's head. I've heard this topic time and time before and I'll admit there have been times when I wondered what it would be like being married to Kimbel, and what if he doesn't satisfy me. But on the other hand, as my best friend told me, you can't miss what you've never had.

Ms. Conrad lifted the hooded dryer from her head. I should have known her nosy behind was listening. "I'ma tell y'all, I was married to my husband for twenty years before he decided he wanted his freedom. Charles was the only man I had ever been with so I had no idea what I was missing. But leaving me was the best thing he could have ever done for me. I now got a man in my life, who makes my toes curl."

"Shit, I know that's right. This dude I was with last night had my toes curled and me calling out his name!" screamed some tall chick sitting in the lobby.

Ms. Conrad glared at her. "That's the problem with all you young folks. You're too busy trying to get yours. Relationships are supposed to be about a lot more than just sex."

Debra waved a hot comb in the air as she spoke. "True, but sex is important. If the sex is bad then so is the relationship." She shook her head. "Tiffany, I don't see how you can do."

Toothpick chick gave me a curious grin. "So, is your fiancé a virgin, too?"

Damn they're nosy. "Nope, but he knows I am and he respects that." I wasn't about to tell them Kimbel spent half his time trying to convince me to give it up. Part of me felt the only reason he proposed so soon was because he knew that marrying me was the only way he was going to get some. But Kimbel was rich and he could have any woman he wanted, yet he picked me, a little girl from the projects who grew up in a single parent home. I truly believed he wouldn't have asked me to be his wife if he didn't love me.

"How long y'all been together?" Toothpick asked.

"Six months. He proposed on Valentine's Day." I held out my hand so she could see the three carat solitaire surrounded by emeralds that I wore proudly on my finger.

She barely looked before she frowned. "And you think your man's been faithful all this time?" As soon as I nodded, she started laughing. "Honey, puhleeze! Just 'cause you're not fucking doesn't mean he ain't. He's a man and a man's got needs that someone else is more than willing to fulfill."

I hated bitches like her. I shook my head. "I trust my man."

"I trust mine, too . . . as far as I can see him. Because the second you turn your back there's some hoochie trying to ride his dick. My baby is fine, therefore, I keep his ass on a short leash."

Debra started yanking weave out her head. "That's because Ricky ain't no good. Ursula, shut up."

She rolled her eyes. "Whatever, you know what I'm saying it true."

Ms. Conrad came to my defense. "All of you need to quit. There is nothing wrong with this young lady saving herself for the right man."

Peaches turned on the chair again. "Yeah, but how do you know he's the right man until you find out what he's working with, and, better yet, if he can work it?"

"I know that right!" Toothpick high-fived Peaches and ignored the pissed-off look on my face.

"Just because we don't have sex doesn't mean we don't

do other things." I don't know why I felt like I needed to prove something to these ghetto chicks up in here.

Peaches glanced over her shoulder and gave me a strange look. "Things like what? And I hope you're not talking about oral sex. Because last I checked, that was considered sex as well."

"No, it isn't." Debra said and tossed a sponge roller at her.

"Yes, it is. There was a news report on *Dateline NBC* a while back about all these high school kids giving each other head because it's supposed to be cool. Kids think it's okay to have oral sex."

While they debated the issue, I tuned them out and thought about what they said. I would never admit it to any of them, but there were many times when I was tempted to give in to the moment and let Kimbel have exactly what he wanted but every time I was that close to spreading my legs, I heard my mother's nagging voice in my ear, saying, "why buy the cow if the milk is free." But I'm not going to lie. These heifers in the salon had me thinking. It had been six months since we started dating, which meant Kimbel hadn't had any in half a year. I was confident he wasn't getting any. Some might call me arrogant. Others might call me stupid but I trusted my man. However, the last thing I wanted was for him to get tired of waiting then go out and get him some from one of those trifling chicks in the streets. Now don't get it twisted. I wasn't about to give up my virginity before saying, "I do." Nevertheless, my mama ain't raised no fool. I was just going to have to prove to my man that what I have would definitely be worth the wait.